DAUGHTER OF MINE

FIONA LOWE

PRAISE FOR FIONA LOWE

"A sweeping Australian novel of lost love and tangled family secrets."
—*Australian Country* on *Daughter of Mine*

"A readable and thoughtful book. It has winner written all over it."
—*The Weekly Times* on *Daughter of Mine*

"*Daughter of Mine* is a beautiful story of bonds, family expectations and the insidious and far reaching effects of secrets and lies. It may be the first book I have read by Fiona Lowe but I'm sure it won't be the last." —Beauty & Lace on *Daughter of Mine*

"...a real page-turner" —Cairns Eye on *Daughter of Mine*

"An exceptionally magnificent read" —Talking Books Blog on *Daughter of Mine*

ALSO BY FIONA LOWE

Daughter of Mine

Birthright

Home Fires

Just An Ordinary Family

A Home Like Ours

Coming in 2022

A Family of Strangers

Join My Newsletter

For a free novella, *Summer of Mine;* Doug and Edwina's summer of 1967, please join my VIP Readers newsletter. You'll also be the first to hear about new releases, book sales, competitions and giveaways. Register at

fionalowe.com

Did you know **BookBub** has a new release alert? You can check out the latest deals and get an email when I release my next book by following me at

bookbub.com/authors/fiona-lowe

DAUGHTER OF MINE
First Published by Harlequin Australia in 2017.
This revised 3rd edition published in 2020 by Fiona Lowe.
Copyright © 2017, 2020 by Fiona Lowe. All rights reserved.
www.fionalowe.com

Daughter of Mine

Cover Design by Lana Pecherczyk from Bookcoverology. Cover concepts and ornamental breaks by Barton Lowe.

Published by Fiona Lowe

DEDICATION

In memory of Debbie who, on being told this book was to be published,
replied with her characteristic response of 'Sensational!'
Miss you, Deb. Rest in Peace.

Sisters may share the same mother and father but appear to
come from different families.

Anonymous

CHAPTER ONE

"Auntie Harry, look at my frog."

Harriet Chirnwell recoiled as her eight-year-old nephew, Hugh, thrust a muddy bug catcher under her chin. She could just make out a tiny frog nestled in the greenery.

"It's *our* frog," Ollie corrected. He was the younger twin by four minutes.

Harriet's nose wrinkled as the rancid scent of mud and sheep dung hit her nostrils. "And you found it down at the water hole."

"Yes!" the twins chorused, sounding surprised she'd guessed correctly.

"Why is there mud on my clean floor?" Xara, Harriet's middle sister, walked into the kitchen. She pushed her daughter, Tasha—the twins' sister—in her specially designed wheelchair.

"We're showing Auntie Har—"

"It was a rhetorical question, Hughie." Xara shook her head indulgently. "Trust you to find the only mud on the farm during a drought. Go back to the mudroom and take off those boots. You too, Ollie. Now."

Ignoring the groans of her sons, Xara lifted Tasha from the

wheelchair and positioned her in a foam chair in her favorite spot by the window. "Hi, Harry. I didn't hear you drive up."

"European engineering's incredibly quiet." Harriet got a thrill just thinking about her new car. "And those sheep in the home paddock are bleating so loudly I'm surprised you can hear yourself think."

Xara threw an old towel down on the muddy floor and while she mopped it around with her foot, she stirred a pot on the wood stove that smelled deliciously like beef and ginger. "I keep telling Steve it's time Chump, Chops and Racka went on the truck but you know how pathetic he is with the ones we hand raise." She reached left, opened a cabinet, grabbed two thick-rimmed mugs and threw a teabag into each.

Harriet flinched. She preferred her tea in a bone china cup and made with leaves, not dust. "Do you still have those Royal Albert mugs I gave you for your birthday?"

"Sorry." Xara sounded completely unapologetic. "I usually hide your mugs at the back of the cabinet but after your last visit, I forgot. Steve took one down to the shearing shed and Hughie dropped the other one."

The twins rushed back in whooping, "Cake, cake, cake," and Tasha squealed, joining their enthusiasm. The ear-piercing shrieks formed a wall of sound and every nerve ending in Harriet's body fired off a salvo of tingling aversion.

She wasn't particularly fond of children. As a general rule they were sticky and damp, loud and unruly, and they came with an inexhaustible supply of questions, which she found disconcerting. Of course, she was fond of her daughter, Charlotte. She loved her, especially now that that she was no longer sticky and clingy. Harriet considered Charlotte, now almost eighteen, to be one of her greatest achievements; the others were the day she become a fellow of the Royal College of Surgeons and the year she joined her father in his medical practice.

Over the last decade, she'd taken the practice into the twenty-first century while maintaining a successful and happy marriage to James. She had no time for women who said it was impossible to have it all and her usual response to such statements was that it came down to choice. She'd chosen James because his drive and determination matched her own and he wanted what she wanted.

Now, twenty years after saying "I do," they were Billawarre's power couple: rich, respected, well educated, philanthropic and with the added prestige of being descended from the founding families of the district.

Her mother's family, the Mannerings, arrived in the district in 1838. They'd gone on to establish a farming dynasty as well as diversifying into manufacturing. Harriet loved that she could trace her Australian heritage back to William and John, who'd arrived from England with a mob of sheep and a vision. Since those early pastoralist days when the brothers had bred sheep, cattle, racehorses and children, their descendants included a very successful gold prospector, businessmen, war heroes and heroines, parliamentarians, doctors, an Olympic equestrian and a novelist.

It was a family to be proud of, and throughout the 175 years since the Mannering brothers had crossed the Moorabool River, there'd always been at least one branch of the family living in Billawarre. It gave Harriet a reassuring sense of tradition and a great deal of family pride. Like her mother before her, Harriet had been named after her great-grandmother. She'd continued the tradition, naming Charlotte after her own great-grandmother, and she hoped that when the time came—in another fifteen years or so—Charlotte would consider doing the same.

Harriet glanced around the farmhouse kitchen and pursed her lips. She had no idea how Xara could be so laid back in the presence of so much chaos. When Tasha had been born with severe cerebral palsy and requiring twenty-four-hour care, Harriet had assumed Xara would stop at one child. After all, Harriet had stopped at one.

She'd been stunned by the amount of time and attention a child took and Charlotte was healthy and developmentally normal—gifted, even, in some areas. Between piano lessons, ballet lessons, pony club, private tutors and general school commitments, Harriet and James had juggled their careers and employed Nya Devali to fill the inevitable gaps when neither of them was available.

It had been a huge relief when Charlotte had turned thirteen and gone to boarding school, just like Harriet had at that age. The school vacations were always a bit of a struggle, but Charlotte enjoyed spending time with her aunts and Harriet always scheduled a few days off in the middle of the break, whisking her away to Lorne or Noosa depending on the time of year. Of course they took an overseas vacation every year, alternating between skiing in Europe or Canada and visiting somewhere warm. Last year, Harriet had even conceded to Charlotte's request to go to Bali and she'd been pleasantly surprised by the beautiful north-coast resort.

Harriet honestly couldn't imagine her life with more than one child. She could still recall how stunned she'd been when Xara had announced she was not only pregnant again but with twins. That night, as she and James had been getting ready for bed, Harriet had said, "What on earth were Xara and Steve thinking, getting pregnant again?"

James had come up behind her, pulled her in against him and pressed his lips against the crook of her neck in the exact spot that made her melt. "I doubt at the time they were thinking at all." His deep, rumbling voice had vibrated against her skin, making her shiver in anticipation.

Soon after that, she and James hadn't been thinking at all either. She smiled at the memory, but her cheeks suddenly tightened as a thought struck her: how long had it been since James had kissed her like that?

"I'll buy you some new mugs," Harriet said quickly, thrusting the uncomfortable and unwelcome thoughts about James and their sex life to the back of her mind.

"Perhaps it would be safer if you brought your own when you

visit." Xara handed her a mug decorated with a picture of a sheep playing the bagpipes. "So what's up?"

Harriet ignored the tone in Xara's voice that said, *You only drive out to the farm when you want something,* and instead brushed crumbs and a shriveled pea off the kitchen chair before smoothing her black pencil skirt and sitting. She sometimes questioned if she and her middle sister shared any DNA at all given her own need for order and Xara's total disregard for it.

"Edwina's birthday's a month away. We need to finalize the details for her party." Harriet had been referring to her mother by her first name since her fifteenth birthday. The celebration had coincided with another one of Edwina's "episodes," as her father had always referred to them. Harriet had never been particularly close to her mother and Edwina remained a frustrating mystery. She'd never quite worked out if her mother was depressed or if she conveniently hid behind these random episodes to avoid the familial and social responsibilities she didn't enjoy.

"Finalize what details?" Xara asked. "This is the first time we've talked about it. I can tell you right now, Mom won't want a party."

"Don't be silly. Of course she'll want a party. She needs something to look forward to now that Dad's—"

Damn it. Her throat thickened as though a chunk of Xara's beef stew were caught in it and she had to force herself to swallow around the lump. These days she could usually talk about her father without a problem so she hated the moments when her grief hit her without warning. It instantly took her back to the day he'd died thirteen months ago, forcing her to relive those awful hours again. She missed him desperately, not only because she loved him, but also because, unlike her mother and sisters, her father had been the one person in the family who truly understood her.

She cleared her throat. "A party will be good for Edwina."

Xara didn't look convinced. "Mom's more comfortable with a low-key approach. This year her birthday's right on top of Easter so Georgie and Charlie will be home on vacation. Georgie can drive from Melbourne and pick up Charlie from school on her way through Geelong. We can all have dinner here."

Harriet took in the fine film of dust that coated everything—the scattered toys and books, the half-folded laundry that graced chairs, the dresser and every other available surface. She immediately thought of her beautifully renovated Victorian homestead kept immaculately clean by Nya. No, her plan was much better. Besides, her house was designed for entertaining.

"We did low key last year because it was so close to the funeral. This year her birthday needs to be a big splash like the parties Dad threw her." Harriet drummed her fingers on the table. "We've always thrown big parties and people are expecting one. I've already had Primrose McGowan asking me if we've got plans."

"God, Harry, our role in life isn't to entertain the district." Xara gave the saucepan another vigorous stir.

"I remember you doing a pretty good job of it from seventeen to twenty-three," Harriet said waspishly, feeling the familiar bubble of annoyance rising in her chest. It frustrated her that Xara didn't value her heritage or honor the responsibilities that came with being part of a respected establishment family.

Xara laughed and quoted Jane Austen at her. "'For what do we live, but to make sport for our neighbors, and laugh at them in our turn.' This isn't the fifties, Harry. You take all this stuff way so seriously."

"I'm taking our mother's situation very seriously," Harriet said crisply, tension raising her shoulders. This always happened whenever she thought about her mother's vagueness and periods of detachment. Edwina's episodes could last from a few hours to weeks. They'd come and gone as far back as Harriet could remember and since her father's death, she felt both an obligation to him and a begrudging responsibility to her mother to take care of her.

"You know what she's like, Zar. She needs a push now and then to be involved in things. Now Dad's not here to do it, it's up to us. This party will help."

"I'm not sure a party's the best way."

"It's worked before," Harriet said firmly.

Xara rolled her eyes. "Is there any point at all suggesting that you ask Mom if she wants this party?"

"And ruin the surprise? Honestly, Xara, sometimes I wonder about you. Edwina's surprise parties are both legend and tradition."

"They were *Dad's* tradition," Xara said, an edge creeping into her voice.

Harriet shook her head. "No, they're a *family* tradition and by default a town tradition. I'm not letting them slide just because Dad's not here to host them." Her voice cracked and she cleared her throat. "And Georgie agrees with me."

Xara's untamed eyebrows rose over her chipped mug. "Georgie has an opinion? Are we talking about our baby sister, Georgie, or another Georgie entirely?"

"She suggested making Edwina's favorite mini chocolate mud cakes with ganache." Harriet tweaked the truth around the edges to firm up her argument—one she refused to lose. She hadn't actually texted Georgie about the party nor had she asked her to make the cakes, but she would the moment she'd won Xara over.

"Wow, and you're actually going to let her?" A hint of sarcasm threaded through Xara's words. "I thought you'd want the party to be color coordinated and catered."

"Of course it will be color coordinated and catered." Harriet ignored the jibe and made a mental note to tell Lucinda Petronella, the caterer, that she wanted turquoise and silver to be the signature colors. "I just thought if Georgie made the cakes it would add a personal touch."

Xara's eyes narrowed into a *gotcha* glare. "So she didn't actually offer to make them at all, did she?"

Harriet shrugged. Sometimes the only way to get things done her way was to work people using both their strengths and weaknesses. "Why are you getting all bogged down in semantics? Does it matter if I give Georgie the recipe? I mean, she loves to bake, so end of story."

Xara huffed out a breath. "She always takes the path of least resistance."

Unlike you.

"Do you think she's okay? I mean, it's not something you just get over, is it?"

An uncomfortable feeling tried settling over Harriet, but she fought it off. She refused to feel any guilt about being the only one of her siblings to have a healthy and happy daughter. An idea slid in under her discomfort, offering her the perfect way to close her argument and bring Xara on board. "Do you talk to Georgie much?"

A look of self-reproach crossed Xara's face. "I try, but the days go so fast."

"Exactly, and Georgie hasn't been home in ages. There's no way she can refuse to come to this party, especially as the date is at the start of the school break. When we've gotten her face to face, we can really check up on her."

She leaned forward. "Come on, Zar, it will be fun. You know James and I throw great parties. You know Charlotte loves being the princess of the cousins and she'll keep them entertained." Harriet wheeled out her closing argument: "You and Steve deserve a night away from wool prices, the drought and being parents. You deserve a night to let your hair down and be yourselves."

Xara grimaced as if she was in pain—suggesting she had just struck a deal with the devil. "Is James serving French champagne?"

"*Bien sûr.*" Harriet smiled, knowing she'd just won. "I'll text you your to-do list."

"I caved over French champagne," Xara told Steve ruefully as she climbed into bed with exhaustion clawing every muscle, tendon and bone.

Her husband glanced up from his book, his green eyes laughing at her from behind his black-rimmed reading glasses. "You always cave if Möet or Veuve Clicquot are on the table. The reality is, I married a fickle debutante."

"Hey, sheep farmer." She elbowed him in the ribs before snuggling in against him. "I happily gave up my silver spoon fifteen years ago to slum it with you."

He squeezed her shoulder affectionately and kissed her hair. "Did you ask Harry to follow up with James about the status of the respite-care house check?"

She slapped her forehead. "Sorry. I meant to ask but the whole party thing threw me for a loop. You know what she's like when she's in full-on Harriet-gets-what-Harriet-wants mode, railroading everyone and everything in her path. After I caved, she started telling me how Charlie's coping *brilliantly*," her voice mimicked Harriet's, "being house captain, a champion rower and of course, still on track to get the grades she needs to study pre-med."

Steve shot her a knowing look. "Tell me you resisted the urge to push her buttons by asking if Charlie's really on-board with the college plans?"

"Oh, I had the urge alright," Xara said, feeling the familiar burn of frustration, "but just as I was about to say, 'Are you sure Charlie wants to do pre-med?,' the twins flooded the bathroom. Harry left as I was mopping up the mess." She rubbed her face, thinking about the respite-care house. "I'll ring James."

"That's not a good idea. No matter how hard you try, you'll go all attorney on him. You know how much he hates that."

"Once," she spluttered indignantly, remembering the infamous family lunch. "It only happened once."

Steve tilted his head, looking at her over the top of his glasses. "Yeah, and he's never forgotten. Besides, I've already tried calling and leaving messages. Our best bet is to go through Harry."

"She's operating all day tomorrow but if James still hasn't gotten back to you by then, I'll call her."

"And if that doesn't work, I guess I can always talk to him about it at the party. There has to be some perks being the brother-in-law of the mayor."

She gave a faux gasp. "Steven Paxton, I'm shocked. You're always taking pot shots at the old boys' club and their networks. Now you're planning on doing the same thing."

The moonlight caught the gray streaks in his once jet-black hair and his face sobered as he closed his book. "I'll do whatever it takes for Tashie."

Her heart filled and ached all at the same time. "And that's what I love about you." She kissed him softly on the lips in the way couples do when they've known each other a very long time. Their life was nothing like they'd imagined when they'd naively plunged into marriage all those years ago, but then, was anyone's?

A memory of a hot summer's night on the veranda of her grandparents' old beach shack at Apollo Bay rushed back. It was a week before she'd started seventh grade and her first year of boarding school, which had coincided with Harry's final year of school. As always, her big sister had been full of unsolicited advice on who to make friends with, the pitfalls to avoid in the first few weeks and suggestions on how to cope with living with forty other girls.

"Never forget you belong there," Harriet had said confidently. "Mannering House exists because our great-great-grandfather donated the money to the school."

The thought of telling people that had made Xara's stomach cramp. During her six years at the school, she'd never mentioned the family's connection unless asked directly. Her behavior had been in stark contrast to Harriet's—her sister was always quick to tell people the Mannerings were instrumental in starting the school over a century earlier. Harriet had owned the school during her years there: head girl, an honors student, captain of the girls' rowing and the girl on everyone's invitation list. Now she owned Billawarre: surgeon, wife of the mayor and the woman on everyone's invitation list.

Xara recalled having asked her that night years ago if she was worried about leaving school. Harriet's face had taken on a slightly bewildered look, fast followed by pity, as if the concept of being anxious were foreign to her. "I'm going to ace the college entrance tests, go to Melbourne University, become a doctor and be the first female surgeon in Billawarre."

Xara, who'd just discovered the heady sensations of being kissed by a boy, had said, "If you do that, you're going to be living in Melbourne a really long time. What happens if you fall in love with a city guy?"

Harriet's laugh was dismissive. "I'll only fall in love with a man who's prepared to live in Billawarre and who earns as much as or more than me."

And in typical Harriet style, she'd done all those things. James, who'd grown up in rural New South Wales, had not only adopted Billawarre as his own, but he successfully ran an accounting, financial planning and investment business, which earned him far more than Harriet made—and she was no slouch in the income department. Two years ago, James had run for City Council and just under a year ago, he'd been elected mayor.

Perfect marriage. Perfect child. Perfect life.

Xara pulled her thoughts away from her older sister, not wanting to wander down the toxic green path of envy that often seduced her and always left her feeling nauseous and unsettled. Most days she didn't want Harriet's life—perfection bored her, which was fortunate given what life threw at her on a daily basis. But she'd be lying if she said she didn't want a little bit of Harriet's disposable income and the freedom it gave her.

Who wouldn't experience twinges of jealously for the annual and occasionally twice-yearly overseas vacation, not to mention the conference junkets, the quiet and comfortable European car, the seeming ease with which Harry and James paid Charlotte's phenomenal school fees—an amount equal to what some people earned in a year. Then there was Harriet's wardrobe of designer clothes.

Not that Xara attended even one tenth of the functions Harriet did, but a girl always liked to look good, even if there wasn't a big call for Prada out on the farm. Xara's day-to-day wardrobe was far more prosaic and included Carhartt boots and sturdy cotton work pants.

To be honest, she'd pass on the clothes if it meant the extension to the farmhouse got finished. It had been creeping forward at a snail's pace for eighteen months, because the funds earmarked for it had been channeled into buying feed and surviving the current drought. Life on the farm was a cycle of golden fleeces, high lamb prices and perfect weather conditions for both pasture and sheep, invariably followed by a glut of wool, crashing lamb prices and soul-sucking drought. Money earned in the good years got reinvested back into the farm in an attempt to cushion the impact of the droughts. Yet slowly but surely they were reaping the benefits.

A good farmer needed to be a canny small businessman, skilled in animal husbandry, part mechanic, part nurturer, part accountant, proactive rather than reactive, open to change, at ease with the isolation and above all, an optimist. Steve was all of those things and as far as the farm was concerned, their life was pretty much as she'd imagined—a continuously fluid financial state and a whopping overdraft.

Farm life and family went hand in glove, and she had no regrets there. Unlike Harriet, Zara had been unexpectedly completed by motherhood. It still stunned her how much she loved it. There was something wonderful about being needed and being loved so unconditionally, although that would likely change the moment the twins hit puberty, so she was enjoying it while it lasted. Despite or perhaps because of the challenges, her family gave her a sense of satisfaction unlike any other job she'd ever done. They also drove her crazier than any other job and at times frustrated her until she was tearing her hair out. But somehow the combination made her feel valued and, for the most part, happy.

The one thing neither she nor Steve had anticipated was having a child who'd never be able to care for herself. Tasha's arrival had been a combination of overwhelming love accompanied with crushed dreams, and all wrapped up in a huge red bow of guilt. Guilt that she'd done something to cause the cerebral palsy. Guilt that she ached for the child Tasha may have been without her disability. Guilt and sorrow for even feeling that way. It had taken the twins' safe and healthy arrival to temper her feelings of failure as a creator of life.

She knew people thought her crazy to have gone on to have more children when Tasha needed so much care, but she was incapable of stopping at one child. On a rational level, she knew that on top of the care Tasha required, increasing the size of their family would effectively kill her career as an attorney. But when had rational ever been part of the equation of creating a family? More than anything, she'd needed to prove to herself that she and Steve could create a healthy child. She'd needed that to ease her sense of inadequacy as a biological mother.

She knew Harriet thought another baby was a stress Xara and Steve didn't need, but Xara saw the twins as double confirmation that she wasn't broken. She loved their energy and enthusiasm, but their arrival had brought a whole new level of mother-guilt down upon her as she juggled their needs with Tasha's overwhelming ones.

Caring for Tasha's physical and emotional wellbeing was in many ways the same as caring for the twins, except the boys eventually learned to do things for themselves. Mind you, she had her doubts they'd ever master tying shoelaces. No, it was the added burden of constantly having to write annual, as well as one-time, applications for government disability grants that was wearing her and Steve down.

The constant need to justify and fight for precious funding meant things like Tasha's ongoing therapy, her special education teaching assistant, or added extras like a new wheelchair all became a battleground with bureaucrats or the health-insurance provider. Xara may have given up law, but she'd become her daughter's lobbyist as well as an advocate for other parents in the district who had children with disabilities.

Over the years they'd had their grant wins and their losses.

Fortunately, when one of them was broken, dejected, and worn down by the constant fight, the other still had enough faith to drag the sad one along in the slipstream until new energy could be harnessed. If her destiny had always been to have a special-needs child then she was glad it was with Steve.

He was like a dog with a bone when it came to getting services and support for Tasha and she knew he worried as much as she did about the far-flung future when neither of them would be alive to take care of her. That was why respite-care house was so important, a first step in future planning.

After a lot of fundraising, they'd applied for funding through City Hall to build a custom-built respite-care house in Billawarre, specially designed for people with disabilities. Although the local tradesmen were all donating their time to build the house, they needed the funding to purchase the building materials. City Hall had approved the money, but Xara and Steve were yet to receive the promised check, which was why they were both chasing James to find out the reason for the delay.

Steve kissed her shoulder. "You feeling frisky?"

She tried not to groan. "Just tired."

"Me too, but we should probably make an effort." He ran the tip of his tongue along her collarbone.

She'd been up for seventeen hours and all she craved was sleep. "How about I lie here and you keep making the effort. But I'm not promising anything."

"Challenge accepted." Grinning, he vanished under the cover and then his strong, work-callused fingers were pressing firmly into the soles of her feet. His fingers kept up their rhythm, moving from her feet to her calves and her thighs and a long and languid sigh rolled out of her as a warm river of relaxation stole into her weariness.

A muffled but wicked laugh sounded from under the covers. "I'm good."

A smile tugged at her lips. "I'm still not promising anything." But it was a half-hearted protest and as his gentle touch kneaded her inner thigh, a flicker of need flared. It broke through her fatigue, bringing with it the promise of some precious moments of heady bliss. She rolled into him.

Steve was right. It really was worth the effort.

†

"Ms. Chirnwell, can I bring my pet rats for show and tell tomorrow?"

Georgie tried hard to stall the shudder that whipped through her. Growing up in the country, where rats gnawed easily through the fuel line of a truck and mice plagues turned solid ground into a wriggling and heaving gray mass, rodents as pets were anathema to her. Not so to the kids of her inner-city school, where space was at a premium. "That sounds great, Jai," she said with forced enthusiasm. "I'm looking forward to it."

Yeah. No. She was looking forward to pet rats as much as she was looking forward to the farewell baby shower for Lucy Patrell. It was the reason she'd lingered after the break bell instead of shooing her second grade outside and striding across the already softening black top steaming in the summer heat to the teachers' lounge. Ordinarily, the promise of a cheese platter with Erica Gubbin's homemade quince preserve and Chi Li's carrot cake was enough to make her feign deafness to all student entreaties as she crossed the yard. Not today. Today, self-preservation was in a tug of war with duty and self-preservation was winning.

She heard the click-clack of hurried and determined footsteps in the corridor outside her classroom but before she could dive behind the smart board, her name was being called. Sharon Saunders, the office dragon, had a habit of rounding up stray and recalcitrant faculty members. "Come on, Georgie," she said briskly, pausing in the doorway of her classroom, lips pursed and a critical frown on her pinched face. "Lucy will be disappointed if you're not there to see her open her presents."

Georgie doubted that. It was Sharon who'd be disappointed given she'd organized the baby shower and lived for the accompanying praise: "Great choice of presents, Sharon. What would we do without you?" Georgie's naive hope that kicking in twenty dollars to the farewell gift fund and signing the card would be enough faded fast. Experience had taught her that Sharon wouldn't budge from the doorway until Georgie had exited the classroom.

She swallowed her sigh and picked up her *Keep Calm and Pretend it's on the Lesson Plan* mug. "I was just on my way."

She walked into the crowded teachers' lounge where a beaming Lucy sat surrounded by women and a staggering pile of gifts. Georgie busied herself putting a teabag in her mug and carefully filling it with water from the instant hot-water tap before joining the outer circle. This consisted entirely of the male faculty members and she could hear the low rumble of a sports discussion about cricket between the principal and the visiting psychologist.

She found herself standing next to the new substitute gym teacher and realized with quiet regret that she couldn't remember his name. Was it Brad or Brent? She was almost certain it started with a B but then again, she might be grasping at straws. She really should pay more attention when the substitute faculty members were introduced.

"Do you want to squeeze in?" he asked, angling his body slightly so she could step forward.

She shook her head. "I'm fine here."

Someone squealed and clapped. "Oh my God! Did you knit that, Sharon? It's so tiny."

Georgie gulped tea and immediately regretted it as it burned all the way down.

"You sure you don't want to see?" The gym teacher, whose height dwarfed hers, gave her a cheeky grin. "I hear there's a hand-smocked nightie although my favorite so far is the bib that says, 'Party in my crib at 2:00 a.m., bring a bottle.'"

She summoned a bright smile, dredging it up from who knows

where, and dragged it past the permanent brick of grief that was firmly cemented in her chest with a dull and empty ache. Locking the smile onto tight cheeks she said, "I'm guessing the student teachers bought that one."

His chocolate caramel eyes crinkled around the edges. "Are you implying I'm past partying at 2:00 a.m.?"

Georgie always found it hard to estimate anyone's age, but she'd hazard a guess that Brandon, Barton, Brendon—*God, what was his name?*—was thirty at the very least. She'd been thirty once. "I'm thinking you can make it to midnight once a week as long as the next day isn't a school day."

He laughed. "That's both harsh and sadly true. I can't even blame getting up in the night for kids. Do you have any?"

Given they were strangers at a baby shower it was a perfectly normal question; a societal standard like where did you go to school? Are you married? How long have you been teaching? A polite question and one whose answer he probably had very little interest in. It was a question she should have been prepared for. After all, she had rock-solid protective armor in place with no gaps for attack. It was just his question hit like a rogue grenade, knocking her off balance and throwing her back to a time and place that had stained her soul with the indelible ink of loss.

She badly wanted to answer yes, because it felt disrespectful to say no, but a yes would only bring more questions. Questions that would slide off his tongue with the ease of rolling mercury. Questions that would batter and bruise her until she was blotchy and riddled with pain. So she lied like she always did with strangers. "Only the terrors of my class."

"That class is nature's contraception." He gave her a look that combined both respect and sympathy. "And I've only taught them twice for an hour each time."

She found her tight smile relaxing into something more genuine. "Thanks for running them ragged for me. Rahul actually managed to sit still for the next lesson. I think he was too exhausted to get out of his seat."

"I've got a lot of time for little boys who aren't designed to sit," he said with a rueful smile.

She caught a glimpse of a curly-haired little boy with big brown eyes and an impish grin. She was about to ask if he'd caused his teachers angst when another round of *oohs, ahhhs* and "So cute!" bounced off the walls. She focused on not wincing.

"I don't get it. It just looks like a blanket to me," Brock or Brady said, sounding bemused as he reported what he could easily see over the top of everyone else's heads.

"It will be hand embroidered with a ring of flowers, and accompanying bears or sheep," she offered by way of explanation despite wanting to avoid all discussion of baby accoutrements.

He took another look. "Sheep. You've obviously been to this rodeo before." Turning to the table that was groaning with food he picked up a platter and offered it to her. "Cake, Georgie?"

Oh, God. He knew her name. What the hell was his? *Come on, brain. Spit it out. B … b …b … b …* "Yes, please. Ah, thanks, B … Ben." His name shot out of her mouth.

"Trying to remember my name's been driving you crazy for the entire conversation, hasn't it?"

"Not at all, Ben," she said, trying to sound cool and queenly like her mother but failing miserably.

He laughed and once again his warm brown eyes gazed down at her. How had she failed to notice his lovely eyes before? Probably because she'd been busy wrangling her class to line up so he could take them out for sport.

Her cell phone vibrated in her pocket and as it was break time, she pulled it out and read the message.

This is the recipe you're making for Edwina's 65th party. Harriet x.

She sighed.

"Bad news?" Ben asked between mouthfuls of cake.

"No." She slid her cell back into the pocket of her dress. "Just my bossy big sister in seventh heaven, aka, organizing everyone. This time it's for my mother's birthday party, which I didn't even know was being planned."

A streak of understanding shot across Ben's dimpled cheek. "Once the youngest, always the youngest."

"Exactly." A moment of simpatico passed between them, warming her. "You never get to have an opinion and you're always told what to do."

"But you can get away with a lot." Mischief danced in his eyes. "I reckon Mom and Dad had run out of parenting energy by the time I arrived."

"You don't sound very scarred by that."

He shrugged. "Flying under the radar has its benefits."

Georgie thought about her own parents. She'd certainly been the surprise baby. Had they been tired of the job by the time she'd arrived? Come to think of it, that might explain a lot.

The pre-bell music blared out of the speakers, signaling that break was almost over, and Lucy made a quick thank-you speech, her hand unconsciously rubbing her pregnant belly. Everyone cheered. Georgie clapped politely. The bell finally rang and relief washed through her like a balm; she'd survived and was home free. Walking purposefully to the door, she escaped into the corridor and took her first deep breath in fifteen minutes.

Ben caught her up. "You going to drinks tonight at the pub after work?"

She rarely went to Friday-night drinks and she opened her mouth to say no, but instead she got a flash of her tiny rented house. If she didn't count the mold in the shower, the only living things waiting for her there were her potted anthurium and her cat. "Maybe."

Ben smiled. "Maybe I'll see you there."

He pushed open the outside door and she stood watching him run sure-footedly down the bank of concrete steps, the sun-kissed tips of his curly hair glinting in the sunshine.

CHAPTER TWO

Unless she'd been called out for an emergency, Harriet started most days with a run through the native grasslands and along the banks of the manna gum–lined creek. Today was no different. She'd run for years; it cleared her head, helped her prioritize the day's tasks and it kept her slim. At forty-five, her daily run was more important than ever. She'd noticed any weight that snuck on thanks to vacation treats now sat high on her abdomen and she refused to be one of those women with a belly that started under her breasts.

Against the mocking laugh of the kookaburras, she turned back toward Miligili. It had always been a dream of hers to own one of the original Mannering homesteads and a decade ago she and James bought the house and its accompanying five acres. Her ancestors had wanted to recreate a piece of England in this rugged, stony land with its sprawling gum trees and scrubby vegetation. In the 1870's, and with money earned off the sheep's back, they'd built spectacular mansions between Camperdown, Colac and Geelong. Miligili may have been the smallest but its grand Italianate style rivalled the great houses in Melbourne. She loved the house almost too much and every time she drove through the ornate iron gates, she got a buzz of happiness that it was their home.

Some people called her lucky, but Harriet didn't think luck had anything to do with it. She worked hard and she planned, and that meant she was able to take advantage of opportunities when they presented themselves. She felt the way she and James lived their lives taught Charlotte the same values. Goals and plans were important; Harriet had learned that from her own father and she was trying to instill it in her daughter. Too many teens had no clue what they wanted to study or they were deluded enough to believe they could earn a living wage in the creative arts. Thank goodness Charlotte had come around to Harriet's suggestions that the family business of medicine was an ideal career.

After a shower, she joined James in the kitchen. He gave her a quick kiss on the cheek and handed her a skinny latte with an extra shot of coffee just like he'd done every morning since he'd bought the Italian espresso machine.

"Thanks." She smiled at him, appreciating that unlike many of his peer group, he hadn't entered his mid-forties, gone to flab and lost his hair. He was still fit, fair and fabulous, and she loved the fact that he was her husband.

"Can we sync our diaries?" she asked as she sipped her coffee. "Complicated emergencies excepted, I'm finishing early on Friday so I can be at the golf tournament's opening cocktail party. My intern's finally finding his feet so hopefully he can handle anything straightforward that comes through the door."

James nodded, his fingers on his cell phone's screen, opening his calendar. "It's a big weekend and the press will be all over it. It would be great if you could be at the presentation on Sunday afternoon to hand out the trophies."

She laughed. "Trophy wife hands out trophies."

James took a moment to smile. "You're far from a trophy wife."

"Well, I love being the mayoress and I'm so proud of you." She rested her hand on his shoulder and gave it an affectionate squeeze.

He tensed under her touch and she thought about how much James liked to win. "Have you been over-practicing your drive?"

He shrugged. "I'll be fine."

"Take some ibuprofen."

"Good idea."

They ran through the rest of the week's commitments, including a visit to her mother, and she realized there was only going to be one night of the week when they'd both be home for dinner. James offered to cook. She accepted. Her husband was a keeper and she gave herself an imaginary hug, proud that twenty years ago she'd made the right choice in accepting an invitation to the Narrandera Bachelor and Spinsters Ball, even if she had dumped her date to spend the night with James.

Finishing her coffee, she turned her attention to granola, fruit and yogurt. As she ate, she checked her cell phone. Charlotte had sent a Snapchat of the girls' rowing team training on the Barwon River complete with a vivid sunrise behind them, and there was a message from Xara.

"James?"

"Hmm?"

She waited for him to glance up from the business section of the newspaper, having learned over the years it was pointless saying anything until she had his undivided attention. "Can you call Steve today? Apparently he's left messages at the office and City Hall about the check for the respite-care house."

James frowned and then uncharacteristically thumped the table with his fist. "Bloody hell. Between the pen pushers at county and Bianca, it's a miracle I get told anything. I'll talk to her and remind her that I'm paying her to be my secretary, not to plan her wedding."

Harriet was used to his tirades against Bianca and she'd suggested more than once he get a new secretary. James was resistant and said that despite Bianca's failings she knew how the office worked. He didn't have time to train someone new, especially now he was juggling his financial planning business with his mayoral duties.

"Can't you just write the check to speed things up?" she asked, knowing how important the respite-care house project was to her sister.

He sighed; a sound that said she was utterly clueless as to how the machinations of City Hall worked. "If it was my money I could write a check right now," he said slowly, precisely and with a whiff of condescension, "but it's City Hall so every i has to be dotted and every t has to be crossed before the check can be processed." He glanced at the big train station clock that dominated the light and airy kitchen. "You hate being late so you better get going."

As if to back up his words, the chimes of the news sounded on the radio, prompting her to stand up, dump her bowl in the sink and gather her wallet, cell phone and key fob. As she put the three items into her handbag, she noticed James had already put Nya's money on the kitchen counter ready for their housekeeper just like he'd done every Wednesday for years. Friends complained about their husbands' lack of organizational skills but never her.

She leaned in to kiss him goodbye, breathing in the fresh, sharp scent of his citrus aftershave. "You're a man in a million."

An unreadable look crossed his face, lingering for a moment in his blue-gray eyes. He blinked and it vanished. "That's me. Now go."

He swatted her pencil-skirt-covered behind and she laughed as she walked out the door.

GEORGIE PUT her head down and walked quickly, pushing against the wind that whipped dust, dirt and snack time trash against her skin, gritty and harsh like an exfoliating scrub. The north wind had blasted its heat over the school all day, making the kids feral and the teachers irritable. Everyone was relieved when the bell rang, heralding not just the end of the day, but the end of another busy week. They'd all beaten a hasty retreat to the comfort of their air conditioner and to the icy cold beverage of their choice. Now, the school grounds were empty of parents, kids and staff, and Georgie's car was one of only three left in the parking lot.

She gave thanks that she wasn't in Billawarre, where wind like this not only created dust storms but flamed wildfires. A momentary twinge of conscience reminded her to call her mother as soon as she got home. Another gust of wind buffeted her and she tightened her grip on the stack of her students' storybooks she was taking home to read and stamp with smiley faces. Just as she reached the car, a loud clap of thunder broke overhead and she jumped. A large, fat raindrop plopped onto her nose and she berated herself for not thinking to get her keys out of her bag before she'd left the classroom.

Georgie leaned her knees against the car door trying to use her body to protect the books and plunged her left hand into her cavernous rice-bag tote. She'd bought it at a fair-trade stall to support women in Cambodia and it held heaps, but without internal compartments everything fell into a big mess at the bottom. Her fingers located old tissues, her cell phone, a nail file, a container of tic tacs, tampons, lipstick, her spare glasses, a bottle of water, some hand wipes and her wallet, but no keys. She was just about to start a new search when she heard, "Hey, Georgie."

She looked up. Ben was next to her with a backpack slung on his shoulder, a bike helmet on his head and his left hand balancing a road bike. Despite a lack of lycra, he looked like the fit gym teacher he was, with a polo shirt fitting snugly across his chest, emphasizing the fact the man worked out.

The last time she'd seen him was at the previous week's Friday-night drinks, along with a dozen other faculty members. Each time she'd tried to start a conversation, someone had interrupted them. A frustrating half an hour later, he'd left—unlike her, he obviously had a social life. She'd experienced a mix of disappointment and relief, as well as some foolishness.

Prior to the event, she'd wasted a lot of emotional energy worrying about being rusty at the dating game but as it turned out, she needn't have bothered. Despite some definite faculty flirting at the baby shower, his suggestion she come to drinks hadn't come close to a date. He'd probably only mentioned the pub to be friendly and she'd read far more into it than existed.

She wasn't sure why she'd done that, especially when she'd vacillated about going, right up to and including when she'd walked through the door of the trendy Fitzroy bar. Even before her life fell apart she'd never been one for bars. The entire episode had been uncomfortable from start to finish so when she'd arrived at school on Monday morning and read the faculty bulletin, she was relieved that Ben was away at sixth grade camp for the week.

It had been another lesson in the complicated dance of millennial dating. Going back into the dating pool at thirty-four was not only terrifying, it was ten times worse than starting out as a pimply and gangly thirteen-year-old. Back then, despite her braces and insecurities, her expectations had been blissfully simple. She'd been full of the hope of meeting a boy who liked her and who wanted to spend time with her.

Now, she found hope hard to come by, and the permanently loud and ticking clock in her brain via her ovaries never gave her a chance to forget she was aging fast. That deafening sound had tainted the few dates she'd forced herself to go on in the last few months, along with booming questions like, is he looking beyond now and a good time? Does he want kids or is he like Jason and he's just saying what he thinks I want to hear? And the kicker: does he want to risk his hopes and dreams on me?

"Looks like you could do with a hand," Ben offered, tilting his head toward her unsteady tower of workbooks.

"Looks like you've got your hands full with the bike."

A teasing smile lit up his eyes. "Don't spread it around, but I can actually do two things at once."

"A man who can multitask? I'd like to see that."

A deafening clap of thunder boomed around them, immediately followed by another drop of rain. It turned into two and then five before a deluge fell from the sky with the intensity of the bucket dump at a water park. She squealed as cold water cascaded off her hair and threatened the workbooks. Shoving them at Ben's chest, she grabbed at her tote bag, pulling it from her side and around to her front. She tried again for the keys, her fingers surfing frantically through the contents as the rain soaked her sundress.

At last she found the key fob and pressed it. Her car blessedly beeped and its lights flashed. "Get in," she yelled as she opened the driver's door and hopped inside.

Ben abandoned his bike and as she closed her door, he opened the front passenger door and rain blew horizontally into the car. Sliding into the seat, he slammed the door shut behind him. Raindrops hung precariously from the ends of his eyelashes and clung to the tips of his hair that stuck out through the spaces in his bike helmet. No man should be allowed to have eyelashes that thick and dark when women paid a fortune to have theirs extended.

"Man, that's coming down." He peered through the windshield, which was a wall of water, then shook his head sending water spraying all over her.

"Hey!" She laughed, putting her hands up to fend off the sprinkles. "Are you part dog?"

He grinned and wiped his dripping face on his sleeve before pulling the workbooks out from under his wet shirt. "Lookie here. Hardly damp at all." He leaned sideways, brushing her arm as he deposited the books on the back seat.

"Thanks." The word came out a tiny bit strangled as a wave of goosebumps rose on her skin with a tingling whoosh.

In the small hatchback, she was suddenly very aware of Ben with his scent of sweat, rain and a soupçon of cologne. She shivered again, the sensations of heat and cold disconcerting her. In some ways it was a familiar rush and yet it had been absent for so long its return was vague and foreign. She put it down to an adrenaline surge sparked by being half-drowned and diving out of the rain.

Feeling ridiculously self-conscious, she glanced down at her lap and froze. Her free-flowing cotton sundress was now transparent and sticking to her like it had been vacuum sealed against her skin. She was fully clothed yet naked. To add insult to injury, her rain-cooled nipples clearly stood to attention. *Just fabulous.* She'd kill for a towel or a blanket, or for any sort of covering at all, but since moving to Melbourne she didn't need to keep a fire blanket or a horse blanket in the car. She had nothing.

Honestly, Georgie. You're a walking disaster for embarrassing situations.

She shoved Harriet's voice out of her head and started the car.

"You're not going to kick me out into that are you?"

The rain was rock-band loud, hammering on the car's roof but the embarrassed part of her wanted to be alone. "Well, you're already wet so ..."

"That's a bit harsh." He opened his big brown eyes wide and gave her a hangdog look. "Especially after I heroically saved your class's books."

"That's true," she said, feeling her smile slide off her face under the onslaught of chattering teeth. She turned the heater on full blast in an attempt to warm up. "But I'm frozen."

He glanced at her. "You need to get out of that dress."

And expose stretch marks and surgical scars? "Yeah, that won't be happening."

Despite his deep tan, the tips of his ears turned bright pink. "I didn't mean right now." His embarrassment rode off him in waves. The fact that it came with a certain old-worldliness made her regret her quip, which had been all to do with her issues and nothing to do with him.

"Sorry. Cheap shot."

His wide mouth tweaked up on the left as if to say, *Yup, I agree.* "What I meant was, you need a hot shower. I live just around the corner, so you're welcome to warm up and dry your dress. Or I can lend you some clothes to get you home."

His kindness made her feel even worse for the off-hand comment but the thought of hot water warming her icy skin was too good an offer to refuse. "Thank you, that's very kind. But what about your bike?"

He jerked his thumb toward the back of the car. "You've got those magic seats. If I put them down, the bike will be a sweet fit."

"Sounds like a plan."

Twenty minutes later, Georgie was wrapped up in one of Ben's shirts and wearing a pair of soft cotton track pants that she'd rolled up four inches. She was ensconced on his couch, sipping a mug of hot tea and feeling a lot more relaxed than she'd been in the car.

"So while we wait for your dress to dry, do you want pizza, Chinese, Thai, Indian, fish and chips, Japanese, Vietnamese, Turkish, Greek, Italian ...?" Ben asked, shuffling menus like a deck of cards.

"And *this* is what I love about Melbourne," she raised her mug in his direction, "there's so much choice. I grew up in the country and our takeout options were limited to fish and chips, a tough as shoe leather steak sandwich or Chinese."

"Me too." His eyes creased at the edges as a smile raced into them. "When we had Chinese, Dad always ordered number forty-three."

She laughed, feeling absurdly excited he was familiar with the numbered menu that was found in many small-town Chinese restaurants around the country. "Beef in black bean sauce."

"Yes." Ben grinned at her. "It's decided. We're reliving our childhood and having Chinese."

"Can I have my dumplings steamed?"

"Steamed?" he said with mock horror. "Sounds like someone's forgotten her country roots."

His teasing was easy and friendly, and with some good-natured bickering, they finally settled on their order of dumplings, spring rolls, special fried rice, honey chicken and beef with ginger and spring onions. Ben ordered it on the app before walking into his small kitchen.

"So country girl, do you want a rum and coke?"

In her twenties, she'd been to enough Bachelor and Spinster balls to know that rum was the drink of choice of many of her contemporaries, but she'd been raised around good-quality wines, which she preferred over spirits. Over the past five years, Jason's job as a wine rep had cemented her choice. "Do you have any white wine?"

His hand paused on the door of the refridgerator. "First no fried dumplings and now you want wine? Exactly where did you grow up?"

She gave an apologetic grimace. "The western district."

"Ah." The knowing sound echoed around his flat. "Let me guess? You're the daughter of a rich rancher, you went to boarding school and you grew up in the country, but you identify more with the city."

She was used to this type of reaction and once she would have defended herself against the implied criticism, but as she'd already leaped to one incorrect conclusion about Ben today she let this one wash over her. "Your crystal ball's a little foggy. One grandfather was both a rancher and a well-known Victorian parliamentarian, but Dad was a doctor."

"And your mom?"

How did she explain her mother? Since the death of her father a year ago, Georgie had given more thought to her mother than she had in her previous thirty-three years. "She's a woman of her generation. Her job was raising me and my two sisters as well as being the woman behind the man. Before I was born she did a lot of socializing to help build the practice. Dad was new to Billawarre and her family had the connections. Now she golfs, belongs to the Country Women's Association and the historical society, and she raises money for a children's charity. My middle sister's daughter has cerebral palsy."

"That's tough," he said holding up a bottle of sauvignon blanc. "This okay?"

"Lovely, thanks."

He poured her a glass and opened a beer for himself. Carrying both drinks over, he handed her the wine before settling next to her on the couch. "Cheers."

She raised her glass and took a sip. The wine was overly cold and the chill muted the crisp fruity flavors. She set it on the coffee table to warm up. "What about you? Where did you grow up?" She was more interested in hearing his story than she'd been about anyone else's in a long time.

"Mildura." He gave a self-deprecating shrug. "I don't have quite the same illustrious family history as you. For starters, I can't claim a parliamentarian."

She laughed. "I'm not sure I claim Gramps either. He was a staunch conservative. He died years ago but if he were still alive we'd have clashed a lot on ideology."

"So you're the radical member of your family?" he asked with a mischievous glint in his lovely brown eyes.

She thought about Harriet's obsession with family history—the way she lived her life entrenched in tradition—and Xara's seeming disregard for it. Had Georgie rebelled against anything or had she just done what she wanted with no one seeming to notice? "Remember, I'm the youngest just like you."

His face lit up with understanding. "Hard to be radical isn't it? By the time we were old enough to do anything outrageous our siblings had already done it all. Didn't leave us with much to rebel against, eh?"

"I think there might be something to your theory." She pulled her knees up to her chin. "Even though you can't claim a parliamentarian, I bet you have someone interesting in your family. What about a convict?" She thought about her childhood disappointment. "I was a kid in the bicentennial year and I was desperate for a convict relative, but all I've got are dour Presbyterians."

"Going to have to disappoint you there. We don't have any convicts either." He met her gaze. "A branch of my father's family wasn't a big fan of white settlement."

His tone was very matter-of-fact and she suddenly saw his deep tan, big brown eyes and dark curly hair in a whole new light; his heritage wasn't Mediterranean as she'd previously thought. Ben was Aboriginal.

Her mind immediately and uncomfortably slid to the Mannering family folklore. How her great-great-grandfather and his brothers had arrived, squatted on the fertile Western District's plains and dispossessed the local Aboriginal of their land. The story of how Thomas Mannering had bravely fought off an attack by the Gulidjan tribe and saved William from being murdered was proudly recorded in the family bible.

Not so long after the one-sided clashes with the Gulidjan, the brothers had weathered the drastic loss of staff rushing to the goldfields by being pragmatic and employing Aboriginal as ranch hands. It was a tradition that had lasted a century or more, but by the time Georgie had been born, the large ranches had been whittled down—lands taken for soldier settlements, lands sold to pay inheritance taxes, land divided among descendants—and it had probably been three or four decades since an Aboriginal had been on the payroll.

She swallowed against an odd feeling of the past suddenly inserting itself uninvited into the room. On an intellectual level, she knew she wasn't responsible for the sins of her forebears but that didn't stop her from feeling uncomfortable. Part of her wanted to blurt out, I supported the federal Apology, but that would make her sound as if she was begging for absolution and she wasn't. Was she? She'd never been this close and personal with such a fraught topic before and she wasn't quite sure what to say. No wonder people mostly stuck to their tried and true social groups—it avoided discomfort just like this.

She had a couple of Aboriginal kids in her class and she knew enough to know the words "caste" or "part Aboriginal" were no longer used to define Aboriginal heritage, and nor was skin color. A person either identified as Aboriginal or they didn't, and it was all based on their relationships.

She went for the base question. "Do you identify as Aboriginal?"

He shrugged. "Bit hard when I don't know any of my relatives on Dad's side of the family. By the time I was born, his mother and grandmother were dead and he never knew his father. Mom's side of the family are the only extended family I know."

"What about your dad? Does he identify?"

"It's not something we've ever talked about. He married an Italian girl and spent the seventies and eighties establishing a garage in Mildura. I think most people thought he was Italian." He sipped his beer. "I reckon claiming to be an Aboriginal back then would have been professional suicide."

She was both fascinated and intrigued. Her family's history was laid out in a framed tree that went back generations to the Middle Ages in England. It hung in the hall of her mother's house, and in the halls of her uncle's, her cousins' and second cousins' houses across the country. It hung very proudly in Harriet's home and although Xara didn't have it on her wall, Georgie knew she had a copy stashed somewhere. She hadn't bothered to hang hers after moving out of the house she'd shared with Jason because, as her only artwork, it looked pretentious. But her few hundred years of family history were nothing compared with the 60,000 years Ben could claim.

The doorbell pealed and Ben unfolded himself from the couch, picked up his wallet and went to the door. Georgie walked into the kitchen and opened cabinets until she found plates and cutlery.

They met back at the coffee table. "That smells amazing."

"We can only hope it tastes as good." He passed her a wax-lined brown paper bag containing three steamed dumplings swimming in soy sauce. "Here's your poor excuse for a dumpling."

"Yum. Thanks." She popped them on a plate before peeling back the tight plastic lids from the rest of the food. "Dad told me that when he and Mom first got married, they took their saucepans to the Chinese restaurant for takeout."

"Same." Ben smiled.

It was a wide and cheeky—full of the good things in life—and for the first time in a long time, it made her feel almost carefree. She smiled back, enjoying the long-lost sensation. They loaded their plates with food and settled back on the couch, both opting to use a fork instead of the wooden chopsticks that came with the order.

After commenting on the food—great flavors, could have done with more cashews and less spring onions—Georgie brought the conversation back to where they'd left off when the meal arrived. "So you don't have much information about your Aboriginal heritage?"

"I have about as much as I have about my Italian one. The family tree pretty much stalls on both sides at the great-grandparents." His brows suddenly rose over his bowl of fried rice. "Should I be more interested in one over the other?"

"I don't know. I guess not." The question brought up an interesting dilemma for her given she'd totally bypassed his Italian heritage with her questions. "Actually, maybe I thought you'd be more interested in your Aboriginal heritage because you live in Australia. We're always being told about Aboriginal people's connection to country."

A sick feeling swirled her Chinese food around her stomach. *Country my ancestors stole from yours.*

Georgie, for heaven's sake, Harriet's voice echoed in her head. *You don't hear the English saying they feel guilty over what happened in Scotland in the eighteenth century. Besides, we don't even own a tenth of that land anymore.*

Ben leaned toward the coffee table and refilled his plate. "So much of my Aboriginal ancestry is missing so I was never given that connection. There's a sad irony in the way my Italian grandfather used to fill my palm with the soil from under his vines and tell me that all good things came from the earth. I've never known Dad to take much notice of the bush, but he's magic with an engine. He'd fill my palm with oil and tell me how important it was."

"Did he grow up in Mildura?"

He shook his head. "Nah, he came from somewhere in outback New South Wales. His birth certificate says Wilcannia."

"I have no idea where that is."

"I only know cos I looked it up on a map once for a school project. Dad never talks about his life before he met Mom. He's not a big talker, period. I don't know if it's got anything to do with the time he spent in Vietnam or if he was like that before he got conscripted. Either way, Mom did most of the talking for both of them."

She caught the past tense. "Did?"

Ben spun his fork through his rice. "Yeah. She died a couple of years back. Cancer. Dad took it hard."

"I'm sorry."

He gave a silent nod.

She tried her wine again. This time the zip of gooseberries hit her tongue and she remembered her father teaching her how to swill the wine in her mouth so the liquid touched all her taste buds. "My father passed away almost fourteen months ago." She added hastily, "Not that I'm trying to be in competition with you."

He gave her a long look, his eyes filling with bemusement. "Why would you even think that?"

She shrugged. "Probably because after Dad died in a freak accident we had strangers telling us stories about how their relative died. It was like they thought it would cheer us up or make us feel less cheated. I don't really know why they did it, but it happened so often that my sisters and I started rating their stories as being either less or more freaky than Dad's death."

His face was part horrified, part amused and definitely intrigued. "Now you've made me want to ask how he died." He held up his hand like a stop sign. "You don't have to tell me if you don't want to."

"It's okay. I've asked you a heap of nosy questions so it only seems fair." She told him the story in the script she'd developed and adapted over the year. "Dad spent one week a month in Melbourne lecturing at the school of medicine at Melbourne Uni. He always stayed at a serviced apartment and parked his car in the adjacent multistory parking garage. On this particular day just as he returned to the car, a woman was backing out of her space. She had a heart attack at the wheel and the car slammed straight into Dad, crushing him against a concrete pillar. He died instantly."

"God. That must have been traumatic for your family. At least we had a few months to get used to the fact we were losing Mom."

"Yeah, it was tough but it's been the hardest for Harry and Mom." Ben's brow furrowed in confusion and she explained, "Harry's my eldest sister. She's a surgeon and she shared a practice with Dad. Mom was a career wife and she seems all at sea without him, which is why Harry's insistent on throwing this huge birthday party for her."

"Ah, the big sister who texted the other day." Ben refilled her wine. "Maybe we should introduce your mom and my dad so they can keep each other company."

She smiled politely but no matter which way she came at it, she couldn't imagine her immaculately dressed mother with her blond bob, signature string of pearls and perfectly elocuted vowels having anything in common with an auto mechanic. "The 300 mile distance between them could be problematic."

"True." He relieved her of her empty plate and set it down on the table. "Will you be spending all of your vacation in ... Where do you live?"

Was he asking because he wanted to catch up with her during vacation or was he just being polite? "I live in Essendon. My mother and sisters live in Billawarre and to answer your question, I'm hoping to get away with spending the first week up the bush." She forced herself to sound as casual as he did. "What are your plans?"

He shrugged. "I was going to go straight to Mildura but Dad's on a road trip. He loves restoring old cars and he's off somewhere, driving around with a group of old codgers. I suggested he come and visit me but he insisted I go to Mildura in the second week."

"That sounds fun," she said, disappointed that they'd be away at different times.

He gave a wry smile. "Not nearly as much fun as spending a week getting to know you. Still, perhaps we can do that after the break or ..." He ran his hand through his hair as if he was regretting speaking.

She was clutching on tightly to the fact that he'd said getting to know her might be fun. She wasn't going to let that disappear down a rabbit hole never to be heard of again. "What were you going to suggest?"

He shook his head, his curls bouncing wildly. "Don't worry, it probably won't work."

She leaned forward. "Try me."

He sighed, the sound laced with embarrassment. "It means exposing my nonexistent social life and the fact I have nothing planned this weekend except for shopping and laundry. No guy wants to look desperate."

"Then I'm equal to you in the desperate loser stakes."

"Hey!" He held up a warning finger, but his eyes twinkled. "I never said I was a loser. I find it hard to believe that you're desperate or dateless."

She choked on her wine. "I bet you say that to all the girls."

He grinned. "Only the ones with eyes that remind me of the Mildura sky. Do people comment on your eyes?"

She thought about her childhood and how people in the district immediately identified her as a Mannering the moment they saw the blue of her eyes. "My eyes got me into a lot of trouble as a kid because they were so recognizable. I share the color with my mother, sisters and my nieces. Apparently it dates back to my Scottish ancestors." She set down her glass, determined to chase the elusive rabbit down the hole. "So, what did you have in mind for this weekend?"

He'd relaxed the moment she'd confessed to having nothing going on this weekend. Now his arm was slung along the back of the couch and he was all loose limbed and easy grace. "Can you ride a bike?"

"Ah ... yes," she said cautiously, already worried that dating a gym teacher might mean pushing herself out of her semi-slothful comfort zone. "But isn't tomorrow going to be hot again?"

He shot her an indulgent look as if he knew it might have been a while since she'd ridden a bike. "We'll start early and finish for brunch and a swim."

"We're talking a flat bike trail, right?"

He laughed. "Yes."

"With only two weeks to go until vacation, I guess I can delay my Saturday sleep-in."

"Awesome." They traded cell phone numbers and then she stood and collected her still damp sundress. Plucking the shirt she was wearing, she asked, "Can I return these clothes tomorrow?"

"No worries." He rose from the couch and walked her out to her car.

Standing next to him, her gaze level with his chest, she suddenly felt self-conscious. Given up to this moment she'd been more relaxed than she had in a long time, it didn't make much sense. "Ah, thanks for the shower, the loan of your clothes and the wine." She reached for her wallet, pulled out a twenty-dollar bill and pushed it into his hand. "My contribution toward dinner."

He pushed back. "No."

"Please."

He shook his head, his face shadowed in the fast-fading light. "Tell you what. You can buy me pizza one night and we'll be square."

One night sounded good. Very good. "You're on."

She pressed the car's key fob and he shot out his hand, opening the door for her. "Stay dry, Georgie." A grin dimpled his cheeks.

"I'll do my best." She paused for a moment and then, feeling foolish, hopped into the car.

He closed the door behind her as she shoved her key into the ignition. She turned on the engine so she could wind down the window. "Thanks for a lovely evening."

"Any time." He leaned in and brushed his lips against her cheek so quickly it was over before she'd realized it had begun. "Drive safely." He slapped the roof of the car just like every country boy she'd ever known, and then turned and walked away.

Heady warmth tumbled through her and she wanted to hug it

close as much as she wanted to push it away. Hope was a double-edged sword and right now she didn't want to expend any energy on something that might fall over by lunchtime tomorrow. Or not. Either way, it was way too early to be hoping that this might go somewhere.

A shimmer skittered from her scalp to her toes making her buzz more than a shot of espresso; her body at odds with her brain. It was attraction versus logic and hope versus pessimism and the combination left her giddy and a little light-headed. She pulled in a deep breath, flicked the turn signal and pulled out into the quiet street.

For the next twenty minutes she sang loudly to the radio, trying not to replay all of the evening's conversations in her head. She failed dismally. Ben intrigued her and she liked him. Funny how they'd both spent a lot of time talking about their families but not about themselves. Actually, it wasn't funny at all. So often more was said about a person's life by not speaking and she didn't discuss the last two years if she could possibly avoid it.

Her mind wandered back to that bitter night when every dream she'd ever held about motherhood had been obliterated in a terrifying and bloody mess. Of the chilling and never-ending silence that followed. It only took one heartbeat to separate life and death; to cleave a child from its mother with wrenching and irrevocable finality. One. Tiny. Beat.

The familiar knot of heartache tightened in her chest and she gripped the steering wheel harder than necessary. Would she ever be able to think of Eliza without finding it hard to breathe? Would the intense loss of her daughter and the anger she leveled at her own body for letting Eliza down so badly and stealing her chance at motherhood ever metamorphose into something less raw? She didn't know. Part of her didn't want it to change, because the fear of forgetting was worse than remembering.

She pulled into her driveway and set about collecting her gear from the car, including her students' books, before walking the short distance to the front door. As she rounded the closed-in section of the small porch, she caught a flash of movement.

Her heart took off at a gallop. *Intruder!* A scream leaped into her throat and exited loud and fast through wide-open lips that would have made an opera singer proud. The high-pitched and piercing sound tore around the small space, threatening the early twentieth-century colored glass.

"It's only me, Auntie G. I didn't mean to frighten you."

"Charlie?" She peered into the gloom as the booming sound of her blood in her ears receded. "God. You just gave me a heart attack."

"Sorry."

Her niece was tall, willowy and as graceful as a gazelle, courtesy of years of ballet classes and Harriet's determination that no child of hers would slouch. Right now though, the gazelle looked slumped and the toes of her ballet flats were doing a decent job of trying to bore a hole through the boards.

Georgie's rattled brain rapidly recovered from its fright and started sifting through the information. It was nine-thirty on a Friday night in the middle of the rowing season and Charlotte was fifty miles from school. Harriet hadn't texted or called her to mention a visit. Her gaze slid to the side and she caught sight of Charlotte's designer duffle bag; the overnight bag of choice for every female boarder at her school.

Her niece was as social as her mother and just like Harriet, Charlotte always expected to get her own way. Harriet had probably said no to a party and Charlotte had taken matters into her own hands. Georgie swallowed a sigh. She really didn't want to have to ring Harriet and have a difficult conversation.

"Charlie, it's lovely to see you but exactly why are you here?"

Her confident niece promptly burst into tears.

A sinking feeling pressed in on her, sending her stomach plummeting to her toes. Something was going on and whatever it was, it had just scuttled tomorrow morning's bike ride with Ben.

CHAPTER THREE

Xara watched Tasha's school bus disappear around the bend and then checked the large roadside mailbox. She quickly riffled through the half-dozen envelopes looking for something with the Billawarre City Hall logo printed on it.

There were two letters from the bank, one from their HMO, a bill from the farm supplies store, a farming magazine and a box of diapers, but nothing from the county. She frowned. Harriet had texted her over a week ago saying James was chasing down the check and how furious he was at the ineptitude of some of the county employees. Based on that information, Xara had expected the check to have already arrived.

She blew out a frustrated breath and hopped back into the truck wondering how much longer they should wait before they inquired again. It was a fine line between being proactive and pushy. In any other situation she'd have drawn on her legal experience and sent a demanding letter; she was good at those. As president of the district's parents' support group for special-needs children, she often helped bewildered parents navigate the pothole-ridden roads of bureaucracy. But because of her family connections, this situation was different and her usual course of action would likely shoot them in the foot. James hated attorneys.

Mulling things over, she drove the mile back up the track to the house. With a hundred yards to go, the dogs greeted her racing the truck with enthusiastic barks and jumps. She slipped out of the truck to a hero's welcome until her boot hit the back veranda and then the whining started.

"We'll work later," she said, immune to their sad faces.

She had a heap of farm jobs waiting for her, along with lobbying letters to write and a meeting with her state lower house member, but like most women, first she needed to deal with the mess that was her kitchen. Xara wasn't a fastidious housekeeper but even she had her limits. Breakfast had been a disaster courtesy of Tasha having a bad morning. The frustrations of puberty were exacerbated when speech was impossible, and this morning Xara had totally misjudged what Tasha had wanted for breakfast. It hadn't been yogurt and the walls bore testament to that.

Killing two birds with one stone, she multitasked. Pushing her Bluetooth earbuds into position, she strapped on a pair of rubber gloves and called her mother while she sprayed and wiped. For as long as she could remember, she'd been calling her mother under the guise of a chat but really it was to check and make sure Edwina wasn't having a bad day. The telephone rang and rang and she was about to hang up when her mother finally answered.

"Hello."

"Hi, Mom. Were you in the shower?"

"Xara." Her mother always said her name with an air of surprise as if she'd suddenly remembered Xara was her daughter. "I was out in the garden cutting the roses before the heat ruins them."

Xara automatically glanced at her beleaguered garden, which, like the rest of the house, needed a lot more of her time than she had to give. Her mother's garden at Glenora had been planted in the 1880's under the supervision of the wife of the then brewery owner, and it was magnificent. The towering Canary Island date palm—a big favorite in Victorian-era gardens—stood out against the sprawling oaks and elms, enormous rhododendrons, glossy gardenias, bright azaleas and a rose garden that rivalled Flemington Racetrack.

One of the oaks had been planted by a former governor and still had the plaque under it to remind all of the honor. The garden was laid out like an English park and spoke of an earlier time when Australians aligned themselves to all things British. It also said "wealth" and "well water." Xara believed the garden was therapeutic for her mother who, at times, lost interest in many things, but never her plants.

"Are you on the flower roster for church this week?"

"No. The roses are table decorations for the hall. The Country Women's Association's catering the classic car rally's breakfast of champions." Edwina laughed. "Old men reliving their youth would be more accurate, but they're paying, and the money will bolster the rural relief fund."

"I thought that was next week." Xara remembered Steve promising the twins he'd take them to see the cars. Both boys loved anything with wheels. Did he know the rally was this afternoon? This morning had been so chaotic he'd left for the livestock auction before they'd said more than good morning and kissed each other goodbye.

"The breakfast's tomorrow but the expo's this afternoon," her mother explained. "They're parking the cars in High Street from four onward and they've already set up a row of white tents for this evening's market. There's going to be music, food and a showcase of local wine and cheese. The traders are thrilled James managed to get the rally to come through town because it's worth a lot of money. Did you hear him being interviewed about it this morning on the radio?"

Xara looked at her now yogurt-free wall. "No. This morning wasn't a great morning."

"Sorry, darling," her mother said with quiet understanding. Edwina was supportive of Xara in her own way. She didn't cope very well with Tasha for more than a couple of hours but occasionally she took the boys for a night.

"I saw Jacinta Beaumont the other day," Edwina continued, "and she told me how grateful Amy and Scott are for all your help with Rachel's new lifting machine. They're all very excited about the respite-care project."

Xara swallowed a sigh. "That's nice. I'll be excited too if we actually get the money."

"I thought you got formal approval weeks ago?"

"We did, but for some reason City Hall's dragging its heels releasing the funds. At this rate the house won't be built by December. We desperately want it to be fully operational for next summer to give families a much-needed break."

Her mother made a tsking sound down the phone line. "It's ridiculous the money's taking so long. Ask James. I'm sure he can speed things up."

Edwina sounded exactly like Harriet. It wasn't often her mother acted like a rich and entitled woman but when she did, Xara took delicious delight in the irony. Harriet was impatient with their mother; she considered Edwina wishy-washy and indecisive but every now and then the Mannering family's basic belief that they were born to rule rose up and spilled over.

Xara didn't bother explaining that she and Steve had already asked James. "Thanks, we'll try that."

"Do you want me to pick the boys up from school and take them to see the cars?"

She thought about her meeting. "That would great. Thanks, Mom. I'll text Steve. He can meet you there, which will save you having to field a thousand questions about cars."

"Oh, I don't know," her mother sniffed. "I can recognize a Ford and a Chevy at twenty paces, and I can tell you if your manifold is cracked."

Xara laughed, unable to picture her prim and proper mother sitting in either one of those symbols of working-class nirvana. Her grandfather had driven a Bentley and her father's first car had been a Triumph Spitfire. "I'll let the school know you're picking up the twins." She hung up, still smiling at the idea of her mother knowing one end of a manifold from another.

⚬

"MARDI, LOOK!"

Edwina turned toward the sound of Ollie's exuberant voice calling her by the name she'd chosen when Charlotte had been born. She'd been forty-seven at the time and far too young to be called Nana or Grandma, so she'd settled on Mardi, having read the name in a book. Richard had thought it ridiculous and insisted she be Granny to his Gramps but in an uncharacteristic show of determination, she'd held firm. She was Mardi to all four of her grandchildren.

"Mardi, did you have a car like this?" He was sitting on the polished leather seat of a gleaming green and black Chrysler Imperial, whose bright red and shining Buffalo wire wheels screamed 1920's.

She half laughed and half groaned. "Ollie, darling, this car was old before I was even born."

Hugh tilted his head, studying her. "So what sort of cars did you drive in the olden days?"

"Your great-grandfather was very precious about his cars and I wasn't allowed to drive them."

Hugh and Ollie scrambled out of the Chrysler with a cheery thank you to the owner before slipping their hands in hers.

"How did you learn to drive then?"

"The same way every farm kid learns to drive and the same way you will: in a pasture jalopy." It wasn't strictly true. She'd learned to drive in a pasture but not in an old wreck.

"Did your dad teach you?" Ollie asked.

She reluctantly recalled her strict and dour father. "By the time I was old enough to learn to drive, your great-grandfather was sitting in Parliament. He had his own driver who took him from Murrumbeet to Melbourne and back."

"So who showed you how?" Hugh's s face filled with interest.

Memories she'd buried long ago struggled to the surface. A dark-haired man with smiling eyes who'd taught her to change gears and change oil—among other things—and how, for a few precious months, she'd dared to change the vision of her life. The memories brought with them fondness, regret and an age-old despair that never completely left her despite the intervening years. Faded and ragged around the edges, the feeling still had the capacity to cut deeply and leave her bleeding for days at a time. Each November she prepared for it like a soldier readying for battle; it was other random times that caught her off guard and inflicted the most damage.

"Mardi, who taught you to drive?" Ollie asked again.

Needing to push the past away, she opened her mouth to say, *One of the ranch hands*, for that was exactly who he'd been, but instead found herself speaking the truth. "A friend."

They walked past the imposing redbrick clock tower that dominated High Street. It had been built in 1896 funded by a bequest from her great-grandfather, along with the planting of a boulevard of elms that ran down the middle of the street.. Edwina took some pride in the philanthropy and civic mindedness of her ancestors even though she knew the price one paid for being a Mannering was steep. Not that she ever mentioned that to the tourists she guided up the clock tower on Wednesday afternoons.

The festival's sound stage backed onto the tower and the high school rock band, bless them, was blasting out what their peers considered music and Edwina considered ear-burning noise. "Can you play 'Friday on My Mind'?" a guy in a driving cap called to the bass player but Lachlan Hamilton shook his head, concentrating on his Hendrix impersonation. That was a travesty in itself, Edwina thought as she hurried the twins quickly past the tent. If the teens of today had to bond with the music of her youth they could have at least chosen an Australian.

"Can we have ice cream?" the boys implored.

Edwina checked her watch. "You won't be allowed near the cars with ice cream. How about we look at the next section and then we have ice cream when Daddy arrives?"

"Yay." The boys cheered and hared off toward the next grouping of cars—ones Edwina had a chance of recognizing at first glance.

She caught up with them running around a shining white Volkswagen with red and white striped seats complete with vinyl piping. A pang of memory pierced her as sharply as a blade and she automatically rubbed her sternum.

"Oh, Edwina!" Primrose McGowan, her dearest friend, surprised her from the other side of the car. She wore a far-away look. "Doesn't this bring back memories? I can still picture it clear as the day you returned from your trip to London and Europe. You drove up the driveway of Irrewillipe in your brand new VW bug and stepped out wearing hot pants and white go-go boots." She let out a soft sigh. "You were the epitome of sophistication while I was stuck on the farm with Dad and 10,000 sheep."

Edwina recalled that day for other reasons and she found her fingers had crept up to touch her pearls. She forced her hand back to her side and said, with a touch of grit, "It was summer. With no air-conditioning, I would've been a hot and sweaty mess."

Primrose rolled her eyes. "Darling, you've never been sweaty in your life. Fortunately, I love you, otherwise I'd have succumbed to jealousy of the Mannerings' Midas touch years ago."

The guilt that was inexorably tied up with their long friendship, and which lay dormant most days now, suddenly flared, scorching Edwina as if it was the summer of 1968 all over again. She was eighteen—beautiful and poised on the outside, dying on the inside, and standing on a white and purple agapanthus–lined gravel driveway, expanding the lie to her friend that had started the year before.

"Rosie, it was just a car."

Primrose shook her head with the certainty of someone who clearly saw the absurdity of the statement. "It was freedom. I never understood why you didn't take what it offered and drove far away. I would have."

It wasn't the first time Primrose had expressed her confusion, but it had been many years since Edwina had last heard her speak of it. Her own reaction hadn't changed and her chest tightened with a familiar twist. She wanted to yell, *It wasn't freedom, it was a shackle without a key,* but she swallowed the words. One didn't shout in public or private and today wasn't the day to change the habits of a lifetime. Or tell Primrose the truth. Instead, she fell back on the lie that had served her for forty-eight years.

"I met Richard."

"Richard and his bloody yellow Triumph," Primrose said with the unmistakable hint of regret. She'd never been overly fond of Richard and in true Primrose style, she'd never bothered to hide it. Edwina appreciated that her friend, unlike other people in town, hadn't suddenly started speaking of Richard reverently now that he was dead. "You know, Edwina, there's a yellow Triumph Spitfire here today."

"Is there?" Edwina mustered some enthusiasm. Richard really had gone to a lot of effort in the weeks before he'd proposed. There'd been fun and laughter in that old Triumph. Sadly, it hadn't lasted. "I should show the boys."

"See you at six then?" Primrose asked, referring to the Country Women's Association breakfast the next morning.

"God, it's a crazy hour."

Primrose, who'd married a dairyman forty years earlier, laughed as she walked away.

The yellow Triumph Spitfire's gleaming chrome shone dazzlingly bright in the afternoon sunshine. It was while Edwina was chatting with the owner that Steve arrived to collect the boys.

"Daddy!" The twins threw themselves against their father. "Gramps asked Mardi to marry him in this car."

Surprise lit up her son-in-law's stubble-covered face as if he was having trouble aligning his taciturn father-in-law with the man who'd once owned a canary yellow racing car. "Really? This car?"

"Not exactly," she said with a half-smile, "but one very similar." The initial memories that had been unlocked by the presence of the car were being followed thick and fast by many more. They buffeted her like waves pounding against golden sands. "He loved that car. I'm not sure he ever forgave me when we had to sell it for the far more practical station wagon after Harriet was born."

"I can understand that." Steve grinned as he ran his hand lovingly over the sleek sporting lines of the vehicle. "I had no idea Richard was into sports cars. What other secrets did he have?"

"Far too many to mention, dear," Edwina said lightly, hoping the smile on her face hadn't cracked, fallen and opened her up to more questions.

"Daddy!" the twins implored. "We're hungry."

"Why doesn't that surprise me?" Steve pulled the brims of the twins' hats down. "Edwina, do you want to come and have some wood-fired pizza with us?"

It was kind of Steve to include her but then again there was nothing about Steve Paxton that wasn't kind and considerate. She could understand why Xara had been drawn to him from the moment she'd met him. Why she'd stood up to Richard when he'd asked her if she could bear to live a life where she out-earned her husband and where the farm would come first in every one of their marriage transactions. Edwina had thought that question particularly rich given Richard's surgical practice took precedence over their marriage. Actually, to be fair, that wasn't strictly true: she'd known from the start she wasn't just marrying Richard but the practice too.

As her father—glass of whiskey in one hand, pipe in the other —had so succinctly pointed out, Richard needed her name and the leg up her social standing in town provided and she needed the respectability of his career. He'd talked of a practical match, warned her that even the best-kept secrets had a way of coming to light at the most inopportune times and really, she had no choice but to accept the up-and-coming doctor. Then he'd eyed her from beneath his bushy gray eyebrows and said, "Given what you've put your mother and me through this last year, it's the very least you can do. It's time to grow up and live a life worthy of a Mannering."

Edwina found herself shaking her head against the memory as if the action would move it and its bitter legacy from her mind. It had been decades since she'd thought about that conversation and yet one small yellow Triumph Spitfire seemed to have brought it all rushing back.

"Another time then."

Steve's matter-of-fact voice broke into her thoughts and she realized he'd taken her headshake as a refusal of his invitation. That hadn't been her intention at all; pizza with the twins and Steve was something she'd enjoy. But given the barrage of memories she was currently wrestling, it was probably better if she spent the evening in the sanctuary of Glenora.

She opened her wallet and pressed a five-dollar bill into each boy's palm. "That's for ice cream, and I want to you to call me tomorrow and tell me all about the other cars."

The boys agreed and kissed her goodbye, as did Steve, and she watched them walk into the sizeable crowd. It might be a school night but like any country town, Billawarre embraced events that gave people a chance to ease the isolation of country life and help put some money into the civic coffers. A folk group had replaced the high school band and the sounds of a miked fiddle swam through the warm evening air, making her toes twitch. She crossed the crowd, dodging between couples and families, dogs and strollers, and made her way across the grass.

"Edwina!"

She turned and paused, watching Harriet slip her arm from James's. If he was aware Harriet had pulled away, he didn't show it as his concentration remained firmly on his conversation with two men wearing driving caps. They were probably the organizers of the car rally and James was schmoozing and thanking them for their choice of making Billawarre an overnight stop.

Harriet hurried over to her. "James is about to do the official welcome and then we're going to Lemongrass for dinner. You're welcome to join us."

The idea of making polite conversation with car enthusiasts all evening wasn't enticing. *Your life's been one long polite conversation.* The thought struck her as hard as a clenched fist and she automatically sucked in a surprised breath.

"Are you okay?" Harriet's forehead creased in an impatient frown. This daughter was frequently irritated with her. Sometimes Edwina thought that Harriet had stepped in to take on Richard's role now that he was no longer around to grind his teeth or sigh at her.

"I'm fine, Harry, just a bit tired." She gave a faint laugh. "I've had the twins for the last hour."

"Oh, God, really?" Harriet looked horrified. "Xara should know better."

"I'm sixty-four, Harriet, not ninety," she said more waspishly than she'd intended. "According to recent articles in the *Women's Weekly*, I'm a woman in my prime. I'm more than capable of giving your sister a hand now and then."

Harriet's blue eyes flashed silver. "I work full time, Edwina, and I lend Xara Charlotte during vacation."

Harriet's snappish reaction surprised Edwina. Once again she was faced with the unerring fact that despite forty-five years of being her mother, she didn't understand Harriet at all. Even if Harriet did have time to spare, she was so uncomfortable in the company of children that any attempt at child minding was a disaster. There was an odd irony in the fact that Charlotte was a counterpoint to her mother in this regard: she was a natural with kids. With all the talk of Charlotte pursuing medicine as a career, Edwina had wondered more than once if she'd specialize in pediatrics.

Edwina had an urge to reach out her hand and give her daughter's arm a gentle squeeze to reassure her that Xara didn't expect her to mind the twins, but she didn't. She and Harriet didn't have that sort of mother-daughter relationship. "We all help the best ways we can. Could you have a word to James and get him to find out what the hold-up is for the respite-care house money?"

Harriet gave one of her annoyed sighs. "I've already done that. Honestly, the power-hungry pen pushers in the county need a bomb under them. James deserves a medal for what he's taken on as mayor." As her brief rant came to an end she seemed to remember her original purpose. "Are you coming to dinner?"

It was a duty offer. A knot of sadness tightened inside Edwina that duty was the only thing she and Harriet shared. "Thank you for the invitation, but I think I'll pass. I have to be up before dawn tomorrow for the Country Women's Association breakfast."

"It's good you're involved again," Harriet said briskly and approvingly as if Edwina had just given her one less thing to worry about. "You've locked in family dinner at Miligili Saturday week?"

"Yes, darling, it's in the calendar." She almost said, *Thank you for not organizing a big birthday party*, but she changed her mind at the last minute, not convinced it wasn't still happening. "I'm looking forward to seeing Charlie. I talked to her at Georgie's last week and she seemed a bit low."

Harriet pursed her lips. "I'm still cross with Georgie for not taking Charlotte straight back to school on Friday night. It doesn't look good when the rowing captain goes AWOL just because she's not picked for the team. Yes, her shoulder was a problem, but she knows better than that. I've had a long and serious telephone conversation with her explaining we all have to learn to live with disappointment, be a team player and soldier on."

Edwina wasn't certain Harriet had ever truly experienced disappointment in her life. "She sounded exhausted to me."

"Yes, well, senior year is a big year. If she's tired she needs to wait until vacation to sleep," Harriet said crisply. "Fortunately, I was able to smooth things over with the coach and it helped that Georgie got her back in time to be seen at the regatta. Thankfully, she avoided being stripped of her captaincy and tipped out of the team altogether." A visible shudder ran through Harriet and her hand gripped her handbag just that little bit tighter. "Thank God, she's put it all behind her now. She's training hard for the race of the year and we're driving to Nagambie tomorrow."

Edwina remembered the huge weekend of socializing that accompanied the regatta, starting with the Friday-night cocktail party and ending with the school rowing luncheon. She was glad those days were behind her. "You've got a very busy weekend."

"We have. Do you want to know what I'm looking forward to the most?" It was uncharacteristic for Harriet to pause to ask—generally she just assumed people were interested.

"Seeing Charlie?"

"Well, yes, obviously, although I'll have her at home for two weeks soon." A wistful look crossed her face. "Actually, I'm really looking forward to the three-and-a-half-hour drive to Nagambie, because it means I'll have James to myself." Then as if she'd said too much, she leaned in and quickly air-kissed Edwina's cheek. "I better go and do the mayoress thing."

Harriet strode away over the grass, the uneven ground not daring to cause any upset or mayhem to her high heels. It made Edwina think of Primrose's earlier comment about the Midas touch of the Mannerings. She didn't believe in it but when she thought about Harriet's life, she was tempted to be swayed by the argument.

Stepping down from the raised median onto the road, she found herself standing between two cars. One was a sparkling blue station wagon with a distinctive white roof rack and side venetian blinds. The other was a stunning red Jaguar XK-E.

She blinked to clear the image, convinced that she must be imagining those two particular vehicles side by side, because what were the odds of it actually happening? Her eyes returned to focus, but the cars remained unchanged. It was as if the day was conspiring to keep her pulled firmly back in the past she'd spent so much time avoiding. Part of her wanted to walk away but another part stayed her feet, urging her to stop, sit and remember.

The Ford was in far better condition than the one she'd laid under in 1967. This one didn't reek of oil and dust and its engine was so clean as to be unrecognizable. Her hand lingered on the doorframe as she peered into the all-blue interior, remembering how she'd sat on the bench seat, her hot skin sticking to vinyl as she'd bounced over the pastures struggling to conquer the column shift.

"You can sit in her if you want, love." A portly man was seated on a folding chair under the shade of an elm.

"Are you sure?"

He dragged in hard on his cigarette. "You're a pretty good bet, love. Doubt you'd be able to handle the column shift to make a quick getaway."

Edwina's chin shot up despite herself. "I could give you a run for your money on handling that shift. I learned to drive in a car just like it."

He gave a husky chuckle. "Bet you learned more than just how to stroke the gear shift."

The crude inference made her shoot him her best cool and withering stare—Richard had called it the Mannering putdown. "I learned that European engineering lasts longer," she said icily and with perfect diction before walking away. But the exit line didn't stop the hairs on the back of her neck rising, nor did it prevent flashes of memory—kisses in the moonlight, fumbles in the dark and later, much later, hot and burning tears.

Edwina, when it all gets too much, you need to concentrate on the present.

The words of the counselor she'd seen after Richard's death managed to penetrate the cacophonous noise in her ears and the choppy images in her mind, all of which threatened to overwhelm her. Had overwhelmed her. Her heart hammered hard against her ribs, beads of sweat formed at her hairline and once again she was fighting against the pull of the dark. Fighting against the forces that had conspired against her for forty-eight years, turning her life into a war zone of unending loss and leaving her permanently stranded in no-man's-land.

Her head spun, perspiration glued the lining of her linen dress to her skin and she pressed her hand against the Jaguar to steady herself. She refused to faint in the main street of Billawarre. That would cause a fuss and she hated fuss. Hated being the center of attention, hated inquisitive eyes and never-ending questions. Hated the risk of her carefully constructed life falling down around her.

"Here." A male voice reached her through the thumping noise in her ears. "Sit." She felt a hand on her shoulder and then she was being gently pushed backwards. The edge of a seat pressed behind her knees and she sat, automatically swinging her legs sideways. The familiar scent of leather enveloped her.

"Drink this."

A bottle of water was pressed into her hands. She greedily drank the icy contents before pressing the bottle against her cheeks, welcoming the cold droplets of condensation on her skin. She didn't know how long it took but eventually the suffocating heat that burned every cell of her skin faded and the booming noises in her head quieted.

"Feeling better?"

The deep and solicitous voice should have been soothing, but it shot along her veins like a flame licking gunpowder. Her hand closed hard around the almost empty water bottle, crumpling it with a loud crack. Dear God, but she knew that voice. Surely, it couldn't be ... She turned her head, the movement so sharp and fast it sent her hair flying and sticking to her lips.

A pair of chocolate brown eyes set deep in an aged, sun-spotted face and framed by wiry salt and pepper hair gazed back at her with concern in their depths.

Edwina's breath shortened and her mind raced. *You're being ridiculous.* She was letting her imagination run wild and conspire with the memories those blasted cars of her youth had dredged up. It couldn't possibly be him. There was absolutely no reason for her to even think it might be. Apart from the bulk of 1968, she'd always lived in Billawarre and in forty-eight years he'd never once tried to contact her. She'd never once tried to contact him. Well, not for a very long time. No, this man was a stranger; a kind man doing what kind men do when faced with a woman about to faint.

Logic and reason lengthened her breathing. "I am feeling better. Thank you."

"Are you up for standing?" He stretched out his work-worn hand and she caught sight of neatly clipped nails with half-moon cuticles faintly stained with oil.

A clanging started in her head and she fought to silence it. *It's not him. All car enthusiasts have hands like that.* "Absolutely," she said, ignoring his hand and rising to her feet. "It's a beautiful car. Did you restore it yourself?"

"It's been a labor of love or an old man's folly. It depends on your point of view."

She laughed. "It was certainly a car most young men coveted back in the day, as my granddaughter would say."

"I only ever wanted two things back then; this car and a beautiful girl." His head dipped in a self-deprecating nod and his face creased into a soft and well-worn smile. Memories bracketed his mouth in the deep folds and creases. "Both were out of my league."

Edwina felt a tug deep in the pit of her stomach for a boy with a cheeky smile who'd loved a girl he still remembered decades later. She covered it by quipping, "I'm sure the car's aged better than the girl." Before he could reply she hurried on briskly, "Thank you again for the water."

"No worries," he said, tilting his head as if he was trying to remember something.

"I hope you enjoy your stay in Billawarre and all the planned activities."

He laughed and the sound was filled with humor and tinged with chagrin. It made her feel as though she'd been locked out of a private joke. A shiver shot up her spine. "Did I say something funny?"

"No." His tone was serious. He rubbed the back of his neck as if the sun had burned his skin and it was now itching and peeling. "It's just ... last time I was here I wasn't welcomed quite so enthusiastically."

"I'm sorry to hear that," she offered up automatically, the manners ingrained from childhood coming to the fore. "I hope this time we can reverse your opinion of our town. We're hosting a breakfast tomorrow and I hope you can come."

"Will you be there?"

Something in the way he asked made her flash hot and cold. "Yes." She found she needed to clear her throat. "I'll be in the kitchen but do come and say hello."

"Who will I ask for?"

"Edwina."

"Jesus." He sagged against the car, his face suddenly pallid and gray as his brown eyes intently searched her face. "Edwina Mannering?" His voice cracked over her name. "Eddy?"

He used his nickname for her so softly and so reverently she was hurled back in time to their last night together forty-eight years ago. A night when the full moon had illuminated his face and his love for her. It was the last time she'd ever been truly happy.

CHAPTER FOUR

"Take blood cultures," Harriet instructed her intern, Blake, over the phone as she opened the door to accept the delivery of champagne. "And call me back when you have the results." She hung up without saying goodbye and immediately indicated to the delivery man where he should unload the boxes.

It was the day before Edwina's party and Harriet had a to-do list worthy of an Olympic event. With razor-sharp prioritizing, she was determined to clear it by day's end. For efficiency's sake, she'd dispatched James to Geelong to pick up Charlotte from school. Her daughter was now officially on vacation and home for the next two weeks.

The thought of James driving to Geelong reminded her of last Friday when the two of them were supposed to have driven to Nagambie together. After all her plans and anticipation, it hadn't happened. A pang of disappointment laced with lost opportunity slugged her yet again.

While they'd been packing the car for the trip, James had received a phone call about some City Hall crisis or other. He'd ranted and raved about the moronic people he was required to work with and then stayed back to sort out the mess. Harriet had done her own share of fuming over the ineptitude of some county employees and had driven to Nagambie alone.

James had finally arrived on Saturday just before Charlotte's race and, of course, he'd been instantly absorbed into the crowd of Harriet's old school friends, who adored him. Between time spent at the regatta, the evening's cocktail party in Melbourne and then the rowers' luncheon at school on Sunday, she'd scarcely had any time alone with him. Her plans of seducing him in the luxurious Melbourne hotel she'd booked for them had taken a hit when he'd collapsed in an exhausted heap on the feather-top mattress.

This week had been no better. She'd put herself on the weekday on-call schedule so she had the weekend free for Edwina's party and she'd spent most nights at the hospital due to a cluster of emergencies. So this weekend was it. Come hell or high water, even if she had to tie James down, they were going to have sex.

An anticipatory tingle shot through her and she smiled. The idea of tying him down was quite exciting and it might just be the sort of thing they needed to recharge their languishing sex life. It was a shame she hadn't thought of tying him up earlier, because then she'd have had time to order something. Billawarre didn't have an adult shop but luckily she had a vast collection of silk scarves. One of those would do the trick nicely.

Her cell phone buzzed and she checked her email, rolling her eyes at the school's efficiency in sending the account before the students had even stepped off the campus. She forwarded it to James —he handled all the bill paying—and instead opened the one with the subject line, *Student Academic Progress Report Card*. Clicking through to the school's online portal, she located Charlotte's name, selected the current year, semester one report cards, and quickly scanned the results.

She audibly gasped at the dramatic plunge in grades, the astonishingly poor attitude assessment and the less than stellar quality of work. It was as if she was reading the report of a completely different child from the one who'd gotten a glowing progress report card at the end of the fourth week of semester. What the hell had happened?

No, no, no. Not again. Not now. There'd been a couple of periods when Charlotte was twelve and fourteen where she'd lost focus. On both occasions, real fear had Harriet that Charlotte may be similar to Edwina. That had been enough to cajole, push and threaten Charlotte to keep her on track. The last two years had been drama-free with Charlotte showing signs of being as focused as herself. Harriet had relaxed, concluding that puberty must have been the culprit of those momentary lapses.

As she re-read the report, acid burned her stomach. Charlotte couldn't afford to lose focus in her vital senior year when her college acceptance depended on high grades and attitude. Anger surged in over Harriet's stupefaction; a latent fury at the school for not having notified her earlier. She brought up the number of Charlotte's housemistress in her contact list and stabbed the name with her finger. While the phone rang, she planned a vicious tirade on the duty of care.

"Hello, Harriet." Bella Moretti's calm voice carried down the line. "How can I help?"

"I've just read Charlotte's report."

"Ah." The sound was soft and knowing. "If it's any consolation, you're the fourth rowing parent I've spoken to this morning. I do understand it's a shock when Charlotte's always achieved such high grades but honestly, given the hours they're expected to train, something always gives. In most cases it's the academics."

"I managed both," Harriet said hotly as she paced across the Italian marble tiles of the l'Orangerie, unable to stay still.

Bella didn't skip a beat. "Charlotte's got the vacation to revive, reenergize and catch up. All her teachers have spoken with her and together they've devised a vacation study program. If she follows it, she'll start the new term back on track and," she gave a light laugh, "disaster averted."

The quietly spoken words were a balm to Harriet's shock and indignation. "So there are other girls in the eight in a similar situation?"

"She's not alone. We really do expect a lot from our young people so it's not surprising this sort of thing happens. It's early in the year and if she works hard from now on she'll be back on track. Vacation is the perfect opportunity to discuss with her how to balance extracurricular activities in the coming weeks."

Harriet decoded the meaning. "Oh, God. She's not still talking about auditioning for the school play, is she?"

"Actually, I was talking about the parties," Bella said with a sigh. "Their impact spreads far beyond Saturday night with the effects being felt through to weepie Wednesday."

"Charlotte will need to significantly improve her grades before I'll give permission for any weekend leave," Harriet said tersely. "Thank you for the chat."

"My pleasure. Enjoy having Charlotte home for vacation."

Harriet's phone rang as soon as she'd hung up from Bella and she took the call from her practice manager, trying not to sigh. "Debbie."

"Hi, Harriet, sorry to bother. I know you're busy with the party preparations and—"

"What's the problem?" Harriet asked, trying to keep the loquacious woman on track.

"I've been checking the bank statements and I've got a query about a series of payments."

Hundreds of payments went through the practice each month and Debbie was responsible for the bulk of them. "Which ones?" Harriet walked to the laundry and opened the linen closet, all the while wishing the woman would get to the point.

"They're payments for AAB Medical and they vary from a few hundred dollars to 80,000."

Harriet lifted a pile of plush hand towels from the stack. "Debbie," she said, not bothering to hide the irritation from her voice, "that's the company we purchase all our supplies from."

"We use AB Medical supplies."

"Yes and they merged with another company and changed their name, remember?" A thought struck her. "God. They're not double billing us, are they?"

"I don't know. The thing is, I can't find any invoices from AAB and I'm certain I haven't paid them. That's why I'm ringing. To check if for some reason you'd paid them."

"I leave all that to you." A chill rippled through Harriet. "You haven't left the computer logged in so someone else in the office could access the accounts, have you?"

"No." Debbie's indignation burned down the line. "Of course not."

"Sorry," Harriet said carefully. Office politics really wasn't her strong suit. "Ring this new company and get them to resend the invoices. We'll go from there. There's probably a perfectly reasonable explanation and I'm betting the name change is the culprit. I'll see you at the party tomorrow."

Slipping her cell phone into her pocket, she walked back into the kitchen and saw Nya standing by the sink, obviously waiting for her. The woman had been cleaning all morning to make Miligili glow for tomorrow night's festivities.

"Do you need something, Nya?"

The diminutive woman's hands fluttered nervously in front of her chest. "I'd like to be paid, please."

Harriet didn't follow. As today was an extra shift to help prepare for the party, she'd been the one to pay Nya. Her gaze drifted to the now clean and empty island counter. "I put the money in the usual place for you."

"That's not the money I'm talking about."

Harriet frowned, not understanding, and a bubble of exasperation formed in her gut. Why today? Nya had worked for them for years but at least once a year there was an uncomfortable situation around money. After the last misunderstanding, Harriet had taken to noting down the hours Nya worked so they were both on the same page.

"What money are you talking about?"

"The last two weeks."

Nothing out of the ordinary had happened in the last two weeks. "Nya, Mr. Minchin leaves your money in the kitchen for you each week."

The woman's nodding head stopped moving. "But there's been no money this last two weeks. I thought he just forgot and you'd pay today."

A vague memory of seeing cash on the counter as she left for work came back to her. Was that two weeks ago? Probably. What about the Wednesday just past? She couldn't remember. "Mr. Minchin definitely paid you two weeks ago."

"No," Nya said determinedly. "He did not."

"I saw the money on the counter, Nya."

The woman pursed her lips and Harriet recognized the adamant reaction—the one that preceded Nya digging her heels in and refusing to cooperate. With her mother's party tomorrow she really couldn't afford to have Nya being uncooperative. "Fine." Harriet put down the towels and stalked to the study and retrieved her handbag.

Returning to the kitchen, she pulled bills from her wallet before slapping them into Nya's hand. "But I'll be talking to Mr. Minchin about this and if he says he left the money then this conversation isn't over."

"I'll take these towels for the bathrooms, yes?" Nya picked them up as if they'd been talking about towels rather than squabbling over money.

"Thank you, Nya." Harriet filled the kettle, thinking that a complicated bowel resection was a hell of lot easier than juggling staff. Her male colleagues had it easy—their thoughts rarely turned to anything domestic and if they did, they just asked their wife to take care of it.

She heard the sound of tires on gravel and smiled. *James.*

Darling man. There might be days when having a wife would be handy but she had a husband who understood her career and did his best to share the load. Walking to the large sliding doors, she waved through the glass to her husband and her daughter and immediately noticed the absence of bright yellow learner plates on the windshield of the car. Charlotte usually grabbed as many driving hours as she could, keen to accrue the massive 120 hour requirement before she sat her driving test on her eighteenth birthday in May.

"Not driving today?" Harriet asked as she gave her daughter a welcome-home kiss.

"Too tired," Charlotte replied flatly as she walked into the house and collapsed on the couch. "All I'm doing this vacation is sleeping."

Harriet folded her arms and caught her daughter's gaze, slightly taken aback by the dark rings under her Mannering-blue eyes. "Sleep and *study.*"

Charlotte's arms rose in the air before falling back against the dark green Chesterfield. "Jeez, Mom. I only just walked through the door."

"Give her a couple of days off, H," James said quietly as he carried Charlotte's bags inside. "After Mardi's party, you'll get stuck into your schoolwork, won't you, sweetheart?"

Charlotte gave her father a grateful smile. "Yes, Dad. Meanwhile, I didn't have breakfast and I'm starving. Will you make me a ham and cheese croissant, Daddy dearest?"

"It's a bit close to lunch for that," Harriet said, thinking of the ingredients she had in the refrigerator for a chicken Caesar salad. "Why didn't you have breakfast? You know it's the most important meal of the day."

"And welcome home, Charlie," Charlotte mumbled before shooting to her feet. "God. I'm barely through the door, Mom, and you're at me. I'm going to my room to starve in peace. Call me when the healthy lunch is being served." She flounced down the corridor and the slam of her bedroom door echoed up the long hallway.

"Good going." James picked an apple from the bowl and bit into it with a loud crunch.

"What?" It wasn't like James to criticize her. "You know she should have had breakfast and this outburst is the perfect example of why. She's got low blood sugar, she's irrational and we have to deal with the fallout. Honestly, she's her own worst enemy. And have you seen her report? Those grades? I tell you, come Monday, that girl's knuckling down to some serious study."

Harriet waited for James to murmur his agreement but all he said was, "She's not you."

"No," Harriet said. "But she can be."

"And if she doesn't want to be?"

She stared at James and blinked before realizing he was cracking a joke. She laughed and touched his cheek. "Thank you, I needed that. It's been a shitty morning. I had a funny conversation with Nya. She said you haven't left her any money for two weeks. I know I saw the cash two weeks ago, but did you forget on Wednesday?"

"In ten years, have I ever forgotten?" He picked up his keys. "I have to get to the office."

Harriet barely heard him as a haze of angry vermillion blurred her vision. Of course James hadn't forgotten. "I can't believe Nya stood here in this kitchen and told me you hadn't paid her." The full impact of the deceit hit her and she groaned. "Oh, God, I'll have to sack her. Today. Right on top of Edwina's party and then there's the whole process of finding someone else."

"Don't fire her," James said emphatically as he bounced his keys in his hand. "Hell, for years she's gone above and beyond. Okay, for some reason she's needed some extra cash and she found an inventive way of getting it. Think of it as a bonus and let it go."

Harriet wasn't so certain. "It's not the money, James, it's the lie. How can I trust someone who lies to me?"

"Unless you want this party to be a disaster, you're going to have to find a way." He opened the door and disappeared into the noon heat.

THE BELL RANG AND, over the cheers of the entire school community, the principal wished everyone a very happy vacation. The children scattered, leaving the teachers to wander back to their classrooms and do a final tidy up before they could relax into two lovely weeks of relative freedom. Georgie figured she really only had one week. In many ways her week in Billawarre was going to be a lot like school, only she'd be the little kid being bossed around by the big ones. On one level she loved her sisters. On another, they drove her nuts.

"Knock, knock."

She looked up from packing the storage box to see Ben leaning casually against the doorframe, his gaze fixed on her. With his hands in his pockets, his weight on his left leg and his right crossed over it, he exuded the confidence of a man comfortable in his own skin. His lips curved in a smile that combined pleasure and relaxed charm.

A genuine shot of joy whizzed through her. "Hey."

It was two weeks since she'd telephoned him and canceled their bike ride. At the time, he'd sounded understanding but he hadn't suggested they reschedule and she'd been too worried about Charlotte to think beyond the moment. Since then, he'd divided his time between two schools and she'd hardly seen him to say more than hi and bye in the teachers' lounge.

"Have you been working here today?"

He shook his head. "I finished at Fitzroy Elementary School at lunchtime. Thought I'd stop by and catch you before you leave." He pushed off the doorjamb and walked inside, ducking to avoid taking out the cardboard spiral artwork she'd strung around the room. "How's your niece?"

She pressed the lid onto the storage box and gave him an honest answer. "I really don't know. When I called you, I'd just put a teen to bed who was so hysterical and distraught she couldn't string a sentence together. A totally different young woman woke me up at six o'clock the next morning holding a cup of tea. She looked and sounded perfectly normal and she asked me to take her back to school so she could arrive in time for the rowing regatta."

He spun a little person's chair around, straddled it and lowered himself down, bringing his knees up around his chin. "Did you drive her back?"

"Of course I did. I thought if the two of us were trapped in a car together for seventy minutes, she'd tell me what had upset her so much."

"And?"

She sighed, still bugged by the bizarre event. In the two weeks since she'd dropped Charlotte at the regatta, she'd received a couple of chatty texts from her, including a Snapchat of her on top of the school clock tower. Neither communication had totally reassured her. "I tried everything to get her to talk. I tried being the cool aunt. You know, the one who accepts the situation, says nothing and waits for her to volunteer the information."

"Did it work?"

"No. My next strategy was asking about school and her friends, but I drew a blank there too. After that, I totally blew the cool persona and asked pointed questions. She was contrite, insisting she was sorry she'd worried me. She said she'd been upset about her shoulder and not being picked to race. That a night away from the boarding house and a good sleep was all she'd needed and that everything was now," she raised her fingers into quotation marks, "'all good, Auntie G.'"

"I get that," Ben said nodding thoughtfully. "I couldn't think of anything worse than being sent away to boarding school."

She rolled her eyes at the old chestnut that was lobbed at her by people who'd gone to school where they lived. "Spoken by someone who's never boarded. She wasn't sent, Ben. It's not a punishment. It's an opportunity and she loves it. Most teenage girls do, because they get to spend hours on end with their friends. Charlie's very social, just like her mother, and her worst fear is missing out. Plus, she has her own room so she can get space if she needs it."

"Still," he said sounding dubious, "it must be pretty intense. Perhaps she had a fight with a girl at school?"

"Maybe. The thing is, Charlie's been boarding for long enough to know how to deal with that sort of stuff and she's hardly a victim. She's got a lot of her mother in her."

"Fight with her boyfriend, then?"

She shook her head. "She doesn't have a boyfriend at the moment and she's far too level-headed for that sort of drama."

Ben laughed. "No one is level-headed when it comes to heartbreak."

"I guess not." She thought about Jason and Eliza and her year of seesawing emotions. "Anyway, whatever it was, I'm sorry it got in the way of our outing."

He gave a *whatever* shrug. "That's why I'm here. Dad called last night. Turns out his car rally went through Billawarre."

"Seriously?"

"I know, right? I've never heard of the joint and then I hear about it twice in two weeks. He's decided to stay on for a few days, so I Googled it to see the attraction. Apparently, it's got a historically significant clock tower, an avenue of trees, dry stone walls to rival Yorkshire, a milk factory, and it's the heartbeat of sheep and dairy country."

She pulled down the window blinds in preparation for vacation. "And your father's interested in clocks, trees, walls, cows and sheep?"

He laughed. "No, but he loves restoring cars. He's probably lallygagging to an old farmer about a wreck with potential in some far-flung meadow. He'll be doing a deal to get it towed to the garage." He gave her a sheepish look. "I thought I might surprise the old man and go visit him there. Thing is, I didn't want to surprise you. I wouldn't want you thinking I was stalking you."

"And are you?"

He gave her his cheeky grin; the one that reminded her of what he must have looked like as a mischievous little boy. "Only a little bit and not in a scary way."

She cocked her head, studying him. "For all I know, using honesty might be part of your stalking persona. You know, draw me in so I never suspect."

"Mostly I'm saving myself a trip to Mildura in the second week of the vacation," he said practically. "It means we're both in Melbourne at the same time and we can finally do that bike ride."

A warm and cozy feeling wound through her accompanied by a skitter of excitement. He still wanted to spend time with her. "That sounds great."

"I don't expect to see you in Billawarre," he added tentatively. "I don't want to get in the way. You've got your family and your mother's party and I wouldn't want to complicate things for you. We haven't even had an official date yet so meeting the parents is way ahead of the curve."

His straightforward approach was disarming and charming and right then she knew without a doubt that she wanted to get to know him a lot better. She put her handbag on top of the storage box. "After the party, I'm definitely going to need a day off from my mother and sisters."

He shot to his feet—quick and as fast as a jack-in-the-box—and again she was surprised by his height. He looked down at her from under a recalcitrant curl and with a smile tugging at his lips. "Is that right?"

"Absolutely." Lightness wove through her in a way it hadn't done in over a year and she grabbed onto it, harnessing the joy of flirting. "My family's well known in the district for our hospitality so it would be really remiss of me not to show you the rail trail."

Now he was standing very close to her with his head tilted down to hers. "The bike track with the old railway bridge?"

His breath stroked her cheek and she found it hard to concentrate. "Not just any old bridge. The finest example of a wooden trestle railway bridge in the state."

"My mistake." He picked up her hands, lacing his fingers through hers. "I'm looking forward to you showing it to me."

She looked down at his tanned hands in hers, felt his warmth streaking through her and heating places that hadn't thawed in a very long time. Suddenly Sunday couldn't come quickly enough. "Do you need a ride to Billawarre?"

His enticing brown eyes studied her. "Are you offering?"

She smiled and nodded slowly. "I think I am."

"In that case ..." He released her hands and slid his arms around her waist, pulling her into him. "I accept."

"Excellent." It seemed the most natural thing in the world to rise on her toes and kiss him.

He didn't hesitate in kissing her back.

CHAPTER FIVE

Speeding down the road, Xara tried to make up some of the time she'd lost chasing a newborn calf. With the skill of a magician, it had somehow managed to escape from a pasture with seemingly intact fences. Harriet was going to have a hissy fit if she didn't pick up their mother soon. The plan, which had been imposed on her by Harriet, was to bring Edwina out to the farm for the day. This was to prevent their mother from visiting Harriet at Miligili and discovering the birthday surprise.

Xara had told Harriet that the chances of Edwina dropping by unannounced were a thousand to one, because Edwina always called ahead. It was a lesson their mother had tried to instill in her daughters, explaining it was unfair to anyone to be caught unawares and not have had the chance to put their house in order. Xara felt her mouth tug wryly. If having a house in order was a prerequisite for guests, she'd never see anyone.

When Harriet outlined the plan, Xara had said there was a higher chance of her mother springing a surprise visit on the farm than on Harriet. Her mother and elder sister didn't have a drop-in sort of relationship. But Harriet had pointed out pithily that as Charlotte was home from school, of course there was a chance Edwina might swing by, so the plan had stuck. Xara was to keep Edwina away from town until tonight's party.

As if on cue, her cell phone rang and Harriet's voice filled the car. "Xara, is Georgie with you?"

"Hi, Harriet." She never missed a chance to remind her that she wasn't one of Harriet's junior medical or nursing staff. "How are you?"

Harriet sighed. "Good thanks. You?" She didn't pause for breath. "I'm chasing Georgie."

"I haven't seen her. Did she mention at breakfast she was coming out to the farm?" If Xara had known that was a possibility she'd have saved herself a journey. Georgie could have picked up their mother and collected Xara's dry-cleaned party dress.

"She hasn't arrived yet." Harriet's exasperation rolled down the line. "I was expecting her last night, but she sent a text saying she was baking the cakes and she'd be here early this morning. She's not here. She's not answering her cell phone and she's not replying to texts."

Xara slowed at the speed limit sign on the edge of town. "Perhaps she went to see Mom first?"

"With mini chocolate cakes in the car and frosting that could melt? Not to mention that Edwina doesn't know she's coming."

I will get through today. I will get through today. Xara swallowed a sigh. "I'm sure she'll arrive soon. If I see her in town I'll send her straight over."

"In town?" Harriet's voice was instantly suspicious. "Don't tell me you haven't collected Edwina yet?"

"Sorry, you're breaking up. See you tonight." Xara cut off the call as she turned down her mother's long, tree-lined driveway, enjoying the dappled shade cast by the ancient oaks, elms and the heritage-listed Bhutan pine. Photos in the Billawarre historical society showed early-nineteenth-century tennis parties and picnics on Glenora's lawn with women dressed in white lace dresses and men in their shirtsleeves and vests.

There was one picture of a team of suspender-clad gardeners flanking their mistress in all of her Victorian splendor. In contrast, her mother had a team of two: herself and young Adrian. He'd been helping in the garden for twenty-five years, having started working for his father at sixteen and then taking over the landscaping business ten years later when Adrian senior retired. In all that time he'd never been able to shed the "young" moniker and everyone in town still called him young Adrian, even people half his age.

A peacock strutted across the driveway and she braked quickly. Tasha squealed in delight from the back seat. She loved the peacocks and visiting her grandmother's garden. After the peacock had flashed its impressive tail and vanished behind the trees, Xara drove the remaining distance to the house and pulled the car to a stop on the circular drive. She turned to smile at her daughter. "Let's go and surprise Mardi."

It took her a few minutes to unload Tasha from her new car seat and get her settled into her wheelchair. As much as Tasha loved visiting Mardi, she was less fond of being moved in or out of the car seat. It was supposed to be a state-of-the art piece of equipment but the first time they'd used it, Xara hadn't noticed a bolt protruding from underneath. It had broken the skin on Tasha's leg and as a result she tended to arch her back whenever she entered or exited it.

Avoiding the steep stone steps that rose majestically to the tessellated-tiled veranda and the heavy oak front door, Xara pushed the wheelchair down the path that ran along the side of the house. As they passed the laundry door her mother's Russian Blue cat, Tsar, shot out of the cat door and jumped up onto Tasha's lap, purring loudly.

"Hello to you too, Tsar," Xara said. She leaned over to rub the cat behind the ears before lifting Tasha's hand so it rested on the thick and luxurious fur. Tsar wasn't the only animal that responded to Tasha with affection and it both fascinated and delighted Xara.

As they rounded the corner of the house, she glanced into the kitchen window, anticipating seeing her mother through the glass, but the room was empty. Opening the French doors, she negotiated the wheelchair into the large sunroom, which was also empty. "I wonder where Mardi is?"

Xara didn't know exactly how much Tasha understood, but from the very start she'd explained all situations. The fact that it was always a one-sided conversation had ceased to bother her. As she parked Tasha near the window, she heard the soft rumble of voices drifting from the front of the house.

"Sounds like Mardi's got a visitor. I'll go and tell her we're here so she can come and say hello."

As Xara walked down the hall, the thick carpet runner that had replaced the old worn one of her childhood absorbed the sound of her footsteps. The lack of noise was in stark contrast to the loud and echoing sounds she and her sisters' feet had made pummeling the kauri-pine floorboards. A happy peal of laughter floated down the long corridor and she stopped abruptly, struck by the sound. How long had it been since she'd heard her mother laugh like that? Not since Dad died?

It was before that.

Like most kids growing up, Xara had never given a great deal of thought to her parents' relationship. Mom kept the home fires burning and Dad was a country doctor who appeared late most evenings and did his best to make it to sports carnivals, concerts, plays and award ceremonies. She didn't have strong memories of her parents arguing but then again, she didn't have strong memories of them laughing together either. Her father's presence had always been strong in the house; his opinions louder than her mother's, and she recalled few instances when Edwina had aired her views and stood her ground.

During her childhood, there'd been occasions when she'd been aware that her mother wasn't as happy as she might be, but the most significant period was straight after Georgie's birth. She remembered her father telling her that Mommy loved her, but she was going to need some peace and quiet. Soon after that pronouncement, Mrs.

Abercrombie, their housekeeper, had moved in for eight long months.

During that time there'd been nights when Xara had woken to hear the indistinct rumble of her father's baritone voice rising and falling. At first the tone would be one of supplication before firming to terse demands and then fading in resignation. He'd leave for work early and come home late but he always read her a bedtime story, even if she had to wake up to hear it. He'd lie beside her on her bed with a glass of whiskey in one hand and a copy of the *Roald Dahl Treasury* in the other, and he'd send her off to sleep hopeful that when she woke the next morning she'd find everything back to normal.

Each afternoon after school, she'd sneak into her mother's room, wishing and praying to see Edwina up, dressed, makeup and pearls in place, eyes twinkling and looking like the mother she'd known for five years. She'd almost lost faith that it was ever going to happen and then one day, she ran inside and Edwina was in the kitchen cooking drop scones and asking her about her day. Life returned then to what Xara had considered normal.

Ironically, when her mother got better, her father's presence in her everyday life took a step back. Her fondest memories of him were his visits to see her at boarding school on his way home from his regular week spent lecturing in Melbourne. He always seemed different on those occasions, more relaxed somehow compared with the official visiting days when he came with her mother.

He'd arrive at school unannounced, overrule her housemistress and whisk Xara into Geelong for dinner. Sometimes, she'd manage to convince him not to take her to the stuffy Geelong Club but to let his hair down and buy shawarmas. They'd eat the spiced lamb on its nest of tabbouleh and tahini down at Eastern Beach. Her father would shuck his jacket and tie and they'd watch local families picnicking and racing one another down the steep emerald slopes on huge sheets of cardboard.

Xara had wanted to try speeding down the thick grass with the salty air whipping her cheeks, but her father—ever the doctor—had always said, "It's a one-way ticket to brain damage." So she'd watched in quiet envy, not wanting to mar the treasured and infrequent companionship. Wisely, she'd never told him how many risks she took urging her horse over the jumps she'd built in the far pasture at school, well out of the sight of everyone.

She'd learned her father had very definite views and it was best to dole out information on a need-to-know basis. At seventeen, she'd held off for as long as possible before telling him she was dropping all her science subjects and choosing to focus on French and the humanities. He'd yelled, ranted and sulked and when that hadn't moved her, he'd blustered and threatened that if she was going to waste her talents he wasn't going to pay for her to attend Ormond College.

She'd told him he already had Harriet following in his footsteps and she was treading her own path. Her mother had been oddly silent on this issue, which Xara had put down to the fact her mother had never gone to college. Ironically, Xara had inadvertently appeased him when she'd accepted the offer of arts/law at Melbourne University but then she'd upset him again when she'd refused to join a sorority, preferring instead to live in a shared house in Carlton.

She'd loved her father but there was something about him that made her want to do the exact opposite of anything he suggested. It wasn't until years later when she'd met and married Steve that she'd wondered if her father's dominant personality may have contributed to her mother's periods of disconnection. It was soon after that epiphany that she'd started her "checking in" phone calls to Edwina.

She'd never broached the subject of Richard's personality with her. She and her mother didn't talk about things like that but mostly Xara had never asked because part of her didn't wanted to know. Unlike Harriet, she didn't consider her father perfect but now that he was dead, it seemed disrespectful to even inquire.

She heard her mother laugh again and this time it was followed by a definite chuckle; a deep and sonorous sound. Xara realized the noise wasn't coming from the front room after all but wafting through her mother's open bedroom door. She recalled that Edwina had mentioned she was waiting on a plumber to quote on installing a new toilet in the en-suite bathroom. It sounded like he'd finally turned up.

She walked into the bedroom, saying, "Hi, M—" The greeting died on her lips and her blood swooped to her feet. Her head spun, her stomach roiled and she forgot to breathe. *Oh. My. God.* A silent scream tore across her mind. Her mother was in bed. With. A. Man.

Like a rabbit caught in headlights, Xara didn't seem able to move. Or speak. Or close her eyes to block out the undeniable, uncomfortable and upsetting visual. "I ... oh ... God ... sorry ... I'll ... just ..."

Too stunned to turn, she stumbled backwards out of the room, knocking into the doorframe before running fast down the hall back to Tasha.

She was just releasing the brakes on the wheelchair when she heard her name.

"Xara. Wait."

She looked up to see her mother approaching, wrapped in her ecru silk dressing gown with its intricate Chantilly lace trim; the robe Richard had given her for their fortieth wedding anniversary. The image of Edwina in bed with the unknown man flashed again in Xara's head and she frantically blinked as if the action would be enough to remove it.

Edwina dropped a kiss on Tasha's head. "Hello, Tashie, darling. I see you've got Tsar all snuggled up and cozy."

The normality of the greeting added to the craziness of the moment. Xara gripped the wheelchair's handles. "Mom, I should go."

"Don't be silly," Edwina said with uncharacteristic firmness. "You look like you need a good strong cup of tea."

"I need more than tea." She locked the wheelchair brakes.

Edwina switched on the kettle. "That's a bit dramatic, darling. All you saw were two people sitting up in bed having breakfast. To be honest, it would have been a lot more disturbing for us all if you'd arrived half an hour ago."

"Mom!" Her mother's frankness disarmed her. She sat down abruptly on the couch, dropping her head in her hands, not knowing whether to laugh, cry or throw up.

"I know it's a shock," Edwina patted her shoulder sympathetically, "but you're a mother of three. You know all about sex."

Her head shot up. "Yes! But everyone knows their parents don't have sex more times than the number of children they have. I've gotten away without thinking or being confronted by my mother doing it for forty years."

Edwina had the audacity to smile. "Sorry, darling. I wasn't expecting to see you before tonight."

"Obviously."

"This is why I taught you to call ahead."

The kettle boiled and Edwina busied herself making tea. Xara heard the tap of a spoon against china and knew her mother had added sugar to her mug.

Edwina carried it over. "Here. Drink this. It will help."

"It comes with guaranteed memory loss, does it?" She accepted the proffered Wedgewood mug with a slightly shaking hand. "So who is he? I didn't recognize him. Not that I spent very long looking."

Edwina, who'd taken a seat on the opposite couch, gazed into her mug, seemingly fascinated with her tea.

"Mom?"

Edwina was silent for a few beats longer before blowing out a breath. "He's an old friend."

Friend? Right up until this moment, Xara thought she knew all of her parents' friends. She wracked her brain, seeking a memory of this man, but she kept drawing blanks. "A friend of yours and Dad's?"

"No." She took a couple of sips of her tea before saying quietly and almost reluctantly, "I knew him before I met your father."

Surprise rocketed over Xara's shock, sending goosebumps rising on her arms. "But you always said Dad was your first boyfriend."

The corner of her mother's mouth knotted. "Your father's generation didn't like to be reminded that they might not have been the first friend."

Something about the way her mother said the word "first" made Xara's head jerk up. She tried to catch the fleeting emotion racing across her mother's face, but she wasn't fast enough and it faded quickly. Her thoughts jumbled together before separating and then jumping all over the place again. Had her mother just told her that her father wasn't the first man she'd slept with?

No. The idea went against all the family stories she'd grown up hearing. Xara couldn't even start to absorb an idea that hinted at her family folklore not being exactly as she'd always understood it. And yet she'd just seen her mother in bed with a man who wasn't her father. A man her mother had known before her father.

Xara focused on the word "friend," reassuring herself that it was the friendship with another man that her father wouldn't have liked. That made far more sense than thinking something may have happened between Edwina and this man way back in the day.

Sure, her mother had been a teen in the late 1960's but her life had been far, far removed from flower power, Vietnam War demonstrations and free love. She'd done what was expected of her: attended The Hermitage School for girls before being sent to Switzerland for finishing school. She'd returned home, met Richard, fallen in love and lived the life that was expected of the wife of a respected country doctor.

There wasn't a single photo in the family album of her mother dressed in flowing, tie-dyed dresses or anything else that hinted at rebellion. The closest her mother came to looking like a swinging sixties starlet was a black and white photo of her wearing a Mary Quant mini, though the taut reserve on Edwina's face didn't exactly scream sexual revolution. It was more of a tight-lipped *I don't think so, thank you very much.*

It tied in with a very clear memory. Xara was fifteen and her mother had caught her in the wool shed at Murrumbeet kissing Ricky Switkowski. Edwina's face had paled to alabaster before flaming bright red; her reaction was so shocked and horrified that Xara had been convinced her mother had never kissed anyone until she'd met her father. Given she'd married him at barely twenty, that assumption wasn't so outlandish.

Her father had been outraged at Xara kissing Ricky but for a totally different reason. Apparently, if she'd been kissing sons of established families in the district that would have been okay—kissing the son of the farm manager was decidedly not okay. The incident had set off a decade of her deliberately choosing boyfriends that raised her father's blood pressure, although it had become far more challenging at a school where she'd been surrounded by boys her father considered suitable.

Now her mother—that formerly prudish woman—had a man in her bed. A stranger. Although obviously not a stranger to Edwina, because somehow he fitted into her mother's life.

"What's his name?"

"Doug."

The name didn't summon up a single memory. "You've never mentioned him before."

Edwina shrugged but there was a line of tension running across her shoulders. "We lost contact. It was all a very long time ago."

I knew him before I met your father.

A thousand questions peppered her. Where had her mother met this man? Why had they lost contact? How had they met again? When had they met again? How long had they been having sex? *Nope. Don't want to know the answer to that question.*

"Did you meet him overseas?"

"Is there a cup left in the pot, Eddy?" A very broad Australian accent broke the silence hanging between Xara and her mother.

Eddy? Another mini shock detonated inside Xara. No one called her mother Eddy. Certainly, no one with such a strong diphthong had ever been so familiar with her.

Her mother started to rise. "I'll pour you one."

"I think I can manage," he said with a wink. "You take a load off."

It was hard to estimate his age, but he looked a little older than her mother, although that may have been due to a life lived outdoors. He had a tanned, weather-beaten face but kind, dark eyes that twinkled with a glint of mischief. Thankfully, he was now fully dressed in pressed blue jeans and a collared shirt, which was tucked in over a slightly protruding belly that hinted at a possible fondness for beer. In looks, he was the polar opposite of her father, although he carried himself with similar confidence.

He obviously knew the layout of the kitchen, because he walked to a cabinet, removed a bone china mug and handled the old-fashioned swinging silver tea strainer—a device which confused many—like a pro. It was all done with a minimum of fuss and devoid of any embarrassment. It was as if being discovered in bed by his lover's—*no, no, no*—friend's daughter was an everyday occurrence.

Xara glanced at her mother, whose lips had lifted into a smile of wonder as if she couldn't quite believe Doug was in her kitchen. Edwina's glowing gaze was fixed on the straight-shouldered, salt and pepper–haired, jowl-faced man. A flicker in her compelling blue eyes hinted that she was worried that if she looked away, he might vanish. Had he vanished on her once before?

We lost contact.

Doug took a seat next to Edwina and Xara couldn't help but notice he had extraordinarily large hands, the backs of which were pigmented with half-a-dozen scars. They were work-worn hands with the faint remnants of black oil ingrained in some of the creases. The only thing they shared with her father's long, lean surgical hands was neatly clipped nails.

He set his mug down on the coffee table and slid his left hand into her mother's before stretching his other hand out to Xara. "I'm

Doug." His tone was serious, but his lips tilted up in a smile. "I'm a friend of your mother's."

A friend with benefits, apparently.

Shut up! We're not thinking about that.

"Xara," she managed to say as she accepted his firm handshake. She held his intelligent dark gaze. "The middle daughter. The difficult one who caused the most grief."

"Your mother didn't mention that so you can't have been too terrible. It's great to meet one of Eddy's girls. I hope you're not too traumatized about before."

Xara smiled despite herself. "Just traumatized enough."

Her mother laughed; a merry sound devoid of any awkwardness. "And this is Tashie," she said, reaching out her free hand to stroke her granddaughter's hair, "Xara's daughter."

Xara was used to the full gamut of reactions from people when they met Tasha. Responses covered everything from acute discomfort and intensive glances at the floor to gushing baby talk. Despite years of practice in preparing herself, she still couldn't stop anticipatory nerves shooting along her spine.

Doug fixed his full attention on her child-like teen and said, "G'day, Tash. You're obviously pretty special if you can get Tsar to sit on your lap." He gave her a rueful smile. "He won't have a bar of me."

Tasha's eyes brightened and she smiled, sending saliva dribbling out of her open mouth and onto her bandana. At that moment, despite the fact that Doug had obviously been having sex with her mother—*don't think about it, just don't think about it*—Xara decided that the guy was okay.

"Darling, was there a reason you dropped in?" Edwina asked, her hand still nestled in Doug's beefy paw. "Something you needed?"

With the shock of discovering her mother and Doug in bed, Xara had completely forgotten the plan of whisking her out of town for the day. "Um, yes, of course. I wanted you to come out to the farm and give me some gardening advice."

Her mother's brows rose. "Xara, you don't really have a garden."

"Exactly," she said, agreeing before she realized what she'd said. "Actually, Mom, that's not fair. I have the bones of what could be a fabulous garden if I had the time and the—" She swallowed the word "money." It wasn't something she ever discussed with her mother or Harriet. "I thought today was the day to start planning the resurrection."

"It's moving into autumn, darling, a time when you put gardens to bed. I suppose you could mulch and plant some bulbs ..." Edwina suddenly sighed. "We're not having family dinner tonight, are we? Harriet's gone and organized a party."

"What?" Xara tried to look convincingly perplexed. "No. Why would you think that?"

Edwina's blue-on-blue eyes shone in sympathy. "Because you're not a gardener, Xara, and you're not very good at acting either. You'd have kept me off the scent better if you'd asked me to come out and mind the twins."

Xara's hands rose and fell and she silently cursed herself, then Harriet. "Okay, you've got me. Harriet sent me to keep you away from Miligili and out of town for the day. She was worried you might stop by to see Charlie even though I told her that was unlikely. I can now see it's totally improbable."

Her mother's lips pressed together at her acerbic tone. "Actually, I was planning on visiting Charlotte this afternoon. The reason I hadn't rushed over was because I was giving her some time to sleep in. She's exhausted after a huge few weeks."

Visiting with or without Doug? The question spawned a hundred more. Xara suddenly wanted to know exactly how long her mother had been seeing Doug. Hell, she wanted to know way more than that but asking now, with Doug sitting right there next to her, was impossible. She leaned forward.

"Well, I'm hardly going to force you out to the farm. Just promise me you'll avoid town. Oh, and to make my life easier, if Harriet calls, please say you're with me?"

"I can do that." Her mother touched her nose with her forefinger.

"And while we're talking favors, please don't mention Doug to your sisters."

The request hooked into her like a leech, making her both uncomfortable and strangely disloyal. Words clanged together as she tried formulating a reply that was neither rude to Doug nor upsetting to her mother. She struggled with the sticky point of Edwina asking her to lie by omission.

"It's not quite as it sounds," Doug said as though reading her mind. "Eddy wants to introduce me to your family tonight when everyone's together."

A rush of protective love for her mother engulfed her and she suddenly needed to know if Doug was forcing Edwina to do this. "Is this true, Mom? Are you sure?"

"Yes, darling. We've discussed it at length and that's the plan."

It's not just dinner. Xara found her thumb had migrated to her mouth and she gave in to chewing the edge of the nail. She leveled her gaze intently at Edwina, blocking out Doug. "Do you want to rethink this? It's not just family dinner anymore. Hell, Mom, it's not just your close friends. James and Harriet will have added in anyone they feel may be useful to James's tilt at the party nomination for parliament. It's everyone who's influential in town and the rest of the shire."

"I know exactly what sort of party it will be, Xara," her mother said quietly. "Remember, I'm the one who taught your sister how to entertain."

"So you know what I'm talking about," Xara said, desperate to add, *And if you bring Doug tonight, you're making a very public statement you can't back down from.*

"Xara's right," Doug said, rubbing his jaw. "It might be better for you to go to the party alone. I'll meet your girls tomorrow."

Doug shot up another notch in Xara's estimation. "Good idea."

"This isn't just about me," Edwina said vehemently as she turned to face Doug. "It's about us."

Xara's heart rate picked up. *Us* sounded far more together than "just sex." The sex she wasn't thinking about.

"There's no hurry to do this, Eddy." Doug patted her knee. "Think about it. You sure you're ready to introduce me to the who's who of Billawarre?"

Her mother nodded, her blond bob swinging gently. "I think it's long past time."

Had Edwina wanted to introduce Doug before? The thought dug into Xara like a burr and for the first time she wondered if she really knew her mother.

"Well, if you're fair dinkum," Doug said, his face serious, "I'll be there."

Xara pictured Doug and her mother walking hand in hand through the balloon-festooned entrance of Miligili. It was immediately followed by a 3D image of the look on Harriet's face. She grinned. If her mother was determined to do this, it was a real shame she had to wait eight hours to see it.

CHAPTER SIX

"So thrilled you could come, Primrose." Harriet greeted her honorary aunt with a brief kiss on the cheek, while looking over the older woman's shoulder and scanning the room. Where on earth was James? A steady stream of guests had been arriving for the last ten minutes and both Charlotte and James should have been standing here with her in the time-honored tradition of hosts. However, despite her constant urging, neither of them had been ready when the old Victorian doorbell gave its long, loud ring. In fact, when it had rung, she'd been talking to Charlotte through a closed bathroom door. Talking was probably a stretch—she'd been yelling.

How could such a bright young woman be so infuriating? When she'd realized Charlotte wasn't even close to being dressed, despite a day of spending more time in her room than out of it, Harriet had stalked into her daughter's walk-in robe and pulled clothes off hangers. If too much choice was the cause of Charlotte's tardiness then Harriet would speed things up by giving her three options.

She'd just finished laying out the clothes and accessories when Charlotte appeared from her bathroom. Her daughter had taken one look at her, stopped short, dropped the towel in surprise and gone ballistic. As she'd crossed one arm over herself and scrambled to retrieve the towel from the floor, she'd screamed at Harriet, "Get out of my room." She'd ranted about the invasion of privacy and the rights of the child before retreating into the bathroom and slamming the door shut behind her.

Frustrated and furious, Harriet rattled the doorknob. "For pity's sake, Charlotte. We're expecting a hundred people in ten minutes and you're behaving like a child. Get dressed and come downstairs."

Charlotte's sulky reply barely penetrated the heavy door. "It's your party, Mom. Not mine."

Why did everyone keep saying it was her party? "It's your grandmother's party and you owe it to her and Gramps to behave in an appropriate manner." She'd almost said, *You owe it to me too*, but she swallowed the words.

"I'm tired," Charlotte moaned.

"You've done nothing all day!"

"So? I still feel tired."

Harriet determined right there and then that come Monday, Charlotte was having a blood test to check for low hemoglobin and mononucleosis. "You can rest all day tomorrow, but tonight you don't have a choice. You're a Minchin and a Chirnwell. That comes with certain responsibilities in this town, especially now your father's running for office. People expect to see you greeting them with a smile on your face. Daddy and I expect to see you welcoming them.'

She sucked in a breath and decided to try praise to lure her recalcitrant daughter out of the bathroom. "I know how good you are at making people feel welcome and special when you put your mind to it."

And then the doorbell pealed five minutes before the stated time on the printed turquoise-shot paper invitations. As she walked out of Charlotte's bedroom, Georgie was hovering on the wide landing, her face a combination of concern and awkwardness.

"Sorry, Harry. I couldn't help overhearing the shouting. Can I help? I could answer the door or ...?"

"Or what? Find out what the hell is the matter with Charlotte? Good luck with that."

She regretted the snark in her tone the moment she heard it, but she was still cross with Georgie about Charlotte's visit two weeks ago. Her youngest sister liked to think that because she was closer in age to her niece, Charlotte was more likely to confide in her. Worried that this was a distinct possibility, Harriet had drilled Georgie this afternoon. Georgie hadn't mentioned the dismal academic results, thank God, and it appeared her intel was even less than Harriet's. As a mother, this was reassuring, because Harriet had always told Charlotte she could tell her anything.

The bell trilled again, longer and more demanding. "If you can get Charlotte out of the bathroom, dressed and downstairs as soon as possible, that would be a win. Thanks."

As she ran down the stairs to the front door, she knew it would be the Finlaysons. They always broke the rule of arriving a polite five minutes late to give the hosts some breathing space and they were always the last to leave. Their saving grace was they'd been close friends of her parents and Jim had been her father's golf buddy for forty years. Since her father's passing, Harriet enjoyed listening to Jim's stories, because they kept her dad close.

The Finlaysons may have led the advance guard but not by much. Dozens of couples had now arrived and Harriet was stuck standing by the door greeting people and unable to leave. She was still waiting for her husband and daughter to join her.

"You know we wouldn't have missed Edwina's party for the world," Primrose said, glancing at her husband. "Would we, David?"

"Always good to have a night off." The garrulous dairyman expertly extricated a glass of beer from between a forest of champagne flutes on a passing waiter's tray. "Actually, it's good timing because I wanted to talk to James about the rural relief fund and—"

"Plenty of time for that later," Primrose said, throwing Harriet an apologetic glance. "Is your mother here?"

"Not yet." Harriet checked her watch. "Xara's bringing her, and you know Xara and I don't share the same relationship with time."

"Hello, Auntie P."

Charlotte appeared at Harriet's side in an outfit she'd never seen before. Unlike the three short and tight-fitting cocktail dresses Harriet had laid out on her bed, Charlotte was wearing a matching skirt and blouse. The blue and green top draped from the shoulder in silky folds and a section of the sleeves opened enticingly, exposing her tanned and toned upper arms. The material re-joined just above mid-tricep and then covered her arm to the wrist. The blouse fell halfway down the short, fitted skirt, which hugged her behind and showed off her long legs. She looked young, fit, poised and beautiful. Harriet breathed a sigh of relief.

"Charlie, look at you!" Primrose exclaimed looking slightly stunned. "You're all grown up."

Charlotte laughed but gave Harriet a sidelong glance. "Please tell Mom that."

The older woman hugged Charlotte. "Don't rush it, sweetie. You've got years and years ahead of you to be an adult."

Charlotte's smile wobbled at the edges as if pulled down by a weight. "Have a lovely night, Auntie P."

As Primrose and David were absorbed into the growing crowd, Harriet leaned in and said quietly, "Thank you, darling."

Charlotte gave an indifferent shrug. "Where's Dad?"

"I don't know. Can you go and find him?"

Her daughter widened her eyes. "What? And abandon my post and my responsibilities?"

Harriet ground her teeth. "Go and find your father."

"I'm here." James slipped between the two of them. It was his usual practice to slide an arm around each of them but this time his hands stayed by his sides.

"Where have you been?" Harriet asked *sotto voce*. "You missed Phillip Ciobo." Phillip was a mover and shaker in the Liberal Party and someone they needed to schmooze. "I covered for you, but you need to go and find him as soon as Edwina arrives and we've called out surprise."

"Right. Thanks."

Instead of sounding appreciative, James's tone was clipped as if she'd done the wrong thing. She glanced at him and then at Charlotte —the two people she loved most in the world—and she got the strangest sensation something was slipping away from her.

Hugh and Ollie chose that moment to run through the balloon archway, pushing their sister. "Charlie," they whooped when they saw their cousin. Abandoning Tasha's chair, they enthusiastically threw themselves at her in the way only eight-year-old boys can. "Let's play Twister."

"After we've given Mardi her big surprise." Charlotte gave them both a bear hug. "Hi, Tashie." She kissed her cousin on the forehead before automatically straightening the bandana around her neck. "Look at you, all gorgeous in that pink sparkly top."

Tasha's beam lit up her face.

"Boys. Push your sister out of the doorway before Mardi walks in with your mother," Harriet instructed.

"Oh, she's—"

"It looks amazing, Harry," Xara interrupted her sons. She stood arm in arm with Steve and surveyed the room, taking in the one hundred turquoise helium balloons hovering on the ceiling with their lightly swishing silver ribbon tails. "Really gorgeous."

"Thank you," Harriet said, momentarily distracted by the praise before realizing that her mother hadn't walked in with them.

"Xara!" Georgie suddenly appeared from the crowd to envelope her sister in a warm hug before turning her attention to Steve. She kissed him affectionately on the cheek then loudly high-fived the twins while hooting, "Dudes!" After the boys slapped her hand, she squatted next to the wheelchair so she was at eye level with Tasha. "How's my girl?" She tied a helium balloon to the chair. "Now you're ready to party."

Harriet wished Georgie could greet everyone a little less

exuberantly. "Where's Edwina?" She peered behind Xara for their mother.

Xara turned back from the waiter holding two glasses of champagne. "She insisted on driving herself and I couldn't talk her out of it. She should be here any minute."

A throb pulsed in Harriet's temple and she spoke slowly and quietly, working hard at not collaring her sister. "What do you mean she should be here any minute? The arrangements were crystal clear. You were to all arrive together. I've got a hundred people here ready to surprise her. Where is she?" The ache from her clenched teeth joined her throbbing temple.

"She'll be here," Xara said firmly. "When have you ever known Mom to be late to a social function? Oh, I hear a car." She turned. "Ollie, Hughie, sneak out and see if it's Mardi's car but don't let her see you."

"Okay." The boys rushed past and returned quickly. "It's Mardi and she's—"

Harriet clapped loudly—the snapping sound reverberating around the room. "The guest of honor is here."

She heard her mother's heels clicking on the veranda and she raised her arms as if she were conducting a choir.

Edwina appeared in the balloon arch and everyone called out, "Surprise!" Harriet's jaw dropped, stalling the word in her throat. Her mother wasn't alone.

Edwina stood holding a man's hand—a man Harriet had never seen in her life. Worse than that, she was smiling up at him in a way she'd never looked at anyone before.

Memories of her father flooded Harriet and a thick feeling of betrayal clogged her veins. How could her mother do this to her? To them? Here. Now. Tonight. She shot a glance at Georgie. Her younger sister's mouth hung open. Obviously she was as stunned as Harriet. Her gaze sought Xara's. Her middle sister's face wasn't blanched in shock or etched in surprise, but Harriet detected anxiety.

"Cool!" Charlotte said in a loud whisper. "Mardi's got a boyfriend."

No! A hot sensation burned under Harriet's ribs and she grabbed Xara's arm so hard that champagne sloshed onto her fingers. "Who's that man?"

"Doug? You old bastard," David McGowan called out in delighted surprise, his booming voice breaking the crowd's surprised silence. "God, it's been forty-odd years. How the hell are you?"

SOON AFTER HER mother's surprise entrance, Georgie carried three glasses of champagne into the l'Orangerie and sat down in one of the white cane chairs that Xara had pulled into a circle. Gathering together wasn't something the sisters did very often but Harriet had insisted they talk. Her mother's wily maneuver of arriving at the party with an unknown man hadn't gone down well with her elder sister.

Georgie handed a flute to each of her sisters. "So ... wow. Mom's got a boyfriend? Who knew?"

"Xara, apparently," Harriet said tartly, closing the double doors against any guest who might be tempted to wander away from party central.

"Hey, in my defense, I only found out at ten-thirty this morning and believe me, I'd have preferred not to." Xara gulped champagne. "I've wanted to bleach my eyeballs all day."

"Oh, I don't know." Georgie thought Xara was being a bit unfair. "Doug's pretty well preserved for a guy his age and he's not hard to look at. In fact, don't you think he's kind of familiar?"

"He's not familiar at all," Harriet said in her best condescending-big-sister tone. "And Xara wasn't talking about the man's looks, Georgie."

She decided to ignore Harriet. "What do you mean then, Zar?"

Xara's fingers tightened on her glass. "I found them having breakfast together in bed."

"Oh, is that all." Georgie laughed and champagne bubbles fizzed up her nose. "It could have been worse. Did I ever tell you about the time I walked in on Mom and Dad doing it once and—"

"Shut up, Georgie," Xara and Harriet said in unison.

Georgie swallowed an infuriated sigh. She was back home in the heart of her family and yet again she was being firmly placed in her position of youngest and denied an opinion.

"Who is he?" Harriet asked again. "I want to ask David McGowan about him but that means admitting we don't know who he is and Jesus ... how would that look?" She rose and paced. "I'm furious with Edwina. How could she spring him on us like this?"

"To give Doug his due," Xara said, "he suggested meeting us at a family lunch tomorrow. It was Mom who insisted he come tonight."

"Hiding him in a crowd," Harriet muttered, her brows pulling down into a sharp V. "She knew we couldn't give either of them the third degree tonight but tomorrow's another story."

"I think it's great she's got a friend," Georgie said, deliberately baiting Harriet. "She actually looks happy. Isn't that what counts?"

Harriet gave her a death stare. "Not when we don't have any idea who he is. We know nothing about him. God, he could be anyone. What if he's after her money?"

"Oh, the family inheritance under threat." Georgie rolled her eyes. "Of course that was *your* first thought, Harry. Sometimes I think you were born in the wrong era." She tried for logic. "Look, David knows him so he's obviously not a total stranger. I bet that's why he seems familiar. He's probably someone's cousin. You know how they all intermarried back in the day to keep the land inside the six founding families." A thought struck her. "It would be a bit ick though if he was somehow related to us, wouldn't it?"

"With dusky skin, Georgie?" Harriet snapped. "Highly unlikely. If he was a distant cousin twice removed, I'd feel a lot happier. At least that way we'd know who he was."

"Mom told me they were friends a long time ago." Xara stared at the fine bead of her champagne, rising continuously in her glass. "Before she met Dad. I wondered if they'd met during her grand tour of Europe but if David knows him then perhaps they met here."

"Mom introduced him as 'my friend Doug.'" Harriet stopped pacing. "Don't you think it's odd we've never heard of him? And that she didn't mention his surname?"

"No." Georgie wished she'd brought Ben to the party. He'd have been the perfect excuse for her not to be stuck here listening to Harriet's conspiracy theories.

Thinking of Ben made her grin like she'd won the lottery. She'd been floating two inches above the ground for the last thirty hours, ever since he'd kissed her in the middle of her second grade's classroom. After that bone-melting kiss, he'd come back to her house and somehow, despite the magnetic pull that ran between them, they'd managed to keep their hands off each other long enough to bake one hundred mini chocolate cakes. During the glorious ninety minutes they'd had to fill while the cakes cooled enough to be iced, there'd also been a lot of licking and tasting, and not just restricted to chocolate frosting.

An anticipatory quiver shimmied and buzzed deep down inside her, heating her cheeks and tightening her thighs. She squirmed in the chair. Part of her wanted to jump up and tell her sisters she'd spent last night and this morning naked and having the best sex of her life. The rest of her wanted to hold the memories close and keep what she and Ben had shared locked tightly inside a private bubble.

And if her mother was flying as high as she was, then who was Georgie to get upset about this Doug guy? Granted, she'd only met him briefly to shake his hand, but he had a reassuring vibe about him. The thing that really struck her was how very different Doug was in both looks and style from her father. It stood to reason he'd probably be different in personality as well, although that could be a leap. Pop psychology was always spouting that people were attracted to those with similar traits.

But she looks happy.

The thought dried her mouth, leaving a traitorous residue. Georgie had loved her father, although once she'd hit her late twenties, she'd seen him through adult eyes. It had made her wonder if she'd really known him at all. For someone who'd been raised by parents with an intact marriage, she didn't feel close to either of them.

She'd grown up listening to her father cross swords with Xara, especially when she'd told him she wasn't going to be a doctor. Five years later, it was Georgie's turn to tell him that she planned on the less prestigious career of elementary school teaching. She'd had her arguments prepared and been ready to weather his disappointment, which would fall like a guillotine. Part of her had craved the fight and the lecture she was wasting her talents, but all he'd said was, "At least I won't have to pay Ormond College fees."

And that pretty much summed up her childhood. It wasn't that her parents didn't notice her, it was just they didn't get as involved in her life as they had with Harriet and Xara. Mostly, it had been a good thing but sometimes Georgie would have liked the chance to ruffle her father's sanguine demeanor.

Of course, she could have tested it by taking drugs, getting expelled or getting pregnant, but she hadn't wanted to do anything that drastic. Instead, she'd changed her mind about where she was going to study, applied to Trinity College and hit her father for the expensive fees. She'd gotten her double degree at Melbourne University, majoring in creative arts and education.

Looking back, she was never sure if her father had tried reverse psychology on her, but she didn't think so. Certainly her attending Melbourne University had appeased his pretensions but her course had not. Growing up, she'd learned from him that the words "arts major" were always accompanied with an eye roll and always followed by the statement, "and that will make her so very employable."

What was it Ben had said the first time she'd met him? Something about parents running out of energy? The more she thought about it, the more convinced she was this had happened to her parents. She was the accident, the unexpected third daughter, but if they'd tired of parenting by the time she hit her teens, where had their energy been redirected? Looking at her mother's incandescent glow today she knew in her heart that it hadn't been toward each other.

"His surname tells us who he is and who he's related to," Harriet said. "Xara, surely he told you his name when you met him this morning?"

"He probably did but I was still reeling from finding them in bed together. I can't remember."

"Well, you're not much use."

"So sue me," Xara bristled, rising from her chair. "I'll go and get Auntie Primrose, shall I? Or better yet, I'll get Doug so he can tell you."

"Don't," Harriet snapped then sucked in a deep breath. "Sorry, Xara. It's just this has thrown me for a loop. The party was to help Edwina get back to being involved."

"It looks like she's been very involved," Georgie quipped with a wink.

"How can you make jokes about them having sex?" Xara emptied her champagne glass. "Can we get a bottle in here, Harry?"

Perhaps because I'm having sex again for the first time in almost two years and I want everyone to feel this way. "You're not the one I thought would be getting her panties in a twist about Mom having sex. You can't deny those endorphins are working their magic on her better than any pills she's ever taken. She looks different somehow. Lighter. Younger."

"She may as well be wearing a sign around her neck saying, *I'm getting some*," Harriet said bitterly, reappearing with a bottle of Möet & Chandon. "Dear God, she giggled. Our mother *giggled* when Elise Gregson cooed and said, 'No wonder you missed bridge last week. I would have too.'"

Harriet's talented surgical fingers trembled slightly as they ripped the gold foil around the bottle's neck, exposing the muselet. "And did you see what she's wearing? She always wore a cocktail dress to her birthday party."

"She would have looked overdressed next to Doug if she had," Georgie said. "Mind you, he rocks the George Strait look."

"We're not out on the farm," Harriet sniped. "Everyone will be talking about this and not in a good way. It's hardly the impression James and I were aiming for. We've got some heavy hitters from the Liberal Party here tonight and my mother waltzing in with a lover of unknown origin wasn't supposed to be part of it."

Pop! The champagne cork flew from the bottle with an intensity matching Harriet's temper. She refilled all their glasses. "I'm so furious with her I could spit. After everyone's left tonight, she's not allowed to go home until she's faced us. I want to know who he is and how the hell he fits into her life. As soon as I know, I'll start Googling. Edwina's a sitting duck for a con man."

Georgie flinched at the idea of the meeting. "That will only put her back up. Sometimes, Mom can be really stubborn. You know, like you."

"I would never have done something like this!" A couple of specks of saliva flew out of Harriet's mouth. "And what about Dad? I mean, God. Dad threw her so many birthday parties over the years and now she brings another man to this one. It's like she's giving the bird to his memory."

"Don't make this about Dad." Xara gave a long and aggrieved sigh. "This has nothing to do with him and everything to do with Mom. But Georgie's right. Bailing her up has disaster written all over it. Besides, she came with Doug and I'd bet the farm there's no way he'll leave her here. I got the impression the guy has a protective streak a mile wide."

"She did this to avoid us," Harriet's voice rose, "and now you're playing straight into her hands."

"No, I'm not. Out at the farm tomorrow will be a better time to talk. Mom can come at eleven and I'll invite Doug for one."

Georgie glanced at her sisters. On the handful of occasions they chose to work together, they were a formidable team. She'd long been subjected to their razor-sharp interrogations when they'd joined forces to act in *loco parentis* after getting a whiff of her adolescent antics and her young adult escapades. She felt a stab of pity for her mother and Doug.

She was definitely keeping Ben secret for quite a while longer.

CHAPTER SEVEN

HARRIET TURNED AROUND AT THE CREAK OF THE DOOR HANDLE and James walked into the l'Orangerie. Her heart rolled over. What a man. He knew how devastated she was about the way Edwina had dropped her bombshell—airing what should have been a private family announcement in a public forum—and now he'd come to check on her. To make sure she was okay and coping.

He was immaculately dressed in a gray Italian suit with a fine thread of pink and white woven through it. He'd teamed it with a pale pink shirt and a gray, white and pink striped tie. He'd shaved, as he always did for an evening event, and his strong, smooth jaw gave him a crisp, fresh look. She frowned. Crisp and fresh except for his hair. What on earth had happened to his hair? It stood at wild and rakish angles as if he'd been electrocuted.

He stood behind her chair, resting his hands on her shoulders, the grip too firm. "Sorry to break up the party, girls, but I really need Harriet."

"No worries, James." Xara stood. "We've finished. Come on, Georgie, we better rescue Charlie from the kids."

As her sisters walked away, Harriet put her hand over James's and eased the pressure of his fingers off her clavicle. It wasn't just his hair looking frazzled; he sounded stressed. "Everything okay?"

"No." He clawed his hand through his hair. "I've had bloody David McGowan banging on at me about the rural relief fund and Vikram Singh can't take a hint that tonight's not the night to discuss the permit for his proposed new medical center. Sometimes being mayor's ..." He threw her an accusatory look. "You need to get out there and have my back."

A burr of hurt prickled through her. She'd taken half an hour for a vital conversation with her sisters about their mother. He was behaving as if it was his world was rocked and she'd abandoned him.

She stood, smoothing the pleats of her dress. "I'm sorry my family crisis has gotten in the way of your enjoyment of the evening."

"It's hardly a crisis, Harriet," he said dryly. "Edwina brought a guy to her birthday party. Big whoop."

She stared at him. "James, everyone at this party is connected and my mother walked in and lobbed a grenade. You heard the silence and the twitters that followed. Oh, God." The word twitters sparked a horrifying thought. What if someone had already tweeted it? "This is gossip in its purest form and the town will have a field day with it. All it takes is something with a whiff of scandal attached and they circle like vultures. You saw this man, Doug. His accent's so broad it could strip paint and no matter what Georgie says, the fact David McGowan knows him is hardly reassuring or an endorsement."

"Yeah, he's a pain in the ass alright." James lifted her champagne glass out of her hand and drained the contents in two big gulps.

"Exactly, so you see my point." Relief slid in to soothe her; finally they were on the same page. "We only tolerate David because of Primrose, Jenny, Kate and Sarah. For an intelligent woman like Primrose, he was an interesting choice of husband. I know he drove Dad to distraction."

She took back her glass and refilled it for herself. "Did you know that when I was a kid, David would bring odd bods home from the Veterans' League? Men he hardly knew but who'd served in Vietnam.

Sometimes they'd stay for weeks on the farm and poor Primrose had to feed and house them. Once, Jenny moved in with us for the summer because she said the farm was like a halfway house for broken vets."

"Yeah, well he's moved on from vets and his current project's the rural relief fund. I've fobbed him off, but I need you to keep him away from Phillip Ciobo. We didn't invite Phillip to our home to get sprayed by a radical leftie."

She'd never seen James so rattled. "Darling, you're the favorite for party nomination. Everyone knows what an amazing job you're doing as mayor."

He stared out the window as if fascinated by dusk's shadows on the emerald sweep of lawn. "You can't make an omelet without breaking some eggs."

"Meaning?"

He pulled a napkin out of his pocket and thrust it into her hand. Half-a-dozen names were scrawled on it but unlike his usual clear and precise handwriting, it was barely legible.

"What's this?"

"A list of boring people I can't cope with tonight."

She recognized all the names. They included a farmer, a widower and one of her colleagues from the hospital. James was right, most of them were boring but boring people didn't usually bother him. Always a charming host, he was expert at moving through a crowd and disengaging himself from dull people. But right now he looked wrung out and the sharp light in his eyes worried her. Her protective instincts kicked in.

"How's this for a plan? People don't tend to interrupt family so go and find Charlotte and dance with her. Hell, talk to Edwina and see if you can find out what on earth she's playing at. Leave the rest to me."

"Debbie, I'm looking for James Minchin." The authoritative voice of Lewis Rayne, a cardiologist with a very successful multi-practice spread across four towns in the district, drifted in from the hall. "Have you seen him?"

"Quick." Harriet pushed James toward a door that led to the pantry's two-way refrigerators; they backed onto the garage for the easy unloading of food and now they offered an exit. "I'll chat with him and then walk him back to the party. You re-enter the house through the service area."

She closed the door behind him and turned to see Lewis striding across the white marble floor. "Hello, Lewis. No drink?" She approached him and slid her arm through his. "We can't have that. Come, let's go and get you one."

Lewis's feet stilled. "I'm looking for your husband."

"Oh, he's around somewhere," she said airily. "You know what it's like when you're hosting a party. If we head back to the main area we're more likely to find him."

Lewis gave her a shrewd look as if he were calculating the pros and cons of staying or going. He started walking.

As they left the l'Orangerie she asked, "Perhaps I can help?"

He made a grunting sound. "Not unless you know what's going on with the McCluskey development."

"I know that the sales of lots has exceeded expectations." She gave Lewis what she hoped was a soothing smile; soothing not being her strong point. She was very much a surgeon in all things, including emotions—cut it out, stitch it up and don't look back. "If you took James's advice and invested then you'll get a good return."

"Exactly." His craggy face was as stony as the volcanic rises behind Miligili. "So why has the dividend date passed and no monies been paid?"

Harriet's spine stiffened at his tone and she slipped her arm out of his. "I don't know, Lewis, but I'm sure there's a perfectly reasonable explanation." Her voice took on a frosty edge. "What I do know is that my mother's birthday party is *not* the time or place to discuss it."

They'd reached the bar and David McGowan was talking with

one of the young bartenders while waiting for a drink. "David, have you met Lewis Rayne?" Harriet said with practiced social ease. "He runs a few Angus cattle on his hobby farm over near Bostock's Creek. I'm sure he'd value your insight and knowledge."

David's eyes lit up at the chance to talk cattle and before Lewis could open his mouth to object, the farmer was in full oratory flight. The cardiologist threw a narrow-eyed look in Harriet's direction. She didn't care; it served him right to be stuck in an excruciatingly dull conversation.

She flitted around the room in hostess mode, chatting briefly with many and avoiding all possibilities of being drawn into an in-depth conversation with anyone. She refused to discuss her mother outside of the family; she wasn't giving anyone any fuel to add to the bonfire she knew they were building. She desperately wanted to talk to Primrose and gauge what she knew about this Doug person, but she couldn't think of a way to do it without exposing her total ignorance of the situation. As for talking to her mother alone, that seemed impossible: Doug hadn't left her side all evening. It was as if the two of them were a unified front with no break in the line. Harriet wasn't sure she could forgive her mother for this passive-aggressive attack.

In honor of Edwina, the three-piece band played a popular sixties set and the tiny dance floor filled. Harriet was relieved to see James in the center of the crowd doing the Twist with Charlotte. The tension headache that had been part of her since Edwina had almost skipped through the balloon archway now jabbed Harriet behind the eyes like a scalpel blade. Ignoring the fact her medical advice to someone with a headache would be to drink more water, she grabbed another glass of French champagne and headed into the kitchen for a breather from the guests.

The catering staff bustled around her and she ate a tiny caramelized beetroot and goat's cheese tart and then tipped an Asian spoon of smoked salmon in dill vinaigrette into her mouth. Savory flavors had always been her preference, but she had an overwhelming craving for rich, dark chocolate—lots and lots of it. Was it too early for the cake-cutting ceremony and dessert?

Steve walked into the kitchen holding Tasha's special water bottle and his face registered surprise. "Harry? You okay?"

"Fine," she said quickly, not wanting to give into the tempting lure of saying, *No, I'm bloody well not. My husband's having some sort of a meltdown, my mother's brought her unknown lover to the party and exposed us all to ridicule, and on top of everything, my daughter's chosen to start being difficult.* "Just checking in with the caterers."

"All going smoothly this end," Lucinda said with a cat-that-ate-the-cream smile as she handed another tray of delicious apple rings topped with walnut and gorgonzola to a waiting server.

Harriet tensed. The insinuation in the woman's voice was clear: Lucinda, who catered all the A-list parties in the region, knew all was not going smoothly on the other side of the kitchen door. That meant Edwina's escapade would be a discussion point in households far beyond Billawarre by breakfast tomorrow.

"Food's fabulous as always, Luce," Steve said, filling the drink bottle at the sink. "I can't wait for dessert." He snapped the lid on the bottle and tilted his head toward the door. "Harry, come and dance."

"Lovely." She pushed off the kitchen counter, grateful for her brother-in-law's perspicacity. As Steve rarely danced, he was just creating an opportunity for her to exit the kitchen gracefully without having to respond to Lucinda.

As soon as they got through the doorway she said, "Thanks, Steve. I appreciate it."

"No worries. That's what family's for." He shot her a slightly agonized look. "I can dance if you want."

She laughed. "You're off the hook."

He gave a mock swipe of his brow. "Looks like Charlie's giving James a workout."

"Father and daughter time," she said lightly as the weight of the truth behind James's dancing pressed down on her.

"He looks like he needs rescuing from his very fit daughter." Steve held out the water bottle. "If you give this to Zar for me, I'll get James a beer and give him a breather."

The suggestion was perfect. Steve was family and by talking to him, James would still be protected from the bores. "Thanks, Steve. You really are remarkably thoughtful."

His field-green gaze slid away from her face and she realized she'd embarrassed him. She added a teasing dig: "For a man."

His laugh was tight. "That's me. I'll do anything for free beer."

Leaving James in the care of Steve, she skirted the dance floor and took another hallway. At the end was the large room they still referred to as the playroom, despite the fact that Charlotte hadn't played in it for a long time. It was the repository of all the toys, books, games and dress-ups she swore she could never be parted from. Now, it also contained a computer, a games console and a large flat-screen television. Tasha and the twins loved spending time here.

Harriet heard the twins before she saw them jumping up and down and swinging their arms as they moved the game controllers. Virtual racing cars whizzed across the screen to the tune of tinny and annoying music. This was punctuated by loud crashing sounds and the moans and cheers of the boys.

Tasha was propped in a beanbag and draped in a shimmering silvery blue material that Charlotte had always called her fairy cloak. Xara was reading her *The Princess Knight* and going on the look on her niece's face, Tasha was entranced by the idea of being Violetta. Or perhaps just by the fact that she had someone's undivided attention. None of them knew how much Tasha really understood but they did know she loved being the center of someone's attention. Disability or not, who didn't enjoy that?

As Xara's voice gave life to the words on the page, Harriet smiled, remembering how many times she'd read that book to Charlotte. Remembering with a silent sigh how easy and uncomplicated her daughter had been to mother at seven.

"Here's Tasha's water."

"Thanks." Xara finished the last page of the book before setting it down. She picked up the bottle and held it up to Tasha's lips. Most of the water dribbled out onto the bandana.

Harriet frowned. "Is her swallowing worse?"

Xara mopped at the water. "She's choking on soft food now. We're going to the Geelong Hospital after Easter."

"For a PEG feeding tube?" She wondered which pediatric surgeon would be inserting the tube into Tasha's stomach.

"We'll feed her via the tube overnight." Xara sighed. "In some ways it will be easier but what if tasting food is something she loves? It's another loss for her."

Harriet didn't know what to say. She never knew what to say when it came to the ongoing grief that was Tasha. She did what she always did: fell back on what she'd say to a patient. "At least with the feeding tube she'll be getting all the nutrients she needs. Unlike now."

Xara's mouth tightened around the edges, her lips pursing, but she didn't say anything until she'd lifted Tasha out of the beanbag and settled her back into her wheelchair. "Surely it's time for cake?"

Harriet didn't even glance at her watch. "Hell, yes."

Her middle sister stared at her for a moment and then burst out laughing. "Just when I think I've got you pegged, you go and do something like this."

Harriet often had no idea what Xara was talking about and now was no exception. "What?"

Xara's eyes widened in pretend shock. "Break your own rigid rules. I thought the world came to an end if cake was served before the speeches. If you've told me once, you've told me ten times that the speeches can't start before ten."

Harriet's chin shot up. "If Edwina can break the rules by bringing an uninvited guest, then we can start the speeches early and eat cake." She spun around to the twins. "Come on, boys. Finish that game. It's time to sing 'Happy Birthday' to Mardi."

She was on her way back to the bar to give the heads-up to the wait staff to pour champagne for the birthday toast when Debbie stopped her.

"Lovely party, Harriet. The house looks amazing as always."

"Thank you." Harriet smiled at her business manager, thinking she looked different somehow. She was used to seeing Debbie in her work uniform of either black or navy blue pants and a contrasting blouse monogrammed with the practice's logo. Tonight, she wore a deep purple dress with a skirt that swirled around her thick waist in a very flattering way. "That color and style really suits you."

The woman beamed. "Thanks. I thought it was time to shake things up a bit and get noticed by Erica."

"Did it work?"

She giggled in the way all women do when they've met someone and are dreaming of possibilities. "We're going on a bush walk tomorrow."

The lesbian pool wasn't huge in a town the size of Billawarre and Debbie had been alone for a couple of years since her long-time partner had left her for a horse trainer in Hamilton. Harriet felt for her; every woman deserved a partner who made her feel she could take on the world. James had always made her feel that way.

Not so much recently.

She closed her mind to the unwelcome thought and to the even more odious one of while she was in a personal drought, her sixty-five-year-old widowed mother was apparently getting plenty of sex. The moment this disastrous evening was over, she was tying James up and having her way with him. A thick, warm feeling rolled through her, settling between her legs with an insistent and delicious throb. God, she wanted to push everyone out the door right this minute and drag James to bed. Actually, the couch would be far enough.

"Um, Harriet?"

"Hmm?" She was only half listening, not quite ready to abandon the delicious buzz of excitement making her light and carefree.

"Can you come in early on Monday? I want to run through the

accounts with you now I've got those invoices from AB Medical supplies."

Her lust instantly flatlined. "So they've been double billing us?"

Debbie shook her head. "No, it's more complicated than that. AB Medical's invoices all match up with our payments. It's AAB Medical that's the issue. I did some digging and I can't find any evidence the company exists."

Harriet's stomach rolled. "Then what are those payments? Where's the money going?"

"I've asked myself the same questions. All I can think is that it's a shell company." Debbie wrung her hands. "There are only three people with access to the accounts. You, me and James."

A hot flash of indignation heated her skin. "What are you implying?"

Debbie's shoulders stiffened. "Don't shoot the messenger, Harriet. I'm just stating facts. Someone's taking money out of the account at regular intervals under the guise of fake payments."

"Obviously, we've been hacked." Harriet tried squashing the needles of doubt that Debbie was raising this problem to cover her own tracks.

"To the tune of 22,000 dollars."

"Wh-what?" The amount stunned her but at the same time it made her blood boil. Someone was stealing *her* money. Money she worked damn hard to earn. "Have you contacted the bank?"

"They've frozen the account until we can sort things out."

"Good. Thanks. Don't say anything about this to anyone. We'll talk on Monday." It was official; there was no way this night could possibly get any worse. "Excuse me, Debbie, I have to give a happy birthday speech and toast my mother."

Lucinda had arranged Georgie's amazing cupcakes on a five-layer tower stand and placed a tiny red heart on each. At the very top she'd positioned a slab of white chocolate and inscribed Edwina's name and *Happy 65th Birthday* in curly writing. Brown and white wired fondant stars burst out from behind the greeting, making it look like exploding fireworks. The cakes, on their white cloth–draped table, were both a centerpiece and fabulous cake art. People had been commenting all evening and Harriet would happily talk about it *ad infinitum* if it kept the conversation well away from Edwina and Doug.

As she walked past the alcove formed by the turret, she heard a raised male voice saying, "That's bullshit." Wondering who'd had too much to drink, she stopped ready to smooth the situation. The last thing she needed was a drunken scene.

She blinked at the sight in front of her, willing it to change. James had his back to the lead-lined windows, his backside casually resting on the wide windowsill. It was his askew tie, disheveled hair and gleaming white knuckles gripping the sill that told her he was far from relaxed. She recognized the profiles of the three men facing him. They were standing in a half circle, filling the outer rim of the alcove and blocking his exit.

"The check for the respite-care house has been in the mail for five weeks, James." There was an edge to Steve's usually calm voice. "I've spoken to Kevin Duncan at the City Hall. He said it was processed on time and both of you signed it. In fact, you apparently offered to hand deliver it to me, so where the hell is it?"

"I was going to drive out to the farm but things got crazy with the golf weekend and then the car rally, so I mailed it," James said equably. "I think it's safe to say that it must have gotten lost in the mail. I'll set things in motion to cancel the check and draw up another one."

"Don't bother with another check. I want the money direct debited on Monday," Steve said coolly. "In fact, I want to be there to see it happen."

"Mate, I understand you're frustrated. Hell, so am I, but going to City Hall and standing over an employee isn't going to help matters." James spread out his hands, palms upwards. "You're going to have to trust me on this."

Steve stiffened and puffed out his chest. "That's getting increasingly hard to do."

A rip of anger bolted along Harriet's veins. She didn't recognize the belligerent man inside Steve. In the fifteen years she'd known him, her brother-in-law had always been laid back and easygoing. She couldn't recall him ever being confrontational and he'd never taken advantage of family ties in any situation. If she'd known accosting James was his plan, she'd never have taken the damn water bottle to Xara. She took a step, intending to interrupt the conversation and support James.

"I wouldn't trust him as far as I could throw him," David McGowan said gruffly. "There's something dodgy going on with the rural relief fund too."

"Is this another one of your conspiracy theories, David?" James rolled his eyes. "As I've told you more than once, I've audited the books and explained the discrepancy." His mouth curled. "It's not my fault one of your volunteers can't add."

"Gentlemen," Harriet said, "I hate to interrupt but it's time—"

"So the check got lost in the mail and a volunteer can't do math," Lewis said in a tone that would freeze fire. "I'm all ears for your explanation on the lack of dividends from the McCluskey development."

James sighed, a long, put-upon sound that filled the small space. "I know we all had high hopes about that development, Lewis, but sales have been slower than expected. You knew the risks when you invested."

Harriet stared at James, her thoughts a tumbled mixture of confusion and surprise.

"That's not what your wife told me." Lewis looked directly at Harriet. "You told me the sales had exceeded expectations."

James shot her a cautioning look and uncertainty whipped her. She fought it hard with the well-founded premise—the one their marriage was based on—James didn't lie.

"Perhaps, I misunderstood. I'm not privy to the intricate details of James's business."

"The early sales were promising and at the time I told Harriet it was looking like a real winner." James nodded at Lewis as if seeking a shared understanding. "As a husband, I try to protect her from the bad stuff."

A wave of goosebumps rose on Harriet's arms. It was as if he was talking about her parents' marriage, not theirs. Her father had always protected her fragile mother from bad news and, in many ways, from the real world, but she and James were equal partners. They discussed things. They shared information.

With sudden clarity, she realized it had been a long time since James had told her any in-depth details about his business. Was he speaking the truth? She immediately threw off the unworthy doubt. Of course he was telling the truth. She had no reason to doubt him, only to wonder why he'd stopped telling her things.

She dredged her memory and recalled the conversations they'd shared over the last few months, but they'd been more about her seeking his advice regarding financial investments and her medical practice. Given his expertise in the area, she generally followed his recommendations. He managed her retirement fund like he managed many others in the district and he regularly showed her the growth statements—the good news.

She knew her husband. How could she have been married to him for twenty years and not know him? And yet the sheen of sweat on his forehead and his behavior earlier in the evening unsettled her. His recent air of disconnectedness that she'd put down to mismatching schedules unsettled her. Their lack of sex ...

She became aware of a commotion behind her—a man yelling, people whispering loudly. Rory Bateman, a former farmer and now a paraplegic after a quad-bike accident, was wheeling fast toward them. So fast, he almost knocked into the back of David McGowan.

"There you are, Minchin, you weaselly bastard."

"Rory!" Shocked at his unexpected and uninvited arrival, it took

Harriet a moment to find her best acerbic voice. "This is a private party."

A silence loaded with fascinated curiosity descended over the crowd. Everyone stilled, greedy and eager to watch things play out.

"Yeah, well," the man snarled, "your husband's been avoiding me for weeks so excuse me for gate-crashing."

"James will see you in his office on Monday morning," she said curtly. Her hands reached for his chair. "I will see you out."

With the skill born from three years in a wheelchair, Rory spun sideways away from her and the three men parted to allow him room to enter the circle. He pointed at James, his face contorted in rage. "What the hell have you done with my million-dollar payout?"

"Minchin," Lewis said loudly and clearly as if he was addressing a room full of doctors at a cardiac conference. "It's all starting to add up to something rotten in the town of Billawarre and the money trail leads directly to you."

Harriet wanted to scream, *You're wrong!* She wanted to throw herself forward and defend James. More than anything, she wanted to banish these men and their evil accusations from her home. But as she opened her mouth to speak, she caught sight of dawning realization on Debbie's face. Up against the other accusations of missing monies, the transfer of 22,000 dollars into a shell company suddenly pointed to James.

Her heart sped up as memories flashed across her mind: his ranting about City Hall's ineptitude when she'd asked about the respite-care check. Nya's firm insistence James hadn't paid her. James's terse reply and his insistence she not sack Nya for lying. Her mouth dried. Nya hadn't been lying. It was James who'd lied.

He's lying now.

No. Not possible.

But her chest burned, and she struggled to breathe as the truth pressed in on her heavy as lead and just as poisonous. She didn't want to believe James was capable of such acts but no matter which way she came at it, how hard she tried to find a way around it, the truth glowed as bright and white as an incandescent searchlight. James was a thief.

Her blood dropped to her feet and silver spots cascaded in front of her eyes. Her knees softened and she gulped, pushing down the rising tide of champagne and salmon. She felt a hand pressing lightly on her back and she looked up to see Georgie and Xara flanking her, their faces creased with bewilderment and concern. She tried to speak but her throat was too tight and her mouth seemed disconnected from her brain.

"These accusations are libelous." James spoke loudly and from pale lips.

"They're bloody well true." David turned to the crowd for confirmation. "Anyone else invested with Minchin and now missing money?"

"He told me the Tax Office had stuffed up my return," Greg Quartermaine called out, raising his fist and shaking it. "You prick, Minchin."

"Oh, God," Helen Papadopoulos wailed before slumping onto a chair. "When Con got cancer he invested everything with him so I'd be looked after."

The silence of the room broke with accusations, shocked concern and a certain morbid delight. Snippets of conversations reached Harriet, flowing around her like the eddying and sucking treachery of floodwaters.

"I always said his promised returns were too good to be true."

"Do you think there'll be a fire sale? I quite fancy his classic Porsche."

"This has to be the most entertaining party they've ever thrown."

"We'll need a new candidate for party nomination." Phillip Ciobo's disgusted voice rose above the rest like a slap from an open palm, stinging Harriet with the full force of the situation.

Edwina and Charlotte materialized beside her. As expected, her mother's face was pale with shock and she didn't say a word. They rarely said anything significant to each other on a good day, so this wasn't unusual, irrespective of the fact that her life was falling apart. What was unexpected was the steely glint in her mother's vivid blue eyes. It rippled the waters of Harriet's stunned stupor.

"Mom?" Charlotte's voice sounded less like the self-assured young woman she'd been earlier and more like a worried little girl. "Is what they're saying true?"

"All of you," James yelled, sweeping his arm dismissively in a large arc, "leave my house immediately before I call the police."

"Oh, that's rich," Lewis said sarcastically. "I think we're the ones calling the police."

James held out his hands to Charlotte and Harriet, smiling and urging them to come and stand next to him. She knew the strategy—the political ploy of presenting a united front to the world. She knew the power of projecting a tight-knit family, because it was what the Mannerings and Chirnwells had been doing for generations. It was a sure-fire way to cast doubt amid gossiping rumors.

Many time, she'd happily stood hand in hand with James when he ran for mayor, but back then being the good and supportive wife was effortless. She'd believed in him and in what he could do for the district. Right now her mind was a mess of tangled, divergent thoughts and she didn't know what or whom she believed.

He stole from me.

He allegedly stole from me.

Charlotte glanced between Harriet and James, worried and hesitating. Suddenly, the idea of photos of Charlotte standing next James appearing in the local newspaper or on the internet before Harriet had all the facts, appalled her. She shot out an arm, catching Charlotte's hand in hers and stalling her.

"Thank you everyone for coming tonight and helping me celebrate my birthday." Edwina's beautifully cultured voice, with its well-rounded vowels, boomed through the speakers . The room instantly fell silent. "It's certainly the most memorable birthday party I've had, but all good things must to come to an end. Please pick up a delicious chocolate cupcake on your way out and have a safe drive home."

At that moment, as Harriet's world as she knew it crumbled around her, she experienced an unfamiliar and almost foreign appreciation of her mother.

CHAPTER EIGHT

"THE KIDS ARE ASLEEP." XARA WALKED WEARILY INTO THE bedroom and kicked off her heels. "What a night."

Steve paused his pacing, stopping midway along the length of the built-in closets. "Hell, Xara. I'm sorry I blew up your mother's party."

She shook her head slowly, still struggling to come to grips with what had happened. "I think James did that all on his own."

"Yeah, but if I'd known what was going to happen ..." He unzipped her dress. "I should have gone to see him at the office, but I was just so pissed off with the delay. I wanted to have it out with him there and then."

She put her hand on his arm. "None of this is your fault. In fact, there's a possibility you may have done the entire district a civic service."

"What? By inadvertently sparking off a public shaming of my brother-in-law?" He scrubbed his cheeks with his palms.

"Oh God, has he really stolen money from the sick, the elderly, the gullible and the greedy?" She shuddered as she shimmied out of her dress.

"It's hard to wrap your head around it, isn't it? James has always been a bit of a show-off. He likes bright and shiny toys, but I never picked him to rip off his clients."

"Allegedly," the attorney in her felt compelled to say, although it was hard to get past the fact that five unrelated people had accused James of withholding their money. She finally asked Steve the question that had been troubling her—the question she hadn't broached in the car because Georgie and the kids were in the back: "Do you think Harry knew?"

He shook his head slowly. "I doubt it. If she did, she's a bloody good actress. I reckon she realized what was going on pretty much the same time as the rest of us."

"I've never seen her look so rattled. I offered to stay with her, but she blew me off."

"I wouldn't take it personally," Steve said, falling back onto the bed. "I reckon she'll want to talk to James with no one else around to overhear their conversation."

"I guess you're right." She remembered Charlotte and her skin flashed hot and cold, just as it had at Miligili. "And Charlie. God, did you see her face?"

"Yeah, poor kid. Are you sure we did the right thing letting Edwina take her home to Glenora?" He sat up and ran his hand across the back of his permanently sun-browned neck. "Maybe she should have come home with us. Your mother's not exactly known for her coping abilities in a crisis. Your dad was the one who always dealt with the difficult stuff."

"That's true." She thought about when Georgie was eleven and her sister had been rushed to the hospital after being thrown from her horse. That sparked off the memory of the day Tasha was born and how her father had come alone to the hospital. It wasn't until she and Tasha were discharged that her mother visited, and even then she'd cleaned and cooked rather than helping with the baby. For a woman with three daughters, she'd never been great with babies, but as they grew into toddlers and beyond she became a lot more hands on.

"But tonight Mom was amazing." She slipped off her bra and

panties and pulled on her pajamas. "I've got no idea what's going on with her or if it has anything to do with Doug, but she was formidable. No one dared not do as she said and short of a fire, I've never seen a room empty so fast."

"It was impressive. It was a night of bombshells, that's for sure."

"Oh, but it was a train wreck of a party." A hysterical edge tinged Xara's laugh. "There's a horrible irony to the fact that Harry thought Mom bringing Doug to the party was a disaster. Compared with James's alleged activities, Doug's arrival is positively minor in the rumor and gossip stakes."

"I had a quick chat with him. He seems like a good bloke, but then again," bitterness filled his voice, "so did James."

She squeezed his hand, wanting to give him something when nothing much helped. "I'm guessing most people relocated somewhere else to deconstruct the night's events and take delight in James and Harry's alleged fall from grace."

"Not all of them. Lewis, Rory and David went straight to the police." A pained expression crossed his face and he raised his head to meet her gaze. "The senior officer on duty called me while you were settling the twins. He also called Kevin Duncan. He wants both of us to go down and give a statement."

She realized that while she'd been getting ready for bed all he'd done was divest himself of his tie. "What? Now? It's almost eleven."

He shrugged as if the time was irrelevant. "You know more about this than I do, Zar, but I'm thinking the police need enough statements to convince a magistrate to issue a warrant."

"Oh, shit, you're right. The longer it takes to get the warrant, the more time James has to shred and delete."

"I know we're family but we're not enabling that, right?" Steve frowned, his face deeply worried.

She leaned in and kissed him. "No, we're not enabling that in any shape or form. He'll have his chance in court to prove he hasn't stolen money from the respite-care house fund." *And the rest.*

"And if he has, I'll rip his bloody arms off."

"No, you won't or you'll land up in court too." She rested her forehead gently on his, a little alarmed by his violent reaction. "Besides, you're not one of those aggressive, moronic blokes I used to date. You're my wonderful, level-headed, rational guy."

He stood up and resumed pacing. "I don't feel rational, Zar. I feel like I need to go and chop a hell of a lot of wood." He swung around and looked at her, completely nonplussed. "Tell me. What kind of a bloke rips off kids with disabilities?"

A desperate one. Her heart tore at his bewilderment but she knew there was no point having this conversation with him tonight. Not when he was angry and struggling with betrayal.

"He's lower than pond scum."

The night's events caught up with her and suddenly she was incredibly cold. Shivers ran over her skin and she crawled under the covers. "And if he's found guilty, you can tell him that as part of your victim impact statement."

"Oh, he's guilty alright." Steve's usually soft eyes hardened and flashed shards of emerald green. "And the bastard's never setting foot on my farm again."

Xara flinched at his resolute tone. If Steve, who was usually the voice of reason, was this incensed, hurt and raw, how was the rest of the town reacting? James and Harriet were Billawarre's favorite couple. As much as many had wished to be and tried to be included in their circle, and the accepted ones had gloried in it, most people loved nothing more than watching tall poppies fall. James, as mayor and a successful—*allegedly successful*—businessman, had definitely stumbled if not fallen.

Suspicion and allegations were enough for the newsmakers to pounce and when his position as mayor of one of the larger rural cities in the state was added into the mix, this story was bigger than Billawarre. By morning, the haters would have seeded their vitriol across the internet, using social media to act as both judge and jury. Those savage and venomous comments would stay on the net forever, appearing over and over whenever the names

James Minchin or Harriet Chirnwell were typed into a search engine.

The treacherous question she'd thought she'd put to rest bubbled up again. Had Harry known about James's theft?

Alleged, alleged, alleged theft. But the attorney in her was losing the battle to the woman with a strong gut feeling.

For the first time in her life, Xara felt sorry for her talented, bossy, designer-wearing, social climbing sister. Harriet's perfect life was suddenly messier than her own.

GEORGIE SAT on top of a hill with her back resting uncomfortably against a dry stone wall. Long blades of summer-dried grass tickled her bare legs, but the air was blessedly autumn-morning cool. She watched the dawn leech into the sky, sending out its wash of pale pink and orange. It wasn't long before the colors faded; absorbed into the distinctive blue that was the Australian sky.

She'd woken early to the bleating of sheep, the happy warbling of magpies and the raucous and shudder-inducing squawks of cockatoos. She swore all the rustic sounds of the country were louder than the early morning rumblings of city traffic and the buzz, crank and thump of the recycling truck. Perhaps she had become *that city chick* Xara liked to tease her about.

If she had, it had been unintentional. After spending five years at uni, she'd taught for two years in Melbourne before heading off overseas. After three years of traveling and teaching English she'd returned to Australia and immediately been offered a short-term teaching contract at her current school. Almost broke, and never one to ask for money from her parents, she'd accepted the job as a stopgap measure until she got herself more organized. Only, each time the contract ended, someone else went on maternity leave, long-service leave or sick leave and she was asked to stay on. She loved the school and she enjoyed the classroom work, but her true love was teaching art. Sadly, there were few specific art teaching jobs on offer in the country.

Eight months after meeting Jason, she was encouraged by the school to apply for a permanent classroom position. She'd prevaricated but Jason had urged her on, telling her that writing her resume and taking the interview would all be good experience. If she was honest with herself, she'd known his suggestion was more to do with keeping her in the city: he had no bucolic interests at all.

On their infrequent visits to Billawarre, he'd always tried to persuade her to return to Melbourne earlier than planned. When the school offered her the permanent job, he'd proposed she accept it and they move in together. At the time it had seemed like a commitment from him, the first step toward a long and happy future together.

So, she taught kids and Jason sold wine on a huge scale. His job was very Melbourne-centric. For the top end of the market he needed to be in the heart of the upper-middle-class leafy suburbs, snob central, as well as having easy access to the growth corridor where women stranded in the suburbs with young children drank copious amounts of cheap sauv blanc; bitch diesel, as he'd taken to calling it.

She winced and it wasn't just from the pain of the jagged rock pressing against her spine. There was a lot not to miss about Jason. The fact that he kept popping into her thoughts, especially now when she'd just stumbled across a rock-filled field in the dusky dawn light to call Ben, bothered her.

And why do you think this keeps happening, Georgina? The question skittered across her mind in the soft and calm voice of the counselor she'd seen after Eliza's birth. Georgie immediately tried to shy away from the answer, but it caught her by the throat. She and Jason shared a child. He was part of Eliza and Eliza was always going to be a part of her. Her hand closed tightly around her cell phone, welcoming the painful press of the edges against her palm as she both reminded and berated herself that Jason had always been ambivalent about having children.

How had she missed that about him? She'd brought up the topic of kids on and off during their first couple of years together and he'd said, sure, in the future. He'd asked her to wait until the business was fully on its feet and, against the sound of a loudly ticking biological clock, she'd complied. She knew enough about relationships to know that getting pregnant before he was ready was a direct path to rancor and resentment.

When she'd unexpectedly found herself pregnant following a bout of stomach flu—it turned out she'd not only thrown up all food for two days but also her contraceptive pill—she'd been delirious with happiness. Jason had expressed just enough interest in the pregnancy to allay her fears that he didn't feel tricked into becoming a father earlier than he'd preferred. He'd even got as far as downloading a pregnancy for dads' app on his cell phone and agreed to attend classes. But they never made it to class.

Eliza's unexpectedly abrupt arrival and precipitous death hadn't affected Jason in the same way it had Georgie. He'd quickly accepted the outcome. She had not. She'd railed against the devastating unfairness, weeping and wailing and furious at the world. Three months after she'd held her perfectly formed daughter, with her translucent skin and soft covering of downy hair, he'd told her what had happened was for the best. He'd said it was time for her to face facts, take it in her stride and "move on."

God, how she hated that overused, psychobabble. People with no understanding of grief said it so easily. She could almost forgive acquaintances and strangers, but she couldn't forgive Jason. How could a mother just *move on* from the death of her child? She wanted to remember forever and he wanted to forget.

Her cell phone lit up and she realized she must have accidentally pressed Ben's number. She brought it up to her ear just as he answered.

"Georgie." His sleep-filled voice quietly stroked her name.

She quivered as she remembered his large and talented hands stroking her two nights ago. Her pulse quickened. "Sorry, did I wake you?"

"Hang on," he said softly.

She heard some rustling, a thump and then footsteps before the noise of a door closing. "Sorry about that." His voice was normal volume. "Dad and I are sharing a room at the motel and he's still snoring. How are things?"

She thought about everything that had happened since she'd dropped him off yesterday. "Weird."

He laughed. "Is that code for 'family'? I know the feeling. The longer I live away from mine the weirder they seem when I return."

"Actually, my sisters are being totally predictable." She pulled up the blade of grass that was prickling her leg and chewed on it.

"Predictable is good."

"I guess," she said, thinking that nothing else about her visit so far had been predictable.

A flock of sulfur-crested cockatoos swooped past, a white flash against the deepening blue sky. A moment later they landed in a nearby gum tree, announcing their arrival with a loud and distinctive *car-car* sound.

"Where are you?" he asked.

"The home field of my middle sister's farm."

"Xara, right?"

She smiled, both delighted and surprised by his memory. "Well done."

"Hey," he said, his tone both teasing and serious. "I listen. Why are you out there?"

"The house is too small to have a private conversation." *And I'm keeping you private.*

"No. I meant why are you out at the farm? I thought you were staying with Harriet."

"Wow, you really do listen."

"Told you."

She could picture his cheeky and endearing grin and she had an overwhelming urge to see him right this second and kiss those lips that curved crookedly upwards. "Yes, you did and I guess I have to believe you."

"Too right. Why are you out there instead of in town?"

"Um ..." She bit down on the grass, feeling the stem split in her mouth. The monumental events and subsequent fallout of last night were just too enormous to explain over the phone.

A ripple of unease forced her to her feet. Was she really ready to tell Ben that her prim and proper mother had produced a boyfriend who was unlike anyone in her usual social set? Tell him her wealthy and successful brother-in-law had allegedly committed fraud? The idea made her queasy. She and Ben were so new and shiny with so much to discover about each other that she wanted to keep them in their blissful bubble—immune from the world of family and dirty little secrets—for as long as possible.

"You still there—" The roaring sound of an engine tumbled down the line, obliterating Ben's voice. He whistled. "Whoa, that scattered the grazing kangaroos."

She could picture the scene. "Let me guess, the morning milk trucks just rumbled through town heading toward the factory."

"Nope. Wasn't the milk trucks."

"Okay, logging trucks."

"Wrong again. I thought you said this town of yours was quiet."

"It is. In fact, I'd bet money on absolutely nothing happening on a Sunday morning at seven-thirty. You could fire a cannon down the main street and not hit anyone."

He laughed. "In that case, I should ask you to bet me twenty dollars. It would be the easiest money I've ever made."

Curiosity got the better of her. "Spit it out then. What's going on in the thriving metropolis of Billawarre this fine morning besides the reverend and the priest setting up their sandwich boards?"

"Something big, otherwise the five Melbourne television stations wouldn't have sent news crews."

Her mouth dropped open and the dried grass she'd been chewing landed on her feet. *Shit, shit, shit.* The odds of keeping Ben in the bubble just massively shortened.

She didn't want to tell him about James. Would it prejudice him against her? Her mind spun on that thought. If it did make him think worse of her wasn't it better to know that now and walk away? Walk before she'd sunk too much energy and emotion into yet another dead-end relationship. Walk before it hurt too much.

Who are you kidding? You slept with him. It's gonna hurt either way.

Her stomach flipped. Did she even have a choice whether or not to tell him? Her family's dirty laundry was about to be pegged out for all to see via radio, television, print and online newspapers, as well as the goliath that was social media. She searched her brain ways to keep it a secret from him.

A fizz of hope trickled through her. She'd never mentioned James and he had a different surname from hers. *Harriet doesn't.* A pain burned under her ribs. She was seeing a guy who listened and remembered her sisters' names. Hell, he'd asked her why she wasn't at Harriet's place. She wouldn't need to tell him, he'd put two and two together in a heartbeat. It was suddenly vitally important that he heard about this mess from her and not the press or the Sunday morning bakery queue. At least by telling him she might have the opportunity to hose down spot fires flaring from his reaction. Or perhaps this would be the end of something she'd prayed might be good.

Injecting faux-cheeriness into her voice, she said, "Any chance I could treat you to the big breakfast at the Staff of Life café this morning? They do awesome bacon and eggs."

"Can't go an extra twenty-four hours without me, eh?" He sounded pleased.

Any other time she'd have rolled her eyes and delivered a dry, "Dream on, mate."

She was about to tell him she needed to talk to him when he said, "I'd love to but sorry, I can't." Regret rang in his voice. "I promised

Dad I'd help him load the old wreck he's bought onto the trailer. Experience has taught me that's never quick. On the plus side though, he did say he wanted to start early. We should be done by noon."

Bugger. Sneaking out early was one thing. Disappearing in the middle of the day was impossible. Even though she doubted the family lunch Xara had proposed last night would happen, she'd be expected to be around to monitor the situation with Harriet and James and provide support. "I've got a family thing I really can't miss."

"No problem. I'm free tonight and it's chicken parm night at the motel. We could eat here."

By tonight, eating out in Billawarre would be a nightmare. Hell, by lunchtime the media would have spread the word far and wide about Billawarre's infamous mayor. Everyone who knew she was related to James—even if she didn't know them—wouldn't hesitate to walk over to her and Ben's table and demand the juicy details about what was going on.

She could hear the gleeful questions already: Is he guilty? Did Harriet know about the money? How long has it been going on? How can you stand to be related to him? Then, when they'd finally finished picking all the meat off that particular juicy bone, they'd notice Ben. His presence would start another round of inquisitive and overly personal questions. Questions that risked Eliza and Jason being mentioned. It was a subject that Ben needed to learn from her if and when they got to a place in their relationship that warranted it. If they survived James's situation.

No, eating in public, hell, being seen in public was completely out of the question. Every cell in her body tensed. She was going to have to tell him over the phone.

"Ah, Ben, you know how you're really good at listening? How good are you at keeping secrets?"

"Unless the secret comes under the ruling of mandatory reporting or the proceeds of crime, I'm pretty good. Why?"

"Um ... you know those television news crews?" She chewed at her lip, ineffectively delaying the inevitable. "They're in town because of my brother-in-law."

There was a moment's silence before he said slowly, "I'm guessing it's not because of a feel-good news story."

"Ah, no." She pressed a booted foot against the wall and stretched her Achilles tendon, welcoming the pain. It hurt less than the words. "He's been ... he's been accused of fraud."

"Shit." His shock reverberated down the line.

"Exactly. And it well and truly hit the fan last night at Mom's party."

"That sounds like a fun night."

His sympathy buoyed her. "Oh, Ben, it was awful."

"Did you suspect anything?"

She heard the wariness in his voice and cursed James for putting her in this position. She thought of Harriet and guilt slugged her. Here she was trying to protect the tender new shoots of a fledging relationship when Harriet was dealing with the badly damaged roots of a mature marriage. "Nothing. It's so hard to know what to believe.

"Harriet and James have always had an enviable lifestyle. From the outside looking in, not much has changed over the years so there was nothing to be suspicious about until last night's accusations. Obviously, the press has gotten wind of it and I'm sure horrible stuff will be reported today about James and Harriet."

"Is your sister involved?"

"God, I hope not. If she is, she'll lose her medical license." Georgie tugged her windblown hair back behind her ears, trying to stay calm. She'd spent half the night lying awake in the narrow single bed, listening to Tasha's noisy breathing and asking herself similar questions. "Harriet's got her faults but stealing's not one of them. Then again, I never thought in a million years that James might be propping up their lavish lifestyle with other people's money."

"So if all this is going public, exactly what are you asking me to keep secret?"

She sucked in a breath. "I know this sounds really shallow, especially as we're nowhere near ready to meet each other's relatives yet, and you probably haven't even mentioned me to your father ..." She knew she was gabbling but she couldn't stop herself. "I'd really appreciate it if—"

"I didn't tell him I'm seeing the sister-in-law of an alleged criminal? No sweat."

The word "criminal" lashed her and she made an involuntary gagging noise.

"Georgie, are you okay?"

Ben seemed genuinely worried and she sighed. "I really don't think anyone in my family is okay today."

CHAPTER NINE

THE MORNING AFTER THE PARTY, EDWINA WAS IN THE YARD AND working by seven. Despite the early morning chill of autumn air making her hands cramp, being outside was preferable to lying awake in bed and staring at the ceiling. For most of the night, sleep had eluded her. She'd put it down to the monumental events of the previous evening, although she knew deep down that part of her restlessness was due to being alone in the bed for the first time in a week. It surprised her how quickly she'd gotten used to Doug's reassuring bulk snuggled up against her.

As she weeded, she couldn't shake the feeling that Glenora felt empty without Doug's presence. He was incapable of doing anything quietly and he moved around enthusiastically both inside and out. He whistled while he raked leaves, he clanged saucepans and banged cabinet doors when he cooked, constantly humming. The noise was in stark contrast to Richard. She had no need to compare the two men any further, because how they acted in the kitchen was the perfect summation of all their differences.

For the thousandth time she thought about the party. Nothing about the evening—from the reaction of her acquaintances to Doug's presence to the exposure of her son-in-law's possible law-breaking behavior—had matched her expectations. From the moment she and Doug had walked under the balloon arch, he hadn't left her side.

She'd thought taking him to her party was her way of making a statement to a critical group of people—one that said, *I'm with this man, like it or lump it.* As it turned out, he'd been as busy protecting her as she'd been of him. They'd been a team of two and perhaps that solidarity was the reason none of her social circle had dared to make any polite-yet-barbed comments to her face. No doubt there was chatter behind their backs, after all, this was Billawarre.

But amid the curiosity, most people had been relatively welcoming. Granted, it had been her birthday but even so, the response came with an element of irony. Forty-eight years ago, if she'd arrived at a party with Doug, they'd have asked him to leave. Were they welcoming now because so many years had passed or had they forgotten him? David McGowan was the only person who'd remembered him, not as it turned out from his time on Murrumbeet but, from a shared tour of duty in Vietnam.

Their united front had also delayed the inevitable third-degree grilling from Harriet—an unexpected bonus. Now that James's activities had redirected the limelight, she and Doug had some breathing space. It was space Edwina needed, because there was still so much between them left unsaid. Despite almost five decades apart, their reunion held some of the elements of their original time together. The stolen moments. The secret meetings.

Determination straightened her spine. Not anymore. Taking Doug public last night was the first step and the freedom she'd glimpsed was the unanticipated by-product. It had been fleeting, but it had existed. She eventually had to face the girls and their questions but last night alone in bed she'd settled on a story that was rooted in the truth. They only needed the basic information about her and Doug; the intimate details belonged to her.

Xara would have already told her sisters the sketchy information Edwina had shared with her and Georgie was unlikely to ask questions or demand difficult answers. The only regret Edwina had about taking Doug to the party was the timing. In her desire to right a past wrong, she'd inadvertently added to the debit side. She should have told Primrose. She should have told Primrose a lot of things a long time ago.

At eight, her cell phone rang and Doug's name appeared on the screen. She tried to answer it but the screen didn't respond to her gardening glove. Frantically, she pulled it off with her teeth and caught the call just before it went to voice mail. "Hello," she said breathlessly.

"Did I wake you?"

"No, I've been gardening for an hour. I couldn't sleep. I missed you," she said, her honesty surprising her. She'd had a lifetime of keeping her emotions buried deep.

"I missed you too." His gravelly voice rumbled softly down the line reminding her of how he whispered into her ear when they made love. A delicious shiver coiled through her just as it had when she was seventeen.

"Your bed's a hell of a lot more comfortable than the motel's. I reckon it was new when we first met."

"Sorry."

"No need to be sorry. You need to be with your girls. I've got plenty to keep me busy today."

Today was probably the tip of the iceberg of what was ahead for Harriet and Charlotte. She swallowed a sigh. "I'm not sure how long my granddaughter will be staying with me."

Last night in the car, Charlotte was silent on the short drive to Glenora. Her granddaughter had refused the offer of a hot chocolate and gone straight to bed. To bed but not to sleep. Edwina had heard sounds of padding feet and the clicking of door latches until the early hours of the morning.

"I don't want to complicate things for her." The moment the

words left her mouth she worried he might think she was giving him the brush off. "I really want to spend more time with you. We've still got so much to talk about and ..." She changed tack then, veering away from a topic she didn't want to broach on the phone. "I could shoot James for doing this. His timing is lousy."

"I reckon he probably thinks it's lousy timing too."

"Indeed," she said waspishly, not able to muster much sympathy for her son-in-law.

"Remind me never to cross you." A smile danced in Doug's voice. "You're bloody good at that polite voice that could cut—"

"The balls off a bull? Yes, I know."

Doug roared with laughter. "I was going to say cut glass. One day I hope to hear you use those rounded vowels to swear."

"It doesn't happen very often." She thought about how she'd been raised and her position in the town. "Old habits die hard."

"No worries. I plan to be around for a long time."

The past rushed up to choke her. As if sensing the direction of her thoughts, Doug added, "I promise you, Eddy. This time, no matter what, I'm not going anywhere."

This time. Her stomach swooped. She knew it was juvenile—she was sixty-five years old for heaven's sake—but she couldn't stop herself from testing him. "What if your son-in-law's suspected of fraud?"

He snorted. "He's a good bloke and a great dad, but I don't think he's smart enough or organized enough to manage something like that."

"Okay." She took a tense breath. "What if there's some sort of family disaster?"

"Unlikely. But if I have to dash home, I'll tell you before I leave."

Her lips pursed but not hard enough to cut off the words, "And if the government needs you?"

"I'm not going anywhere, Eddy," he said firmly. "Take all the time you need with your family. When you're free, I'll be waiting."

She wanted to believe him, she truly did, but the past was back creating havoc and cleaving her trust. She fought it, remembering the events of last night and how kind he'd been. How kind he was still. "What are your plans for today?" she asked, moving the conversation away from fraught topics.

After the call ended, she stowed her gloves and trowel in the garden shed and walked inside. The house was silent but for the burr and click of the refrigerator and freezer. She put on the kettle and telephoned Harriet. The call went straight to voicemail and her mind blanked in panic. She felt foolish saying, "Just wondering how you are?" Of course Harriet wasn't going to be great, good or even fine. She kept the message brief: "Charlie's still asleep. I'll call again when she's awake."

As she cut the call, it occurred to her that for the first time since she'd given birth to Harriet, she had a fair idea how her daughter might be feeling. Her own world had fallen apart once and it had been like drowning in choking sand.

During that bleak and devastating period, every time Edwina had tried for a foothold, she'd tumbled backwards and slipped further under. Eventually, she'd managed to shore up her life and rebuild the foundations only to find that, without warning, they could shake and shift and send her plummeting back into the breath-sucking sand with no obvious escape route.

The kettle sang and she sloshed hot water around the teapot to warm it. As the kettle boiled again she used the tea scoop to measure the tea—one for each person and one for the pot—and then poured the bubbling water over the fragrant leaves. The clink of the china lid sliding into place was as familiar as time, as was the placement of the tea cozy over the tea pot. This one was a hand-knitted, rose-covered woolen cozy. Georgie had made it for her during a frenzy of craft activities Edwina knew was a form of therapy after losing Eliza and ending things with Jason. She'd also knitted a black-faced, woolly white sheep cozy for Xara and an elegant cardigan cozy, complete with an intricate cable and tiny pearl buttons, for Harriet.

Eliza. Edwina had forced herself to attend the funeral of her youngest granddaughter and had plumbed the depths of her resolve to get through the day. After surviving it, there'd been nothing left over to offer Georgina support. She knew she'd failed her daughter on that bitterly cold July day, when the weather had perfectly reflected the bleakness of the occasion, but to explain why was fraught with debilitating memories, secrets she couldn't divulge, and the risk of inflicting pain on too many people. The rose cozy had become a totem; each time she tucked it around the pot she thought about her very different daughters and their daughters. The tiny baby, who'd struggled so valiantly for life and lost. Tasha, who struggled every day in so many ways. And Charlotte, who was fast approaching adulthood with the world at her feet.

Dear Charlotte, whose father had just turned her world upside down. An unusually silent Charlotte.

Her granddaughter was a normal teenage girl with her fair share of ranting and raving. Given what had happened last night, Edwina had fully expected her to fling out her arms and ask dramatically, how he could do this to me? But apart from the quietly tortured question she'd asked Harriet at the party—*Is it true?*—she'd been almost mute. Surely that wasn't normal?

Leaving the tea to steep, Edwina went to check if Charlotte was awake. She carefully dodged the creaky floorboard that had been a handy herald back in the day for detecting recalcitrant teenage daughters—mostly Xara—who snuck home late. Making her way to Harriet's old room, she pressed her ear up against the closed door, straining to hear. The faint sound of coughing drifted to her and she tapped lightly on the door before opening it and peeking inside. The bed was rumpled but empty.

She heard a retching sound in the en-suite bathroom. "Charlie, darling? Are you alright?"

A strangled sort of a sob followed.

"I'm coming in."

She found her granddaughter slumped on the bathroom floor with her knees under her chin and her arms around them. Any other time she would have suspected period cramps but not today. "Upset tummy?"

Charlotte nodded, her usually brilliant blue eyes dull and listless in her pale face.

Edwina wasn't surprised that her granddaughter was nauseous. "When you were a little girl and you got overtired or upset, your face would drain of color and you'd vomit."

"I don't remember that."

"I do. When you were three and we were in the car after a weekend of excitement at the State Fair, you threw up all over the leather seats in Gramps's Mercedes. Lucky he loved you," she teased as she filled a glass with cold water. "After that, whenever you were in the car with us, he always had an empty ice-cream container on hand."

"Poor Gramps. He always kept his cars so clean." Charlotte drained the water and handed back the glass. "Thanks."

Edwina moistened a face cloth and wiped her granddaughter's sweaty forehead. "Last night was a big shock for you. It's only natural your body's going to react. Some people eat junk food. You vomit."

"I think I'd rather eat chocolate." Charlotte suddenly trembled and dropped her forehead onto her knees. "Mardi?"

She caressed the girl's bent head. "Yes?"

"What if I ... if I knew something? Something that would upset Mom. Should I ... you know ... tell her now ... after last night?"

Edwina knew all too well about the fallout of family secrets and the pressure to keep them hidden away. She wouldn't wish that or its effects on her granddaughter, especially if James was guilty. "If it's something to do with your father and the missing money, you need to tell the police first. Then you can tell your mother."

Charlotte gave a violent sniff. "It's not about Dad."

Edwina passed her a tissue and thought about Harriet. Her daughter was dealing with the possibility that her husband was a criminal and that his actions may have destroyed good people's financial security. If what

Charlotte knew had nothing to do with James, was it something to do with school? If it was then it could probably wait a few more days before she told Harriet unless ... "Is it a life and death situation?"

Charlotte raised her head, her face stricken. "Not exactly."

Concern rippled through Edwina at the vague answer. "Is someone in danger?"

"Not really."

Charlotte's voice sounded hollow and small. Edwina's disquiet intensified. She bent down until she was at eye level. "Charlie, are you using drugs?"

Chagrin flashed across her granddaughter's line-free face. "No! I'm not that stupid."

"You're far from stupid, darling, and I didn't say you were. But at some point in our lives, all of us make a poor choice. We all make mistakes, only some are bigger than others." She sighed and stood, feeling like she was pushing against the hefty weight of life experience. "Sadly, some mistakes can't always be reversed."

Charlotte watched her closely, her face contemplative. "I can't imagine you ever making a mistake, Mardi."

Oh, the naiveté of youth. Forcing a light laugh out of a tight throat, Edwina tried not to think about the one irreversible mistake that continued to haunt her and had done for over four decades. "Can you give your mother a few days' grace before telling her this information you think will upset her?"

Charlotte rose until she stood tall and graceful, looking down at Edwina. "I guess."

"If it helps, you can always tell me. Or one of your aunts?"

Perfectly straight white teeth snagged Charlotte's bottom lip as a blur of emotions played across her face. "Thanks, Mardi, but if I tell you, I know you'll just tell me that I have to tell Mom so ..." She grabbed a towel and dried her face. "What's going to happen to Dad?"

At last. Relief that she was talking about James pushed Edwina's other concerns to the back of her mind. "I imagine the police will interview him."

"And?"

"Come into the kitchen and have some tea and toast. We can talk about it there."

CHAPTER TEN

HARRIET FOCUSED THE BINOCULARS AND HER CHEST immediately tightened. Through the family room window she could see the television trucks parked at the end of her long driveway. She lowered the binoculars, feeling the weight of them dragging down on her neck and pressing heavily on her chest. The real sensation matched the metaphysical one that had been crushing her for the last seventeen hours.

The media had taken up residence outside Miligili's gates around eight this morning and the first reporter had knocked on the front door soon after. By nine, she'd hired young Adrian's burly, weight-lifting son to stand at the gates and act as security. For the most part it had worked although it hadn't prevented one rat-bastard journalist from entering the garden the back way, hiking in from across the Stony Rises.

More than anything she'd wanted to stalk out onto the veranda, tell him in no uncertain terms he was trespassing and demand he leave. But the thought of photos of her looking and sounding shrewish kept her inside—trapped in her own home. She hated this invasion of privacy and she'd called the police, expecting them to come and move the press on. The young officer had listened to her politely before informing her they were very busy with more pressing matters and an officer couldn't be spared just at the moment.

Yesterday, Harriet wouldn't have hesitated in telling the officer that her safety was equally important, but today she knew exactly what those pressing matters were. James was being investigated for fraud and by default so was she. Last night, after everyone left the party, James had left her standing in the detritus of a celebration gone wrong and barricaded himself in the study. She'd rattled the door handle without success and been forced to press her ear up against the oak to try and work out what he was doing. All she'd heard was his low and urgent voice on the phone and the tap of computer keys.

Unable to ask him the questions that burned so hot they branded themselves on her mind, she'd tied on an apron, pulled on some gloves and worked frantically to clear away the party mess. She'd scrubbed surfaces hard and fast, removing the stains and the grime until everything gleamed. Amid her frenzy of spraying and wiping and rubbing and polishing, she'd desperately wished that a bit of elbow grease was all it took to clean away James's treachery.

The pealing of the doorbell at 12:30 a.m. had destroyed that little fantasy. Police officers stood at her door with a search warrant in hand. She'd lost it, screaming, "This is all your fault!" at a stony-faced and silent James. She'd stood by helplessly while the police searched and seized two filing cabinets from the study and all the computers in the house, including Charlotte's laptop. She'd coldly told the officer that it was entirely unnecessary for him to take a school student's computer, especially when she'd been at boarding school all term, but he'd merely cited the terms of the warrant and tucked the slim silver device under his arm.

When they'd taken all they wanted from Miligili, they'd asked James to accompany them to his office in town. Computers, files and cell phone records now resided at the Billawarre police station, being combed for evidence to add to the initial nine charges. A Geelong detective, called in to help the local police, had asked her if James had a gambling problem. The question rammed home the fact her husband was currently a stranger to her. She'd told him she didn't think James had a gambling problem, but given the events of the last twenty-four hours, she couldn't say with any degree of certainty. Was gambling the reason he'd stolen the money? God, she had no idea. No idea about anything.

James had spent part of last night and all of this morning at the police station before being formally charged with obtaining property by deception, obtaining property by financial advantage, theft, and using and making false documents. In one of the most excruciatingly embarrassing moments of her life, she'd had to stand in a courtroom and answer questions about her ability to post bail of 50,000 dollars.

They'd left the court an hour ago, driving home in separate cars and navigating the media crush outside their beautiful and intricate iron gates. Without a word, James shut himself in the study again so he didn't have to face her. Unable to help herself, she'd turned on the television and watched the news reports. The footage outside the courthouse showed her as a well-dressed woman with a tight face walking two steps ahead of her husband. The images of James—head down, unshaven, with wildly ruffled hair and wearing a now very rumpled bespoke suit—devastated and enraged her in equal measure.

How could he have done this to them? The now unceasing question was slowly sending her mad. Her desire to believe James innocent had been shredded and stomped on by the mounting number of people coming forward to claim he owed them money. She hadn't told the police about the 22,000 dollars he'd stolen from her practice or her discovery this morning that her retirement fund was now echoingly empty. She knew she should tell them but something was holding her back. Loyalty? Love?

She kicked out at one of the helium balloons hovering just above the floor, sending it wafting into the air. It lingered for a moment up where it belonged—proud and pretty—before gravity dragged it back down to its forlorn position close to the parquetry. Why was she holding back? James obviously had no loyalty to her or Charlotte. If he had, he wouldn't have turned their lives upside down and inside out, exposing them to the ridicule and prying eyes of the town, the district and beyond. Her cell phone had beeped all day with messages and rung with calls from people she hadn't heard from in years until she'd turned the damn thing off and stuffed it under a cushion on the sofa. The worst call was from the Royal College of Surgeons wanting documentation that proved she wasn't involved in the alleged crime.

Her face suffused with heat as she remembered the cool voice on the end of the line treating her as if she was both a difficult child and a morally bankrupt adult. The fact she couldn't understand how or why James had broken the law added to her torment. Enough was enough. James had been monosyllabic for too long. He owed her a detailed explanation. She stormed down the hall and tried the door of the study. To her surprise it opened and she strode in.

"Talk to me."

For a moment, the tall-backed Victorian office chair didn't move, then it slowly swiveled. James's handsome but haggard face came into view across the wide mahogany desk. He held a glass of whiskey in one hand and he stretched out his other, waving it casually through the stream of sunshine capturing dancing dust motes and casting rainbows on the carpet.

"Lovely weather we're having, H. Although it's a bit dry. If it keeps up, we'll have to hand feed the calves."

"Damn it, James."

He raised his brows. "What? Not what you wanted to chat about?"

"You know exactly what I want to talk about." She pressed her palms against the desk and leaned in. "How much money have you stolen and how many people have you stolen it from?"

He met her gaze, his face loaded with a combination of distress and disappointment. "As my *wife*, you're supposed to believe in my innocence. You're supposed to gather the family together and stand by me. Haven't seen much evidence of that last night or today."

She wanted to lunge at him, but she didn't know if it was to grab him by the throat or to hug him. From the moment she'd refused his extended hand last night, his behavior had been radically different from the man she loved and thought she knew. Her thoughts swung wildly but she knew she couldn't let seesawing emotions get in the way of reason. Reason and logic were all she had left and clinging to them was the only way to make sense of what he told her. The only way she could get to the truth.

"I'm sorry you're feeling abandoned," she said sarcastically. "Let's leave out the dozen accusations of your clients, shall we? As my accountant and my husband, you're not supposed to steal 300,000 dollars of my money."

He downed the dark amber whiskey and refilled the glass from the bottle on the table. Yesterday it had been full. Today it was almost empty. "I didn't steal the money. I borrowed it."

"Borrowed it?" She heard her rising incredulity. "Borrowing is something that's done with consent on both sides. It infers it will be returned."

"Exactly! I borrowed the money with every intention of returning it. I needed a loan."

Confusion snuck in, contaminating her tenuous grip on logic. "I don't understand. Why didn't you ask me? I would have said yes."

"You always say we're equal partners, H, so I took you at your word."

She struggled with the sentiments his words generated. She'd always believed they were equal partners. She valued that about their marriage. How many times over the years had she glibly told people they were a team? She'd frequently felt superior when women complained about their husband's lack of respect and domestic contributions and she'd taken pleasure in saying, "James values my work as I value his."

But real partners told each other things and kept each other in the picture. The gnawing disquiet of the past weeks thundered back, painfully reminding her he'd stopped telling her things a long time ago. With the advantage of hindsight she now realized why—he'd been too busy hiding things from her. "Do you have a gambling addiction?"

"No."

A flutter of relief stirred her mess of complicated feelings. "Then why did you need the loan?"

"To pay the dividends on the McCluskey development."

The softly spoken words may as well have been bullets peppering her body. She sank into a winged armchair and faced him across the desk. "But surely the sale of the land paid them?"

He shrugged. "Unlike your job, business isn't an exact science."

"Don't bullshit me, James. If no land was sold, no dividends would need to be paid. What have you done with the dividend money?"

He was silent for a moment, staring into his glass. "I used some of it to service the business's bank loans. I invested the rest."

It sounded like a Ponzi-style scheme: taking from Peter to pay Paul. "Why on earth would you invest money without permission?"

"Why do you think?" He slammed down the glass and whiskey sloshed onto the green leather desk top. "To save the business and repay the debt."

She stared at him, her mouth falling open. "Save the business?" she repeated inanely as if it would give her clarity. "How long's it been struggling?"

"It's been bleeding money for two years."

"Two years?" Her leaden brain struggled to absorb the news. "You never said a word. Why didn't you tell me?" Anger took hold like wildfire. "You should have told me."

"Yeah, right." He took another slug of his drink. "Of course I couldn't tell you. That meant I was failing and with you, everything has to be so fucking perfect."

Denial burned hot in her chest. "That's not true."

He snorted. "The hell it is. Look at this house, look at the party last night, look at the hell you put your staff through so they meet your exacting standards. Charlie and I aren't staff, but you expect more from us than we can give."

"Leave Charlotte out of this."

"No." His eyes flashed hard as slate. "I've got a news bulletin for you, H. I'm not you. She's not you."

"She sure as hell isn't you," she said in an uncontrollable screech. "She hasn't stolen then lost other people's money."

"Only because she wasn't forced to."

"Who held a gun at your head?"

His handsome face hardened into deep and bitter lines. "You, my darling. You, your pretentious birth right, your family name, your assumed entitlement and your superior sense of self."

His cruel and unanticipated attack blindsided her, sending pain and bewilderment slamming through her. Not once in all their years together had he ever said anything so brutal. Her throat thickened, tears threatened and for one tempting moment she wanted to curl up in a ball. A shiver raced across her skin before burrowing down deep and invading her bones and her marrow. The cold was so insidious she believed she'd never be warm again.

"Surely," she said, her words coming out slowly and precisely, "you're not blaming me for *your* breaking of the law?"

"Don't get all high and mighty on me now, Harriet. For a decade, all you've wanted is for us to be Billawarre's power couple. Everything you've done, every party you've thrown, every dinner invitation you've issued and accepted has been part of that plan. Me becoming mayor was part of that plan. Well, I've got news for you, sweetheart. If I'd gone bankrupt, becoming mayor would have been impossible."

This conversation was like being in a parallel universe. He looked like her husband, but he didn't sound anything like him. "I suggested you run for mayor because I believed you'd be good for Billawarre. I never forced you to stand. You could have said no."

His hard and derisive laugh bounced off the walls. "Your suggestions are a lot like your expectations: they have to be met. Let's turn the spotlight back on you, shall we? Ask yourself this. What would your reaction have been if I'd gone bankrupt two years ago? Be honest, now."

"I would have been upset for you, I would have—"

"Bullshit!" His fist thumped the desk. "That's utter bullshit and you know it. You'd have been furious that I'd failed. Mortified that people were talking about us. You'd have carried on about your family name being dragged through the mud. I did what was necessary to avoid all of that and protect your precious social standing."

Hot white fury exploded inside her, blasting out the cold. "Don't you dare justify breaking the law by pinning the blame on me. You had choices and you made the selfish one. Nothing can justify you stealing money to try to save yourself from bankruptcy and failure." She lurched to her feet. "Oh, and great job on not dragging us through the mud. You well and truly fucked up that ambition. I might have been able to forgive you using my money and my retirement fund to prop up the business, but I can't forgive you for stealing from people in town.

"Those people trusted you and my good name. A name that's meant a lot in this district for 175 years. You've stolen money from my patients. From our friends. God. You went so low you even stole money from the disabled." The nausea she got every time she thought about what he'd done spun her empty stomach. "You stole from Tasha, you bastard."

"The plan was always to pay it back," he said, his anger suddenly gone, leaving behind only exhaustion. He'd aged ten years overnight and the handsome and successful man in his mid-forties was nowhere to be seen. Deep lines cut in around his now bloodshot eyes and the skin that stretched over his cheeks was florid and puffy. Two days ago, back when her world was steady on its axis, if he'd looked like this she'd have been worried he was coming down with a virus. Today, her sympathy was vanquished. Her trust was in tatters and her heart was so battered it limped painfully in her chest.

"Get out."

"Fine." He rose wearily to his feet. "I need a shower anyway."

"No." She shook her head so fast her brain hurt. "I mean pack a bag and leave this house."

"And go where, exactly?" Eyes that once made her smile bored into her adding to her pain. "Remember my bail conditions? The ones we both signed?"

"I don't care where you go," she said, fast losing any semblance of composure. "You've brought shame and pain down on Charlotte and me. You've brought the press to our doorstep. We can't come and go freely without risking images of us being beamed around the country. Go and sleep in one of those half-constructed houses in the McCluskey estate before the bank seizes them. Go anywhere and take the press with you. You're not welcome here."

He folded his arms across his chest, an immoveable force. "This is my house too, Harriet. My name's on the title."

She wanted to scream, she wanted to throw things, she wanted to hit and scratch him, but she knew none of those things would move James. He had a stubborn streak a mile wide and while so much about him today was unrecognizable, she doubted that particular characteristic had changed. But she needed him gone. Staying in her beloved house with him right now was asking far more of her than she was able to give. Plus, she didn't want Charlotte anywhere near him. She didn't trust him not to spew his vitriol about her to their daughter.

Her mind spun, flitting from thought to thought without gaining purchase. *Oh Dad, what do I do?* She missed her father so much and wished he were here to put his solid arms around her and hold her tightly against his chest. Wished he was giving his practical and no-nonsense advice. Did she have any legal rights to force James off the property? Xara would know but she needed something to get him out of the house right now.

"Fine," she said as an idea formed that would give her some breathing space. "You can stay on the property, but you move into the guest house."

"I could," he said coolly, "but then again, I could stay in the house and you could move into the guesthouse."

"No! I'm not the one who fucked up our lives!"

He shrugged. "We can debate that another time."

She stared hard, trying to read him, trying to locate the source of his anger and resentment. "Why are you doing this?"

He sighed. "I don't want to fight you, Harriet, but if you push, I'll push back. You're my wife and things will be a lot easier if you support me on this."

She snorted. "Support you? How on earth can I do that and keep my professional reputation intact?"

His demeanor changed completely and the light of a plan lit up his face. "Come on, H. You know better than I do that it's all about the spin. I'll plead guilty to taking and losing the money. You tell people I did it because I was trying to keep the McCluskey development afloat and viable for the economic good of the town. That puts everything in a totally different light. It makes people stop, think and consider."

The idea stunned her. "You want me to encourage the town and the district to think of your theft as philanthropic?"

He nodded, his face flushed with the excitement of the idea. "How we deal with this together determines our future. People have come back from worse. I'll use the time before the court case to do a lot of volunteering. We'll get some photos of you, Charlie and me doing community activities. Remember D'Angelo? He survived. He's back working in town."

Astonishment and disgust made her slack-jawed. "Yes, but you didn't take from the rich and give to the poor. You used the money to try to save yourself. There's no way in hell you're using our daughter to improve your public image."

"Harriet, you love me."

It wasn't a question. His voice was the honey smooth of old; the seductive tone he'd always used as a prelude to sex. The one he whispered into her ear, warm, enticing and full of promise. The one that made her melt into him every single time. She felt the familiar visceral tug and her longing for him spiraled up from deep down inside her the way it always did whenever he was close. She wavered.

"Harry, if we're partners like we've always been, we can turn this around.' The passion in his eyes held her in its grip. 'We can work together and minimize the fallout and maximize the effect. We can pull it off. We always do. This plan will work. Trust me, babe."

Oh. My. God.

The spell shattered and she was itching like crazy, her skin crawling with his audacity. "Babe" was a word he only used when he was trying to sweet-talk her into something. He'd used it for years and she didn't think he was aware that he did it. It had become a flag for her, a sign that whatever the topic, it was something he wanted badly or something he needed her help with or approval for. Like his purchase of the classic Porsche, the month riding a motorbike alone around Chile, and using her family connections to entice new clients.

Only now he was asking her to lie to her family. Lie to her friends and to the district. Possibly lie in court. He was manipulating her unconditional love for him, expecting her to set aside truth and cross the moral boundaries that framed her life. He was finessing their marriage and using their commitment to each other—something she'd valued as much as life itself—as leverage to drag her down to his level.

The realization slammed into her like a punch to the solar plexus, winding her and leaving her gasping. This was ten times worse than discovering he'd stolen the money. She suddenly saw him in a totally new light. Traits she'd once admired and considered astute and perceptive, she now saw as hard-nosed self-interest with a take-no-prisoners approach. Did he have any remorse for what he'd done? Any sympathy for the people whose lives he'd reduced by stripping them of their money? Was his plan to plead guilty utterly self-serving, driven purely by the fact that it would gain him some credibility? Would he really sacrifice their daughter on the pyre of his own making?

Her breath quickened and the walls of the office closed in on her, pushing down and stealing her air. She tried to suck in a deep breath, but her chest burned and raged against it as questions raced around and around in her head. Amid the tumultuous noise, a faint but stern warning penetrated the chaos.

This is not a good time to have a panic attack. Breathe and leave. Protect Charlotte.

She focused on Charlotte, gulping in air against the pain. One breath in. One breath out. Another in. Blow it out. Slowly, the room came back into focus and when she finally managed to speak, she hardly recognized herself.

"I'm going to stay with my mother."

CHAPTER ELEVEN

At the end of what Harriet had dubbed "shit-storm Sunday" she was in Glenora's library with Charlotte having the most difficult conversation she'd ever had with her daughter. The man they loved and trusted had betrayed them in the worst way and it made the sex and drugs talks seem like a walk in the park.

Sticking to the facts was the only way to keep her emotions in check. "The police have charged James with stealing from the county, the rural relief fund and from four people who'd trusted him to invest their money. But the detective told me these charges are just the tip of the iceberg."

"What does that mean?" Charlotte asked.

"It means they're certain your father's stolen money from a lot more people and they're still investigating. It means it's not over and more charges will be laid in the coming weeks and months, and your father will be back in court." The calm restraint she'd imposed upon herself cracked. "Your father's a criminal! A thief! I don't want you to see him."

Charlotte's arms crossed with teenage truculence. "Isn't that my decision?"

"Not now, Charlotte, please." Harriet rubbed her throbbing temples. "It's been a shitty day. All I'm trying to do is protect you."

"Mom, I'm almost eighteen." There was an edge of desperation to her voice. "You keep telling me that I'm almost an adult and you expect me to behave like one. If you use that logic, I don't need protecting. Besides, I've watched the news and read Twitter."

"Fine." Harriet hurt that her best intentions were being summarily dismissed. "I'll be perfectly blunt then. Don't let him use you."

Frown lines pulled at Charlotte's smooth brow. "What do you mean?"

"He wants us to help him improve his image. An image, I might add, he's tarnished all on his own without any help from either of us. Whatever you do, don't let him sweet talk you into having your photo taken or talk to the press."

"Dad wouldn't do that." Charlotte vibrated with indignation.

"Yes, well, I never thought he'd steal more than a million dollars either, but there you go. I was wrong."

Charlotte's mouth settled into a mulish line. "I have the right to see my father if I choose to."

Harriet thought about all the hurtful things the stranger who was her husband, had hurled at her in the study. She knew he wouldn't hesitate to use Charlotte if he thought it would advance his cause. She wanted to wrap her innocent daughter up in cotton wool and shield her from hurt, disillusionment and pain. But given how erratically Charlotte had been behaving before James destroyed their lives, she couldn't risk alienating her. Couldn't risk James poisoning Charlotte against her.

"I don't want to see him, but I suppose I can't stop you. All I ask is that if you do see him, do it at Glenora when Mardi or Georgie are home. I don't want you going to Miligili."

"But that's home. All my stuff's there," Charlotte wailed. "I need my stuff to feel like me."

So do I. Harriet had only been at Glenora a few hours and already she missed her "stuff." She'd put her heart and soul into restoring Miligili to its former glory along with putting her individual stamp on it. "Talking about stuff, the police have your computer."

"What?" Charlotte shot to her feet, her face ashen. "But it's mine. It's private. I don't want strangers reading my—" She sat down abruptly, her eyes round and imploring. "You have to get it back."

"I've spoken to an attorney. We'll get it back, but it might take a while."

"You don't understand." Agitation whipped off Charlotte like choppy waves on windblown sea. "I need it. It's got all my schoolwork on it. It's got everything I need to study. You know how much work I have to catch up on."

Harriet was both surprised and reassured by Charlotte's reaction. Despite the chaos going on around her, she was finally showing some concern about her schoolwork. Unlike everything else that had happened in the last twenty-four hours, this situation was easily solved. "Don't stress. Isn't all the vacation prep on the school website? We'll email your teachers and your friends to catch what isn't. I promise you, it will work out."

Charlotte's thumbnail crept to her mouth. "What will the police be looking for on my computer?"

"I don't really know. Emails probably."

"Do they tell the press what they find?"

"I really don't know. We can ask Xara."

"I hate this." Charlotte's voice broke and her eyes brimmed with tears. "I really hate this."

"Me too." Harriet leaned over and hugged her. Unexpectedly, Charlotte dropped her head against her shoulder and snuggled in just as she'd done when she was a little girl. In a sea of despair, Harriet treasured this moment and wished she had the power to turn back time.

"I've written up IV antibiotics for Mrs. Grant starting with a bolus dose," Harriet told the unit manager. "Call Blake if her temp goes over thirty-nine."

"Will do, Harriet." As the nurse walked over to the drug cabinet, keys jangling, she called over her shoulder, "Have a good afternoon."

It was Monday and Harriet hurried toward the elevators, stabbing the button twice as if that would summon them faster. It didn't and she took the stairs. Her afternoon session at the practice started at two and although running late was all part of the job, she preferred to start on time if she could. Her practice was only a short walk away and it made crossing back and forth between the hospital and the clinic easy.

This morning had been predictably busy and Harriet was thankful for that small mercy. It had allowed her to block out the weekend and all her associated thoughts. This was absolutely necessary because if she allowed her thoughts to riot, they threatened to immobilize her. Thank God it was Monday—a morning session of surgery and surgery meant routine, order and control. She'd ignored the sideways glances and the conversations that had fallen silent, after all, as an attending, she was used to ignoring the edge of whispered conversations. The only difference today was that she'd had to do it a bit more often.

She pushed open the fire door and stepped onto the street, calling Charlotte to check she was okay. Charlotte didn't pick up. She left a message and as she lowered the phone from her ear she heard someone calling her name. She swung around to see a man hurrying across the street toward her—a patient. His badly infected gall bladder had caused her some angst during a tricky cholecystectomy last year, but his name escaped her. Used to people approaching her in the street, she gave him a practiced smile.

He didn't smile back. "I see you've gotten yourself some Euro trash."

His belligerence reached out and slapped her. "I beg your pardon?"

"You heard me. That bloody expensive German car you're driving." The veins in his neck stood out. "You're livin' the highlife by ripping off decent people."

Her stomach lurched and pins and needles raced across her skin. *Stay calm.* "I paid for that car with money I earned from my medical practice."

"Yeah, well I don't believe ya. My sister trusted that bastard husband of yours and now she's got squat."

Harriet wanted to attack. Wanted to use her best icy voice to freeze his unfair fire but she understood his anger despite its misdirection. "I'm very sorry, Mr.—um ...?"

"Perkins," he spat, "and sorry don't cut it. You know she's diabetic. You know she's got heart problems and now she's probably gonna lose the house."

Silver spots flashed in front of Harriet's eyes and she swallowed against a dry mouth. "I realize it's no consolation, Mr. Perkins, but I had no idea about my husband's business practices. I'm as shocked as everyone else. Has she reported the theft to the police?"

"Of course she bloody has but it won't get her life savings back, will it?" His eyes narrowed and his voice dropped to a threatening timbre. "You better put that fuckin' mansion of yours up for sale, lady, because you owe this town a shitload of money."

He moved abruptly, catching her shoulder on his way past as he stormed away from her. Harriet stood in the street shaking, her heart pounding and the sandwich she'd eaten for lunch a solid lump in the back of her throat. She forced her trembling legs to cover the short distance to the clinic before stumbling inside. The cool air and soothing pastel colors greeted her, enveloping her with the calmness of a sanctuary.

Thankfully, the waiting room was quiet with only one elderly man sitting in one of the eight chairs. She gave him and her receptionist, Nicki, a nod and said overly brightly, "Won't be long!" before disappearing into her office and closing the door behind her.

With shaking hands she poured iced water from a jug, gulping it down then concentrated breathing away the angry and vindictive sound of Perkins's voice. When she'd seen him crossing the street, it had never occurred to her that his intentions were to publicly accuse and berate her. His attack brought the whole sordid story of James's treachery flooding back.

Focus on the patients. She checked her hair and makeup in the small compact mirror she kept in her handbag. A pale face with startled violet-blue eyes stared back at her. Patients expected their doctor to look less sick than they did so she reapplied her blush and lipstick, powdered down and spritzed on some perfume. Looking and feeling more like herself, she walked over to her desk and checked the afternoon appointment list. Today, it looked a little different and she picked it up for closer inspection.

For years it was rare to see any empty spaces on the sheet. Since her father's death, vacancies had become almost nonexistent and she was now the only general surgeon within a hundred miles. If anyone canceled an appointment, it was quickly filled from the long elective surgery waiting list. On today's sheet, red lines crossed out four names and there were two empty spaces. She thought about the chatter that had rolled around her in the OR this morning. There'd been the discussion about the shock elimination of a favorite on *The Bachelor*, the high hopes everyone held for the Billawarre Panthers in the upcoming football season and the fact that a nasty virus was causing chaos with staffing levels all over the hospital.

She rubbed the bridge of her nose. When patients made their first appointment, Nicki always explained the cancellation policy over the phone before mailing a physical copy. As there was a fee for last-minute cancellations, they didn't happen often. Her fingers traced the names under the red lines and she picked up the phone.

"Four cancellations, Nicki? Have they all come down with the virus?"

"Um," Nicki said as she always did before she spoke. "They didn't say they were sick."

"It's very late notice. They must have given you a reason."

"Um, no."

No? She was used to patients arriving and wanting to tell her why they'd rescheduled despite the fact that she had little interest in the reason. "This is Billawarre. We usually get chapter and verse." She tried a light laugh but it sounded strained. "They must have told you something."

There was silence on the line and a moment later Nicki walked into the office, closing the door behind her. "Um ... I didn't want to say anything where people could hear," she said, wringing her hands nervously. Her head dropped as if she was scared to look at Harriet. "I'm really sorry, Ms. Chirnwell. They said they wanted to see another surgeon."

The same pins and needles Harriet had experienced with Perkins returned, only this time with the excruciating pain of a blunt and barbed needle. "Did you explain that seeing another surgeon involves them travelling to either Geelong or Ballarat?"

"Um, yes, but they didn't want to make another appointment." She lifted her head and looked at Harriet with pleading eyes. "I told them that no matter what your husband's done, you're a good surgeon."

Oh God. She pressed a fist into her diaphragm, pushing against the burning pain that radiated into every corner of her body. Her receptionist had reassured her patients she was a good surgeon not a good *person.* "What's the rest of the week looking like?"

"Um, well, when I got in this morning the voice mail had six cancellations on it."

"And?"

"Um, the phone's been ringing all morning."

Her hand wrapped around the edge of her desk to steady her sagging knees. "I need the numbers, Nicki."

"Um, please don't yell."

"Just. Tell. Me."

"Um, I think it's close to eighteen who've canceled."

"New patients?"

Nicki shook her head. "Not all. You've only got two people left on Wednesday's operating list, but you know," she threw Harriet a look that didn't reach reassuring, "Easter's a busy time for people."

This morning when she'd gotten to the hospital, she'd been relieved and reassured that despite everything that had happened, her job hadn't been affected. Perkins's vitriol and the en masse exodus of patients now cast that conclusion in a harsh and delusional light. The fact that the town hated her so much that people were prepared to cancel long awaited elective surgery slayed her.

James, you bastard! You total fucking asshole!

Her breathing threatened to match the speed of a very fast train and she worked hard to keep it slow and steady against the violent pull to pant and gasp. "I think we both know Easter's not the issue.'

Nicki bit her lip. "Um, did you have any idea that Mr. Minchin was using other people's money?"

Fury, hot and strong, blew through Harriet like a raging northerly. She was tempted to fire Nicki on the spot for her total lack of faith but then the icy winds of despair followed. Her receptionist had only voiced the question everyone in town was asking.

"I didn't know anything about it," she said numbly.

But she knew the truth was not enough to save her from a town seeking revenge.

CHAPTER TWELVE

GEORGIE HAD ALL BUT GIVEN UP ON BEING ABLE TO SNEAK AWAY from the farm and see Ben when Xara hung up the phone looking stunned. "Mom says Harriet's arrived at Glenora with three suitcases. She's moved into her old room and Charlie's sleeping in mine."

"Seriously?"

It was a well-known, if unspoken, truth that Edwina and Harriet had a familial-duty relationship rather than a close and affectionate one. Come to think of it, none of them ever turned to their mother in a crisis. When Eliza had died, Georgie had gotten the distinct feeling that Edwina had needed and wanted her support to get through the funeral.

She'd tried telling herself that her perceptions were off-kilter. That a mother with a grieving daughter was hardly going to lean on her for comfort, but despite the logic she hadn't been able to shift the feeling. It lingered still, a nub of resentment that heated and cooled at different times but never totally vanished. Of course Georgie hadn't been able to give any solace to Edwina—it had been all she could do to get through the day and the weeks that followed.

Harriet's support for her had been as expected—brisk and no

nonsense. If the problem wasn't something that could be surgically removed, gotten rid of and forgotten then Harriet struggled to provide empathy. Their father had been exactly the same. Xara had been the one with the closest understanding of what Georgie was going through and she'd turned to her in the early days, leaning heavily. She'd also painted, knitted, sewed, scrapbooked, quilted, mucked about with clay and even toyed with glass art. Anything to keep herself occupied and her hands busy and full so they didn't ache with the same emptiness that filled her heart.

"Harriet at Mom's ... I didn't see that coming." Xara opened a bottle of sauv blanc and poured two glasses. "I mean, maybe if Dad was still alive, but ..." She handed Georgie a glass, took a sip from her own and grimaced. "If anyone should be leaving Miligili, it's James."

"It's probably just until the media storm dies down. Surely their interest in this will only last one more twenty-four-hour cycle."

"If that were the situation, Harry would have packed an overnight bag—not three suitcases."

"Maybe she didn't want Charlie to be alone."

Xara raised her brows—Charlotte was often in the care of Edwina, Georgie or herself.

"Okay." Georgie dragged her finger through the condensation around the base of her wine glass. "Perhaps Harry didn't want to be alone. I mean, she must be devastated. If you believe the news, it's not looking good."

"What's not looking good?" Steve ambled into the room after putting Tasha to bed.

Georgie both admired and envied Xara and Steve's marriage. Although Harriet always talked about how she and James were a team, even before James's fall from grace, Georgie had always seen more evidence of true teamwork between Xara and Steve. Right from the start, Steve had taken on the role of putting Tasha to bed, giving Xara a break. It was now such an entrenched tradition that if he was away and unable to do bath and story time, Tasha stacked on a tantrum.

"The ever-increasing number of people saying James owes them money," Xara said, holding up her full wine glass to Steve in a gesture of inquiry.

He shook his head and cracked open a can of beer. "I've been fielding phone calls all day. I tell you, it wouldn't take much for this to turn into a lynch mob."

"Harriet's gone to Mom's."

"Shit. I didn't see that coming."

"No. It means she believes James is guilty, otherwise I can't imagine she'd have left the house."

"Or him," Steve had said tersely. The fact that he didn't refer to James by name spoke volumes.

Georgie was still trying to wrap her head around the fact Harriet, Edwina and Charlotte were under the same roof when her thoughts slid sideways to her mother's friend, Doug. Although she was certain Harriet wouldn't want her support, her mother might just need it, especially with Harriet in the house. Perhaps she should move into Glenora too.

You'd have more freedom to come and go at Glenora.

Freedom to secretly see Ben.

"Do you think I should—"

"Do you think you could—"

They laughed at having the same thought at the same time. Xara continued, "Go to Glenora and keep an eye on things."

Georgie arrived on her mother's doorstep the following morning with her travel bag slung on her shoulder. "Sharing a room with Tashie is like sleeping with a steam train. Got room for one more, Mom?"

Edwina's eyes widened with surprise along with something that may have been relief, resignation or a combination of the two. She quickly covered it with a smile. "Of course, darling. Come in."

Two days in and it seemed to Georgie the four of them were all living very different lives under Glenora's roof and all of them were keeping their own counsel. She'd got up early on Tuesday, after

Harriet had left on her run but before her mother and Charlotte had surfaced. She used the quiet time to talk to Ben. The rest of the day was spent being available if, when, and where she was needed. Edwina did all her usual things around the house and garden, but there was no denying her distracted air. More than once, Georgie overheard her talking on her cell in the pergola. She assumed it was to Doug, otherwise why not chat inside the house?

Harriet lurched between needing company and totally rejecting it. She came home from work drawn, white and unusually quiet. The only time she showed any signs of her normal self was when they watched a reality television show. No one needed the non-stop TV commentary of *The People's Couch* when they had Harriet. Charlotte slept in each day, arriving in the kitchen around eleven looking like she still needed more sleep. Georgie tried to engage her, but it was hard work.

Yesterday, she'd taken Charlotte out to the farm and together they'd helped the twins and Tasha decorate Easter eggs. Amid the mess of bowls of food coloring, wax, wet newspaper and drying eggs, Charlotte had lost her pensive look. When the boys had declared they preferred eating chocolate eggs to painting real ones, she'd chased them around the home pasture, shrieking and laughing like she always did when she was on vacation. Georgie had watched the chase and the subsequent tickle fest and let out a long breath. She knew it didn't change the fact that Charlotte's life was in upheaval but sometimes it was good to be able to forget even if it was only for an hour or two.

And that's what today's bike ride was all about for Georgie.

She lay on a rug by the river with shadows and sunshine dancing around her as she stared through the old wooden trestle railway bridge up to an indigo sky. Wispy white clouds scudded past, reminding her of dinghies sailing on a summer sea. A bit closer, the weatherworn beams of the bridge crisscrossed above her and Ben, the gray wood punctuated by the enormous rust-brown bolts and plates that were a testament to the engineering of a past era. She had to pinch herself that she was finally here and alone with Ben.

Not that Ben was about forgetting. She hoped and wished that everything to do with him was all about moving forward.

Full of the chicken, chive, mustard and mayonnaise sandwiches she'd made for their picnic lunch, she raised her arm toward the bridge. "Isn't it spectacular?"

"Very." Ben propped himself up on an elbow and smiled down at her while his fingertips swiped a few stray strands of hair off her cheeks. "Beautiful, in fact."

A shot of pleasure whipped her from head to toe. "You planning on seducing me with some of that Italian charm that runs in your veins?"

"Is it working?"

She laughed, loving the way his warm caramel eyes memorized her. "I guess you'll have to keep going to find out."

A mischievous light flared in his eyes. "I've already told you how fabulous your legs look in these cycling shorts." He ran the pad of his forefinger slowly along the outside of her thigh until it rested on her hipbone. It was the lightest of touches and yet it exerted pressure a thousand times more intense. The best type of shiver wound through her.

"That's cheating, although repeat compliments aren't totally out of the question."

"Good, because you're gorgeous and every part of you is distracting me and totally frying my brain." He leaned down, his hair tickling her skin as he nuzzled her neck. Starting in the hollow at the base of her throat, he pressed a series of soft and gentle kisses until he reached her earlobe.

Everything inside her slackened on a sigh of bliss. Lying in the sunshine, she momentarily let go of everything that bound her to her life. Being worshipped by a tide of kisses was heaven and she could stay here forever and never move. Ben's tongue flicked her earlobe then traced the curve of her ear. An electric current of need rocked her and she rolled into him, suddenly frantic to touch him. Feel him.

He pressed his lips against hers, gliding the tip of his tongue along the seams of her lips, requesting entry. She opened her mouth and welcomed him. He tasted of chicken, sunshine, sweat and something she was learning to recognize as quintessentially Ben. His tongue played her mouth like a virtuoso—as if he remembered exactly what she enjoyed best. Ribbons of sensations streamed along her veins, spinning and twisting until they surged and sparked need, joy and— despite her self-protective mantra that *sex was just sex*—hope.

Without any conscious input, her body responded in an age-old way. Her hips rose, her legs entwined around his, pulling him into her, and her hands buried themselves in his thick curly hair. She rolled again until she lay over him, her mouth melding with his, taking what he offered and giving in return.

Ben's hands reached under her top, deliciously kneading her spine one vertebrae at a time until they reached her bra clasp. His fingers fumbled twice and then the elastic slackened. Her breasts tumbled against his chest, tingling and aching for his touch. This time he rolled, tucking her under him.

"God, you're wonderful." His mouth sought the prize his hands had released and his tongue worked its magic, bringing her body and mind thrumming to life. She was alive in a way she didn't remember forgetting.

The sound of children's piping voices drifted toward them on the autumnal air. Ben abruptly rolled away, his chest heaving. The breeze cooled her hot and sweating skin and then Ben was sitting up and pulling down her top.

"Sorry. That got a bit out of control."

She sat up too, disappointment dueling with common-sense. "Don't be sorry."

He gave a wry smile. "Hey, I'm only sorry we're not somewhere more private. I suppose us getting a room at the motel is out of the question?"

She wrinkled her nose. "I went to school with Tanya and Jeff."

"Does that matter?"

"Last week, no. This week, there's enough Chirnwell gossip circulating in town without me adding to the whirlpool."

He nodded glumly and pulled her in close. "I guess we're stuck pretending we're teens and sticking to hand holding, earnest talking and chaste kisses."

"Earnest talking and chaste kisses?" She gave him a gentle nudge. "What sort of teen were you?"

"Slow." He grinned. "I spent hours listening to a variety of teenage girls telling me how much they hated some guy. All of them eventually ended up having sex with said guy."

"You were a boy best friend?" she asked, surprised. "I would have pegged you as a cool jock."

"Obviously that's me now." He flashed her that beguiling half boy-half man smile she loved so much. "I was a late bloomer. I lost my virginity on my twentieth birthday when I was seduced by an older and more experienced woman."

"That all sounds very Mrs. Robinson."

"Thankfully, not even close. She was twenty-one and I met her at my impromptu birthday party—"

"Let me guess. Three blokes sharing a house so you got some beers and some pizza and called it a party."

"Were you there?" He shot her a wink and her stomach swooped and fizzed. "I didn't know Jade, but she arrived at the party with a group of friends. As the night wore on there was the inevitable drunken teasing from my mates about how I hadn't been laid. Somehow, I found myself in my bedroom with Jade and she offered to rectify the situation."

"And being a gentleman, you couldn't refuse her."

He laughed. "Pretty much. It was both momentous and forgettable all at the same time. I never saw her again and I was faced with having to have a barrage of STD tests. Lesson learned." He reached into a pannier and pulled out a Thermos. "What about you?"

"Similar drunken situation only it involved a black-tie ball, an expensive university college single bed and a condom."

"Wise woman."

"I was eighteen and he was twenty-one. It happened two more times. The sex I mean, not the ball. Then he met a girl with a better pedigree than me and that was that." She gave him an arch look. "We've just traded first sexual encounter stories. Does this mean we're officially dating?"

"Yes, please."

CHAPTER THIRTEEN

EDWINA WATCHED THE TWINS CHARGING AROUND GLENORA'S garden. She tried not to flinch as their feet strayed from the path and hovered far too close to the last crop of this season's strawberries.

"You're cold," she called out in a rescue mission of diversion. "Ice cold."

"Told you." Hugh grabbed Ollie's arm and they spun around, plunging back onto the path. "What about now?"

"Warmer."

Charlotte rounded the corner, pushing Tasha in her wheelchair. "Race you to the palm tree," she yelled, dashing past the twins. Tasha squealed in delight.

"Thanks for setting up the hunt, Mom." Xara she sat in the shade of the centenary oak, sipping gin and tonics with her sisters.

"You won't be thanking me when they're high on chocolate tonight," Edwina said wryly.

"You always made us wait until Easter Sunday for the egg hunt," Harriet commented, an edge of criticism in her voice.

"I thought Charlie needed the distraction today." *I think we all need the distraction.*

"She needs to knuckle down and study if she wants to get into pre-med," Harriet muttered and refilled her glass from the pitcher.

Edwina chose not to reply. Apart from going to the hospital for a ward round at seven this morning and spending an hour sequestered in Glenora's library on the phone with a Melbourne attorney, Harriet had spent Maundy Thursday at a loss. It hadn't gone well.

Just like Richard, Harriet floundered without structure and in her attempt to create a system to make herself feel better, she'd tried to organize everyone else. So far today she'd tied Charlotte to the desk while she devised a detailed study program for her, and she'd lectured Edwina on the state of her messy pantry.

Edwina had taken the path of least resistance knowing Harriet needed the distraction, and she'd left her to it. Stacking Tupperware and sorting spices was much easier for Harriet to think about than the fact that her husband had lied to her and the district, torpedoed their marriage, put her beloved house in peril and upended her social standing.

Edwina knew all about the short-term benefits a frenzy of cleaning and reorganization offered, but she also knew they didn't last. Once everything was cleaned, stacked, restocked and alphabetized and there was nothing else left to do, all the thoughts and feelings the work had held at bay rushed back in like a king tide: longer, stronger, higher and with an undertow that sucked you under, leaving you gasping. When the inevitable tide finally hit Harriet, Edwina knew her daughter would need a lifeguard.

After decades of entrenched emotional aloofness stretching between them—thanks to guilt on her side and resistance on Harriet's—this time Edwina planned to be that lifeguard. Committing to it, however, didn't lessen the dismay she felt at the prospect of Harriet being at Glenora full time across the four-day Easter break. Not that Edwina wished an emergency or an accident on anyone, but for all their sakes, if Harriet was called in to the hospital and was required to be in the OR for a few hours, it would give the rest of them some much-needed breathing space. Edwina had spent the day biting her tongue so when Xara had arrived with the children, it had seemed the ideal time to break out the Easter eggs for the kids and the G&T for the adults.

"Are we still doing the full-on family Easter Sunday lunch this year?" Georgie asked, changing the subject.

"Steve wouldn't miss it. He's bringing the lamb," Xara said.

"James will *not* be attending," Harriet said icily. "James can rot in hell."

"You won't get an argument from me." Xara raised her glass to Harriet's.

Her sister clinked it and drained her glass. Edwina refilled it, before pouring herself one. She sat in a teak armchair and squared her shoulders. This was the opportunity she'd been waiting for and she wasn't going to let it slip past.

"We'll still be ten for lunch. I've invited Doug."

Three sets of violet-blue eyes turned to her. They held the full spectrum of emotions and she detected delight, intrigue and anger. "And he's accepted my invitation."

"God, Mom. Really? On top of everything else? Can't it wait? Why do we have to do this now?" Harriet protested.

"Because he's *my* friend and it's time you all met him properly." Edwina thought about all the times in her life she'd allowed herself to be talked out of things that were important to her and held firm. "I know you're all upset I ambushed you at my party so this is the perfect opportunity for you to sit down and get to know him."

"I think it's a great idea," Georgie said, ever the peacemaker. "He seemed nice, based on the brief conversation I had with him about party decorations."

"Thank you, darling." Edwina appreciated that she had at least one ally.

Xara stirred the slice of orange in her glass. "He's a brave man if he's prepared to meet us all at once. We better sit him next to Steve for solidarity."

"But if Doug's coming, it's hardly a *family* Easter," Harriet said tartly. "Is it?"

"Harry, we know you feel like crap, but without James, it was never going to be a normal family Easter," Xara said. "At least meeting Doug gives us all a new focus."

Harriet's eyes lit up. "You're right. And I do have a lot of questions to ask him."

"Be nice," Georgie warned.

"When have you ever known me not to be polite?"

But Edwina, who'd been raised to put good manners ahead of everything, knew polite words masked nothing: they could be wielded as ruthlessly and cause as much hurt and damage as the unambiguous crassness of swearing. She couldn't stop hurtful words being spoken but this time, with age and experience on their side, she was determined she and Doug would survive them.

The full moon spilled into the library at Glenora. With it came the clicking and croaking sounds of contented frogs nestled in the ponds and the dark, damp hollows of the garden. The house was quiet in a way only a house built of stone could be when most everyone in it slept. As Harriet sat at her father's antique walnut desk, sipping wine, she appreciated the silence. Since the police still had her laptop, she was using her mother's desktop, preferring the large screen to her smartphone. With four women in the house sharing one computer, they almost needed a booking system.

On her first night at Glenora, when she'd come into the library and sat at the desk surrounded by the musky scent of leather and the dusty bouquet of old books, she'd felt as if her father was back in the room with her discussing the latest surgical techniques. The library was a comforting haven and visiting it now an evening ritual. Each night she retreated to its bookcase-lined walls just like her father had done, only she sipped wine instead of top-shelf whiskey.

She refilled her glass, took a solid sip and steeled herself to check her mail. For the past week, she'd been bombarded with emails with subject lines ranging from *OMG Harriet!* to *Die Evil Scum Die*. Most of the vitriol was from self-appointed defenders of the people James had defrauded. The bulk of the sympathy notes were faux and voyeuristic, sent from people who wanted the full story so they could rejoice in the fact their husband hadn't done something illegal and brought them down with him.

For her own peace of mind and to prevent herself from being sucked into the quagmire of rancor, she'd disabled receiving emails on her cell phone. She'd also taken the step of creating a new email account reserved for her attorney and Debbie, her practice manager, so important documents didn't get lost in the maelstrom of splenetic mail.

Yesterday, after she'd refused to take James's calls, he'd vented in a vicious email. He hadn't appreciated the letter from her attorney proposing new financial arrangements between them. Nor had he responded well to the fact she'd emptied their joint bank account before he'd got to it first. She didn't care. In fact, she took perverse pleasure in having done to him what he'd done to her and so many others.

She moved the mouse and the computer screen flickered to life with a click and a whirr, waking from inky hibernation. Whoever used it last hadn't closed down the browser so she immediately directed the cursor to the URL box. She was about to type in her webmail address when she noticed the distinctive blue and white banner of Facebook.

She recognized some of Charlotte's school friends in happy fun vacation photos. Curious, she scrolled down to see more but as she read a post, her eyes drifted right. The three advertisements on the side of the screen reached out and grabbed her. Leaning in closer, she blinked. The first was a picture of two pregnancy test sticks, one showing a plus sign, the other a minus sign. The middle promotion was a picture of a glowing pregnant woman wearing a bright red poncho and the words "Chic Maternity Fashion" written underneath. The final advertisement was for a family planning clinic.

A low moan escaped across suddenly dry lips. She knew these advertisements were no random thing. She understood companies used cookies and had the ability to store information about internet searches and target advertisements accordingly. She could have shrugged them away if they'd appeared on a search engine. She could have considered that perhaps Georgie had been looking at baby stuff as a way of grieving. But when she matched these very specific advertisements with Charlotte's Facebook page, her fatigue, thinness, emotional lability and recent erratic behavior, she couldn't ignore the very strong possibility her daughter was pregnant.

No! The word screamed so loud in her head, she flinched. *God damn it, Charlotte.* She pushed back from the desk as rage enveloped her. Not caring what time it was or that her stomping footsteps were booming through the silent house, she stormed into Charlotte's room and flicked on the light.

"Wake up!"

One of Charlotte's hands flew to her squinting eyes while the other pulled the sheet over her head. "Turn it off!" Her muffled indignation rose from under the covers. "I'm asleep."

"Sit up." Harriet pulled at the sheet. "I need to talk to you."

Charlotte tugged in return and the sheet stretched taut between them. "In the morning."

"No. We're talking now."

There was silence and then a grumbled, "This better be good," before Charlotte begrudgingly wriggled up against the pillows. She stonily crossed her arms over her breasts. "What?"

Harriet crossed her own arms to match Charlotte's hostile pose but mostly she did it to keep herself shaking. She forced out the words she didn't want to speak. "Are you pregnant?"

Charlotte's eyes shot wide, her inky pupils almost obliterating the distinctive blue of her irises. "Wha—what sort of question is that?"

But the stunned shock that preceded Charlotte's chagrin gave

Harriet her answer. Her roiling stomach stilled; the contents now a lead weight pressing low and hard in her belly. A raw and biting chill crawled through her veins until it encased her heart.

"You stupid, stupid, girl."

Charlotte blinked rapidly. "I only had real sex once."

"And that's all it takes!" Harriet threw out her hands, wanting to hit something, wanting to feel the shattering pain of her fist against plaster and welcome the jolt radiating up her arm. It would be easier to bear than this gut-wrenching twist of devastation. "For God's sake, Charlotte. Didn't you heed a single thing I ever told you about contraception?"

"Yes." Her daughter's voice sounded small. "And we used a condom."

"But it didn't work, did it." Harriet's voice rose. "Because you're almost eighteen and pregnant. You're in your final year of high school with your life stretching out in front of you and you're pregnant. You're going to med school next year but you're pregnant." The words fell hard, fast and brutal. "You're my daughter and you're bloody well pregnant! How could you do this to me?"

Tears spilled, streaking down Charlotte's cheeks, making her look younger than her years and desperately forlorn. "I d—didn't m—mean —" She gave an almighty, shuddering sniff. "I didn't mean for it to happen."

Harriet knew she should feel sympathy, but she was numb with the enormity of the news. God help her, she was still dazed and spinning from the magnitude of James's deceit and the week's events. All of it had drained her ability to provide comfort to a level below empty. A week ago she couldn't have conceived James would betray her and put her in financial jeopardy, that her family name would be mud and that she'd be a social pariah. Now Charlotte was pregnant? What had she done to deserve all of this? What other axe was yet to fall and strike her down?

"Jesus, Charlotte! You may not have meant for this to happen but it doesn't change the fact that it has. Who's the father?"

"You don't know him."

"Who. Is. The. Father?"

"A Melbourne Grammar boy. I met him last year at the rowing ball." Charlotte winced as a combination of guilt, embarrassment and hurt slid across her face. "We're not really together. We just like ..." her gaze slid away, "... hook up at parties."

Harriet plowed her hands through her hair savagely, needing to feel the sting of the strands tugging hard against her scalp. If the district found out Charlotte was pregnant the weight of that disgrace would sink any remnants of the now tattered Chirnwell reputation.

Think! She went into damage control. "Who knows about ..." The word "baby" embedded itself in her throat, refusing to be voiced. "Who knows about this?"

Charlotte wound the covers tightly around her hands. "I tried to tell Auntie G when I went to Melbourne but I couldn't. I was too scared to tell you over the phone. I thought I'd tell you after Mardi's party but then Dad—"

"What about Mardi?" Harriet blurted, horrified Edwina might already know.

Somehow the idea her mother knew about the pregnancy was infinitely worse than anyone else in the family being privy to it. Edwina had always lived in a sanitized version of the world—first growing up on Murrumbeet protected and sheltered by the wealth and position of her family, and then the safety of her marriage to Harriet's father. Not only wouldn't Edwina cope with this ruinous news, she'd be absolutely horrified and aghast.

"Tell me you haven't told your grandmother."

Charlotte shook her head. "I haven't told anyone."

"Thank God for small mercies." She paced, needing to move to think. "How pregnant are you?"

"I ... um ... the test said eight weeks."

"Right. We can't do anything about it until after Easter. I'll call in a few favors and we'll go to Melbourne on Tuesday to sort things out."

Charlotte's hands stilled on the tangled sheet. "What do you mean?"

Staggered by the question, Harriet stared at her bright and intelligent daughter. "Isn't it obvious? You need a termination."

"No!" Charlotte leaped from the bed, her cheeks bright pink. "I'm not doing that."

"Oh, yes you are."

Charlotte squared her shoulders. "No. I. Am. Not."

"God, help me, you're seventeen and clueless about responsibility. You got drunk, had sex and got pregnant. You leave your wet towels on the bathroom floor as if a genie will magically fly in and pick them up, you spend all your allowance on designer clothes and you don't know how to boil an egg. You're not even mature enough to have prevented this nightmare." She sucked in a breath. "You're underage and you will do as I say!"

"Harriet!" Edwina's voice behind her sounded shocked and yet sternly parental at the same time. "What on earth's going on? I can hear you screeching like a fishwife through two closed doors."

Harriet spun around on a surge of fear. Her mother stood just inside the room, tying the sash of her silk dressing gown. Her lips pressed together in a tight line of exasperation but her eyes held concern. Exactly what had she heard?

"Nothing's going on," Harriet said breathlessly, desperately trying to still her trembling limbs.

Edwina glanced at Charlotte, who was now standing—her feet wide apart and her face stony—before shifting her gaze back to Harriet. "It doesn't look or sound like nothing."

Harriet shot Charlotte a warning look. "I was just reminding Charlotte that while she's living at Glenora she needs to pick up after herself and help out more."

Edwina frowned. "And you chose to do this at eleven forty-five at night after she's been in bed for ninety minutes? Honestly, Harriet, how much wine have you drunk?"

"Believe me, nowhere near enough," Harriet muttered before

turning back to her daughter. In a tone that brooked no argument she said, "We will talk more about this in the morning."

Charlotte stood motionless, her eyes bright with a familiar combative gleam. Too late, Harriet recognized the look. She moved fast to intercept the grenade, but Charlotte was pulling the pin. "Go back to bed, Ed—"

"Mardi, I'm pregnant!"

The shouted words held no ambiguity. They echoed around the high-ceilinged room before falling like acid rain, cloaking and burning the silent occupants.

Harriet heard an agonized howl and realized it was coming from her mouth.

Edwina sagged against the wall as if she'd been punched and was fighting for air. Her arm was pulled tight across her belly, her fingers clutching the silky material of her dressing gown. She stayed there, frozen—immobilized by shock—and with pain etched on every part of her. A long moment passed before she straightened up and directed her full attention to her granddaughter.

"Are you, darling?"

"Yes." Charlotte bit her lower lip. "I am."

"You must be terrified." Edwina opened her arms wide.

Charlotte burst into loud sobs and rushed into her grandmother's embrace, burying her head on her chest. Against the muffled noise of Charlotte's gulping distress, Harriet heard the creaking sound of a door opening followed by the soft thud of feet on the carpet runner and then Georgie was in the room wearing short pajamas and a pained expression.

"Charlie's pregnant?"

Edwina nodded her confirmation as she continued to make soothing sounds and stroke Charlotte's hair. Harriet's gaze was held tight—hypnotized by the uncommon sight of her mother's display of affection and love. She had no memories of Edwina ever soothing or consoling her like this as a child. Nor as an adult. God, even this week when everything had imploded, Edwina hadn't hugged her. Hugging had been her father's domain, but he was no longer here to take care of her.

As Harriet watched Edwina kiss the top of Charlotte's head, the almighty gulf that existed between her and her mother widened to an unbreachable distance. An excruciating feeling of abject isolation hit her, buckling her knees. She slumped on the bed, dropped her head into her hands and gave herself over to the sobs she'd held at bay for a week.

CHAPTER FOURTEEN

GEORGIE'S DISTRAUGHT PHONE CALL WOKE XARA AROUND ONE in the morning. By the time she'd cut the call, Steve was wide awake, his forehead creased with worry. "Someone sick? Hurt? What?"

"It was Georgie..." Xara was struggling to absorb the momentous news.

"And?"

"And ... Charlie's pregnant."

"Crikey! Harriet will go mental."

"According to Georgie, that's already happened. God, what is going on with this family?" A crazy sort of laugh burst out of her.

"What's so funny?"

She opened her mouth to tell him but every time she tried, another rip of laughter shot out of her. Absolutely nothing about Charlotte being pregnant or one single thing that James had done was remotely funny but the harder she'd tried to stop the laughter, the more it came. Tears trickled down her cheeks, the salty taste registering on her lips before dripping off her chin and her ribs ached and strained as if she'd just run three miles.

Steve looked baffled but instead of saying anything, he wrapped his arms around her and snuggled in close. It was only when her head started spinning and she was panting for breath that she finally managed to get herself under control.

"Steve?"

"Hmm?"

"Do you realize that for the first time ever, our branch of the family with its accompanying chaos is actually looking the most functional?"

He laughed and kissed the top of her head. "That's pretty bloody, scary."

"Tell me about it." Her mind had raced with logistics, trying to come up with the best way she could help. "I need to go to Glenora first thing."

"Xara to the rescue?"

"More like protecting everyone from Harriet. Can you deal with the kids in the morning?"

"Sure. They can come out in the truck while I check the stock. Tashie loves that. And we'll go fishing for our Good Friday dinner."

"I already bought fresh salmon."

"Are you doubting our ability to catch enough fish to feed us all for dinner?"

She snorted. "I'm doubting you can catch *a* fish period, let alone enough fish."

"For that lack of faith, I'll have to teach you a lesson."

His hands had shot out and tickled her aching ribs. She'd let out a token squeal of protest before letting him pull her over and then under him. As she'd welcomed the reassuring weight of him against her, her mouth met his and she'd given heartfelt thanks for having him in her life and on her side.

She left the farm before the kids woke, swung by the bakery for fresh hot cross buns and let herself into Glenora. The atmosphere at breakfast would be strained and fraught so she was determined there would be food. Lots of food. She got busy flipping pancakes, scrambling eggs and baking bacon.

Remembering how sick she'd been in the mornings when she was pregnant with the twins, she made a pot of ginger and lemon tea and filled a rack with toast for Charlotte. To avoid Harriet complaining there was nothing for her to eat and using that as an excuse to leave, Xara added muesli, skim milk and yogurt to the table. Satisfied she'd thought of everything, she walked to the bedroom wing and opened doors.

"Breakfast is ready and the dress code is pajamas."

"Go away, Xara," Harriet said curtly before rolling away from her.

"No." She threw open the curtains and sunshine streamed into the room unrelenting and squintingly bright. She picked up what Harriet called her "post-exercise cool-down pants" and everyone else called sweatpants, scrunched them into a ball and threw them at her sister's head. "Put these on."

"No."

Years of being Harriet's sister had taught her that soothing and sympathy rarely worked with her and today wasn't the day to start. "I have no hesitation in getting a bucket of cold water like I did that time in Apollo Bay. Remember?"

"Grow up, Xara."

She thought about Harriet's week. "Sometimes being grown up sucks, Harry." She pulled back the covers until they completely fell off the bed and Harriet shivered. "See you in the kitchen."

Xara found Charlotte already awake and hugging the toilet bowl. "I've got ginger tea and toast waiting for you in the kitchen, dear. Wash your face and come through."

"Is Mom up?"

Xara heard her niece's apprehension. "It's a Chirnwell women's breakfast. All five of us." She reached out a hand. "Hop up, wash your face and come to the kitchen."

The next door was Georgie's. She was sitting up in bed, reading.

"Family breakfast, baby sis."

"Zar!" Georgie shot out of bed and hugged her. "Thanks for

coming. I know I should be understanding and supportive and I'm trying but—" Her voice cracked. "God, Xara. A baby."

Xara returned the hug, remembering Georgie's tiny baby and feeling the old weight of grief and loss she always carried for the child Tasha might have been. "I know it's hard but I really need you at breakfast. I cooked you crispy bacon."

Georgie gave her a hangdog look. "That's dirty pool, Zar."

She grinned. "Whatever it takes."

Xara made her way to the front of the house only to find her mother's room empty and her bed neatly made. As she returned to the kitchen, Edwina strolled in from the garden. "Morning, Mom. Big night I hear."

"Hello, darling." Edwina was dressed in her gardening clothes but instead of holding her gloves, she was clutching her cell phone. She gave Xara an absent kiss on the cheek. "Do I smell coffee?"

"And the rest." Xara pulled plates from the plate warmer. "I thought you all needed a hearty breakfast."

"Very thoughtful." Her mother gave a faint smile and sat down. "I haven't had pancakes in years."

Xara recognized her mother's coping mechanism—polite and insignificant chitchat—so she stuck to the superficial. "Try them with Nutella. It's the twins' favorite."

Harriet strode in wearing a thunderous look. She scraped a chair noisily over the slate, took a seat opposite her mother and silently poured muesli into a bowl.

"Latte, Harry?" Xara switched on the coffee machine.

Her sister threw her a mutinous look and she raced for an acerbic serve but then Harriet's shoulders slumped. "I want to say no, but coffee's essential this morning. Make it an espresso."

Georgie arrived with Charlotte, who eyed her mother with a mixture of anxiety and distrust then said, "Morning, Mardi." She gave a quick nod to Harriet. "Mom." She took the seat next to her grandmother.

Georgie passed Charlotte the toast and poured her a mug of tea.

"Breathe in the aroma of the ginger to lessen the smell of coffee."

"Thanks." Charlotte shot her a grateful smile.

Xara made coffees to order and let the others eat before she finally sat down and helped herself to some crispy bacon. The natural thing to say when someone was pregnant was "congratulations" but in this situation and at this point when everything was up in the air, good wishes would be starkly out of place. She gave her niece an encouraging smile instead.

"Charlie, you're pregnant and Georgie tells me you've known for a month. I guess you've been doing a lot of thinking. What are your plans?"

Charlotte's eyes widened in surprise as if the question wasn't one she'd been expecting. She licked her lips and said softly, "I want to keep the baby."

Harriet sucked in a breath so fast it hissed between gritted teeth. "That is *not* going to happen."

Two bright pink spots burned on Charlotte's cheeks. "You can't make me get rid of it."

"You can't make me take care of it." Harriet's tone could cut glass.

"Do you know when the baby's due?" Xara interceded. She wanted the conversation to be useful, not to degenerate into a slinging match from the second sentence.

"The middle of November."

"Oh, now that is spectacular planning, Charlotte," Harriet said. "How convenient that your baby's due right in the middle of your final exams."

Charlotte's knuckles whitened on the handle of her tea mug. "I know it's not perfect—"

"Perfect!" Harriet yelled, her arms flying out wide. "Nothing about this is perfect. It's all a fucking mess."

"Harriet!" Edwina's voice cut in with the same tone she'd used when her eldest daughter was fourteen and swearing. "Obviously Charlie being pregnant isn't ideal, but we need to discuss this calmly."

"Calmly?" Harriet's head snapped around so fast there was an audible click. "My daughter's planning to ruin her life and you want me to be calm? Jesus, Edwina! How can I be calm?" She pointed the butter knife accusingly at her mother. "And why are you so calm? After all, you're the one who taught me about family duty, responsibility and social standing. Exactly how does having a seventeen-year-old pregnant granddaughter fit with that? Or has spending time with this Doug person, with his blue-collar accent, suddenly change a lifetime of beliefs?"

Edwina flinched and the color drained from her face.

Xara gently pressed her hand against Harriet's arm, lowering the butter knife to the table. "Leave Doug out of this, Harry."

"One of the things besides money that's always elevated the Mannerings above the hoi polloi is that we don't get knocked up." Harriet didn't take her eyes off Edwina or pause for breath. "We don't have teenage pregnancies and we don't have unmarried mothers. We're scandal free and yet in one week my husband and my daughter have managed to destroy everything we stand for. So no, Edwina, I can't be calm. *Nothing* about this situation calls for calm."

Ripping open a hot cross bun, Harriet hacked at the butter. "Tell me, Charlotte, if you keep this baby, where are you going to live?" The silver knife flashed back and forth against the bun. "How are you going to pay the rent? How are you going to finish school? Get a decent job so you can raise this child?"

Xara felt battered by the barrage of questions and they weren't even directed at her. She poured Charlotte more tea.

"I don't know yet," Charlotte said miserably. "I was hoping you'd support me like you're planning to next year."

"*That* was when you were going to university to become a doctor!"

"I have my trust fund."

"Not anymore you don't. Your father raided that too."

Georgie raised her head from her intense study of the peony rose botanical painting on her plate. "You can live with me, Charlie. I can work part-time and that way you can finish school and go to uni. We can bring up the baby together." She got a faraway look in her eyes. "I'll be great Auntie G."

Xara frowned but before she could formulate her worried thoughts into words, Edwina said quietly, "It's Charlie's baby, Georgina."

Georgie's chin jutted. "I *know* the baby is Charlie's, Mom. But it sounds like Harriet's kicking her out of home so I'm trying to help. I'm the one who lives in Melbourne where the universities are so it's a viable option."

"Thank you, Auntie G. I appreciate the offer," Charlotte's gaze remained on her mother with a new and calculating glint. "Dad will let me live with him."

"In jail?" Harriet said icily. "How lovely for you and your baby."

Charlotte blinked rapidly but her shoulders remained set. "I'm doing this with or without your support, Mom."

"Charlotte." Harriet sighed then continued speaking but without the piercing criticism. "The timing's all wrong. You're in your final year of high school and none of your goals included being pregnant. You need to get the highest score you possibly can, go to university and study pre-med. None of that has to change." Her tone crept up a register. "What I don't understand is, even though you're not in a relationship with the father, you're preparing to have a child who will grow up feeling that loss all of its life?"

"I'm going to tell Hamish about the baby. He might want to be involved," Charlotte said almost too quickly. "His parents might, like, um, you know ..."

Xara exchanged a quick look with Georgie. The naiveté of the remark was certain to rupture Harriet's barely leashed control.

"Charlie, honey. Jason and I broke up because he didn't want another baby." Georgie's voice wavered. "To be honest, he didn't really want Eliza. We'd been together a long time and we loved each other but it wasn't enough. The chances of your party hook-up guy wanting to be a dad or supporting you are almost nonexistent."

Harriet looked as if she wanted to kiss Georgie. "Charlotte, this cluster of cells inside you is a mistake. It's a mistake that will cost you your dreams. Don't let one mistake stain your life forever."

Charlotte shook her head so hard strands of her long blond hair flew out behind her. "Mom, you're the one who wants me to be a doctor, not me. I'm not sure what I want to do. I've been thinking about teaching like Auntie Georgie or doing early childhood development. The one thing I know is that I love being with kids."

"A baby's not a doll," Harriet said thickly. "It's not something you can play with and put down when you've had enough. It's not like taking care of other people's children and getting to walk away at the end of the day."

"I know that."

"Do you really?" Harriet stabbed some bacon with a fork. "I don't think you do."

"Yes! I do." Charlotte's spine straightened. "While you've been working, I've spent heaps of time on the farm with Xara and Steve. I've watched them with Tashie. I've helped them look after her and I've spent hours playing with the twins."

"But you haven't been responsible for them. Being a mother is the hardest job you'll ever do." Harriet looked around the table, imploring Xara to chime in. "Tell her!"

"It's tough, Charlie," Xara said honestly, knowing today wasn't the time for sugar coating. Whatever decision Charlotte made, she wanted her to make it with the full facts in front of her. "There's no time for you to do the stuff you take for granted now like playing computer games, watching movies, just hanging out with friends, riding your horse or going to parties."

"If it's so hard then why did you have the twins after Tashie?"

Oh, God. Her niece was as sharp as a tack. "I love kids. Steve and I both have siblings and we always planned to have at least two. Stopping after Tashie might have been practical but nothing about the decision to have children is practical. It's biological and emotional and probably a little bit irrational ..."

She caught Harriet's fury coming at her like a flame thrower. "But, Charlie—and this is a big but—I have Steve. We're a team. There's no way I could do what I do without Steve's love and support. It's going to be very tough for you on your own even with a healthy child."

"Did you hear that, Charlotte?" Harriet's tone held a triumphant edge. "It's tough being a mother even when you have a partner. Which you don't. Having a termination is the only sensible thing to do."

Charlotte's nostril's flared and her lips thinned into a tight line. For the briefest of moments she looked exactly like Harriet at seventeen—tenacious and determined. "I know me getting pregnant is a horrible shock for you, Mom, but I've had four weeks to think about it. It's *all* I've been able to think about. I've spent weeks being petrified, worried about how I'll manage with a baby. But none of that fear comes close to the panic I get when I think about having an abortion."

She laced her fingers, the action speaking volumes. "This time, Mom, I won't let you push me around. This time, I'm not allowing you to make the decision for me. I'm sorry you're not happy but I'm having this baby."

Xara marveled at Charlotte's eloquence and wondered if she was more mature than any of them gave her credit.

"God, I've raised a spoilt princess." Harriet's hands fisted so tight her knuckles shone translucent. "You, young lady, have no idea what you're doing. I refuse to let you ruin your potential and destroy your life. You are getting rid of this baby."

"Harriet." Edwina's voice rumbled in the room with the ominous foreboding of thunder. "This is *not* your decision."

Startled, Xara stared at her mother. Edwina rarely stood up to Harriet. In fact, she rarely stood up to anyone or for anyone, including herself.

Harriet blinked, momentarily nonplussed. "You do realize,

Edwina, this will not only ruin Charlotte's life, it means you'll be the grandmother of a single mother. The great-grandmother of a bastard?" She shook her head as though trying to make sense of what her mother had said. "And this from the woman who was considered one half of the moral compass of this town for decades. Someone people have looked up to. Think about it! Think about what Dad would have said."

Edwina's fingers reached for her pearls but, in their absence, touched bare skin. "Richard isn't here to do or say anything. It's unwise to even suggest what opinions he may have offered."

"You'll have to face Primrose. You'll have to deal with the rest of the town's comments. If you think they'll be kind, think again." Harriet tapped the exquisite Jarrah wooden tabletop with a teaspoon; the dull, relentless clunk reinforcing her words. "Believe me, this week I've learned people can be vicious with their opinions. They can be cruel about a lot of things but they're merciless about teenage mothers. God, you only have to walk down the main street and linger near the war memorial park to hear the judging comments. Hell, they make them in front of the girls and their children. Do you want that for Charlotte, Edwina?"

"I want her to be at peace with her decision."

"At peace?" Incredulity streaked across Harriet's face. "How very new age of you, Mother. There's no peace for her in keeping this baby. She becomes part of Billawarre's infamous statistic of having the highest teen pregnancy rate in the state. She's opening herself up to shame and ignominy. She's adding to the scandal and humiliation James is subjecting us to.

"And you, Edwina. You who gets the—"Harriet's fingers made quotes in the air—"'can't copes' at the drop of a hat and retreats from the world, leaving the rest of us to deal with things, you're saying it's her decision? What happened to family responsibility? How can you let her tarnish the family name you've spent a lifetime upholding? How can you sit there and let her take a road to poverty paved with lost opportunities?"

"Be fair, Harry," Georgie said reasonably. "Don't make this about your obsession with the past and the Mannerings. It's about Charlie."

Edwina, who'd kept her eyes on Harriet throughout the ruthless blast turned to her granddaughter. "Darling, have you talked to a counselor about all of this?"

Charlotte nodded. "That night I stayed at Georgie's. I saw a counselor that day."

"Do you want to talk to her again?"

"No. I need to see a doctor now and have a check-up."

Harriet cast the teaspoon scudding down the table, pinging against porcelain. "If you go through with this pregnancy, Charlotte, you have to move out. I'm not having *anything* to do with this."

Charlotte's eyes burned bright with defiance but the skin on her face tightened, giving her the stricken and wounded look of an animal in distress. Xara saw it was only her niece's sheer strength of will that kept her head high and tears at bay.

"You can stay with us," Xara offered at exactly the same time Georgie said, "You can stay with me."

"I think you're all forgetting something." Edwina briskly spread Nutella on another pancake. "At the moment both Charlie and Harriet are living in my house, therefore I'm the person who decides who moves in or who moves out. Charlie, do you want to stay at Glenora for the time being?"

Charlotte fervently gripped her grandmother's hand. "Yes, please, Mardi."

Harriet made a choking sound, which Edwina ignored, instead concentrating on rolling the pancake with her fork and slicing it into dainty mouthfuls. "Harriet, I'll leave your decision to go or stay up to you. Please know you're very welcome here as long as you respect your daughter's decision to have this baby."

White with rage, Harriet stood, knocking the table and setting the cups rattling against their saucers. Vibrating with fury, she spat, "Tell me, Edwina. Why did you choose today to suddenly grow a pair?"

"Harry!" Shock rocked Xara, and waves of queasiness pitched the toast in her stomach. "Enough. Don't say anything else you'll regret."

"It's alright, Xara." Edwina sounded remarkably composed despite the raw antagonism cutting and slicing the air around her.

Xara struggled to align the here and now with the known world where, for as long as she could remember, her mother had done everything in her power to avoid conflict. Edwina had just willingly thrown herself into the middle of what might become the biggest rift the family had ever known.

Edwina continued, "To answer your crude question, Harriet, I've grown a pair because it's time."

"Well, your timing sucks," Harriet muttered bitterly, sounding far more like Charlotte than herself.

"And talking of time, if you'll all excuse me, I have to go out for a few hours." Edwina rose elegantly from her chair.

"On Good Friday?" Georgie asked, flabbergasted.

Ignoring her youngest daughter in the queenly way Edwina excelled at when she didn't want to answer a question, she said, "Xara, can you brew me some coffee and put it in a Thermos? Oh, and wrap up some hot cross buns, please."

Under the fraught circumstances, the perfectly polite request held a surreal quality. Xara took a couple of seconds to murmur her acquiescence.

As Edwina walked down the hall, Harriet screamed after her, "You've got to be kidding me! You're going to see that Doug, aren't you? Off you go then, Edwina. Put yourself first like you've done all of my life. Walk away from me the only time I've ever asked you for support. I wish to God it was you who'd died and not Dad."

Harriet stormed into the garden, slamming the French doors so hard the vibrations shattered a pane of glass. Charlotte, who'd held back her tears during the inquisition, sobbed quietly.

Georgie gathered her into a hug and glanced at Xara over the top of their niece's blond head. Xara read *Fuck almighty* in her sister's bright blue eyes.

Amen to that.

CHAPTER FIFTEEN

EDWINA PULLED UP OUTSIDE THE MOTEL RIGHT ON TEN AND
Doug was waiting as per the crisp instructions she'd given him over
the phone before her distressing family breakfast.

He swung up into the passenger seat, a smile on his face and he
leaned over, kissed her on the cheek, fastened his seatbelt and said, "A
beautiful day, a beautiful woman and a beautiful car. Life is good."

She tensed. "Don't tempt fate."

He gave her a sideways glance, his kind eyes curious and
concerned. "Everything okay?"

"Fine."

She turned on the radio and the car filled with Bach's *Saint
Matthew's Passion*. She pointed the car out of town, keeping her
thoughts to herself. Her family was caught in the strong and swirling
waters of an emotional maelstrom that cast the damage James had
inflicted well and truly in the shadows.

Charlotte was pregnant.

Overnight, the word had pounded so loud in her head it became a
tattoo, indelibly inking itself on her mind and soul. At breakfast,
another word had joined it in a curly, flowing script: *Baby*. Georgie

was daydreaming about co-parenting with Charlotte and in the process convincing herself it was the savior to her heartache for Eliza.

Edwina recognized the rose-colored thoughts and knew better than anyone it wasn't the answer. Amid the furor, Xara was trying to keep things rational and reasonable, but she was no match for her elder sister. *Oh, Harriet.* Harriet was spinning in a tornado of fury and the lashing and sucking vortex was centered squarely on Edwina.

I wish to God it was you who'd died.

Her gut twisted. As painful and as hard as it was to accept, some of Harriet's invective was fair. Deserved even. Theirs was a rocky mother–daughter bond and always had been. From the moment she'd held newborn Harriet in her arms, Edwina had struggled. She'd gazed into her baby's slightly frowning face and waited with confidence for feelings of love to burst in her chest like the bright white light of fireworks before raining down to ignite that intense mother–child connection.

They hadn't come.

She'd waited for them, prayed for them, cried for them and desperately craved them, but for a very long time the place where love should have sprouted and grown was nothing but an echoing and empty void. A nothingness that engendered debilitating guilt. Over time, that space had gradually filled, but the legacy of the void was an integral part of her and Harriet's lives.

Edwina turned off the highway and changed down into second gear as the four-wheel drive bounced along a corrugated track. She felt the pull of the seatbelt tighten against her chest, holding her firmly against the soft leather seat.

"You have to hand it to the Germans. They know suspension," Doug said.

She turned hard on the steering wheel to avoid a deep rut but the wheel caught the edge of it. "It was a waste on this car. Richard never took it off the black top."

Doug's hands gripped the handle above the door to stop his head hitting the roof. "And you're making up for that today?"

"Yes." She wasn't ready to explain her brusqueness so she hid behind her intense concentration on the steep descent.

"Well, you haven't lost your touch," he said admiringly. "I remember how well you handled the old Ford long before power steering was invented."

"That column shift hated me."

"Yeah, it was a mongrel, but that car had other qualities. I've got very fond memories of that Ford."

He grinned at her and his palm briefly skimmed the back of her hand.

The look in his eyes rolled back the years in a heartbeat and she was suddenly a girl again, dizzy, elated and high on being in love. She'd spent hours in that car dreaming about the future. Only in the confines of the blue vinyl interior was she able to visualize the life she craved. With hindsight, she saw how heavily those dreams had been washed in a rose-colored tint. Her reality had turned out to be starkly black and white and heavily stamped with duty, responsibility and family obligation.

Harriet's words from breakfast regained volume in her head and her concentration slipped. She braked hard at a closed gate. Without a word, Doug slipped out, strode to the latch, unhooked it and walked the gate open. She put the vehicle into gear and thudded over the cattle guard, watching him through the rear-view mirror. His big hands threaded the chain through the closest square of wire and pulled it toward the knob. It didn't quite reach so he shoved his boot under the bottom of the gate and lifted the top. He tugged the chain and adroitly hooked it back over the knob, gave the gate a shake and then brushed his hands on his jeans. She smiled, delight catching her like an unexpected sunbeam. Some things time didn't change.

Doug swung back into the vehicle. "That gate brought back memories. There was one just like it with a sticky close on Murrumbeet. Used to cause me merry hell on winter mornings."

Edwina shifted the gear stick into first and released the clutch. "It's the same gate."

"No." Doug glanced left and right before shifting in his seat to look out the rear window. "Can't be. The gate I'm talking about had a gnarly old gum growing next to it."

"It got struck by lightning twenty years ago."

"So we're actually on Murrumbeet?" He sounded bemused. "Why didn't we come through the main gates?"

"We're on what used to be the southern boundary. My brother sold this land to pay debts when the wool market collapsed."

The car crested a rise and Doug smiled. "Ah! Now I know exactly where I am."

A mob of sheep eyed the vehicle both hesitantly and indecisively. Off to the left and in the far distance was the silver shimmer of the corrugated iron roof of the shearing shed and below them, just beyond another fence line, was the salty lake, shining a dazzling blue in the morning sunshine. The surrounding vegetation was scrubby, low and sparse but for the stand of cypress pines her grandfather had planted to provide shade for picnics.

"Is this the first stop on a tour of revisiting our favorite haunts?"

"Could be." It wasn't. She had no plans to take him anywhere else, but he seemed so happy with the idea she chose not to dissuade him. Killing the engine, she pressed the button to pop the trunk and hopped out of the car. Doug met her at the open trunk and she handed him the wicker basket with the Thermos of coffee and hot cross buns. She carried the picnic blanket.

Doug lumbered over the stile before turning and offering his hand. It wasn't that she didn't appreciate the gesture—she did—but she was more than capable of crossing it unaided and part of her yearned to do just that. For years people had done things for her, made decisions for her, and she'd allowed it all to happen. She'd let her life roll on without much input from herself.

Since meeting Doug again, the yearning to take back control of her life was growing stronger. The party was her first fledgling step— like a toddler on bare and unsteady feet. The news of Charlotte's pregnancy had clad those feet in cross-trainers and brought her to the lake. Placing the blanket in Doug's outstretched hand, she climbed up and over the stile unassisted.

Under the cool and dappled shade of the old trees, Doug flicked out the rubber-backed tartan. It hit the ground disturbing the decades-thick layer of brown needles and the pungent but fresh scent of pine permeated the air. It was the perfume of hot summer nights, the giddy heights of first love, stolen moments that held the world at bay and the intoxication of tantalizing hope. He sat down with an affectionate smile and accepted the mug of coffee she'd poured for him.

"You know, I remember us swimming here. I remember cooking sausages over a fire and ..." his smile widened with the same impish tilt of his lips that had captivated her all those years ago, "... I remember kissing you until I couldn't see straight. But I don't ever remember us drinking coffee."

She lowered herself next to him, feeling the protesting ache of her hips that she refused to acknowledge. "I remember you drinking beer but for some reason you always bought me Porphyry Pearl."

"That's what I thought rich, cultured and sophisticated girls drank back then."

"I was barely eighteen, Doug," she said quietly. "I was hardly sophisticated."

"Not from where I was standing." His dark eyes took on a dreamy look. "I'd never met anyone like you. From the first time I saw you astride that horse, I was captivated by your grace and style. It spun around you like an aura. You had it then, you've got it now. It's who you are."

"It's not really me." She fingered her grandmother's plump pearls —feeling the roundness of them roll between her thumb and index finger—in the same way she'd been doing since they'd been strung around her neck an hour before her wedding to Richard. "It's who I thought I had to be."

Confusion crossed his face. "Who you thought you had to be back then?"

Who I thought I've had to be all of my life. She tossed the dregs of her coffee onto the grass. "Do you remember the last night we spent together here?"

"I've never forgotten it." Memories lived and breathed in the cadence of his voice and his hand stroked her back in an intimate and affectionate way. "The moon was so bright it reflected silver in your amazing eyes. I spent that night memorizing you so I didn't forget what you looked like. Didn't forget the soft and silky feel of your skin or your sweet scent."

He cleared his throat. "I carried all of it with me the whole time I was in Vietnam."

For two weeks they'd skirted around the elephant in the room. Both of them being excruciatingly careful not to mar the wonderful and heady moments reconnecting was giving them after so many years apart. Since they'd stumbled across each other at the car rally, they'd outlined the bare bones of their lives in the intervening years. Things like the names of their spouses and their quirks and interests.

They'd talked of his business, her charity work, and the number and names of their kids. They'd exchanged the highs and lows of raising children, discussed the careers their children pursued, and they'd shown each other photos of their grandchildren. Eventually, they'd talked of their experiences of losing their spouse.

Edwina gleaned Doug missed Sophia more than she missed Richard, and in a strange way, that was comforting. It seemed less of a waste than if both of them had spent all those years unhappy. Mostly though, they'd talked about common interests, deliberately giving a wide birth to the time when they'd lost each other.

They'd been almost too eager to accept that despite life having intervened to separate them for forty-eight years, now they were together again the past didn't matter. Only it did matter. It mattered a lot. Especially today.

Being with Doug made Edwina feel like that hopeful eighteen-year-old girl again—confident that all she needed to be happy was the love of this good and honorable man who adored her. Oh, how badly she wanted to believe it, but she wasn't eighteen anymore. She was world weary and painfully aware that if she gave in to the tempting daydream, it would only end in heartache and tears for both of them. Real life had derailed them once, setting in motion a chain of events that had not only separated them but had changed her life forever.

"Doug?"

"Yes?"

"That night under the full moon, you knew you were leaving, didn't you?" The hurt and pain she'd been certain had fossilized years ago caught her by surprise. "You must have known for a month you had to report to Puckapunyal for basic training, but you never said a word. I've never understood why you let me go to Melbourne knowing you'd be gone when I got back. How could you disappear without a word?"

"I'm sorry, Eddy." His entire body wore his regret like an old, threadbare coat. "I should have told you but I was just a stupid kid. I had no idea you'd take it so badly. I tried to tell you. Jesus, how I tried, but we were so happy that night. I wanted to take that perfect memory with me to keep me going until I got back. I didn't want to remember you crying and me scared shitless."

He rubbed his hands against his denim-clad thighs. "And I'm not good with words. I didn't trust myself to say it right. I wrote to you instead and took the letter up to the homestead on my last afternoon. Stewie, the old shearer, told me giving it to the housekeeper was my best bet but when I rang the bell your father answered the door."

"My father?" She didn't think she had a single memory of Fraser Mannering ever answering the front door of Murrumbeet. Mrs. Chester, their housekeeper, yes. Her mother, certainly, on the few occasions Mrs. Chester was indisposed, but her father? Never. If he was home and the loud doorbell ever shrilled a second time, his booming voice would sound from his study summoning a female—family member or otherwise—to answer the door.

Doug nodded. "Yeah. I wasn't expecting it either. The guys always reckoned the boss was a bit of a ..."

Edwina heard his hesitation and knew it was in deference to her feelings, but she had no illusions left as to the type of man her father had been. "Bastard? Go right ahead and call a spade a spade. It won't offend me."

Doug gave a shrug. "Thing is, back then, I didn't think he was a bastard. The few times I'd had anything to do with him in the shearing shed or out in the pasture, he'd been fair. When I explained I was leaving for nasho, he invited me in. We had a beer. He asked me about my family and my future plans. I told him I was good with engines and I planned on opening a garage one day. I told him I loved you and I hoped my future included you."

Her heart lurched with a combination of shock, appreciation and dust-covered acceptance. She'd kept Doug a secret from her family and friends but now his words summoned up missing pieces of an old and faded puzzle; they vied to fit into the spaces that had lain empty for decades. "I had no idea you'd told my father about us."

"What was I supposed to do?" He ran his hand across the back of his neck. "I was sitting in his house, drinking his beer and holding a letter addressed to his daughter. I thought telling him was the right thing to do."

Weary resignation rolled through her. In another time and with another man it would have been the right thing to do but not in 1968 in the heart of country Victoria's landed gentry. Part of her wanted to berate him for his twenty-year-old naiveté but how could she? He'd always been a decent man who valued integrity, loyalty and hard work. He believed a man proved himself on those merits.

Not once during those halcyon days when they'd shut out the world, dreamed, talked and planned their future together, had she told him her parents would never accept him. There'd been no point. He'd been conscripted and was committed to the army for two years, and despite her father's grumblings to the contrary, she was determined to go to university. After Doug was discharged they'd only need to wait one more year and she'd be free to marry him without her parents' consent. Why hurt him unduly by raising her father's racist and elitist beliefs? Why tell him her parents would die rather than allow her to marry a farmhand who had Irish, English and Aboriginal blood running in his veins?

"What did my father say to you when you told him about us?"

"He shook my hand and wished me well."

Old anger reignited, popping and crackling like burning red gum and raining showers of sparks into her veins. "He never gave me the letter. He never even told me you'd visited."

"He assured me he'd give it to you."

"He lied." She couldn't stop the accusatory tone from seeping into her voice. "Why would you believe him?"

He frowned and she saw hurt and confusion dueling with exasperation. "He gave his word. I had no reason not to believe him. Hell, it wasn't the only letter, Eddy. I wrote from basic and corps training. A letter a week for months."

He looked down at his hands. "At first I thought you were just pissed off at me for leaving without telling you, but then I got worried. I tried to get back here before I flew out but because you weren't family the army wouldn't pay for my travel. I didn't have the money to fly from Canungra to Melbourne and I didn't have the time to bus it down here and get back without going AWOL.

"I spent a fortune on a long-distance phone call to Murrumbeet but Mrs. Chester said you weren't home. I got her to write down that I'd been posted to the ordnance depot at Vung Tau. Spelled the bloody name out letter by letter but still I heard nothing. It was like you'd fallen off the face of the earth. I stopped writing after that. I reckoned your silence was telling me it was over."

Her dormant pain grew jagged barbs, crawling through her as fresh and strong as if her heart had been broken yesterday. She knew all about the ominous and terrifying sounds of silence. She'd lived with them too. "I loved you."

Sadness shone in his eyes, matching hers. "And I loved you too. But living in a war zone is surreal. Nothing's familiar. Nothing seems real and yet everything's more real than home. Your silence let the doubts roar in. Loud, malicious doubts that told me I was a dickhead to think I had a chance with you. That you'd been slumming it with me. Just a rich girl getting her kicks with one of the workers. It didn't help that I was living with guys whose answer to any problem was to get drunk or bang a local or both."

His words, full of anguish, hailed down on her. The young man she'd loved all those years ago was here now and hurting. She wanted to interrupt him, tell him that all those doubts were wrong; that he'd been exactly the caliber of man she'd have been honored to share her life with, but she stayed silent. He needed to tell his story and she needed to hear it. She needed those missing pieces to complete the puzzle of their separation. She needed to try to understand and, in the process, patch and darn her own pain of those dreadful months.

"I tried to forget you, Ed," he said wearily as if revisiting that time and space was exhausting him. "I hated myself for still loving you when you'd obviously forgotten me so easily. I tried to hate you, but I didn't have it in me. No matter how hard I tried to forget you, it was thoughts of you that got me through patrols. I never knew if I was going to cop a Viet Cong bullet or live to hear yet another chopper full of casualties land at the hospital.

"Six months in, I was supposed to do a stint up at Radar Hill but a mate asked me to swap shifts so he could see his girl that night." He picked up a stick and his faintly oil-stained fingers snapped it into neat lengths. "Poor bugger stood on a mine. Lost both legs. That night in the hospital, I sat with him, watching the empty space where his legs used to be and all I could think of was you. I needed the truth. I swallowed my shattered pride and wrote one last letter asking if I still had a chance with you. Or if it was really over."

He rubbed his forehead. "I got a letter from your father. He said he didn't want to disappoint a man fighting for freedom, but you were up at university and you'd just gotten engaged. He said don't write again."

A metallic taste filled her mouth. She tried to picture Doug in the oppressive tropical heat surrounded by the sounds of war and reading a letter she'd never known had been written, let alone sent. "He lied, Doug. I was never at university."

"But the engagement wasn't a lie," he said with a trace of accusation in his voice. "When I finished my tour, I came back to Murrumbeet. I had to see you and make sure you were happy. Check that this Richard character was who you really wanted. I avoided the homestead but Stewie told me you were on your honeymoon. Turns out, I'd missed your wedding by five days."

Her hand flew to her mouth as her insides were pulverized by the weight of appalling timing. "Oh, God, Doug. I had no idea. I'm so sorry."

His mouth tightened. "That night I got drunker than I'd ever gotten in 'Nam. And believe me, that's saying something. I spent the night in the Billawarre lockup sleeping it off."

He turned to her, his gentle and caring eyes filled with difficult questions. "I know we were young, Eddy. Hell, you were just out of school, but I never took you for someone who'd change her mind so fast. Never thought you were the type who'd punish me so harshly for the stupid mistake of not saying goodbye. That you'd marry someone else fourteen months later. I didn't understand any of it, but you were married so what could I do? Nothin'. I left town. I didn't let myself think about us again. And I haven't."

He dug his booted heel into the pine needles. "Well, I didn't until I drove into Billawarre with the rally and then it all came back. I never expected to find you still here but there you were, looking as beautiful as ever. These last two weeks have been wonderful. Makes me feel like we've never been apart but ..." He gave a heavy sigh and his shoulders slumped. "It's flummoxed me all over again. What the hell happened? I really need to know."

Memories of those long-gone awful days, memories she'd forced into a box before slamming the lid hard and bolting it shut, blew their lock. They rolled through her, kicking and biting and bringing with them distress not remotely attenuated by the passage of time. She was hurled back hard and fast into the past. Her nostrils twitched as if she smelled the smoke from the burn-off that had hung like a pall over Murrumbeet that long-ago autumn.

In her mind she heard the rhythmic chug-chug-chug of the old John Deere tractor plowing up and down the pasture, readying the rich, dark soil to accept the seeds of wheat like a lush and fertile womb. Her mind played images like a projector casting them onto a screen. She saw terrified and shaking lambs bleating for their mothers as they were herded onto trucks bound for the abattoirs. Riding roughshod over time and place was the breath-sucking anxiety that Doug had left her for good.

She gripped his forearm hard, hoping the pressure would convey to him how much she needed him to listen carefully. "I loved you, Doug. I didn't marry Richard because I'd changed my mind. I married him because ..." She halted, not wanting to get ahead of herself. "Please know I wrote to you. I called the army. I tried to find a relative of yours to get word to you. No one knew where you were from or who your family were. I never got a reply to any of my letters. I thought you'd abandoned me for a different life."

He tugged at his salt and pepper curls as if they would offer an answer to a perplexing question. "How the hell can that many letters go missing?"

She wrapped her arms around her knees and sighed. "They didn't go missing. Now I know my father knew about us I can see him clear as day dropping that first letter into the fire before the front door had even closed behind you. After that, he would have instructed my mother and the housekeeper to vet my mail and destroy anything from you. In his eyes you lacked the pedigree to marry me."

"Bastard." His jaw tightened as he absorbed the news. "But that doesn't explain why I never got any of your letters."

"No." Different memories—ones that were never too far away—surfaced. "For a long time, I didn't have access to a letterbox. I depended on other people to post my letters. Obviously, my father must have gotten to them too."

"What do you mean you couldn't get to a letterbox?"

She gazed out at the lake, watching a pelican coming in to land—blue- gray feet outstretched, wings akimbo; a living, breathing jumbo jet.

"Were you sick, Eddy? Did you break your legs?"

If only.

CHAPTER SIXTEEN

When Harriet had stormed from Glenora after Good Friday's breakfast, Georgie had given her thirty-one hours to cool down. Then, uninvited, she'd driven to Miligili's guesthouse. She believed the only way for Harriet and Charlotte's relationship to have a chance of surviving was if they lived in the same house.

"Please come back. Glenora's not the same without you."

"I can't do that. Edwina's betrayed me and Charlotte ..." Harriet's haughty tone cracked. "I can't sit around and pretend to play happy families. Not when my daughter's throwing her life away and my mother's enabling it."

Although Georgie didn't agree with Harriet's refusal to support Charlotte, she conceded some understanding of Harriet's anger with their mother. All their lives they'd seen Edwina in her role as one of Billawarre's elite—a position given to her courtesy of the Mannering family name and wealth. Although it wasn't a position either Georgie or Xara wanted, Edwina had retained it by living her life according to those unspoken rules inherent with the position: duty, responsibility, honor and moral guardianship. Harriet had happily followed suit. For Edwina to appear so calm about her granddaughter's teenage pregnancy, as well as being so adamant that Harriet accept Charlotte's decision, was so far out of the realms of normal and known behavior it was unrecognizable.

Edwina's stance made absolutely no sense and Georgie and Xara had discussed it at length, but their conversation hadn't thrown up any clear answers. If anything, it raised more questions. Georgie had two reasons for not having a similar conversation with Harriet: it would only exacerbate her sister's antagonism toward Edwina and it wouldn't change her mind about returning to Glenora.

She noticed a pile of weekend newspapers and caught sight of a headline, Disgraced Mayor Hides in Mansion.

It gave her an idea and she changed tack. "What about James?"

"What about him?"

"How can you stand being back at Miligili when he's here?"

Harriet's shoulders stiffened and her mouth puckered into a wrinkled and bitter line as if she'd sucked on a lime. "He's in the main house. I'm here. There's a full-size tennis court, a swimming pool and a pool house separating us. I intend to keep it that way."

"Yes, but people won't know you're living in the guesthouse. They'll think you've moved back into the main house and forgiven him." She dived into dirty pool territory—anything to get Harriet back to Glenora. "People talk and they judge. You know how much you hate that."

Harriet's hand trembled as she sloshed shiraz into a wine glass. The rich red fluid swirled fast around the deep bowl, the force driving out a drop, which spread its indelible stain across Harriet's white silk blouse. "People are already talking and believe me, they're not letting the truth get in the way of their opinions. They're also walking."

She gulped wine, breaking her not-until-six-pm rule a good hour early. "At the moment I've got ten patients booked in to see me next week. Come Tuesday, it's likely to be less."

"Oh, Harry." Georgie moved to hug her but Harriet held out the large glass like a shield. "I'm so sorry. I'm sure it's just a knee-jerk reaction. Things will settle down, especially when they realize the travel that's involved to see another surgeon."

"I doubt it." Harriet stared out at her autumnal garden with unfocused eyes. "I've never been hated before, Georgie. It's ..." But she didn't finish the sentence. She swallowed more wine instead.

A wave of helplessness washed over Georgie. She'd never seen Harriet so adrift. Knowing that the usual platitudes didn't work with her big sister, she turned to practicalities. "Do you want me to stay here with you tonight?"

"Don't be ridiculous! I'm not sick."

Georgie refrained from muttering, *You're not exactly well* and threw together a tuna stir-fry. She stayed until Harriet ate enough to soak up some of the wine. As she left the guesthouse, she said, "You're still coming to Sunday lunch, right?"

Harriet's glare blistered her skin.

She returned to Glenora alone. The moment her car's tires crunched on the driveway, Charlotte rushed out onto the veranda with hope bright on her face. It faded as soon as Georgie stepped out of the car alone. Resigned sadness—the type of despondency people could more easily accept in their older relatives—settled over her, slumping her shoulders and pulling down her lips.

Georgie fought back tears for them all. For Charlotte, who craved her mother's approval and support. For Harriet, who was pushing her daughter away and risking a rift that could deepen into something permanent. For herself; Charlotte had the chance at motherhood Georgie coveted more than anything. Accepting that was proving very difficult. The constant ache inside her twisted cruelly, but with fortitude she wasn't aware dwelled in her, she pushed her grief aside, buried her jealousy and hugged her niece.

"It's early days, honey. She's still in shock."

"But you know what she's like," Charlotte said wearily. "It's easier to reverse the spin of the earth's rotation than change her mind. Dad's betrayed her and now she thinks I have too. I've let her down."

"Hey." Georgie held Charlotte's shoulders firmly gave her a little shake. "Even when things are going well, Harry makes it hard for us mere mortals not to let her down. Right now she's upset. She's not seeing things as clearly as she might, but that's her problem. It's not yours. The best thing you can do is honor your decision and prove to her that you're in charge of your own life."

Charlotte chewed at her lip, her face dubious. "God, what's happened to my parents? They're supposed to be the adults but they're so screwed up. Dad's been calling and texting for days. He wants to see me tomorrow, but I don't know if I want to see him. Every time I think about what he's done to all those people, I hate him for it. Just when I'm sure I hate him, I remember all the awesome things he's done for me and that reminds me how much I love him." Her voice cracked. "Then I hate him all over again for wrecking everything."

Georgie ached for her niece. "All those feelings are normal, Charlie. Your father's betrayed more than just the people he stole money from. He's betrayed the people who love him. You, your mom, Xara and Steve—all of us."

"I'm going to have to tell him about the baby soon though, right? I mean, I told Mom so it's only fair I tell him too?"

Georgie wasn't sure "fair" extended to a man who'd ripped off hard-working people and in the process, destroyed his family. "Do you trust him?"

"Yes. No. I want to." Charlie wrung her hands. "Crap! I don't know anything anymore. I don't trust either of them."

No matter how stark the truth was, Georgie decided to tell it. She knew if Harriet said what she was about to say, Charlotte would refuse to believe it so she crossed her fingers hoping her niece would take it on board from her. "You know your mom's worried James wants to use you to improve his image? Well, he might say stuff about the baby that you want to hear just to get back at Harriet.

"Please know that no matter what he says, no matter what he offers you, he probably doesn't have any money. Xara says that the amount of money he's stolen means it's almost certain he's going to jail. If he promises you things for when the baby's born, know that he probably won't be around to fulfill them. I know it's hard to understand and accept but no matter how much you want to, you can't rely on him."

Charlotte's eyes widened into shimmering blue pools that glistened with a film of tears. "All of this sucks."

"It does, but it's time to be honest with yourself. You know that if you'd told your parents you were pregnant before James blew everything up, neither of them would be thrilled about this baby."

"Yes, but Daddy would have worked on Mom."

Georgie tried not to sigh at the fantasy Charlotte had woven in her head to bolster her decision. "No. He wouldn't have done that. Status is important to James. He was running for party nomination and political parties like their candidates to have squeaky-clean families. With or without your father committing these crimes, I'm pretty sure that you'd have ended up out of home and here at Glenora with Mardi."

Charlotte bit her lip. "She's been amazing."

"Yeah," Georgie said with a half laugh, half sigh. "And we've got no idea why, so accept it as the gift it truly is." Shadows flitted across Charlotte's face as she pulled open the wooden Victorian screen door.

"Tell you what," Georgie added, "I'll make popcorn and you and Mardi choose a movie."

The three of them had sat on the big old leather couch with covers on their knees and Tsar snuggled up on Charlotte's lap. Georgie had given thanks for her mother's choice of movie—one that had required little concentration and even less thought. Given how much her mind was spinning, that had been a blessing.

After saying goodnight and when the sounds of doors closing and water pipes rumbling had faded to silence, Georgie called Ben before meeting him at Glenora's gates.

"Hey."

"Hey." He pulled her into his arms and kissed her hello until her knees softened, the world had slowed, and every sense heightened, bringing with it an indefinable feeling that hovered outside the very definable lust she had for this man. She caught his buoyant smile in the moonlight, absorbed the solid strength of him pressed up against her, breathed in his scent of fresh cologne with a slight tang of sweat, and savored his fresh minty taste. He'd obviously cleaned his teeth just before he'd left the motel and she gave him points for consideration.

"Come on." She grabbed his hand.

"Where?"

He was the first man she'd ever snuck into her room. Not that she'd ever sneaked a boy in, although perhaps she should have as it turned out that her old bedroom window was conveniently large. Ben's long legs were made for clambering over the wide sandstone sill, and he did it with ease until he forgot to duck and banged his head on the window sash.

"Aren't we too old for all this sneaking about?" He rubbed his scalp.

"Sorry. It's just with everything going on ..."

"It's okay." He wrapped his arms around her and she'd leaned into him in a way that was fast becoming normal. "I'd rather meet your family at a time when they're not wondering what the hell is going to happen next."

"Only good things are going to happen next," she said firmly, winding her fingers into his curls, locating the bump on his head. "I can get you an icepack for this mini Easter egg. Might make it feel better."

He shook his head and the pale shaft of moonlight illuminated a wicked twinkle in his dark caramel eyes. "I know another way to make it feel better."

Her body leaped, blood pulsing, muscles twitching and excitement throbbing intoxicatingly through her before settling deep down with a pull as strong as the tide. She'd linked her fingers at the back of his neck and pulled his face closer.

"Do you now?"

"I do."

Without taking his gaze off her face, he walked her backwards until the edge of the single mattress hit the back of her knees. She let herself fall, taking him with her, and they went down in a tangle of limbs and clothes. Stifling giggles, they pulled and pushed at each other's garments, kicked off shoes and peeled off socks until skin touched glorious skin. She sighed as his warmth infused her and for a moment, amid the freneticism that pulsed between them, fueled by a week of longing, she was filled with a sense of belonging with this man. It buoyed her and scared her in equal measure.

She gripped his face and kissed him hard, driving out the hopes and fears and concentrating on the here and now. On him. His body. On not making any noise and on the precarious balancing act of sex in a single bed.

"Shh." Georgie pressed two fingers to Ben's lips, feeling the laughter shaking his body vibrating into her own.

There was barely enough room to breathe or wriggle a big toe, but she didn't care. She was flying high on the wonder of it all. She'd never had a secret lover and as she snuggled into his arms, she decided everyone should have the opportunity at least once in their life just for the sheer thrill of it.

"This is crazy," he whispered, kissing her nose. "Amazing but crazy."

Her cheeks ached from smiling so widely but she was powerless to stop her almost permanent grin. "There's definitely something erotic about having to keep quiet."

He raised a brow. "That's one word for the bite mark on my hand."

"Sorry." She flicked out her tongue and licked the dented skin, tasting salt and sweat.

He tensed and she felt him harden against her thigh. A banner of joy unfurled inside her and she gloried in it. It had been a very long time since she'd believed in her allure and power as a woman. When her body had failed Eliza—and by default herself—she'd lost faith in it.

She'd hated it; hated the red-raw slash above her pubic bone and the pink stretch marks on her breasts that falsely claimed she'd suckled and nurtured a baby. She loathed the emptiness of her uterus that echoed loudly around her body, never letting her forget what she'd lost. Who she'd let down so badly.

During the death throes of her relationship with Jason she'd felt like an empty vessel unable to give and too numb to receive. During sex she'd feel Jason inside her, feel his sweat against her skin and hear the panting of his breath in her ear, but she was absent. Her thoughts were with her baby girl; instead of holding her close to her chest where she belonged, she'd had to bury her. Georgie's lack of response during sex had precipitated the end. Jason had needed sex to feel close to her again; she'd needed his love and understanding. For months after they'd separated she hadn't missed sex. She hadn't even thought about it but more recently, every now and then, she'd notice the occasional flicker of sensation whenever she was watching a love scene in a movie. When Ben had flirted with her at school it was like he'd flicked a switch on her libido.

He trailed a finger lazily between her breasts and she shivered at the delicious swoop of sensation. He circled her belly button twice and then with a sweeping zigzag motion, he crossed her belly until the pad of his finger traced the length of her scar.

She involuntarily tensed, the action so sharp it jerked her body against his.

He whipped his hand away. "Sorry. Did that hurt?"

She shook her head.

He gazed down at her. "It's a long scar. What happened?"

Her throat tightened. The first time they'd had sex she'd been on edge, expecting him to ask about the scar. He hadn't said a word. Nor had he mentioned it the second or the third time. Confident he wasn't going to ask, she'd let down her guard. Now, all snuggled up in her cocoon of bliss and totally unprepared, the question hit her like a sniper's bullet. It tore through her, ripping, burning, brutal.

She raised her hand to a faint, white scar that ran across the top of his eyebrow. "What happened here?"

"One of my sisters dropped me on my head when I was three."

"That explains a lot."

"You're a comedian too? Who knew?" The light caught his impish grin. "Apparently there was blood everywhere and I was rushed to the hospital. I needed eight stitches. Mom always said Josie was more traumatized by it than I was. Big sis has spent thirty years vowing it was an accident but I'm not so sure. I mean, with these curls, I was pretty damn cute as kid. And what with being the long awaited son and all, I guess her jealousy was just too much."

"Hang on." She tapped his chest with her fingers. "I thought you said you were an accident." *Like me.*

"I don't recall my parents ever telling me I was an accident or a mistake. I mean, look at me ..." He winked and gave her a double thumbs-up. "I have three older sisters and I'm the only son of an Italian mother. In a lot of ways I'm the epitome of the indulged youngest child."

"I'm learning all sorts of things about you tonight, including that modesty is one of your character strengths."

He laughed, the sound deep and enticing. She basked in it but shushed him all the same. The walls of Glenora were thick but Charlotte's room was close and she really didn't want to have to deal with being discovered with a man in her bed.

He looked at her expectantly and tucked loose strands of hair behind her ear. "I've told you my war story so now you have to tell me yours."

Her stomach lurched. She'd hoped her teasing would have distracted him from her scar. She'd have to try something else so she defaulted to deflection, aiming for every guy's Achilles heel. Drawing on years of experience with men, she knew exactly how to end the conversation quickly and cleanly. She quietly cleared her throat.

"Women's business."

He didn't even blink. "Endometriosis? Ovarian cysts?"

Stunned, she stared at him. "Who are you?"

"I've got sisters. I hear things." He gave a mock shudder. "I get told things."

She giggled softly and then turned her head, pressing a kiss to his chest and flicking his nipple with her tongue. In the past when she'd done that he'd forgotten everything except the fact that he wanted her.

He let out a puff of air—the soft sigh of a moan—and then he pressed a kiss into her hair. "People who are getting to know one another generally share information about themselves."

At his slightly censuring tone she pulled her tongue back into her mouth and dragged in a deep breath. "I thought we're having fun."

He frowned. "I thought we were dating."

"We are. The two aren't mutually exclusive, are they?" Her voice betrayed her by ending on a rising inflection. *Damn it.*

He was still for a moment, those dark eyes of his illuminated by the churning cogs of his brain. "Don't get me wrong. I'm all for some fun but I've been there and done that. I'm not twenty-five anymore, Georgie. I'm here for more than just sex."

His words should have made her deliciously happy. Wasn't that what every single woman in her thirties wanted to hear? A seemingly normal guy looking to commit? "It's still early days."

"So? Have you got some sort of information-release system?" For the first time in all their conversations, she heard irritation weaving into his voice. "A mathematically predetermined date circled on the calendar for disclosures? X number of days or weeks have to pass before you'll tell me?"

Oh God. Was he inside her head?

His usual laid back demeanor had vanished. "If you won't tell me about some surgery now, exactly how far in do you mention the big things like a criminal record?"

"I don't have a criminal record." She shoot for a light and breezy tone despite feeling hammered by his question. "Although I did get pulled over once for speeding." She sat up, needing some space but instantly missed his heat as the chilly night air swept in over her Ben-warmed skin.

"Georgie ..." His hand lightly touched her back.

Ignoring the plea in his voice, she pulled away and clambered across him. She swung her legs over the edge of the bed, feeling the smooth and familiar boards under her feet. As she bent down and picked up her pajama pants, she noticed her hand was trembling.

"I've upset you." He sounded sad and he sat up and placed his feet on the floor, the sheet spilling across his lap. "I'd apologize but I can't do that until I understand why I've upset you."

She picked up his shirt; the one she'd popped a button off earlier when she'd been desperate to lay her palms against his broad chest and feel the play of muscles under her fingers. She went to hand it to him as a hint it was time for him to leave but instead of passing it over, she found herself staring at it.

Moonlight turned its color to sepia and her thoughts lurched this way and that. If Ben left with his question unanswered, she doubted he'd let it slide away quietly. No, it would sit between them, large, imposing and with sharp corners, demanding an answer the next time they met. It meant they'd never reach her imagined point of her being ready to tell him what had happened or him being ready to hear it.

Truth was, she was never ready to talk about Eliza, so why did she think she'd be happy to do it in a week's or a month's time? Still holding his shirt, her gaze slid to her toes. Her thoughts rolled back to the time her toes had peeked out from under Ben's sweatpants when he'd lent her his clothes after the rain had drowned her. The evening she'd had her suspicions confirmed that he was kind, funny and sexy as hell.

Was she really going to walk away from him because he was asking her a question she didn't want to answer? Walk away to avoid telling a story that was part of who she was? Walk before she'd worked out if this thing between them was more than just lust and given it a chance to grow? Given *him* a chance?

"That time I got pulled over for speeding ..." she glanced sideways at him from under her hair, "I was driving myself to hospital."

He didn't say a word, but he laced his fingers into hers as if he sensed the story was big and she needed his support. She dropped her eyes back to her toes and idly thought she should paint tiny eggs on them for tomorrow. *Today*. Tasha would get a kick out of it.

"That scar's my permanent reminder that I was once a mother for three hours."

"Oh, fuck." Horror and embarrassment wove themselves into his voice and she glanced up as he added, "God. Georgie. I'm sorry." Stricken, he dragged his free hand through his hair before dropping it to her cheek. "When did this happen?"

"Some days it feels like yesterday. Other days it's like I dreamed it." She saw the lines creasing his forehead and remembered he was a guy and they needed real dates. "It will be two years this July."

He nodded slowly as if he was processing all the information. "Did you have a son or a daughter?"

Her heart rolled not so much in grief for Eliza but in appreciation that he'd thought to ask. Most people didn't. Most people got so embarrassed when they discovered her child had died they immediately shifted the conversation to something trite and inane. But happy; always happy. Generally, the only people who inquired about her baby were other grieving parents, which was why she'd found the bereavement support group so helpful.

"I had a little girl. Eliza Jane. She was born at twenty-six weeks because—" She stopped. She wasn't at a support group meeting now. "It doesn't matter."

"You can tell me if you want to." His thumb stroked her cheek and his mouth tweaked up. "You won't freak me out. Remember, I've got sisters who tell me stuff."

A laugh bubbled up from nowhere and then she was leaning into him like he was a quiet cove on a dark and stormy sea. He wrapped his arms around her and together they fell back on the bed, only this time it was nothing to do with sex and everything to do with comfort. She told him about the undiagnosed placenta previa, the terrifying and soaking amounts of blood, the emergency caesarean section and waking up to a baby who was so tiny she was scared to hold her in case she crushed her. When the inevitable tears rolled down her face, Ben didn't say anything, just wiped them away with the sheet.

An owl hooted, the sound loud and spine chilling in the quiet room. "Did you do all this on your own?" Ben asked.

"I didn't think I was, but it turned out that way."

"Shit. Sorry. Again." He sighed. "Is the father why you didn't want to tell me?"

"No, not at all." That was an easy question to answer. "Talking about Jason doesn't upset me. After Eliza ... We wanted different things."

It was very important to clarify so the truth wasn't hidden. "Actually, it turns out we'd always wanted different things, but I'd convinced myself otherwise. Eliza's birth and death shone a bright light on the fact I'd been deluding myself for a long time. It forced us to be honest. I wanted children. He didn't. The end of our five years together was quietly unremarkable and far less devastating to me than losing my baby."

She splayed her fingers on his chest, watching the shadows flitting between them. "And that's my pathetic story."

"It's not pathetic," he said quietly but firmly.

"Well, it's not exactly inspiring. I attached myself to a guy for years in the hope he'd change his mind about parenthood."

"It's no less inspiring than being dumped because you're boring."

Surprised, she pulled back to bring his face into focus. "Someone thought you were boring?"

"Pretty unbelievable, eh?" He smiled that mischievous smile of his, the one that made her feel like she'd forgive him anything. "But sadly true." He shrugged, his face unperturbed. "You learn from your mistakes, right? And Ashley's bald words taught me something. I've stopped dating student teachers and anyone under twenty-six."

"Phew. Lucky for me I just snuck in under the wire then."

He laughed softly, his hand stroking her hair. "What was that you were saying about not deluding yourself anymore?"

She knew he was teasing her, but the words prickled and scratched. She was thirty-four and Ben was right, her timeline theory was stupid. It was getting in the way of what she wanted in her life. On paper, the sum of their relationship was half a dozen one-on-one meetings—probably nowhere near enough to have reached that mythical place magazine advice columnists talked about. But how long did she wait? How much time did she waste before she discovered his life plans didn't remotely match up with hers? This wasn't like asking him the big question on a first date; they'd gone way past that now. If it freaked him out, wasn't it better to know sooner rather than later?

She trashed her timeline theory. "Ben, do you see kids in your future?"

"I'm a teacher, Georgie. Kids are my here and now."

"Ha, ha." She dug him in the ribs. "I'm being serious. I don't want to waste any more time deluding myself. You just shredded my dumb timeline theory on what and when things can be asked and shared so ..." Her heart rate picked up and words stuck to the roof of her mouth like marshmallows.

His dark eyes watched her carefully. "Yes?"

"Is having kids one day something you want?"

His lips curved in a sheepish smile. "It's why I was called boring."

Hope soared. "So if you met the right person?"

His finger drew soft circles on her shoulder. "I'd want to do the whole boring gig of getting married, having kids and coaching the local soccer team."

Her heart seemed to be pounding in her throat. "That sounds like a good life. I hope you find her."

"I do too. I've got a feeling I'm a lot closer to finding her than I've ever been before."

She wanted to squeal and whoop but she couldn't make any noise and risk waking Charlotte and Edwina. Instead, she smiled and as she did, something close to peace stole into her. Peace and relief. Now they could relax and explore this wonderful thing that sparked between them. They could open themselves up to all that it offered and see where it took them, knowing they wanted the same things out of life.

"What time can we head back to Melbourne tomorrow?" Ben asked before amending, "Actually, it's today."

"Ah ..."

He frowned. "Please tell me you're coming back to Melbourne with me so we can have our week together?"

She snagged her bottom lip. "I want to, Ben. I really do, but I think I need to stay here. Charlie's pretty vulnerable right now and Harry ..." God, how did she even try to explain Harriet?

"Can we compromise." He said it in the tone of a statement rather than a question. "How about we drive back to Melbourne as planned but you come back here on Thursday? That means we have three days together without the distraction of family and you get to see how everyone down here copes without you. It still gives you another few days with them before you have to go back to work. You'd have time to set up anything that needs doing."

Thoughts and ideas jostled in her head as she silently considered his suggestions.

"What?" he said after a long silence. "Bad idea?"

"No. It's just I'm not used to the radical concept of compromise. Jason wasn't big on it."

He grinned at her, looking as pleased as if he'd just won the competition against the other guy. "So?"

"I think it's a great idea, but I can't leave until four. Today's Easter lunch and it's always a bit of a big deal." *This year it's going to be big in a whole new way.*

"Fair enough. I'll be a good son and do something with Dad. I'm pretty sure he's not heading home until Monday. I'll be ready at four."

"Thank you." She gave him an appreciative kiss. "I'm hoping we might both be at Easter lunch next year."

"Sounds good to me." He ran his fingers up and down her spine. "So exactly how long have I got before you kick me out of this bed?"

She walked her fingers down his chest. "Long enough."

"Good to know."

He tucked her under him and proceeded to use the time very wisely.

CHAPTER SEVENTEEN

WITH THE EXCEPTION OF HER TWO YEARS LIVING AND WORKING in London, Harriet had always spent Easter Sunday at Glenora. Today she was breaking that tradition and she was fine with it. After all, why spend time with people who undermined her and caused her grief?

She'd been called into the hospital at two in the morning to operate on a woman with a lacerated liver courtesy of a drunk driver slamming into her. Despite the tense situation when the woman had almost bled out on the table, there'd been a peace in the utter concentration required by the surgery. The chaos in Harriet's life had blessedly receded, pushed back by the need to focus on finding the damaged vessels. One woman's trauma was Harriet's mental health break and that would be laughable if it weren't so tragic. She'd left the hospital at four, slept a few hours, then gone for a run across the Stony Rises.

Now her gaze slid from her recently returned computer to the wicker Easter basket. Georgie had brought it over when she'd invited her yet again to come to lunch. The basket overflowed with fresh flowers from Glenora's garden, packets of Harriet's preferred coffee, a book she'd expressed an interest in reading and some of Georgie's handmade chocolates along with a chocolate bunny. It was a thoughtful gesture but that was Georgie: she knew how much Harriet liked to mark family occasions. Now the basket hovered like fog, hiding the jagged rocks that lay beyond it.

As a child, Easter Sunday had been a happily anticipated day and there'd always been an Easter egg hunt. Harriet still stored a vivid memory from the Easter when she was four years old and the awe she'd experienced on finding huge rabbit paw prints on the paths that wound through what she'd considered back then to be her magic garden. Long after she'd worked out that the Easter Bunny wasn't real, the paw prints still made their annual appearance, only stopping when Georgie turned thirteen.

When Charlotte was a tot, the paw prints had again returned to Glenora and that was when Harriet discovered her father was the artist. It had made sense to her adult self, because drawing paw prints wasn't the sort of thing Edwina would do. Edwina hadn't been the fun parent—she'd been the passive parent. Always. Well, up until now. Why the bloody hell had Edwina chosen this week to have opinions?

Oh, Dad.

Harriet rubbed her temples, missing her father more than ever. If he were alive, he'd have taken charge like he'd always done and her mother wouldn't be aiding and abetting Charlotte in exchanging a good life for one of hardship and lost opportunities. But he wasn't here and she wasn't at Glenora, and everything in her life had gone to hell in a hand basket.

She had an irrational desire to go back to being that little girl who, when she slid her hand into her father's large warm palm, felt invincible. When she was growing up, her father had always been the one more likely to put down whatever he was doing and join her and her sisters in an activity. She couldn't think of any times her mother had done the same thing.

Yet since Edwina had become a grandmother, she did have moments when she played. Once when Charlotte was seven, Harriet had come home early from work to find Edwina dressed up in a hat and an old ball gown, drinking tea at the plastic play table. She'd been so surprised by the sight that she'd taken a photo. Charlotte still had it pinned on the cork board in her room.

Edwina was in many ways a far better grandmother than she'd ever been a mother, but Harriet's friends said the same things about their parents. Once, after a few wines, Jenny had told her that the relaxed version of Primrose who'd always surfaced at the family's annual Warrnambool beach vacation and who'd always vanished once they were back on the farm, was permanently present in Grandmother Primrose. Harriet often envied the relationship Jenny had with Primrose but never the one she had with David.

Up until five years ago, Harriet often commented how she and Jenny shared diagonally opposite relationships with their parents. Things had changed when Jenny took a trip with David to Vietnam. Jenny said the vacation had made a huge difference to their relationship and she now understood her father better. Harriet only understood Edwina enough to know that despite sharing some DNA, they had nothing else in common. She didn't want to admit that she envied the easy relationship Charlotte and her nephews shared with Edwina.

Last Easter, the first one without her father, Harriet had offered to organize the hunt, but Edwina had thanked her and declined Harriet's help—she had it all under control. Growing up, Harriet had always assumed her mother had been too busy playing hostess at Easter to join in the hunt. Only when she matched up Harriet's actions to the behavior of her maternal grandparents, had she wondered if the Easter egg hunt had been a Chirnwell tradition her father had brought into the family.

Although her Mannering grandfather and uncles played cricket at family gatherings, they'd never joined in the egg hunt, preferring instead to observe from the veranda with a drink in hand. It was only when Richard had declared all the eggs collected that her Mannering grandfather would become involved, meeting her at the top of the steps and insisting on helping her count her stash. Each year he'd advise her to eat one or two and save the rest for later.

She'd taken him on his word and in later years when her younger sisters were older, his advice had proved salient: Xara and Georgie always scarfed down their eggs on the day and her saved ones become good earners for her when they wanted more. With her supply in high demand, she'd been able to up her price and trade them for coins and other things she'd wanted—it had been her first lesson in market economy. Her grandfather had also told her that winners were grinners, money made money and if she wanted to be a true Mannering, she had to know how to make money.

Harriet slammed her laptop shut, closing out the stark and relentless view of her seriously depleted financial status. Not only had James stolen hundreds of thousands of dollars from her and others, in the process he'd seriously damaged her ability to earn money. Debbie had carefully outlined the situation to her on Wednesday without sugar coating a thing.

Taking the practice into the twenty-first century had been necessary but it also meant it was heavily leveraged. This hadn't been a problem when she had a large volume of private patients coming through the door. Now those numbers had diminished drastically, and if it continued, her earning capacity would barely cover her payroll and running costs.

She fingered the letter from the bank that was addressed to Mr. James Minchin and Ms. Harriet Chirnwell. It outlined how two payments on Miligili's mortgage had been missed and it stated the *urgent need* for them to contact the bank as soon as possible. "I didn't miss them. He did!" she yelled at the letter as if saying it out loud could actually change something.

The fact that her share of the payments had vanished from her account each month meant nothing when it hadn't been used to pay the mortgage. Pushing back her chair, she walked to the front door of the guesthouse, opened it and stood looking at her beloved home; a house she hadn't stepped inside in a week. A house that rat bastard was still living in.

Miligili was so much more to her than just a house—it was her heritage, a piece of Mannering history, and she loved it dearly. It was also the biggest asset she shared with James. Going by the emails and the verbal abuse from the community she'd suffered this week, the people he'd stolen money from would force it to be sold so they could seize his share of the profits. James had already taken so much from her she wasn't going to allow his actions to cost her the house as well.

Rolling a plan around in her mind, she pushed off the door frame and marched toward Miligili. She'd do whatever it took to keep it safe. Jogging up the steps, she hesitated for a moment, wondering if she should knock. *Hell no.* She tugged hard on the fly wire door and walked into the laundry, stepping over a pile of dirty clothes as she entered the kitchen. As she took in the unholy mess—plates with remnants of dried food lay scattered across the counter and in the sink, the trash can overflowed with detritus and the fetid stench of rotting food wafted from it—she felt the sharp pain of an arrow pierce her heart. Her beloved house had never looked so unkempt and uncared for under her watch.

She pushed open the kitchen door and walked into the large living space, calling out, "James?" There was no reply so she walked farther into the house, but after exploring all the rooms and drawing a blank she checked the garage. It was empty. Tracking back through the l'Orangerie, she noticed scissors and wrapping paper abandoned on the rectangular marble table and the remnants of ribbon that had drifted to the floor. She automatically stooped to pick up the gold material and while she was down there she discovered a bag and a receipt for Charlotte's favorite chocolates.

Her plans evaporated. She'd bet James's last dollar he was at Glenora. The fact that he hadn't called her or visited was a pretty fair indication he was yet to be told about the pregnancy. If he visited Glenora today all that would change. Once she'd have been confident of James's reaction to the news but not now.

Nothing about him was familiar; it was like he'd undergone a personality change. He, on the other hand, would know exactly how she felt about their daughter being pregnant at seventeen. Would he use it against her by siding with Charlotte? Offer her pipe dreams as a base on which she could continue to construct her fantasies? It was bad enough that Edwina and her sisters were supporting Charlotte without adding James.

She shuddered. Surely her family wouldn't welcome James at Glenora. No. They wouldn't. Suspicion crept in, gnawing at her convictions. There was the knotty issue of her screaming at Edwina that she wished she'd been the parent to die. It was unlikely that had helped keep Edwina on her team.

On the other hand, Steve wouldn't tolerate James after he'd stolen the respite-care house grant money, but her brother-in-law was one of life's nice guys. Even if he objected strongly to James being at Glenora, he was a guest in his mother-in-law's home; his only protest would be to leave the house while James was inside it. Edwina, irrespective of how she felt about Harriet, was just as likely to invite James in because he was Charlotte's father.

A picture of James—all charm and contrition—sitting down and ingratiating himself with her sisters slapped her hard followed by an equally disturbing image of her sisters happily chatting with that Doug person. It was too much. If she stayed away from lunch she had no control over what happened with James or the untenable situation with that man. No control over anything. One thing this fraught week had taught her was she was utterly over having no control.

Right then. It looks like I'm going to lunch.

Her mother had taught her that a guest never arrived empty-handed so she carefully negotiated the old stone stairs worn smooth by generations of Mannerings. Making her way into the cool, dark cellar, she smiled as she carefully selected a bottle of her father's favorite cabernet sauvignon. It was a wine that would perfectly match the lamb she knew was being served at lunch. It was a wine she knew Edwina disliked and never drank.

"Doug cut off his finger," Hugh announced importantly to Xara and Steve.

"Oh God! And Harry's not here." Xara dived across her mother's kitchen to reach the cabinet where the first aid kit was stored.

Steve frantically pulled open the freezer, grabbing ice cubes for the severed finger. "How the hell did he do that?"

"Like this." Hugh bent his left index finger, tucking it around his thumb, which was resting across his palm. He then crooked his right thumb and wriggled it around. His little face creased in concentration as he stared hard at his hands. "Aww, I forget. Wait here. I'll come back and show you." He ran outside.

Xara slumped against the counter, her hand over her racing heart. "That kid's going to kill me."

Steve laughed, returning the ice to the freezer. "Doug's a hit with the kids. I guess that's one hurdle jumped."

Xara gloved her hand with an oven mitt and checked the roasting vegetables. "He's a good bloke."

"He is. So why not say it like you mean it?"

"I do mean it." She sighed as she closed the oven door. "It's just ... Don't you find it odd seeing Mom all starry-eyed like that?"

"Yeah. It takes a bit of getting used to but good for her."

"Yes, but ..."

"What?" He raised his brows as he handed her a glass of champagne. "Aren't you happy she's happy?"

"Of course I'm happy she's happy." She took a sip, savoring the fizz of bubbles on her tongue and the unexpected zip of lemongrass.

"But?" Steve pressed.

She wrinkled her nose. This man she loved knew her too well and he wasn't going to let her get away with anything. "I'm sad because seeing her like this means she's obviously been unhappy for years. It means that her life with Dad was ..." She'd been about to say miserable, but she had no idea if miserable was the right word. Truth be told, like most children, she'd never given much thought to her parents' marriage.

"God. What if all those periods of her being sad weren't a legacy from her postnatal depression after Georgie? What if she was miserable all her married life? And if she was, well ... that's just awful. And Dad? Poor Dad. Did he know Mom had loved Doug? And if she loved him, why did she marry Dad? I've got all these questions and they won't stop going around in my head."

"Complicated things, relationships. Once you start thinking about other people's it makes you think about your own." He kissed her. "Are you happy?"

She leaned her forehead against his. "A few weeks ago I would have told you I wanted a disposable income like Harry's. Considering everything that's gone down this week, I'm thinking you, me, the kids and the sheep, we're not doing too badly."

He pulled back and looked at her, his usually calm green eyes swirling with indecipherable emotions. "You didn't answer the question. Are you happy?"

It was a complicated question and the answer was tricky and she didn't want to brush him off with *Sure, of course.* "What's happy? It changes on an hourly basis. I'm sad Tashie's no longer able to enjoy the taste of Easter chocolate. I'm happy the boys are high on the stuff and that Doug's teaching them tricks. I'm furious that because of James, we're back to raising money again for the respite-care house. I miss not working as an attorney, but I love spearheading the special-needs advocacy group. Mostly I love my jobs on the farm and farm life although I could live without the unpredictability of the weather."

She cupped his cheek. "Happy, sad, miserable, jealous, excited or tired, one thing doesn't change, Steven Paxton. I never want my life without you in it."

Something close to relief skittered across his face. "Guess it's settled then. You have to die first."

She gave him a gentle shove as the wireless meat thermometer beeped. "The lamb's ready. Bring it inside and turn off the barbecue."

"Slave driver." Not moving, he grinned at her. Then he leaned down and kissed her as if they were in the first weeks of a new relationship instead of one and a half decades down the track.

They heard a woman clearing her throat and raised their heads to find Edwina standing on the other side of the counter.

"Are you sure you two don't need any help?"

"We've got the roast covered, Edwina." Steve patted Xara on the behind as he strode toward the door.

Xara's cheeks burned and she was embarrassed being caught in a clinch by her mother and cross with herself for feeling that way. "Dessert's your domain, Mom."

"Yes, I'm aware of that and I've got—"

"Oh, good. I'm not late."

They swung around to find Harriet crossing the sunroom and holding a bottle of wine. She was exquisitely dressed as usual, but there was a brittle quality to her. It made Xara feel both guilty and grateful that her own life wasn't quite as much in the toilet as her sister's.

"Harry! You're here. That's great."

Her older sister's chin shot up. Given that the last time she'd spoken to their mother had been brutal, she was probably steeling herself. She extended her arm. "Edwina, I brought you some wine."

"Thank you." Edwina accepted the proffered bottle with a smile that combined hesitancy and relief. She glanced briefly at the label before setting it down on the counter.

Xara noticed it was red wine and her heart sank. Not only did their mother not drink red wine, this particular bottle was one of their father's favorites. Nothing about the gift was a peace offering; it was all about firing another salvo at Edwina.

Oh, Harry. Today's not the day to bring Dad along.

"Doug's quite partial to a bold cab sav," Edwina said smoothly. "We'll offer it at lunch."

Thwarted, Harriet glared at her mother but said nothing. It was checkmate. It was a well-known fact that once the gift had been given, the giver lost all rights to it. Edwina had just turned the tables on her ungracious daughter. Xara sighed. Everyone thought Harriet was more like their father, but she shared enough of the less endearing qualities of their mother to clash with her. When pushed, Edwina could win Olympic gold in the viciously polite event.

"Has James been here?" Harriet asked, ignoring the atmosphere that vibrated between her and her mother.

"He called in earlier." Edwina inclined her head toward a rectangular gift on the sideboard. "He didn't cross the threshold and all of us stood with Charlie for the full five minutes he was here."

"Not me." Steve returned with the leg of lamb and plunged the carving fork deep into the meat. "The only time I want to be in the same space as that prick is in court."

Xara threw him a shut-up-now look.

Edwina continued as if she hadn't been interrupted. "Charlie didn't tell him her news. I think she's waiting for things to improve between the two of you before she says anything."

Thank Mom for protecting Charlie, Xara willed Harriet.

Harriet's lips thinned. "If she goes ahead with this pregnancy she's going to be waiting a very long time."

So much for ESP.

Harriet readjusted the gold chain of her handbag on her shoulder. "Well, Edwina, I suppose you'd better introduce me to this Doug friend of yours before we sit down for lunch."

"He's out in the garden. The twins have put him into service as their entertainment. He's coping admirably."

As her mother and sister walked outside, Steve tilted his head toward the plate-warming drawer. "I thought the last time Harry was here she told Edwina she wished her dead."

Xara set the hot plates on the island counter. "She did."

"Given that went down, they sound pretty cordial now."

"Oh, Steve." She flicked him with a tea towel. "You poor deluded man. It always sounds civil between Harriet and Mom, but it never is."

CHAPTER EIGHTEEN

SITTING UNDER THE ARBOR, WHICH NOW SHIMMERED WITH vibrant vermillion and vivid orange courtesy of the grapevine's autumnal leaves, Edwina scanned the long dining table. At noon it had been pristine, covered by a white cloth and decorated with evenly spaced vases of flowers. A chocolate Easter bunny, wrapped in gold foil and with a red ribbon and tiny gold bell around its neck, had sat by each place setting. Now, with the meal complete, everyone was sitting back full of food and the table was littered with both scrunched balls and smooth rectangles of colored Easter egg foil. The remains of a large Pavlova heavily weighted with strawberries and cream was in the middle of the table and the silver server was buried deep in its fluffy meringue. She smiled as Doug helped himself to a second slice.

Over the last two weeks—first with Doug and then with her house unexpectedly full of daughters—she'd been reminded of the joy she experienced cooking for others. She hadn't done a lot of cooking since Richard's death because it was hard to muster the enthusiasm to cook for one. Their marriage had been far from perfect and certainly faults lay on both sides, but food had been one area they'd gotten right. She'd always cooked for Richard with consideration and he'd always appreciated the meals she'd prepared. Now, watching Doug eat, she felt an inordinate amount of pleasure warming her. She'd lost him for so many years, yet here he was at her table and meeting her family.

Her mouth suddenly dried at the thought of the task they were yet to undertake. She took a large sip of water as Friday's conversation rushed her as it had done for the last two days. When it happened, it consumed her: the memory as real as the original conversation and the emotions as intense. She didn't fight it. She allowed herself to be pulled back to the lake, smelling the scent of pine and hearing the sound of Doug's life-changing question.

"What do you mean you couldn't get to a mailbox?"

Her heart jumped and she kept her eyes fixed on the pelican to stop herself from falling apart. Who'd have thought that, after all the intervening decades, telling him would be so difficult?

"Do you remember on our last night in the old Ford I told you I was going up to Melbourne to visit a friend from school?"

"I remember the trip but not the name of the friend."

"It was Patricia Templeton, but visiting her wasn't the real reason for the visit. I'd made an appointment to see a doctor to have some tests." She finally turned her head to look at him. "The rabbit died, Doug. He confirmed my suspicions that I was pregnant."

"Jesus, Eddy." He stared at her, dark eyes wide with shock and his mouth slack jawed. "You never even hinted."

She gave a slow, regretful shrug. "I wanted to be absolutely certain before I said anything to you. The moment I got the news I cut short my trip and spent the train journey to Billawarre working out how I was going to tell you. Planning the exact words I was going to say. When I got home, you were gone."

She scooped up a handful of pine needles, watching them fall from her palm. "I reassured myself you'd taken some time off and you'd be back on Sunday, the day I'd told you I'd be home. When you didn't arrive, I went and spoke to the other hands. That's when they told me you'd gone to Puckapunyal."

Her spine stiffened as though the news was fresh and she was once again living those long and apprehensive days. "I won't lie and tell you I wasn't furious at you for leaving without telling me. I was so angry I could barely see straight, but it never crossed my mind that you wouldn't write to me. Or call. Or visit.

"While I waited for you to contact me, I distracted myself by planning everything in my innocent and inexperienced head. I reasoned that although my parents wouldn't be thrilled at the news, the fact you had a reliable army income meant they'd give their begrudging permission. We'd get married at the end of your basic training."

"I'd have been on-board with that," he offered up earnestly. The look in his eyes begged her to believe him.

"I thought so too, only that naive plan went up in flames three weeks later when my mother found me vomiting behind the hydrangeas. That was when, as they say in the classics, the shit well and truly hit the fan." She gave him a faint smile.

"Flaming hell, Eddy." He touched her then, picking up her hand and encasing it in his beefier one.

She tilted her chin, trying to stay strong and stave off the battering ram of tumultuous emotions. Emotions she knew all too well held the power to render her inert for hours, days, weeks at a time. "Apparently, an unmarried pregnant daughter was far more scandalous and damaging to my father's political career than his hushed-up affair with the wife of one of his colleagues. Or my mother's predilection for gin.

"He badgered me to name you. I refused, believing we'd have more power if we told him together. I said everything would be fine and the father of the baby would marry me. That was the only time in my life he ever struck me. Today I learned why. After your visit to the house, he'd guessed it was you."

Anger stormed Doug's face. "Bastard! I thought he was a decent bloke. He talked such a good line but it was all show, wasn't it? The truth was, you marrying a farm hand with mixed blood and aspirations was worse than you being unmarried and pregnant."

She squeezed his hand, both sad and relieved that he understood. "His worst nightmare was someone finding out I was pregnant and the news being leaked. Fraser Mannering did everything in his power to keep his scandals well hidden. He decreed I must go away. Melbourne and Sydney were considered out of the question, because someone we knew might see me. I was sent to a mother and baby home in Hobart. My father told everyone I'd gone to finishing school before taking a grand tour of Europe with my aunt."

"They isolated you?" His voice cracked as the significance sank in. All veterans knew the tenets of torture. "Those mongrels!"

Years of despair bubbled up in her voice. "I tried so hard to contact you. I felt sure if you got word I was pregnant you'd move heaven and earth to get back to me. For months I refused to sign the adoption papers they shoved under my nose every single day. I tried to block out the bullying and the mind games but they were good. Expert. They specialized in sowing seeds of uncertainty."

The matron's sugar-sweet voice leaped into her mind, the phrases loud and clear as if the words were freshly spoken. *If he loves you so much, he'd be here with you now, wouldn't he? Men are evil creatures. They take advantage of innocent girls. You're a very lucky girl to have a family who loves you so much. Look at all the effort they're going to so that that after this little vacation you can start again.*

She choked on the word vacation and a violent urge to gag gripped her. "When the good-cop routine didn't make me sign, they brought in the doctor. He was a stern-looking man much the same age as my father. He always made me sit down and then he stood in front of me in his white coat and authoritative glasses. He told me my behavior was unconscionable. That I was an unlovable slut who couldn't be trusted to keep my legs shut. Said I was useless. That I didn't deserve to be a mother. If I tried to keep the baby I'd fail and have to give it up anyway. He'd look down over the top of his glasses and finish with the kicker: why ruin the child's life as well as my own?"

Doug rocked slowly back and forth. "Flaming hell. I should have been there."

Her eyes prickled with bulging tears. She blinked hard, needing to stall them. Knowing that once they started, they wouldn't stop and there was still so much more she needed to say. "It was an awful labor. So long. I think I fought every single contraction. I wanted to hold onto our baby forever. It was the only way I could keep her safe."

She gave an involuntary shudder. "In the end they pulled her out of me with forceps. I was screaming for her but they wouldn't let me see her, let alone hold her. A kind nurse told me I'd had a little girl and she was alive before they whisked her out of the room and away from my outstretched arms. Later, in the ward with a blood transfusion plunged into my arm and so weak from lack of blood I could hardly see straight let alone think, they came at me again with the papers. This time they held a black fountain pen."

She made an odd huffing sound. "I've never been able to use one since. I asked to see my baby. Begged. They told me yes and my heart soared. Then they hit me with the conditions. I could only see her if I signed the papers first. I knew it was blackmail but what choice did I have? I was eighteen with no income. I had nowhere to live and no support. My family had abandoned me on an island, cut me off from everyone I knew and all I had were a few dollars in my State Savings Bank account. I didn't even have enough money to get back to Victoria."

Her throat thickened, the words clogging and snagging. "All I wanted was to hold my baby. Oh Doug ..." She turned her wet face to him. "She was beautiful. She lay in my arms as serene as an angel, gazing up at me from bright and inquisitive eyes. I stared at her so hard I didn't want to blink in case I missed a precious second of her. Her little hands had dimples in them and her fingers closed around mine with a grip so strong it bruised my heart. The rush of love came so fast I thought I'd explode with the joy of it." A tear splashed onto her hand. "Ten minutes later, she was gone. I never saw her again. No one ever spoke about her again."

She dug her nails into her palms. *Almost there.* "My parents arrived two days later as if nothing out of the ordinary had happened and took me back to Murrumbeet. I was given a new wardrobe worthy of any young woman who'd been to London and Europe and they bought me a car. Their plan had worked. No one suspected I hadn't been overseas but just in case, they didn't let the grass grow under their feet. They quickly paraded me in front of suitable and eligible men who'd made their approved list.

"I was grief-stricken and incapable of fighting them. Richard had the medical talent and I had the pedigree to help him build a very successful surgical practice in Billawarre. I'd lost you and I'd lost our baby. I didn't really care what happened to me, but Richard was a decent man, so when he proposed, I said yes.

"I thought things would get easier, but they didn't. I've never forgotten our baby, Doug. When I lost her, I lost part of me."

Doug made a strangled sound deep in his throat. His arms closed clumsily around her, pulling her close and holding her so tight it hurt. His cheek rested against hers and their tears mingled: salty, warm and harrowingly sad.

After their tears trickled to a stop, they mopped their cheeks and blew their noses. Doug kept saying over and over in a voice full of utter bewilderment, "We have a daughter. A daughter." As though saying it out loud and hearing it again and again was helping him absorb the astonishing news.

"Did you name her?"

She nodded. "Susan."

"Susan." He rolled the name around his mouth as if he was auditioning it. "Nice name, Eddy."

"I always think of her as Susan, but I suppose she's grown up with a completely different name."

"Has she ever tried to contact you?"

"No." She laced her fingers tightly, welcoming the uncomfortable press of bone on bone. "When the law changed in 1989 I thought she might try. I was on tenterhooks for a long time. The thing is, I don't even know if she's been told she's adopted. I don't even know if she's alive."

The wind blew his salt and pepper curls into his eyes. "What about you? Have you searched for her?"

His questions brought back her life-long agony. "Today it's all very different—they have open adoption—but back then it was closed and locked down tighter than a drum. Once they successfully forced you to give away your child, you lost all rights to access any details. They sealed the original birth certificate and issued an amended one so that I couldn't see the adopting family's name and they couldn't see mine. They made everything leak proof. They didn't want you trying to make contact with the child, and if you applied for any information, you were flatly denied."

Edwina didn't tell him that the year Susan turned nine she'd hired a private investigator. Nor did she mention Richard's reaction when he'd discovered what she'd done. She'd relived enough traumas for one day. "We had a family vacation in Tasmania the year Susan turned twelve and I found myself staring at every girl we saw around that age, looking to see if she had my eyes. I know it was silly, but I was desperate. I don't even know if a Tasmanian family adopted her, although it's likely, I suppose. Now though, she could be anywhere."

"I can't believe we have a daughter," he said for at least the fiftieth time as he picked up her hand again and pressed it gently between both of his.

"I've just found out I'm about to become a great-grandmother," she admitted. "Charlie, Harriet's daughter, is pregnant. She's almost the same age I was ..."

He gave her a knowing glance. "Is that why you chose today to tell me about our daughter?"

She puffed out a sound. "I'd always planned to tell you, Doug. Always. But you know as well as I do that we've both been studiously avoiding going back to that awful time. Hearing Charlie's news forced me to take the bull by the horns."

His mouth curved into a sad smile. "I'm glad you did. At least life today's a lot different. Things will be easier for Charlie."

She thought about the town and what Harriet had said at breakfast. "I'm not so sure it's all that different. Scratch the surface and the stigma, shame, prejudice and judgment of unmarried mothers are still lurking, ready to pounce."

"But surely she's got more choice than you had?"

"Yes and no. Choice is only helpful if it offers you an alternative you wish to pursue. My parents and the hospital forced me to give up our child for adoption. If an abortion had been an option in 1968 I wouldn't have wanted to take it, but my parents would have forced me to. Harriet wants Charlie to terminate the pregnancy. She believes that having a baby at eighteen will ruin Charlie's life."

A harsh bark of laughter tumbled over her lips. "Actually, I'm sure Harriet feels the pregnancy is a stain on her own life but considering what James has just done to her, in the eyes of the town she's covered in indelible ink anyway. She's threatened to withdraw all support if Charlie has the baby and she's refusing to speak to her until she capitulates. None of it's so very different from what my parents did to me."

A rush of emotion hit her and she took a moment to steady her breathing. "There might be a generation between my parents and Harriet, but the apple doesn't fall far from the tree. What Harriet doesn't understand is that for Charlie, having a termination will damage her in ways that will affect the rest of her life."

Sympathy and understanding filled his dark eyes. "Have you told her that?"

I wish you'd died instead of Dad. Harriet's words sliced into Edwina again as sharp and as painful as when they'd first been hurled at her. Her relationship with Harriet had never been strong but now it was a burnt-out shell.

"No. Even if I had, she wouldn't have listened. Harriet always thinks she knows best. She was born that way and being a Mannering and a surgeon has only embedded that into a firm belief. In her eyes I lack credibility. The closest I got was telling her I'm supporting Charlie's decision to keep the baby."

"Good for you."

"Harriet doesn't agree. Of course, if she refuses to be involved then I'll support Charlie financially too. My announcement's rocked the girls, I saw it on their faces. They're struggling to align my life and the person they believe me to be with what they see as a very out-of-character decision. I know there's going to be questions, but I refuse to let what happened to me happen to Charlie. Losing a child is ... Enough damage has been done ..."

He gripped her hands tightly and his face took on a pensive look. "I want to try to find her."

"Find her?"

"Yes. Find our daughter." Anxiety hovered in his eyes. "Do you?"

Her heart turned over with joy then flipped back with relief but it wasn't enough to silence all doubt. She scanned his face, seeking evidence that gave truth to his words, fearing she couldn't cope if he changed his mind. "Are you sure?"

He didn't hesitate. "Of course I'm sure."

He made it sound so easy, but it was far from that. She'd had years to mull over the very real consequences of introducing her love child to her family, although with Richard's death, one of those consequences was now invalid. "Searching for her doesn't mean we'll find her. Even if we do, it doesn't mean she'll want to meet us. She might be happy with her life and this could throw her. She might hate me for giving her up. She—"

"All of those things and more are possible, but I don't want to die without having tried," he said gently. "Do you?"

When the Tasmanian government had made a formal apology to the mothers, children and families affected by forced adoption and opened the doors for access to adoption records, she'd almost contacted the department, but Richard was still alive and she'd already sacrificed enough. If his death hadn't come six months after Eliza's she probably would have written then, but for a few months it had been as much as she could manage just getting up, getting dressed and getting through the day.

Now she was no longer on her own. She and Doug could search together. During the process when hope wavered and turned toward hopelessness, they could hold each other up. With him by her side she could find the strength to do this.

"Yes. I want to find her."

Relief spilled into his smile. "Thank God. I suppose we start searching on the internet, do we? I'm not too flash with computers. What about you?"

"I'm not too shabby. I've even bought things online," she said with a laugh before sobering. "Doug, I want to try to find her. But what about your family and my girls? Telling them they have a half-sister they've never heard of will be like dropping a bomb on them."

Doug slowly rubbed his jaw with the backs of his fingers. "It's gonna be a shock for them, for sure. I doubt mine have given any thought to their old man loving anyone but their mother, let alone the fact there's a new sister out there somewhere. But they already know life's full of surprises—some are good and some are bad. Your girls know that too. They've lost their dad." His voice quieted. "And we lost Sophia far too early."

A crazy dart of something akin to jealousy flashed green and pierced her. She gave herself a shake. It was a waste of energy envying a dead woman even if she'd gotten to spend her adult life with Doug. He was right about surprises: life was full of them. Meeting him again after all these years was the best type of surprise even if they had to navigate the rocky shoals of their children's responses to their new-but-old relationship.

"You're not worried how your children will react to me and the news of our daughter?"

His eyes widened. "Are you kidding? Of course I'm worried. One thing I've learned from raising four kids is that if you dare predict how they'll react, you're always wrong."

She knew exactly what he meant. "I think it's easier if we keep the secret for now. There's no point upsetting everyone if our search hits a brick wall. I mean, we may not be able to find her. Or if we do, she may not want to have anything to do with us."

Doug frowned. "I don't like secrets, Eddy. The last time I was part of a secret with you it caused us years of separation. Crikey, we lost our daughter and keeping her secret has hurt you for years. All that's got to stop. If we're searching for her, I want to be totally up front with our families."

Fear and resignation mingled in her veins, making her shake. "Being upfront and dealing with things head on isn't something my family's very good at. It isn't something I'm very good at."

"Sounds like it might be time to get the ball rolling then. What's the worst thing that can happen?"

Her fingers tugged at her pearls as a slightly hysterical sound rose in her throat. "My daughters will never speak to me again."

"I guess that might happen to me too. Let's hope you're underestimating them."

"I'm not underestimating Harriet."

"Your granddaughter will understand."

"That goes directly against your theory of not predicting reactions."

"You got me there. Still, she'd be foolish to reject the one woman who's lovingly accepting her decision to keep her baby."

She couldn't help but smile. He had a way of making her feel optimistic even when things were bleak. As much as she didn't want to face the girls, she knew he was right. Once they started searching for Sus—their daughter, there was the possibility the girls might accidentally discover they had a half-sister. She'd seen the fallout of Harriet discovering Charlotte's pregnancy by stumbling onto Facebook. It would be far worse if they found out from another source. At least if Edwina sat them down and told them together she'd know they had all the facts.

"Alright then," she said, sounding far more confident than she felt, "the secret's coming out. When will you tell your family?"

He rubbed his hands together briskly like a man with a plan. "We'll tell them together. It makes sense to tell your girls at lunch on Sunday. Once we've gotten that out of the way, we'll organize a time next week to tell mine face to face. Then we'll start searching for our girl. From now on, Eddy, we're doing everything together."

Her heart filled and ached with the weight of his love and support but as wonderful as it was, it overwhelmed her. Tears coursed down her cheeks again. She found it odd that she'd cried more in two hours than she'd done in years. When she finally managed to pull herself together, she gave him a watery kiss. "I love you, Doug."

"I love you too, Eddy. This time, nothing short of death is going to separate us."

The idea of him dying when she'd only just found him terrified her. "Well, you'd better stay healthy then," she said briskly, covering her tremulous emotions. "And think about some exercise and cutting back on the beer, because I'm demanding at least twenty years with you."

He grinned widely. "I won't argue with you about that."

"EARTH TO EDWINA?" Harriet's annoyed voice pulled Edwina back to lunch and away from Friday's momentous conversation.

"Doug, be warned," Harriet continued. "Our mother has these concerning moments of vagueness."

Edwina ignored the jibe and instead glanced along the table at her family. Anxiety tangoed with the lure of shedding the crushing weight of a long-held secret. It made her feel both skittish and strangely calm all at the same time. Doug caught her gaze and under the protection of the tablecloth, he gave her knee a gentle squeeze. Sunday was now.

CHAPTER NINETEEN

HARRIET TAPPED HER FOOT AGAINST THE TEAK TABLE LEG, feeling her impatience rise. When she'd arrived at Glenora and discovered that James had thankfully been prevented from having a heart to heart with Charlotte, most of her had wanted to leave. However, as she'd come under the guise of attending the lunch, she'd stayed. Her plan to give Doug the third degree had instantly been derailed when Xara and Steve served the roast as soon as she'd been introduced to the man. As she'd taken her seat, both Xara and Georgie had said, *sotto voce,* "Don't grill Doug while the children are at the table." She wondered whether that included her child.

Charlotte had pointedly seated herself at the opposite end of the table, as far away from Harriet as possible. It suited her—she had nothing left to say to Charlotte until she came to her senses. Over lunch, her daughter had been silent on more than just the topic of her pregnancy; she'd hardly contributed to the conversation at all. Her beautiful face was pale and drawn and for a fleeting moment, Harriet was torn between wanting to hug her and wanting to slap her for creating such a mess of her life.

Really? And your life is in such great shape.

Shut up. She'd over-ruled the unwanted commentary from her psyche—she wasn't the one responsible for creating the mess she currently found herself in. Knowing that wasn't enough to prevent James's words coming at her like sharp and poisonous arrows.

I did what was necessary to protect your precious social standing.

She called bullshit on that. None of this was her fault. All she'd ever done was try to live her life as a pillar of the community and lead by example.

Having been banned from launching a Q&A at Doug, the lunch conversation had been fairly predictable. The meal was deconstructed—the lamb deemed tender, the creamy potatoes perfect and the Weber praised for its roasting abilities. The twins had been their precocious selves, peppering Doug with questions about his Jaguar XK-E. He'd answered with good humor and with far more patience than she'd have been able to muster, but then again, he was probably pulling out all the stops to make a good impression on the Chirnwell daughters.

Good luck with that, Doug.

As livid as Harriet was with Edwina, it was hard not to notice the glow of happiness her mother wore like a new coat with dazzlingly gold buttons. It intensified whenever Doug was near. But Harriet and her sisters knew only too well how fickle their mother's emotional state was and how it could flatline at any moment. Edwina's "episodes" had punctuated their lives and her father had been a saint in the way he'd coped with them.

During the long lunch, Harriet caught some of Edwina and Doug's covert glances and she was certain they'd held hands under the cover of the tablecloth. It was unsettling how age had little, if any, limiting effects on the heady feelings of lust. Apparently wisdom evaporated under its assault, making people in their sixties look ludicrous as they carried on like teens.

Her mother's current elevation in mood was obviously a direct result of her body being flooded with oxytocin, adrenaline, dopamine and serotonin—brain chemistry. In Harriet's book, that was not enough to get Doug over the line. Lust faded and when it did the scales would fall from her mother's eyes.

Until then, it was up to Harriet to prevent anything serious happening between them. His working-class values had already radicalized Edwina; it was the only reason Harriet could come up with for her mother's support of Charlotte. Doug was nothing like her father and he didn't belong in the family or her mother's social circle. She couldn't recall either of her parents ever befriending anyone like him. Employing him, yes. Socializing with him, no. It was a no brainer really: he had to go.

The twins now wriggled in their chairs and Edwina excused them from the table. As they raced away, Tasha screamed in protest.

Charlotte was instantly on her feet. "Let's go for a walk." As she released the wheelchair's brakes, she looked at Edwina. "Is that okay with you, Mardi?"

Harriet took a long drink of wine, but it wasn't enough to stop the burn of anger and the renewed sting of an old but rock-solid sense of betrayal. Her daughter and her mother had formed an alliance—a close bond—something she'd never shared with Edwina. God, she missed her father.

"If it's fine with Xara then it's fine by me," Edwina said. "Just be back by 3:00 for egg hunt part two."

"It's totally fine by me." Xara had kicked back after serving lunch and was now enjoying a third glass of champagne. "Knock yourselves out. Tashie loves watching the mechanical rabbit in Harry Hooper's window, so allow a good five minutes for that. If you rush it, she'll let you know."

"Steve, dear, would you mind taking charge of the tea and coffee?" Edwina asked.

Georgie shot to her feet. "I'll help."

"I'm sure Steve can handle it on his own." Edwina was using her best queenly tone. "Please stay."

Clearly puzzled, Georgie sat down slowly and the three sisters exchanged glances. Harriet took the opportunity to seize control of the conversation. Doug had ignored her previous quip about Edwina's vagueness so she went for a direct question.

"Doug, tell me. What do you do for a living?"

He gave her an easy smile. "I own a large automotive service center. Built it up from nothing and now it chugs along with a staff of ten. It means I can indulge my passion of buying and selling classic cars. It's a hobby of mine to collect old wrecks and restore them.'

"Is that your plan with my mother?"

Edwina snorted wine.

"Harry!" Georgie spluttered.

"Stop it, Harry," Xara said as if she was admonishing the twins. "That's too much."

Unrepentant, Harriet kept her gaze on Doug's face.

"Your mother's a beautiful woman, Harriet." He spoke quietly but his voice held an edge that said, *Cross me and I'll fight right back.* "I loved her when she was seventeen and I love her now. I think you'll agree that nothing about her is old or a wreck."

"Seventeen?" Her mother had been at boarding school in Geelong when she'd turned seventeen. She leaned forward. "How did you two meet?"

"I was working on Murrumbeet doing everything from fixing farm machinery to fixing fences." He gave Edwina a wink. "I taught your mother to drive and how to change the oil. She had a natural gift."

"Ah!" Xara suddenly sat up straight, her face alight with interest. "So that's why the twins came home from the rally full of car stories I'd never heard. I hate to tell you, Doug, but over the years she hasn't put her oil-changing knowledge to much use."

"Changing oil doesn't quite go with Chanel and pearls, now does it?" Harriet glared at Xara. Today wasn't about getting chummy with Doug, it was about sending him away. "I can't imagine Grandpa was thrilled his daughter was friendly with a deeply tanned farmhand?"

Edwina flinched but she didn't stay silent as Harriet had expected. "I kept my friendship with Doug a secret from everyone. I regret that now, but at the time I did it because your grandfather wouldn't have welcomed him."

Harriet almost choked. "That's got to be the understatement of the day, Edwina." She turned back to Doug. "With your dark eyes and curly hair, I'm guessing either your mother or father was Aboriginal?"

"In the twenties and the forties there were probably very few white women forcing themselves onto Aboriginal men," Doug said smoothly but making his point nonetheless. "My mother's father was apparently Irish and my father was an Englishman. I didn't know either of them."

Harriet noticed that Edwina's forehead creased in a light frown. Good. "Your Irish heritage would have been just as upsetting to Grandpa as your Aboriginal blood."

"I met your grandfather before I went to Vietnam for my tour of duty." Doug accepted a cup of coffee from Steve. "He was happy enough to shake my hand as a soldier."

"Now *that* sounds like Grandpa," Xara said sarcastically. "He'd have been in seventh heaven today with all the photo opportunities selfies offer politicians."

"I really regret the old codger died before I met Xara." Steve resumed his seat. "Given Georgie's political persuasions, it would have made for some memorable family dinners."

"Fireworks would have looked dim in comparison," Edwina said dryly. "You were very quick with the coffee, dear."

"Did you need me to take longer?"

"I did my best for you, Steve, by arguing with Dad," Georgie added with a laugh.

Steve grinned. "Too right and I appreciated it. I reckon Doug and Harriet might just continue the tradition."

No way in hell. Harriet mustered a thin smile. "Was it while you were in Vietnam with enforced distance from Edwina that you realized you were socially out of your depth?"

"Harriet! That's enough," Edwina said. "Now you're just being obnoxious."

"I'm just trying to get a picture of what happened. It's not like you've ever mentioned Doug to us before. He's a total mystery man." Harriet turned back to him. "Sorry," she said disingenuously, "but you obviously went on to recover from unrequited teenage love."

"I wasn't a teen when I met your mother."

She ignored the correction. "And you've been married?"

"Yes. Sophia and I shared forty-three mostly happy years and four kids before she died."

"Sorry," Georgie, Xara and Steve offered up in unison.

"Cancer took her, Harriet." A wicked twinkle flashed in Doug's eyes. "I thought I'd mention that just in case you're worried I murdered her."

Georgie laughed. Edwina smiled. Steve and Xara exchanged an intimate shorthand look full of meaning. Harriet was unimpressed by her siblings' willingness to embrace this inappropriate stranger into their lives.

"That's reassuring to know, Doug, considering my mother's worth a lot of money."

"You don't have to worry about that, love," he said, his accent suddenly broadening. Harriet couldn't tell if he was doing it deliberately or not. "Business has been good to me the last few years and I'm not interested in your mother's money."

James's treachery seared her and she stiffened. "Forgive me if I take *that* with a grain of salt."

"Well, I think it's lovely you've reconnected with Mom after all this time," Xara said expansively, courtesy of the champagne. "Are any of your kids bratty like Harriet?"

As Steve poured Xara a coffee, Edwina and Doug exchanged a look. A nod. An agreement. A public hand squeeze. Harriet experienced an unexpected chill in the warm afternoon air.

Edwina cleared her throat and her fingers crawled toward her pearls. "Doug and I have something we need to tell all of you."

The goosebumps intensified to rafts of painful pinpricks shooting all over her body. "No!" Harriet heard herself yell. She didn't know what it was her mother was about to say but she knew down to the depths of her soul she didn't want to hear it. Everything about Edwina's demeanor was portentous, heralding a big announcement. She didn't want a big announcement, especially if it pertained to a future featuring Edwina and Doug as a couple. She wanted to separate them and send Doug far, far away.

"Harriet, be quiet. Let Mom speak," Xara said.

Georgie's hand touched Harriet's arm—the gesture intended to be reassuring, but she immediately threw it off. She didn't want reassuring. She didn't want to be placated. She didn't want her sisters encouraging Edwina in any way, shape or form. She refused to sit here a moment longer and be forced to acknowledge her mother and Doug as a couple. She rose to her feet. "I'm going."

"Leaving won't change what we have to say," Edwina said in a voice that would cut through ice. "I know I'm not your favorite person, but I respectfully ask you to sit down and listen. I want you to hear this from me and not from anyone else."

Harriet shook her head. "If I don't hear what you have to say then I'm not party to it. I can't sit here and smile and pretend that I'm happy about the two of you being together."

"This isn't about that," Edwina said hurriedly. "It's ..." She licked her lips. "It's about your sister."

Harriet glanced between Xara and Georgie but they were busy looking at each other, apparently as equally in the dark as her. "Which one?"

Edwina closed her eyes for a moment, her shoulders rising and falling as she inhaled deep breaths. When she opened them, she looked at Xara, then Georgie and finally Harriet. "Your older sister."

The reins on her exasperation gave way completely and she pulled her handbag off the back of the chair. "And here I was thinking it was Xara who'd been drinking too much. You know as well as I do that I don't have an older sister."

"You have a half-sister." Edwina's words struck the air, clanging as loudly as the old fire bell on a stiflingly hot February afternoon. "In November 1968, I had Doug's baby while he was in Vietnam. She was forcibly removed from me and adopted out. He never knew about her existence until I told him on Friday. I'm telling all of you today."

Time slowed the way it does when the foundations of life are shaken to the core and Harriet became hyperaware of everything going on around her. Doug remained silent but his arm now rested across Edwina's shoulders, his fingers cupping the top of her arm and his body tilting toward hers like a protective shield.

"Oh my God," Georgie said softly. "I ... that's ..."

Xara's mouth opened and closed and she reached for her champagne flute, quickly draining the contents. Steve's eyes widened in shock, holding the same dazed look as a kangaroo caught in the blinding gleam of headlights. He too remained mute.

Harriet looked at her mother, taking in her smooth blond bob, her tailored pants, the floral chiffon blouse she'd teamed perfectly with a contrasting watermelon camisole before finally coming to rest on the string of pearls at her throat—always the signature pearls. Despite all the familiarity, Harriet didn't recognize her. Everything she'd ever believed to be true about her mother was now exposed as a carefully created façade. Edwina was like a piece of crazed porcelain whose faulty glaze had fought long and hard to hold the cracks together but had finally given way.

Edwina Mannering had lived a lie.

Harriet's blood ran cold. She should have questions. She should be demanding answers but it was as if she'd risen out of herself and was now looking down on proceedings as a completely separate entity. Silently, she turned and walked briskly away.

CHAPTER TWENTY

GEORGIE STOOD IN THE SHADE OF THE SPRAWLING NORFOLK pine and reflected that the joy of children was the euphoric pleasure they got from simple things. Thank goodness for the twins. For them life was uncomplicated. Easter meant holidays, chocolate and egg hunts, and nothing was going to stand between them and their quest for chocolate. Not even the fact that their mother and aunts' world had just been turned on its head by the news of an older sister they never knew existed.

They twins had barreled back through the Glenora gates just before three, whooping and shouting it was time for the hunt. Georgie had wanted to hug them for their enthusiasm and for the fact it broke her out of her stupor. It had propelled her and Xara out of their chairs and away from their mother, Doug and the shadow of a secret sister. Georgie didn't know what to think of the revelation and yet she couldn't think of anything else. What she wanted most was to sit down with Xara and Harriet and talk it all through, but she'd promised Ben she'd be ready to leave at four. The idea of driving back to Melbourne now was untenable.

He wouldn't like it if she delayed. Cuddled up with him in her bed in the wee hours of this morning, she'd felt his disapproval at her plan to stay longer. But surely if she told him of this new development he'd understand—this time the news affected her directly. A shot of acid burned under her ribs. Why did all this family crap have to happen now, just as she'd met a fabulous guy who wanted the same things she did?

Ben may have thought the timing of James's fraud coming to light when he was in town was bad luck and Charlotte's pregnancy news simply bad timing, but this? The announcement of a lost sister was the frosting on the cake of nine days of craziness. He'd declare her family an unmitigated disaster when really they were just as happily dysfunctional as the next family. Weren't they? She reassured herself that things came in threes and they'd had their three. Surely they were off the hook for any more dramas in the near future.

A thought skated across her mind—the year of disasters the McGowans had experienced a decade ago. First came crippling drought, then the devastating loss of the farmhouse in a wildfire and finally, Primrose's cancer diagnosis. The McGowans' run of misfortune had all happened in a short space of time too. Remembering reassured Georgie that the universe wasn't singling her family out. It cheerfully dumped on everyone.

After Harriet's abrupt departure, Edwina and Doug had given her and Xara the bare bones of their story: young lovers separated by a disapproving family who feared scandal and the social stigma that came with it. Georgie was bursting with questions, including whether her father had known about the baby, but due to the twins' return, they remained unasked.

She couldn't stop thinking how she'd lost Eliza to death and her mother had lost her baby to life. Was knowing that a child of yours lived somewhere without you worse than knowing your dreams had died with your child? She wouldn't wish either situation on anyone.

The twins dashed past. "We've got ten eggs. We're gonna win," Hugh yelled.

"No eggs back there," Ollie added.

Their confidence kickstarted her competitive streak, thankfully flattening her unsettling thoughts. There were bound to be eggs in the back of the garden; her mother was wily that way. She re-joined the hunt and paused on her way past the potting shed. She jiggled the small round handle and leaned her weight against the old wooden door, swollen with age, until it shifted.

When she pushed it open, the earthy scent of mushroom compost rushed to meet her. As her eyes adjusted to the dim light, she deciphered the shapes of seedling trays on the workbench. Despite the sunshine, the light through the tiny windows barely penetrated the accumulation of a year's worth of grime; it looked like it was time for young Adrian to clean them again.

She reached for her cell phone and the torch app, but her fingers hit an empty pocket. Damn it. Lunch was a cell-phone-free affair and she'd forgotten she'd left the sleek device in her room so as not to be tempted to sneak a peek. Ben liked to send Snapchats of things in the area that tickled his fancy, like the road sign where someone had drawn a shark fin on a cow and written "Bull shark" or the dead-end sign on Cemetery Road. The photos made her smile and laugh. He also sent texts, which didn't make her laugh but sent flashing hot tingles through her. She didn't need anyone in her family catching her mid lust fest so it was safer all around for her cell phone to be tucked away in her room.

A thin beam of sunshine penetrated the grunge, lighting up a flash of blue foil nestled in the corner of the windowsill. Bingo. She scooped up the egg then spider walked her fingers across the top of the sill, finding two small eggs. After that, she turned her attention to the stack of black pots under the table, checking for creepy-crawlies first.

Six eggs later, she stepped out of the shed and closed the door behind her, looking forward to teasing the twins about her haul. Following the direction of their voices, she ran toward the house, finding the boys on the large expanse of lawn near the tennis court.

"Hey guys, you were wrong. There are eggs back here. Big ones too."

The twins rushed her and she danced around laughing, holding the eggs in a pot above her head. They leaped and jumped, trying to get to them and when they couldn't reach they resorted to the guerrilla tactic of tickling. Shrieking, she collapsed onto the grass, rolling around with them until she was puffing and panting, her lungs burning. Aching for breath, she called time out. The twins tore off again to another section of the garden and she rolled onto her knees, sucking in air.

"You right there?"

Her head shot up at the familiar deep voice and the small amount of breath she had left in her lungs evaporated. She blinked, trying to clear her vision, but nothing changed the image of a pair of men's casual canvas shoes, tanned muscular legs covered in a smattering of dark hair and an outstretched hand with a small boomerang scar on the base of the thumb.

Smiling, Ben reached down and hauled her to her feet. "Looks like you've been having fun."

Oxygen was once again reaching her brain and she was filled with joy and an odd sense of relief. Compared with the complicated mess that was her family, Ben represented sanity and normality. She rose on her toes, cupped his cheeks with her hands and kissed him.

"That's a welcome I could get used to." He pulled a twig from her hair.

She laid her cheek against his chest and breathed him in. "You have no idea how good it is to see you. Today's been—"

She stopped, suddenly very aware that she couldn't tell him yet. How could she, when she'd barely had enough time to absorb the news herself? She had another sister and it begged the question: had she ever really known her mother?

She had an overwhelming sense that everything she'd ever believed to be true about Edwina was totally incorrect. Everything was up for scrutiny and questioning. The only parts of her mother's life she recognized as truly authentic were the episodic periods of misery and withdrawal.

That made her sad. It also made her mad, which she didn't understand and that upset her more. Shouldn't she be full of sympathy for her? Her mother had lost a baby too. Georgie knew what that was like but it didn't stop her from being angry with Edwina for never telling them.

Would it have changed anything?

Yes. No. I don't know. Maybe.

Flipping hell, she sounded like Charlotte when she'd been talking about James. All of it was baffling and unfathomable. She needed to talk to her sisters—her known sisters—before she could begin to articulate her muddled thoughts and feelings to Ben.

"Intense?" Ben suggested, finishing her sentence for her. "My family's lunches are always like that. I think it's the Italian legacy. My sisters battle it out for culinary supremacy and Dad and I end up mediating and eating way too much food."

"We had lamb," she said inanely, trying to corral her thoughts.

"If I'd known lamb was on the menu I'd have insisted on an invitation."

His teasing made her suddenly remember he wasn't supposed to be at Glenora. She glanced at her watch. 3:20. "I thought we were we meeting at the motel at four?"

His dark caramel eyes filled with query. "Didn't you get my text?"

She shook her head. "Unless you're a doctor on-call, Mom has a no-phone policy at lunch."

"It's probably just as well you didn't see it. My preference was to tell you in person but then again I didn't want to surprise you by turning up unannounced. Guess that didn't work."

He'd piqued her curiosity. "Tell me what?"

"Just after three, I got a surprising text ..."

The rise and fall of voices distracted her and she turned toward the noise. The combination of treble and bass sounded like her mother and Doug, and going on the increasing volume they were getting closer. One more turn in the path and the two of them would be in plain sight. Given she and Ben were standing smack bang in the middle of the broad expanse of lawn, they would be too.

Panic sent waves of agitation thrumming through her, deafening her to Ben's words. She wasn't up to introducing him to everyone—not today. "Quick." She grabbed his hand and tugged him in the direction of the thick-trunked oak that stood regally behind them. Its breadth offered a hiding place.

A sharp pain wrenched her shoulder, radiating down her arm. Ben hadn't budged an inch. In fact, his attention was no longer focused on her and she saw her mother and Doug had rounded the corner. They were walking straight to them in a brisk and determined manner. *Bugger.*

Ben raised his free arm in greeting. The action surprised her given he was yet to meet her mother. Perhaps he was nervous and overcompensating?

"I guess we're busted."

"Guess so."

She squeezed his hand. "Brace yourself to meet my mother and her new friend. Actually, he's an old friend of hers. More than that really ..." She knew she was gabbling so she finished up lamely, "It's complicated."

"Yeah. About that." His brows drew down and he suddenly looked worried. "The thing is, Georgie—"

"Got lost in the garden, did you?" Doug said heartily.

Georgie wondered at the comment given this was the garden she'd grown up in and she knew it like the back of her hand. Before she could reply, her mother's gaze landed on Georgie and Ben's linked hands. A slight frown marred her hostess smile.

Georgie dropped his hand and immediately hated herself. Hell's bells, she was thirty-four years old and if she wanted to hold Ben's hand it shouldn't matter if her mother approved or not. Edwina had no right to have an opinion about whose hand Georgie held given the bomb she'd dropped on them all today.

"Hello," her mother said in her precise and well-mannered way. "I'm Edwina Chirnwell. Welcome to Glenora."

"Sorry," Georgie said quickly, realizing her indignation had put her behind in the introduction stakes. She was about to say more when she realized Doug was making the exact apology.

"I'd like you to meet Ben."

Her voice collided with Doug's, their words rolling over each other. Startled, she stared at him. Was this some sort of odd joke—like the parrot game kids played, repeating everything someone said?

But as Ben shook her mother's hand and murmured, "It's lovely to meet you, Edwina," Georgie realized with a jolt that Doug must know Ben.

No. That was crazy. They couldn't possibly know each other. She was letting the day's madness get to her. But her mind whipped her back to Ben standing in her classroom and saying, "Dad's car rally went through Billawarre."

Doug slapped Ben familiarly on the shoulder and gave him a wink. "Something you want to tell me?"

Flashes of hot and rafts of cold raced across Georgie's skin and she frantically glanced between Ben and Doug. Both had dark curly hair, caramel eyes and a laconic smile. If you superimposed streaks of silver onto Ben's hair, gave him more wrinkles around the eyes and added jowly cheeks, they'd be twins.

No. It's too random.

But her stomach was in free-fall, overriding her desperate attempts to ignore the truth that was staring her in the face. No wonder she'd sensed a familiarity in Doug the first time she'd met him at Edwina's party. No wonder her mother had frowned at her and Ben holding hands.

Doug was Ben's father.

Her breathing sped. Thoughts squealed in her head like the feedback from a microphone and her hands rose to cover her ears as if it would silence the noise. It didn't. Nothing would silence that. Doug wasn't just Ben's father. He was also the father of her unknown sister. She gagged and stumbled backwards, driven by some unknown but powerful force that made it imperative to put a lot of space between herself and Ben.

CHAPTER TWENTY-ONE

SISTERS! HONESTLY, RIGHT NOW XARA'S WERE CAUSING HER constant heartburn. It was the end of longest Easter Sunday she'd ever known and all she wanted to do was retreat to the farm, Steve and the kids. Instead, she was at the Miligili guesthouse with Harriet and Georgie.

Since Edwina's party, Georgie had been on board, supporting Xara in trying to hold things together. They'd joined forces, trying to prevent Harriet from blasting irreparable holes in the fabric of the family, but all that had changed this afternoon when Edwina and Doug announced the existence of an unknown sister. Georgie had demanded a sister meeting and Georgie never demanded anything. She arrived at the guesthouse a spitting roiling apoplectic mess, sounding far more like Harriet than Harriet herself. In the four hours between Harriet leaving Glenora and their arrival at Miligili, their older sister had become coldly indifferent to the news.

"She should have told us!" Georgie raged. "We needed to know because what if one of us—How could she do this to me?"

"She didn't do anything to you, Georgie." Xara shoot a confused glance at Harriet. Georgie had lost a baby—shouldn't that make her more understanding of their mother?

"Fine. To *us*," Georgie thumped her chest with a fist. "How could she do this to us?"

"She had a baby forcibly removed from her." Xara couldn't conceive how devastating that must have been for Edwina. "I think that deserves some sympathy."

"I'm not unsympathetic. I'm just furious she left it until today to tell us about her and Doug and the baby. I hate that she didn't tell us sooner."

Xara was at a loss to understand why Georgie appeared to be taking the timing of the news as a personal insult. "I think Doug's arrival and Charlie's pregnancy were the catalysts. I'm not sure that her telling us sooner would have lessened our shock."

"You don't understand." Georgie's face contorted in anguish.

Her sister's distress reminded Xara of Georgie's demeanor back in the dark days and months after Eliza's death and her breakup with Jason. It suddenly struck her that the gray shadows that had become a permanent part of Georgie since she'd lost Eliza had been absent this vacation.

"So explain it to me. I want to understand."

Georgie sank onto the couch and hugged a cushion. Sucking in her lips, she blinked furiously and when she'd finally opened her mouth she closed it almost immediately without uttering a sound.

Her sister's generally open and smiling face was hard, the planes of her cheeks sharp and everything that was normally soft and loving had turned ugly and harsh. "Georgie?"

She hurled the cushion across the room. "Mom got postnatal depression after having me."

Despite nothing ever being said and no label ever being attached to that time, the girls had worked it out years ago. "We all know that, Georgie. I'm not sure what you're getting at."

Harriet, who'd been quiet until that point, said, "I'm pretty sure she got it after having Xara too."

"Really? I thought she only got postnatal depression after Georgie."

Harriet shrugged. "I think it's likely. I wasn't quite five so I don't remember much, but I've got a memory of Dad dressing me in my new coat and taking me to visit Edwina somewhere."

Trust Harriet to have attached a garment to the memory. "He was probably taking you to the hospital to meet me when I was born."

"You were at home."

"See? This is what I mean," Georgie's staccato delivery punched the air. "For years I've been told the stories about Mrs. Abercrombie moving in when I was born—"

"Ah, Mrs. A," Harriet had said fondly. "I loved her."

Georgie glared at Xara. "You didn't. You reminded me of that often enough when we were growing up."

"Oh, for Pete's sake." Xara lost patience. "Let it go, Georgie. Kids say dumb stuff. You're my baby sister and I love you. I even love you when you're being ridiculous like you are now right now."

"Ridiculous?" Georgie's voice quavered. "I had parents who never had the same level of interest in me as they did in the two of you. I grew up knowing I was the mistake that sent Mom into a deep and debilitating depression. I've spent years lurching between feeling guilty about it and just plain sad. Now I discover it wasn't my fault at all." Her hand trembled as she reached for her glass. "Do you think Dad knew about the baby?"

"No," Harriet said firmly.

"What makes you so certain?"

"Think about it. He wouldn't have proposed to her if he'd known. Their marriage was a big deal. The wedding was at Scots Church and their photos appeared in the society pages." She sighed. "Poor Dad. I bet he wouldn't have signed up if he'd known what lay ahead."

"That's harsh." Xara felt the need to support her mother.

"It is what it is. Edwina failed him as a wife and she failed us as a mother."

Xara knew Harriet wore blinders when it came to their father.

Even as a child, she'd always sided with him, irrespective of the argument. Over time that collusion welded her to him and their bond had strengthened when she'd joined him in his medical practice. They'd stood as a united front in family affairs, frequently taking a stance against Edwina. Georgie had been too young to have an opinion and even if she did, no one ever listened to her so from fourteen, Xara had found herself catapulted into the role of shoring up the underdog; in this instance, her mother. It was probably part of the reason she'd pursued law and was now an advocate for families with special-needs children.

Hearing Harriet blithely absolve their father of any marital responsibility flamed the embers of an old anger. "Mom did her best and believe me, there are worse mothers out there. Did it ever occur to you that Dad might have failed her? What if he never investigated the reasons for her mood swings? He told us time and time again she was fragile as if that was just an accepted thing. He was always saying, "Buck up, Edwina. Worse things have happened to other people," and then he'd quote some horrible medical story. I doubt it was useful."

Harriet's glass clunked hard against the coffee table. "He worked bloody hard at cheering her up. Think of all those parties he threw for her."

"Parties she hated."

"The expensive gifts he bought her," Harriet said smugly as if she was keeping score. "She still wears that ruby and diamond ring, so she can't hate it."

Xara was leery of saying she thought the gifts came with strings attached. "I don't think we can make assumptions about *anything*. We grew up and formed an impression of our parents and their marriage. Now everything we've believed about them is clouded in uncertainty. Apparently, significant things can be hidden. If Mom kept a baby secret, it makes me wonder what Dad kept from us. Marriages are complicated. No one really knows what goes on inside them."

"Thank you so much for that that enlightening statement," Harriet said acerbically. "It's kind of you to remind me that I had no idea my husband was embezzling money."

Xara sighed at her prickly sister. "That's not what I meant at all, Harry. You're deliberately misconstruing me. But if you want to be offended then I'll give you something to be outraged about. If Mom suffered from depression for years because she gave up a baby, how can you ask Charlie to have an abortion?"

Harriet's torso straightened so fast she gained a good inch in height. "The two situations are not remotely comparable. One," she flicked her left thumb with her right index finger, "Charlotte and Hamish met at three parties, whereas Edwina appears to have—" she shuddered "—known Doug considerably longer. Two, Charlotte is pregnant with a cluster of cells, not a baby, whereas Edwina went through an entire pregnancy. Three, a termination wasn't easily available in 1968 so don't go leaping to conclusions that Edwina had a choice about whether or not to have the baby. Four, medical studies have proven that postnatal depression is—"

"Will you two shut up," Georgie yelled, her voice filled with anguish. "We've got a sister out there who's almost forty-eight. Chances are she's got kids. It's not out of the realms of possibility that she's a grandmother. Doug and Edwina are going to try to find her and then what? If she wants to meet us, are we going to have to just fall in line, no questions asked? And what about Doug's kids? I'm so pissed off with Mom for dumping this on us and ruining my life."

Harriet rolled her eyes. "Now you're sounding like a teen."

"Oh, that's rich. This from someone who walked away when she was told we have a sister. And what? Four hours later you're suddenly fine with it?"

"Oh, grow up, Georgie!" Red-hot fury played across Harriet's face, deepening the lines around her eyes. "Of course I'm not fine with it. Let me count the ways. Everything we've been raised to believe, everything I've built my life on, has collapsed around me like a house of cards. My marriage appears to have been a sham for quite some time without me being aware of it. James has buried my name in the mud and decimated my private practice. My daughter's pregnant and planning on being a teenage mother. Now the frosting on the cake is our mother has a working-class lover of dubious origin and a love child."

She dragged in a quick breath. "Edwina's secret has festered inside this family all of our lives. For large tracts of time she's been an emotionally absent mother and we've had to look after ourselves. When she did function, she parented by foisting duty and responsibility on us when the entire time she'd failed at it herself. This secret's tainted us. Now it's tainting Charlotte.

"I have absolutely no intention of meeting the woman Edwina gave birth to just as I have no intention of acknowledging her relationship with *that man*. I loved my father and I intend to honor him." Harriet poured a glass of whiskey from the crystal decanter and raised it to the ceiling acknowledging Richard before downing it in one gulp. "I really don't care if I never see Edwina again."

"You don't mean that," Xara said without thinking. Telling Harriet she didn't think or want something was akin to throwing down the gauntlet.

Harry's beautiful eyes hardened to navy slate. "Oh, I mean it."

For the first time Xara could remember, it felt like Georgie and Harriet had joined forces against their mother and, in a way, against her. The feeling came with an unanticipated sense of isolation.

She'd gone home to Steve and crawled into the warm space beside him in their bed, feeling unusually needy. "Families suck."

"And yet we love them," he said in his usual unruffled way. "Doesn't mean you have to like everyone in them all of the time."

"Yes, but aren't you supposed to at least like one of them some of the time?"

A week, later, Xara stood on the emerald green grounds of her old school, feeling the salt-laden air grazing her face. The wind carried a soupçon of Antarctic chill across the playing fields, whispering quietly but insistently that autumn would soon turn to winter. She remembered her six winters at the school: the crunch of ice under her feet as she'd trudged out in the pre-dawn darkness to check on her horse; the burn and itch of chilblains on her fingers from forgetting her gloves; and the need to learn how to hustle—arms akimbo, elbows sharp—for space around the heater. It was that or be permanently cold. How times had changed. Charlotte's five winters at the school were spent in a centrally heated boarding house.

Charlotte was staying with her and Steve while Edwina and Doug were in Mildura meeting Doug's daughters. Xara had met his son briefly at Glenora on Easter Sunday. Apparently he'd been in town and his father had obviously told him the news about his new sister, because by the time Xara had been introduced to him, he was ashen faced. He'd refused the offer of a drink and something to eat and excused himself, saying it was a holiday train schedule and he couldn't miss the last train back to Melbourne. Edwina and Doug hadn't urged him to stay or offered to make other arrangements to get him back to Melbourne. Her mother's lack of hospitality had been odd but then again, everyone had been off their game that day. Trying to digest the facts of a sister given away almost half a century ago had distracted all of them.

It wasn't until much later that the thought occurred to her that if Ben had stayed the night, all four of them could have talked together. He was as much affected by this news as they were. She wondered how Ben's sisters were coping. At least the Chirnwell sisters had known for a week that Doug existed and had recognized the signs that he was going to be a part of their mother's life. The Pedersons would be suffering from a double whammy of shock. She felt for those unknown people now connected to her in such a random way and wondered how they felt about their father.

Xara couldn't accurately define how she felt about her mother or her sisters. Georgie had stayed on with Harriet for a few days before returning to Melbourne for work. Although she'd told Xara she'd visit the farm before she left, she didn't. They'd traded a couple of texts but something was different; the banality of the messages wasn't enough to hide the new and uncomfortable distance. It sat between them bulky and with sharp edges that jabbed. Xara didn't want to acknowledge the hurt, especially after their last two years of closeness, but it felt very much like Georgie was actively pushing her away.

She turned her back on the blue of the bay and gazed up at the clock tower. The beautifully crafted metal clock hands showed she had five more minutes before Charlotte had promised to meet her after packing her things and saying goodbye to her friends. She'd promised her on pain of death to be on time because Tasha was having her feeding tube inserted today. If all went well, the procedure would be over soon and Xara wanted to be by her side when she woke up.

When Xara had visited Miligili yesterday to outline the plan for the day—combining the trip to the hospital with one to the school—Harriet had gripped the edge of the sink so hard the bones of her knuckles had threatened to burst through her skin.

"So, Charlotte's not only pregnant, she's dropping out of school too. Oh, it just keeps getting better and better."

"It's not quite like that, Harry. If you talked to her, you'd know."

Harriet's eyes flashed as hot and white as burning magnesium. "I've said everything I have to say on the matter."

And Xara knew exactly how stubborn Harriet could be. "To her credit, Charlie's worried how you'll manage to pay the school fees. She doesn't want to add to your financial stress. She's talked to the counselor and the school's been trying to accommodate her but it's unlikely she'd be allowed to continue past September. They're all a bit toey about her third trimester, so she decided it was best to withdraw now. She's enrolling at Billawarre Secondary."

Harriet flinched. "And her descent into mediocrity begins."

"Oh, for heaven's sake, Harry. Stop being such a snob. Give Charlie some credit for dealing with a difficult situation and focus on the fact she's doing what you want and completing her senior year."

"What I want is for her *not* to be pregnant. You know as well as I do she could go into labor during the exam period and then what?"

"She can apply for special consideration."

"All that means is a pass. It doesn't get her into pre-med."

"She isn't interested in studying pre-med, Harry." Xara touched her sister on the shoulder and finally said what she'd been thinking for a long time. "Isn't it time to let that unobtainable dream die?"

Harriet stepped away from her touch. "She had so much potential."

"She's not dead, Harry. She's still got loads of potential, including being a good mother. Aren't you worried that by not talking to her you're leaving things wide open for James to swoop in?"

"Edwina won't allow that."

"I don't understand you at all. You've clashed with Mom all your life, you're furious with her for standing between you and Charlie and you're barely talking to her. But you trust her to protect Charlie from James?"

Without looking at her, Harriet rubbed at the already clean pantry door with jerky sweeps of the cloth. "Close the door on your way out."

Now, standing on the track where Xara had once won the sprint relay, her cell phone beeped twice. She pulled the device from the pocket of her denim jacket. The first text was from Charlotte. *At car.* The second was from Steve. *She's in recovery. All good. Be here in 20 to meet her when she's out. Sx*

Xara released the breath she'd been holding all day. Tasha's health was hardly robust and any procedure came with extra risks compared with a healthy kid, but they'd cleared another hurdle. Their gorgeous girl was okay. Everything to do with her daughter was part compromise, part hope and part heartbreak. She hoped the trade-off of Tasha no longer tasting much food but receiving the parenteral nutrition would benefit her immune system.

Tasha had taught Xara and Steve that nothing in life was perfect and that expecting and demanding perfection only led to heartache. Xara immediately thought of Harriet as a case in point. Her sister's quest for perfection in all things was costing her a relationship with her daughter and her future grandchild.

Xara didn't want to speculate if perfection had played a role in Harriet's marriage. Even if her high standards had contributed—compelling James to consider stealing all that money—he'd been the one to make the illegal choice. Harriet's life had spectacularly crashed and burned and she'd reacted by cutting herself off from family. Xara wished her sister could see that the family was her one safe place.

She didn't consider herself religious, in fact she'd spent most of her school years dodging compulsory church services, but as she walked around the school chapel on her way back to the parking lot, she entered and sat briefly in the quiet, feeling the cool air swirl around her ankles.

Shafts of light, infused by the red, blue and yellow fragments of glass in the rose window, danced on the stone pillars, giving color to the somber gray. She gave thanks for Steve and the kids before sending up a plea that her mother, her sisters and herself would find a way through this devastating mess and come out the other side with their family still intact.

CHAPTER TWENTY-TWO

GEORGIE STEPPED BACK FROM THE EASEL AND BIT DOWN HARD on her bottom lip, not quite certain if she was doing it to stop the tears that threatened or if she welcomed the pain. She stared at the canvas, dismayed at what she saw. What had started out as an abstract representation of fluffy white clouds high above the old trestle railway bridge was now a mess of violent color: a shocking red bleeding heart hanging off a wooden beam and surrounded by dark pewter skies. So much for art taking her mind off things.

Off Ben.

Two weeks had passed since her world fell apart in the garden at Glenora. Her memories of exactly what had happened that day were hazy. All she could recall was the barrage of shock that had pummeled her and the accompanying gross feelings that now tainted every memory of Ben. He'd called and texted her for two days straight but during that numb period, each time she saw his name, she'd flinched. No matter how hard she screwed up her eyes or chanted *om, om, om,* it wasn't enough to stop disturbing images flashing through her mind.

Sometimes it was her mother and Doug having sex. Other times it was a baby. Once it was Ben, her mother and a baby. These flashes appalled her—if they were her mind's way of processing the shock, it wasn't helping. Nothing helped. Not even teaching the terrors of 2C, whose demands had always been a challenging distraction from her out-of-school life.

A swift volcanic rage suddenly hit her, quickening her pulse and shortening her breath. Hot, cross and despairing, she set down the paint palette, stomped into the kitchen and ripped open a family-size block of Dairy Milk Chocolate. The velvet confectionary melted on her tongue, the sweet flavor giving her a moment's relief.

This is so freaking unfair.

Meeting Ben was supposed to have been the turning point away from eighteen months of heartache and sadness, only now he'd come to embody exactly what she wanted to leave behind. All of it was Edwina's fault. Her ineffectual mother had created this unholy mess and cast her adrift in a sea of contrary emotions that left her lurching between utterly bereft and hell-fire hot fury.

She hated being at the mercy of such savage feelings. Wasn't it enough that she'd lost Eliza? Why did the universe think she should lose the first man she'd met since Jason who she'd dared to dream about sharing a future? She'd never been a daughter to have particularly strong reactions to either of her parents, mostly because in so many ways they'd always seemed to be on the periphery of her life. But these surges of wrath against her mother struck her out of the blue with the same crushing intensity of that awful moment in the garden at Glenora when her newly minted happiness had been brutally cut down.

She leaned heavily against the counter as the exhaustion that always followed the rage arrived. It left behind an immense sense of desolation. The intensity of these episodes made the resentment she'd experienced toward Edwina after Eliza's funeral seem inconsequential. But her fury wasn't restricted to Edwina—it extended to include Doug and Ben. All of them had plunged her into a daytime soap opera.

Without her knowledge, she'd been sleeping with her mother's lover's son and they shared a sister. *Oh God.* Yet again, her mouth dried and her skin crawled. She wasn't that type of person—one of those people who ended up on appalling and sensationalist television shows airing their dirty linen in public and screaming abuse at one another.

An overwhelming urge to scrub herself clean with a loofah hit her and she turned to the bathroom. She stopped. Over the past two weeks she'd succumbed a few times to the need to scour herself clean but the only thing it had achieved was red and stinging skin. It hadn't done a thing to prevent the uncomfortable feelings of shame, humiliation and indignity from rushing straight back and settling deep inside her.

Fear she was losing control of everything gripped her. She'd got close after losing Eliza and she didn't want to go there again. Glancing at the easel, she considered adding more drops of red paint to the pulverized heart but how would that help her? It just made her horror and heartache more real.

Talk to someone. Zar?

She brought up the number on her cell, stared at it then put it down. Again. The idea of telling someone wasn't new. Her educated brain knew talking about it might help, but her reptilian brain's survival instincts over-ruled her the very moment she tried to think of what she would say: "Oh, by the way. The guy I've been dating and having amazing sex with is Doug's son. Possibly our future stepbrother. Who'd have thunk it?"

Xara could be oddly prudish about sex and Georgie immediately pictured the look of horror that would tug at her sister's face before she made a nauseated gasp.. *What about Harry?* Harriet's reaction on the ick scale was an unknown quantity. What was predictable though was her reaction on the I-hate-everything-to-do-with-Doug scale. Her eldest sister would shriek down the phone, "Have you lost your freaking mind?"

Ruling out Harriet left talking to friends, but she was leery of that. No matter the friend, it was the sort of information that made people goggle-eyed and eager to know all the salacious details. The moment the conversation was over they'd share the sordid story with others to improve their gossip status. If she made them promise to keep it a secret, it would be the first thing to come out the next time they got drunk.

Oh, my God! Wait until you hear this. You will not believe what happened to Georgie!

Colleagues at school? Never ever. She didn't have to imagine the chatter in the teacher's lounge if they found out. The gossip about her and Ben would top the football, *The Greatest Loser* and *MasterChef* as the favorite lunchtime discussions. They'd be the hot topic, providing both delicious titillation and sheer relief it hadn't happened to them. At some point, someone would be bound to break into song with a rendition of the country music classic "I'm My Own Grandpa."

Harriet had become embroiled in a social scandal that wasn't of her own making and Billawarre was using her as both its entertainment and its scapegoat. Unlike her sister, Georgie planned to keep control over her story and she'd move heaven and earth to prevent it becoming anyone's amusement. She doubted Ben wanted their situation made public, but where did that leave her? The only person she could possibly talk to about it was Ben, but every time she thought about doing that she died a thousand deaths.

Her almost hysterical pleas at Glenora for him to "just go" made her shudder in mortification. If Ben was experiencing the same acute embarrassment about their situation that she was, how would they get past hello? How would she survive hearing him say, "You blew it, Georgie"? The only saving grace in this entire mess was that he wasn't working at her school this semester.

It didn't stop her missing him.

Her cell phone beeped and despite knowing it was unlikely to be Ben, her heart leaped. She checked the name—Melissa, her fellow second grade teacher—and disappointment flooded her. Hope was a bastard.

Want to see the new James Cameron movie with me and Jacob?

Georgie's body sagged and she gave in to the desolation for an indulgent moment before rolling her shoulders back. Why not go to the movie? At least it would get her out of the house and break up the agonizingly slow weekend. It would be a relief to concentrate on the storyline of the movie instead of the endless loop of her life.

Feeling good about being proactive, she typed back: *Sure. Where & when?*

We'll meet you at the Nova at 2.30.

She knew Melissa and Jacob would have gone shopping together this morning at the Queen Vic Market, sipping great coffee as they bantered with the stallholders and debated over which feta cheese would work best in their spinach and feta lasagna. Right now they'd be having brunch in one of the Lygon Street brasseries, reading the paper and debating the current political crisis and feeling good about throwing her a bone.

A sob broke over her lips as she texted back, *Great.* She was thirty-four years old, single and back to accepting charity dates from married friends.

There are days when magic happens and the imagination soars to tantalize with the promise of glorious and endless possibilities. Days when all the elements line up to reassure you that life is more than good: it's extraordinary and wondrous. Harriet's day hadn't come close. Hell, it had struggled to reach fair, let alone mediocre. Now, at eight o'clock on a Thursday night, she was desperately seeking a win.

After four weeks of losing more patients than she'd gained, she'd taken Debbie's sage advice and let her receptionist go. Nicki had worked with Harriet for a long time and this afternoon's conversation had been both difficult and excruciating. None of it had been made any easier by the fact that Nicki's sister had been James's PA.

"Um, I thought because I worked for you my job would be safe," Nicki had said, her fingers shredding a tear-dampened tissue. "What if I cut back my hours?"

Harriet had experienced the same jaw-tensing sensation she got whenever a patient or relative became upset. She liked to fix things and as a surgeon she was very good at doing just that. There was no better high than fighting death and winning—slicing out cancer; easing pain; giving hope. The buzz that came from removing and repairing was addictive but when she couldn't fix or mend, failure crept through her, casting doubt. She hated that. Right now she hated that she was the instrument of Nicki's distress.

"I wish I could keep you on but until the town has a change of heart, I'm at its mercy. You've seen the fall in patients and you've barely had anything to keep you occupied this week."

"Um, I could take my vacation. I'm owed two weeks."

"You could but I can't promise there'll be a job for you to come back to. If there's a miraculous improvement then of course I'd rehire you, but this town has a long memory. Right now everything's still very raw. I think it will stay like this until after the court case."

"Um, when will that be?" A flicker of hope had flared on Nicki's pale face.

Harriet had hated that she was going to douse that hope like a fireman wielding a high-powered hose. "At the earliest, six months, but it's likely to be as long as a year away. The police are still combing through documents, looking for more evidence." She'd cleared her throat against the familiar lump of fury, pain, distress and despair that rose up every time she thought about what James had done. "I'm not going to give you false hope. I don't want you waiting around for a job that might never happen. I've written you a glowing reference and if you wish, I can make inquiries at the hospital about job openings." *Oh, and won't that be fun. You can do it at the same time you meet with the medical director to ask for increased hospital hours.*

Four hours later, she was still regretting she'd made that offer to Nicki. Reg Davies would do everything he possibly could to make that meeting the most excruciating one of her life. He was still ticked off over her decision three years ago to drop back her public patient load and skew her practice toward predominantly private patients.

Now she needed more public patients so she could work and pay her bills. He'd positively gloat with delight when she went cap in hand to see him and she knew exactly how much he'd make her squirm. He'd schedule her on-call for every weekend as if she was an intern again and she'd have to take it.

The only thing in her favor was the recent federal government funding to help whittle down surgical waiting lists—there was plenty of work in the hospital and although the patients could refuse to have her treat them, they had less choice than the private patients. They may just swallow their pride as she was swallowing hers.

Reg Davies wasn't the only hospital employee who'd be delighting in her predicament. Every enemy she'd made—wittingly or unwittingly—over the last decade was now taking pleasure in her situation. Even her timid intern had queried her over a decision today, which he'd probably regretted after the tongue-lashing she'd given him. Yes, her husband had upended her life and placed her in a precarious financial situation. Yes, her social standing had lost more points than the Billawarre Panthers had lost in last year's appalling season. Yes, she was estranged from her mother and her daughter, but she knew surgery inside out. Right now, that was the only thing keeping her sane, but she needed more of it.

The only upside to her diminished work hours was she had plenty of time to finesse her plans to try and keep Miligili. The message on her cell phone today had given flesh to that hope. She sliced open a box of water crackers and set them in a dish, positioning them next to a cheese platter that included a very ripe blue vein from Tasmania. After adding some pear spread, a handful of roasted almonds and a bunch of green grapes, she stepped back and surveyed her handiwork.

The elegant white platter contrasted beautifully with the Baltic pine table and her grandmother's gleaming silver cheese knife. She poured two glasses of pinot grigio, giving them time to lose a little of the chill and wake up the flavors. She was just returning the bottle to the refrigerator when a knock sounded on the door. She grimaced. Odd how James's moral compass had a totally new setting but his punctuality remained the same.

"Come in."

He strode through the door and into the small living space, heading straight to her as if he was going to kiss her hello. *No way on God's green earth, mate.* She held out her arm, wrist cocked like a traffic cop, and he stopped abruptly, wearing a look of discombobulation.

"No kiss hello? Okay. It's hard to break a habit of a lifetime."

"Oh, I don't know. You didn't seem to have any trouble breaking the law-abiding habit." She gestured to the table. "Have a seat."

Surprisingly, he didn't fire a salvo back but sat and surveyed the table and the wine. "This looks very civilized."

"I thought we could try." She sat opposite him and cut a hunk of brie off the wheel.

"Thanks for seeing me."

She bit off the customary "You're welcome" and got straight to the point. "Going by your voice mail, I believe you had a trip to Geelong for nothing."

His polite façade faltered. "What the hell's going on? Why isn't Charlie back at school and why is she still at Glenora?"

She noticed flecks of silver in his hair that hadn't been there a month ago. His blue eyes, which had always drawn and held her gaze, had paled and in the process lost their enticing power. The lines around his eyes were definitely deeper and carved into his temples. It appeared crime aged a man quickly and decisively.

"You haven't spoken to her?"

His shoulders slumped. "I've tried. She doesn't want to see me and your mother isn't helping. Edwina's guarding her more closely than a eunuch guards a virgin."

Harriet couldn't stop her ironic laugh, but she flinched as the sound bounced back to her. "Your daughter's hardly that."

He frowned. "Hardly what?"

"Charlotte isn't a virgin."

He winced. "I don't want to know that about my little girl."

She took a slug of wine, knowing exactly what he meant but she refused to let him know she felt the same way. She had no intention of softening their daughter's news or the way it was delivered. "You may wish to stick your head in the sand about her being sexually active, but you won't be able to ignore the results. She's pregnant."

For a moment James was ominously still and then his hands hit the table, sending the crockery rocking against the wood. "What the hell! How?"

She rolled her eyes. "Remember that party she wanted to go to in her second week back? The one I said no to but you signed the permission slip after she schmoozed you? Well, that bit of parenting backfired."

"Pregnant? Christ, that's not what I wanted for her."

She mustered everything to stay aloof and disconnected. The last thing she needed was to bond with him over their mutual horror about the pregnancy. He'd lost all rights to sharing anything with her. His fingers tore at a patch of hair on the crown of his head and the uncharitable thought crossed her mind that it was thinner than it had been.

"Fuck, H."

"I believe that is exactly what she was doing."

He leaned forward and she caught the zip of the cologne she'd given him for Christmas, the cologne she always loved on him. The bastard knew how she felt about that fragrance and he'd deliberately showered before coming over to see her. She knew from the tips of her hair to the painted nails of her toes she needed to keep one step ahead of him at all times in whatever this unnamed game was they were playing.

Right now though, sitting slumped and winded, James didn't look like he was playing any games. He looked like a distraught father and his gaze implored her to reassure him. "But you're taking care of things, right? You know the best doctors to ask and after the abortion she'll return to school."

She leaned back, spinning the glass in her fingers and trying to keep her heart rate steady. It always galloped whenever she thought about Charlotte and Edwina. "She's insisting on keeping the baby."

"That's crazy. She's a kid." His eyes narrowed. "What's your game? Is this a way of getting to me?"

She gave a bark of laughter. "Has your foray into fraud made you paranoid? Of course I don't want her to have a baby at eighteen. It's Edwina who's enabling her decision."

"You're joking."

She shook her head slowly.

"None of this makes any sense."

"Actually, it does." The incandescent rage she felt for her mother made her pull a grape off the bunch with more force than necessary. "Charlotte has an unexpected ally supporting her and her choice. It appears your esteemed mother-in-law, the doyen of Billawarre, got knocked up back in 1968. She was forced to give up the baby so now, forty-eight years too late, she's taking a stand."

"Jesus." For a few moments bewilderment played across his face, chasing itself in puzzled circles before rapidly clearing. His mouth curved up into a smile full of white teeth and devastating charm. "At least Edwina's dirty little secret makes my misdemeanors slightly less conspicuous."

Like a blast of liquid nitrogen, the blood in her veins chilled. "One can't confuse a teenage pregnancy with fraud, James. They're two very different beasts." She turned and reached for the manila folder she'd placed on the side table behind her. "Charlotte's withdrawal from school solves the problem of finding the money to pay school fees."

His face pinched. "She can't give up school."

"No." She deliberately drank more wine. She intended to give the impression she was far more informed about their daughter's life than she was and conveniently hide from James that all her information about Charlotte currently came from Xara. "She has plans for her education."

"What plans? I'm her father. I should be involved."

"I think fathers who commit criminal offenses automatically lose a certain amount of parental influence. Mind you, if she ever needs help with creative accounting, you'll probably be her first port of call."

His mouth thinned. "God, you're a first-class bitch when you choose to be."

"I'm sorry. Am I incorrect in assuming you're an expert at creative accountancy? So you've failed at that as well?" She pushed the folder toward him. "Seeing as we're talking about money ..."

A flush started at his collar and quickly spread up his face, giving him the florid look of someone who drank far too much. "Your attorney's claim for your share of the property settlement is ridiculous. Hell, if Charlie's not even living with you then I don't need to pay you a cent for her support."

She raised her brows. "That statement implies you actually have money to pay."

A flicker of furtiveness lit up his eyes before fading quickly. Whether from guilt, secrecy or relief, she couldn't tell, but it gave her pause. Had he stashed some funds somewhere? The Caymans? Switzerland? Was he hiding money to avoid it being seized? A sharp pain caught her between the ribs. That she thought him capable of doing something that low and despicable rammed home that her marriage was truly over.

Before James's duplicity, the concept of their marriage ending in divorce never crossed her radar and yet now it was her reality. It hovered in the air she breathed, pressed down hard on her bones and dragged so heavily it almost impeded her movements. For almost a quarter of a century their marriage had been such a source of pleasure and inspiration for her. Now it was reduced to this bitter wheeling and dealing and loss of mutual respect. She refused to show him how devastated she was that he'd torpedoed their life together but when she was alone, she wept for all they'd lost.

"All my accounts are frozen," he said tersely, "and you emptied the joint account. By rights, H, you should be the one paying me a weekly allowance."

You'll burn in hell before I do that. She stayed focused on her plan, which doubled as her map, compass and flashlight in this heavily contested battle. She tapped the folder. "I have a proposal for you."

The businessman in him sat up. "I'm listening."

"I want sole ownership of Miligili."

He didn't even blink. "I'm sure you do, but that's sounding more like a demand than a proposal."

"My proposal is that you sign over your share of the house to me."

He laughed. "Why would I do that?"

"Oh, I don't know ..." She linked her fingers together tightly to stop her hands from shaking. "... perhaps to protect your share of the house. If it's in my name, your share can't be pursued as part of a civil fraudulent conversion claim."

He fished up a handful of almonds, the casual action belying the tension riddling his body. "You've been doing your legal homework."

She had, although her attorney didn't know it. "If Miligili stays in joint names and we're forced to sell, you don't get any money and I'll lose the house. We both end up losing."

His slightly raised brows told her he didn't totally buy her altruism. "The house and land are valued at three million. If I sign it over, you immediately gain one and a half million."

"One and a half million that won't be contested or lost. Isn't it better I keep it safe for you?"

"You're asking me to trust you with that amount of money?"

Her chin shot up. "I'm not the one who broke the trust in our marriage."

"How about you just buy me out?"

When hell freezes over. Irrespective of the fact she couldn't raise that sort of money, she believed he owed her ownership of the house in exchange for what he'd done to them. Miligili was her heritage, not his. It belonged to her far more than it belonged to him.

"There's the issue of my missing retirement, the theft from the practice, and the large withdrawals earmarked for the mortgage repayments that never got paid." Years of working under pressure in highly charged situations kept her voice even but her heart thumped as hard and as fast as a Labrador's tail on bare boards.

He didn't flinch or wince. "It doesn't add up to one and half million."

"If you add interest and pain and suffering, it comes pretty damn close. The thing is, James, the initial charges laid against you will increase by a factor of ten. My deal is this. You sign over the house to me and I won't tell the police about the theft from my retirement fund or the practice account." She tilted her head in contemplation. "Surely reduced jail time's worth that?"

He considered her offer. "It's not like I'll get a year for every theft. I've been doing some legal research too, H, and in similar cases they bundle up the charges. I tell you what. I'll sign Miligili over to you for the bargain rate of one million. How does that sound?"

She wanted to dive across the table and scratch his eyes out. "I don't think so."

He shrugged, sat back and crossed his arms. "Then you really don't want Miligili badly enough."

She'd thought the threat of jail time would move him but she'd been way off the mark—it was money that drove him. How had she lived with him for so long and not seen that? She'd thought his passion came from a combination of his desire to make money and his philanthropic endeavors but nothing about him hinted at munificence. Time to tweak the plan. She zeroed in on his now evident personality flaw.

"There's no point me paying. It will just be taken off you like your stock portfolio."

"It won't if the money's sent overseas."

She didn't know whether to high-five herself at her earlier prediction or sink into a pit of misery. "The police would be very interested in hearing about that."

"I doubt it. There's no direct link between me and the money and no way to prove it." He shot her a crocodile smile. "So do you want Miligili or not?"

Cool. Calm. Detached. She repeated the mantra over and over because looking needy was weak and the weak got trampled every time. "I do." There was more than one way to skin a cat.

She gave a long, put-upon sigh, hoping she could pull off her last gambit and make it look like she was doing him a favor. "I know you're not happy with my attorney's opinion of what's a fair and equitable distribution of assets."

He snorted. "That's understating it."

"Which is where my proposal really comes in. There's a way we can do this without involving the Family Court or any attorneys."

He took the bait. "How?"

"We act quickly. Choose a small conveyancing firm where we're not known and sign a gift deed to make a transfer of love, care and affection. This puts Miligili into my name. I'll clear the two missed mortgage payments and the bank won't object to the transfer. If you do this, I'll absolve you of all financial responsibility to Charlotte and me."

He studied her intently. "And you'll call off your bitch of an attorney."

"I will."

"I need more."

She really didn't want to sign anything promising him a share of the house down the track—a share she had no intention of giving him. "What?"

"I continue living at Miligili rent free."

No. No. No. Her gut cramped. The whole point of the plan was to get him out of her house and out of her life. But she wouldn't have a house if he didn't sign the papers.

"I've seen the state of the house. How about you move in here, live rent free and I'll pay for Nya to clean it." *And spy for me.*

"Okay."

"Okay?" Her amazement at his far-too-easy capitulation seeped into her voice, undoing all of her studied aloofness. She swiped the unlock screen on her cell phone and brought up her diary. "Shall we do this tomorrow?"

"I want to see Charlie."

Apprehension crawled in her veins. "That's up to Charlotte."

His expression said he didn't agree. "Convince her to meet me for a real visit. I'm not talking five minutes at the door flanked by her grandmother and aunts. It has to be lunch or dinner. Do that and I'll sign."

Harriet's mouth dried. She'd told her daughter in no uncertain terms she was unwelcome in her home unless she terminated her pregnancy. This left her with no bargaining power to convince Charlotte that supporting her quest to save Miligili was the best thing for the both of them. And if she did try to cut a deal with Charlotte and force her to see James when her daughter clearly didn't want to, didn't that make her as morally bankrupt as him?

How is it different from insisting she have an abortion?

The thought came out of nowhere and dug in despite her trying to shift it.

It's totally different. I'm older, wiser and I'm her mother. I'm trying to protect her. Stop her from making the wrong decision. This baby will ruin her life.

She heard her mother's voice in the back of her mind. *Respect her decision.*

And that was the crux of her dilemma. Some decisions, like Charlotte not wanting to see James, were easier to respect than others. Suddenly, the idea of getting her hands on one million dollars to secure Miligili seemed the easier option.

CHAPTER TWENTY-THREE

It had been a whirlwind month for Edwina. She and Doug had driven to Mildura straight after Easter and faced Doug's daughters. Their reactions to Edwina's presence in their father's life had been as varied as her girls' responses to Doug, yet different. Polite but wary most accurately summed up their reactions. There'd been none of Harriet's slit-eyed hostility or Georgie's initial enthusiasm.

They'd visited all three of his daughters' homes and the unifying motif was the photos of Sophia, which hung on their walls and sat on side tables as a solid reminder of her role in their lives and of their love for her. On an intellectual level, Edwina understood their reaction. She was the interloper—the unexpected person impinging on their lives and monopolizing their father's attention. However, knowing that hadn't been enough to stop her from wishing for the pie-in-the-sky ideal that the Pederson girls would instantly warm to her.

In reality, that was unlikely to ever happen. Any seeds of warmth that may have been sown at their first meeting had been trampled by the shock news of their secret sister. On this topic their reactions perfectly matched her daughters': shocked surprise. The difference lay in the fact that it was easier for them to forgive their father, who, until recently, hadn't known of the child's existence, than it was for her daughters to forgive her for having kept the secret for so long.

Doug's son, Ben, had been more forthright when they'd been forced to tell him at Glenora. Sitting next to a white-faced Georgie, he'd asked, "Are you going to try to find her?"

When they'd replied in the affirmative, he'd said, "Good luck." There was a lot of Doug in Ben and his words had been genuinely warm without a trace of sarcasm. Georgie's reaction hadn't been as charitable.

Edwina sighed at the memory. What a mess. She'd had no clue Georgie was seeing anyone, let alone Doug's son. The randomness of it still flabbergasted her and she really didn't know much more about their relationship other than what she'd seen at Glenora—the two of them holding hands.

She'd tried to discuss the situation with Georgie but her daughter had refused, joining Harriet in the not-talking-to-Edwina stakes. She'd asked Doug if he knew anything about Ben and Georgie but he had very little information other than they taught at the same school and they'd been dating a short time.

Edwina had left messages, emailed and texted Georgie, but days turned into weeks and the silence continued. She missed the regular phone calls from her youngest daughter, who'd always brightened her week with entertaining stories of the terrors of 2C.

Would she have any daughters left talking to her by the end of this? The question begged her to define "this" and "end." All she knew was "this" was her life and her need to make peace with the past was currently shattering her present. She huffed out a breath and gave herself a shake. Her past had always shattered her present. The difference now was that she was taking control and living her life the way she wanted rather than having it dictated to her.

It came with consequences but so did not taking any action, and she had a PhD in that. She loved her daughters dearly and if she had the power not to hurt them she would use it, but her pain was their pain and that had been the case for all of their lives. The legacy of the loss of her first-born daughter always hovered over them, circling and impacting on her relationship with the three of them. Was there ever a good time to reveal a secret like a lost child?

Of course not, but she'd rationalized that as her daughters were now adult women with their own life experiences and daughters of their own, they may be able to see things from her point of view. Instead, two of them had reverted to being little girls again, unable to see past their own small worlds to view the bigger picture. She appreciated Xara's unstinting support but at the same time she understood her middle daughter's conflict regarding her sisters.

As soon as she and Doug had returned from Mildura, they'd flown to Hobart. The counselor, Tim, had told them their baby had lived her childhood years in Launceston as Michelle van Leeuwen. He then went on to caution them not to expect too much too soon—or anything at all. He'd emphasized that searches could take a very long time and sometimes the person was never found, or if they were, it was via a death certificate. After hosing down their expectations, he'd checked the adoption information register. Miracle of miracles, Michelle had registered two years earlier, wishing to make contact with her birth parents.

Edwina couldn't believe their luck and she'd trashed caution, thrilled beyond her wildest dreams their daughter wanted to find them. When Tim handed her the folder containing Michelle's adoption details, she'd held it as reverently as if it was fragile lace that would disintegrate under her touch. To be holding concrete evidence of her baby after decades in the wilderness validated the hazy memories of that tiny child with her dimpled fingers and chocolate lashes.

Tim said he'd mail Michelle a brief and standard letter informing her that her birth parents wished to make contact. Thanking Tim, they left the office floating on air and checked into their Georgian bed and breakfast, impervious to the magnificent sandstone façade, the Doric columns, the perfect period reproduction furniture and the luxuriously deep claw-foot bathtub with its large selection of spa products. They'd spent the rest of the day drafting a letter to Michelle, eager to have it ready to send to her the moment they got word from Tim that she'd made contact. They'd written multiple drafts of the letter before they were happy with it. Mentally exhausted but utterly elated, they'd gone out to dinner and celebrated their good fortune by drinking Tasmanian sparkling wine and dining on Tasmanian salmon.

That dinner had been three weeks ago and the much-revised letter lay languishing in her leather writing bag, still waiting to be mailed. Despite having registered for contact two years ago, Michelle was yet to respond to Tim's letter. The disappointment crushed Edwina's soul, a bruising blow on top of the grief she'd carried with her all her life but unlike in the past, this time she hadn't tumbled into the dark abyss. This time she wasn't alone with her grief, and she clung to Doug like a limpet on a rock buffeted by stormy seas. He in turn drew strength from her as they tried to balance hope with impatience and despair with reason.

The antique pendulum clock nestled inside its glass dome chimed four. Shutting down her computer, she watched the screen fade to black against an inbox full of correspondence, but none of it the email she craved. She walked into the kitchen to find Doug and Charlotte whipping up a batch of scones. Doug was currently splitting his time 70/30 between Billawarre and Mildura. The garage had a reliable manager and his classic car sales were mostly done online, giving him the freedom to be in Billawarre, for which she was grateful.

"How was the driving lesson?"

Charlotte laughed. "The drive home from school took ten minutes but I only need another five hours and I'll hit the magic 120 hours for my driver's license. The rest of the time was car anatomy. I've learned how to check the tire pressure, check the oil and I know where to add more windshield washer fluid."

"Tomorrow, it's coolant, keeping battery terminals clean and learning how to use jumper cables," Doug said, his expression serious. "Too many people drive cars and have no idea how to look after them."

"I don't think Mom even knows where her battery is in the new Merc," Charlotte said and immediately winced.

She hadn't mentioned Harriet for days and Edwina hoped as she'd just spoken about her mother she might want to talk more about her. She took a seat at the table. "Your mother's first car was a secondhand Corolla and Gramps taught her all the things Doug's teaching you."

Edwina laughed, suddenly remembering Harriet regaling her and Richard with a story. "Harriet once impressed a group of young male doctors with her car battery knowledge. They were clustered around a car that wouldn't start and she took off her very elegant high-heeled shoe and banged the battery terminals with it. You can imagine how they rolled their eyes, but she had the last laugh when the car roared into life."

"I can see Mom doing that," Charlotte said almost wistfully before turning her attention to the tight jam jar lid. "I appreciate the lessons, Doug. But I'm not sure I can even afford to buy a secondhand car let alone run one."

"Don't worry about that now," Edwina said. "We'll sit down and work out a financial arrangement you can afford. Your job is to sit your test as soon as you turn eighteen. Having your license will make life with a baby a lot easier."

"I've got the boys in the garage keeping an eye out for a decent secondhand car for you," Doug said.

Charlotte hugged him then kissed Edwina. "Thank you, Mardi. Any news from Michelle?"

Unlike her mother and aunts, Charlotte had taken the news about another aunt in her stride. Edwina wondered if it was to do with her youth or her current situation. Whatever the reason, she was just grateful for her granddaughter's non-judgmental attitude and for the easy way she referred to Michelle by name.

Edwina caught Doug's eye and the hopeful flash in their dark depths. She shook her head and watched the anticipation fade. "Nothing yet. Tim said he'd pass on our contact details when she emailed him so all we can do is be patient."

"Don't you think it's strange she wanted to contact you two years ago and now she doesn't?" Charlotte asked.

"A lot can happen in two years." Doug pulled golden scones from the oven. "She might have moved and forgotten to update the register. Her situation may have changed and with it her need to meet us. Life can change in a heartbeat, Charlie girl."

"I get it, Doug. My life changed in the amount of time it took for two pink lines to appear on a white stick." Charlotte set down a small bowl of jam and one of cream. "Now I'm at a new school, my mother's not talking to me, I'm living here and trying to imagine my life with a baby."

Edwina poured tea. "How's school?"

She shrugged. "Different."

"The work?"

"No, the subjects are fine. I'm on top of the study and the teachers are okay. It's just a bit lonely. I'm used to everyone being at school 24/7 and always having someone to talk to. It's hard getting to know people when they leave the grounds if they don't have classes."

"I always see a crowd of senior students at the Staff of Life café when I buy bread." Doug slathered jam on a steaming scone. "You should go there to meet people."

"Mom would have a fit." Charlotte visibly sagged. "I guess I don't have to worry about that anymore."

Edwina squeezed her hand. "I want to say Harriet will change her mind ..."

"Yeah, I know. But there's a big chance she never will. On the flip side though, she did text me today."

Surprise caused Edwina to blink. As far as she knew, it was the first time Harriet had contacted Charlotte. "What did she say?"

"It's a bit weird." Charlotte pulled out her cell phone, swiped the screen until she found the text then read aloud, "'I told your father about the pregnancy. He wants to have lunch or dinner with you soon. Text him yes or no so he knows where he stands with you.'"

Edwina schooled her face to neutral. She didn't know what to make of the text either, but she didn't disclose that to Charlotte. "Why do you think it's odd?"

"Because Mom *always* tells me what to do. What food to eat, which clothes to wear, what career to study, who to make friends with, to terminate my baby ..."

She locked her cell phone and put it face down. "The night after your party she was emphatic that she didn't want me to see Dad. I was angry and I said I wanted to see him. She huffed and eventually said I wasn't to see him alone. Remember how she arrived for Easter Sunday lunch? She only came because she thought Dad would bribe me with chocolates to get me on my own. Now she's basically saying it's my choice whether I see him or not. My choice. That isn't Mom at all."

"It could be a good sign. She might be coming around," Doug said.

"Ha! *Ha!* You don't know my mother." Charlotte exchanged a glance with Edwina then snagged her bottom lip. "I think it's more proof she's cutting me out of her life." Her voice wobbled. "The fact she doesn't care if I meet Dad or not is huge."

"What are you going to do?"

"About Dad? I don't know. I just want to hide here at Glenora with you." Charlotte pressed her hands together under her nose. "Also, Hamish's parents want to meet me in July when they're visiting Melbourne from Qatar. Hamish said they're seriously pissed at him. Should I go?"

"They are the baby's grandparents." Edwina thought through the logistics. "You already know the worst possible reaction because you've experienced it from your mother. The Langs might just surprise you."

"Yoo-hoo. Knock knock." Primrose walked in holding a huge multi-colored bouquet of chrysanthemums.

"Rosie." Edwina jumped to her feet and hugged her friend with a combination of guilt and pleasure. "Are these your 'mums?'"

Primrose grinned. "The garden's a blaze of color. After last year's debacle, I read the riot act to David. I told him if any calves got into the home pasture I'd move to Melbourne."

"The threat obviously worked. They're glorious. We've just made afternoon tea. Join us."

"I will." Primrose sat at the table. "I know we've talked on the phone but I haven't seen you since your party. That's far too long. You're looking good though. Sex obviously suits you."

Doug threw back his head and roared laughing.

Charlotte's mouth fell open. "Auntie P!" she spluttered, sounding exactly like her mother.

Edwina caught the gaze of her long-time friend and gave a rueful smile. "Primrose is cross with me, Charlie. She always behaves badly when she feels she's missing out on things."

"Your grandmother and I have known each other since we were seven and we can say anything to each other," Primrose replied with equanimity. She suddenly startled. "Hang on a minute, Charlie. Why are you wearing Billawarre High's uniform?"

Charlotte's shoulders straightened. "I go there now. This is my third week. I'm pregnant and living with Mardi."

This time it was Primrose's turn to gape.

A surge of pride washed through Edwina at Charlotte's courage, but at the same time it amplified her own deficits. If Charlotte was brave enough to tell people she was pregnant then it was time for Edwina to reverse the lie she'd lived under for so long. She owed Primrose the truth.

As if sensing that Charlotte's statement was portentous for Edwina and Primrose, Doug rose to his feet. "Excuse me, ladies. I've got to call a man about a 1951 Maserati convertible. I'll leave you to chat."

Charlotte stood too. "I've got to study for an assignment, Auntie P, but Mardi will answer your questions."

The usually unflappable Primrose—a stalwart woman who'd weathered droughts and wildfires and cared for veterans with PTSD —grappled for words. "I ... that's ... well ..." She smiled. "Congratulations, Charlie."

Charlotte stilled and a tear spilled down her cheek. "Thanks." She hugged Primrose. "You're the first person who's said that to me."

Primrose patted Charlotte's back and gave Edwina a concerned glance over the top of her head. "It won't be easy, dear, but if you're determined, that will carry you a long way."

The moment Charlotte had left the room, Primrose said, "Good heavens, Edwina. No wonder I haven't seen you. I imagine all hell's broken loose with Harriet."

"You could say that."

Primrose studied her with what Edwina called her analytical social worker gaze. "I have to say, part of me's surprised Charlotte's living here."

Old habits die hard and Edwina heard herself saying, "Living with James was hardly advisable and Xara's flat out with her brood."

"All of that's a given but none of it's an automatic agreement for you to take Charlie in. In fact, if I'd been asked to bet on it, I'd have backed no as being more likely."

"Perhaps you don't know me as well as you think." Except Edwina knew full well Primrose only knew the side of herself she'd been prepared to share.

Primrose sipped her tea. "If Richard were alive and Harriet had kicked Charlie out, you'd have asked me to take her in."

"That's very true."

"Oh, Edwina." She shook her head slowly, smiling broadly. "I've waited forty-odd years for the Edwina Mannering I knew as a girl to come back. You had such spark. You were so full of fun until you married Richard and decided to live your mother's life. Now the real you is back with vengeance and hooray for that. First you flout a lifetime of propriety by openly cohabitating with Doug Pederson and now Charlie's living here. The town's already agog. It will be positively apoplectic when the news of Charlie's pregnancy breaks."

"Do you want a gin and tonic?" Edwina needed one.

"At four in the afternoon?"

"Why not? The sun's well and truly over the yardarm."

Primrose laughed. "Well, when you put it like that. I'll go and pick a lemon."

By the time Primrose returned, Edwina had mixed the drinks and set them on a tray alongside a blue bottle of gin and extra tonic. She deftly sliced the sun-warmed lemon and dropped a slice in each glass. "Let's drink these outside."

They settled in the gazebo and Edwina took a fortifying slug from her drink. "Rosie, there's something I have to tell you. Remember the day I arrived at Irrewillipe in the white VW bug?"

CHAPTER TWENTY-FOUR

"OH, EDWINA." PRIMROSE'S EYES BRIMMED WITH TEARS. "PART of me always envied you the Mannering wealth and style. But all that privilege came with suffocating duty and conditions, didn't it?"

Edwina stirred her second gin and tonic, relaxing into the relief that flowed through her now she'd told Primrose the truth about Doug, Richard and Michelle. She needed her friend's counsel now more than ever. "As much as I hate all the Mannering pride and family duty, I've unwittingly inflicted some of it onto the girls. Harriet especially. She's the one who's embraced the family traditions."

"Hang on, Edwina. She had Richard encouraging her all the way. Harriet is his creation. He made her into what he valued the most. She's a talented doctor like he was, a person of influence like both of you and a hostess with all of your grace and style. She wanted all of it and that's okay."

"That may be, but she's furious with me for the duplicity about Sus—Michelle and for supporting Charlie's decision to keep her baby."

"Poor Harriet. As well as inheriting the best traits of her parents, she also picked up the worst ones. But given everything you've been through, I understand your stance with Charlie."

"I don't have a choice," Edwina reflected. "The loss of Michelle affected how I bonded with my girls. I love them, of course I love them, but when they were born it was different. As much as I tried to love them wholeheartedly, I held something back. I didn't want to, but I had no control. It was almost like I'd taken out heart protection insurance so if they were taken from me, I'd still have something left to keep me standing. How crazy is that? If I'd lost any of them it would have destroyed me."

"You suffered a huge trauma, Edwina. Our brain tries to protect us from that pain and anguish ever happening again. Sadly it can come with nasty side effects."

"Oh, I've had all of those," Edwina said savagely. "My brain didn't protect me. All it did was put distance between me and my daughters. Each time I gave birth, Richard was the one left holding the baby and picking up the pieces of me."

"He had help," Primrose said briskly. "He had a lot of help, if I remember rightly. Stop beating yourself up so much. God, you weren't given any support after you lost Michelle."

"I was told to forget."

"And that's never helpful." Primrose frowned. "Didn't your mother go away for a few months after Ian was born? Back then, everyone said it was a vacation because no one ever mentioned mental illness outside of the family, or inside for that matter. Even if you hadn't been forced to give up your baby, you don't know for sure that you wouldn't have gotten postnatal depression when you had the girls."

"I've wondered the same thing, but all I know is that when I held my first baby everything was different. Despite the traumatic delivery and the fact she was going to be stolen from me, my whole body tingled with an overwhelming love for her. It was so strong, I couldn't comprehend such a feeling existed. When I held Harriet, Xara and

Georgie, all I ever felt was cold, hard dread. The love always came a lot later."

Her voice cracked and she sucked in a steadying breath. "Rosie, I still break out in a cold sweat when I see a newborn baby. It not only made me a poor mother, it made me a poor grandmother until the children were walking and talking. When Georgie lost Eliza, I should have been the one supporting her. Instead I fell back into the pit of despair that has claimed me too often over the years. It left Georgie floundering and relying on her sisters when she should have been depending on me."

She fingered her pearls. "Now, Harriet's risking cutting her only child and future grandchild out of her life. She doesn't realize how much grief that course of action will cause her down the track. And none of it's helped by James's actions. Harriet's spent her life being popular and now she's dealing with the town turning on her."

"There's a definite edge of tall poppy syndrome in the way the town's reacting." Primrose gave a huff of frustration. "Sexism as well. If Harriet had committed the crime and defrauded everyone, James would have been circled with concern and given hot dinners. Instead, the vultures came out and zeroed in on Harriet as if she's carrion."

"It's very unfair and it's so hard to watch. I talked to Doug about going public about Michelle, thinking that if they were busy gossiping about me, it might take the heat off Harriet. He wisely pointed out that until we hear from Michelle it's best not to tell anyone beyond the family."

"And me." Primrose raised her glass.

"You're family, Rosie. You're better than family because you make less emotional demands on me and you give me so much." She shifted in her seat and smoothed down her skirt. "Anyway, all of it's left me aching for Harriet. Granted, her forthright manner hasn't always made her welcome everywhere in town. Remember last November when she was interviewed about the rural obesity epidemic? She said there were causal links between obesity and some cancers and people needed to take it seriously and lose weight. It didn't go down well."

"It's got nothing to do with the message and everything to do with Harriet being a rich, educated, successful and well-dressed woman."

Indignation simmered on Primrose's pink-veined cheeks. "David's made a career out of being obstreperous and outspoken, and Richard was embroiled in his fair share of verbal clashes. Your father was an old-style politician who called a spade a spade and didn't suffer fools. And let's not forget Billawarre's long history of rich and bloody-minded businessmen and farmers who thought because they had the cash, they owned the town.

"All of them men and none of them were treated like Harriet. I told Irene Bennison exactly that the other day when she was mouthing off at the community center. I said I was disappointed in her as a feminist and a citizen."

"Thank you, Rosie, but you probably just risked the future of your life skills course. Irene does the scheduling for the community center."

"If she tries to bump out any of my groups she might just find herself experiencing some of what Harriet's going through," Primrose exclaimed hotly. "What I hate most is how people are behaving. At its core it's just spiteful envy. They're gleefully rejoicing in the struggles of one of Billawarre's upstanding families and cheerfully ignoring Harriet's innocence in the fraud. They're totally overlooking how much she contributes to the community."

"And that's why I love you," Edwina said gratefully. "You're sensible and such a champion for women. I'm taking a page out of your playbook. As much as I love Harriet, I won't allow Charlie's life to be blighted by being forced to lose a baby she desperately wants. If my life is going to count for something, that pain must stop with me."

Primrose silently considered Edwina for a long moment. "Even if it means you and Harriet never reconcile?"

The thought tore down deep, stealing her breath and shredding her soul. "Our current estrangement is an extension of the distance that's always existed between us. Of course, I long for us to be closer, but in forty-five years I can count on one hand the moments when there was a narrowing of the gap. I'd get excited, then Richard would do something smarter, shinier and more interesting, and, puff, it was gone. Since his death, Harriet's idolized him and I can never win against that. I'm not prepared to sacrifice Charlie for a cause that's already lost."

"So what are you going to do?"

Edwina took a fortifying draft of her drink. "I'm going to act like a mother, slice open an artery and talk to Harriet."

HI, Georgie

How are things? We're pretty good here. It rained each day last week just in time for some grass to grow before winter so YAY! Twins LOVING their first football season while I freak out on the sidelines about a kick to the kidneys or a boot to the head. We've had some initial problems with Tashie's feeding tube but she's gained weight.

I'm now volunteering as a Justice of the Peace, witnessing documents on Thursday mornings at the police station. It's basically a good gossip session although I've had to go in to bat for Harry a few times. I don't get people a lot of the time, although I don't have a problem agreeing with them when they say, "that bastard, James." The respite care committee's gone rogue on me and it's taking all my mediation skills to hold it together.

I've got an appointment at Parliament House, Melbourne in two weeks to meet with a grant committee, so fingers crossed! It would be great if we could catch up that night. Perhaps you could take your country sister to the bright lights of the city? I read a review in Epicure *about an Afghani restaurant that sounded great. I hope the plans for the second grader's family food fun day are coming along. Looking forward to hearing all about it.*

Love Xara xx

PS Have you spoken to Harry lately?

As XARA RE-READ her message she felt Steve's hands on her shoulders gently massaging. She tilted her head back. "What?"

"It's chatty."

"Of course it's chatty," she said defensively. "What else is it supposed to be?"

He shrugged. "My brothers and I wrestled. You could try that."

"Not helpful," she called to his retreating back. "Neither is standing next to your sibling silently drinking beer and staring out across the pasture."

"Just call her. You know you want to." He disappeared out the door.

I did call her. She'd called twice and both times she'd gotten an auto text in reply. Later Georgie had texted a real reply: *Sorry! Busy, busy with school. Catch up soon.*

A week had passed without any follow up. With a sigh, Xara picked up the cell phone, pressed the call button and waited impatiently as it rang in her ear.

"Yes, Xara, what is it?" Harriet's clipped voice came down the line.

Xara sighed, but what did she really expect? "I'm good, how are you?"

"Busy."

She reminded herself that even before Easter, phone conversations with Harriet had never been chatty or confiding. They'd always been brief and to the point, usually ironing out details about Charlotte coming to the farm or organizing the next family gathering or discussing concerns about Edwina. Only now Harriet refused to speak their mother's name and her family wasn't gathering at all.

She got to the point. "Have you spoken to Georgie?"

"Not since she was here. Why? Is something up?"

I don't know. My little sister's not talking to me and she usually does. "Not that I know of. I thought that as the two of you have bonded over not speaking to Mom, you might be talking to each other."

"Oh, for pity's sake, Xara." Harriet's exasperation burned down the line. "Georgie's allowed to be pissed off. She's not one of your feel-good projects. Surely you've got enough of those with Edwina, the kids and your advocacy work? And what were you thinking taking on witnessing documents? I really don't understand—"

"Tashie's screaming. I have to go." Xara cut the call feeling worse than before she'd made it. Everything about the conversation with Harriet reinforced what she missed about Georgie.

She stabbed the cell phone and sent the message. *Please send a chatty reply, Georgie, so I know you're okay.*

CHAPTER TWENTY-FIVE

GEORGIE HAD LEFT THE ART GALLERY AND WAS CROSSING Federation Square when she thought she heard someone call her name. She paused, glancing around, and quickly reminded herself she was in Melbourne not Billawarre. Although she couldn't take ten steps down the main street of her hometown without meeting someone she knew, life in Melbourne was very different. The late Sunday afternoon crowds surged around her as football fans mixed with theatregoers, art lovers, cyclists and the café crowd; everyone out enjoying the crisp May weather.

As she waited at the crosswalk lights for a tram to trundle past, her cell phone rang. She fished it out of her bag and her heart lurched. *Ben.* Immune to the loud pealing of her ring tone, she stared in shock at the device.

Answer it.

No.

You know you want to talk to him. Take the call.

"You gonna answer that love or just deafen us with that bloody awful sound?" asked a bemused man wearing a team scarf.

"I ... um ..." Her finger hovered over the accept button as she tried to muster calm. She didn't want her voice to crack on hello.

"Georgie!"

Her chest cramped. This time there was no confusion. This time she recognized the voice. Turning slowly, she watched Ben walking quickly toward her, his cell phone pressed to his ear.

The lights changed and people pushed past her, buffeting her from both directions. One woman swore at her, telling her to move. Panic shot through her although she had no idea if it was because of Ben or the crowd. Then a hand was on her arm and she was being tugged forward against the tide of humanity. The lights changed again, the crowd thinned and she found herself standing face to face with Ben. His hand dropped from her arm.

She steeled herself, waiting for the rush of recoil she'd experienced the last time she'd seen him. It didn't come. All she felt was an acre of excruciating awkwardness separating them, complete with a flowering crop of embarrassment.

Act normal. "Ha-he-llo, Ben." *Oh, yeah. That was smooth.*

"Hello, Georgie." His face was impassive and his normally wide and friendly mouth was a firm, straight line.

The absence of his cheeky smile—the one she loved so much—struck her like a punch to the solar plexus. He looked different and it took her a moment to work out he wasn't wearing casual sports gear. He was city-trendy in black leather shoes, navy chinos and a fire-engine red sweater that made his eyes an even richer caramel. The hint of a checked collared shirt peeked out around the opened zipper at the neck of the sweater and he had his hands shoved deep into the pockets of a navy woolen coat. He looked amazing.

God, she'd missed him so much. She was caught by an aching need to lean into him, feel the tautness of his muscles under her fingers and inhale his woodsy scent. She stiffened against it. "You look good," she finally managed.

His broad shoulders rose and fell and he ran a hand through his hair. "I'm glad I ran into you. I've got something I need to tell you before you hear it from anyone else. This saves me from making a phone call you probably wouldn't answer."

The criticism whipped her so she drew on ingrained manners in an attempt to make amends. "Shall we have coffee then?"

"Um." He checked his watch. "Sure, but I don't have long. I'm meeting someone."

A fire-breathing dragon consumed her, sending green flames licking along her veins. She didn't want him meeting someone—anyone—but his smart clothing suddenly made devastating sense. He'd moved on. He'd found someone who wasn't almost related to him and didn't make his skin crawl. Her throat involuntarily tightened at the thought of him with this unknown woman and she coughed.

He frowned. "You okay?"

She nodded, still coughing, and walked briskly into the nearest café. The service was blessedly quick and a few minutes later they were seated with their coffees—an espresso for him and a latte for her.

Ben didn't beat around the bush. "I wanted to give you the heads up that I was interviewed and I've accepted the permanent PE position."

She stared at him, speech deserting her as the ramifications of his news broke over her. Ben was going to be at school—her school—five days a week. "That's, um ..." She swallowed and tried again. "That's ... Congratulations." Her flat delivery destroyed the intended sentiment.

"Thanks." Ben's clear gaze hooked hers with an unrepentant look.

She tapped her teaspoon against the coffee glass, trying to formulate the questions a normal person not having a mini-meltdown would ask. "When do you start?"

"Monday."

Her stomach churned. "Wow. That soon?"

He shrugged. "I've been looking for a permanent job for two years. I'd be a fool not to accept it."

"I guess. It's just ..."

His dark brows rose in a sardonic arch. "What? You didn't think I'd apply for the perfect job because of you?"

She flinched. "Not me. Us. Because of us."

"Us?" There was a sharp edge to his usually melodic tone. "There is no us."

The ache of what they'd lost intensified. "But there was."

He sighed and fiddled with the sugar packet. "Yeah. There was."

"And now we're going to be working together." *Oh, what fun.* The universe must seriously hate her. "We need to find a way to act normally around each other. I'd die a thousand deaths if anyone at work ever found out about ... Well, you know. The whole freaking sideshow."

"I'm glad to hear it's all about you."

His terse words sliced her. "What's that supposed to mean?"

"It means exactly how it sounds. Instead of thinking about us as a unit, you've totally ignored all my feelings and made it about you."

Indignation puffed out of her. "You can't sit here and tell me you weren't grossed out. I mean, first that our parents are having sex and—"

"Actually, I refuse to think about that."

"How very evolved of you."

He scowled. "Hey. It works better than your approach of thinking about it all the time and driving yourself crazy."

She wanted to argue but damn it, maybe he had a point. "What about the fact we share a half-sister and we're step-siblings?"

His mouth twitched into a sad smile. "We're only step-siblings if Dad and Edwina get married."

"Do you know something I don't?"

"I know that whatever happens between Dad and Edwina is their affair. You don't have to let it affect us unless you want to."

She shivered, only this time the sensation of bugs crawling over her skin was less intense. "Aren't you even a little bit freaked out by all of it?"

"Sure. It's a little weird."

"Weird?" Her laugh was weak. "All of it makes me itchingly uncomfortable."

"I'd never have guessed." But a tired smile softened his words. "Georgie. Of course our family connection is unusual, but there's nothing illegal or immoral about it." He glanced at his watch.

Panic skittered through her. He was going to leave and she wasn't remotely ready for that to happen. "I'm sorry."

Her blurted words hung in the air between them and his hand paused on his scarf. "What are you sorry for?"

This is it. Don't screw it up. "For giving in to panic, shame and embarrassment. For not returning your calls. For making this whole mess more about me than you." She opened her hands, palm upwards. "For everything. I don't quite know why I reacted this way.

"I'm usually the person who sees both sides of a situation but this sideswiped me, coming on top of just being told I had a half-sister. When I discovered Doug was your father, all I could think was we were related. I totally freaked out."

"You don't say." He was silent for a moment, his jaw tight and defensive. "That day at Glenora, you leaped away from me like I was a leper. Every time I went to touch you, you dodged me. When I tried to kiss you goodbye, you shuddered."

Her heart tore at his anguish and hurt. She wrapped her fingers around his wide forearm. "I'm so sorry. I spent two weeks in shock, replaying everything over and over in my head before it started fading. Since then, all I've wanted to do is call you."

"Why didn't you?"

"I was so humiliated and mortified that each time I tried to call, I got cold feet. If I'm honest, I was petrified you'd reject me."

He sighed. "So you rejected me first?"

"Not consciously. But I guess that's true." Her lips suddenly felt dry and she licked them nervously. "I've handled this all wrong."

"Yeah." He stared at his hands. "If you had your time over, how would you handle it?"

Oh, for a do-over. This academic process was probably as close as she'd get to one. "I'd put us first. I'd work on caring less about what other people might think of our complicated and unusual family situation."

He watched her intently. "Even if people teased you about marrying your stepbrother? If they said stuff like your stepfather's your father-in-law?"

"Oh God, is that a scenario?" Her chest tightened a touch, thinking about the country song and then she blew a breath out. "What does it matter? Perhaps I could turn it into a party piece and dine out on it. You know, satisfy people's morbid curiosity."

His cell phone buzzed loudly and her heart ached. "You're meeting someone so I'm guessing all this is just semantics."

Confusion crossed his face. "You think I'm meeting someone? As in another woman?"

"In those clothes and wearing that cologne? What else am I going to think?"

"Well, you're half right."

"Oh?" She failed at feigning nonchalance.

"I'm meeting three women."

"That's a little bit excessive."

"I'm meeting my sisters."

Relief reeled so fast her head spun, "That's nice," she managed weakly.

"Oh, Georgie." A faint smile was enough to generate a dimple. "You have no idea how gratifying it is to see jealousy bright on your face.

"My sisters have come down for the weekend. They want to talk. They're still spinning out about Dad, Edwina and Michelle."

"I don't blame them," she said. "It's what women do."

"So I'm learning."

"Poor Ben," she said sincerely. "Surrounded by emotional women on all fronts."

"I've had more fun at the dentist." He looked straight at her. "Georgie, I don't fall out of love in six weeks."

"No," she said, returning his gaze with her heart in her mouth. "Neither do I."

Relief flared in his eyes then faded, leaving behind the pain she'd inflicted on him. "It doesn't mean I'm not angry with you. If I'm honest, I've never felt so hurt and heartsick in my life."

"I'm so sorry. I know it's no consolation but I've been gutted and miserable too."

He pressed his lips together and gave her a quick nod. "Perhaps I'm a fool but despite the hurt, despite everything, I still love you."

The promise of a reprieve collided with the hope of possibilities. "Oh, Ben. I love you too."

"What worries me is how we got to this point. That future we talked about exploring ... How can it happen if you shut down and won't talk to me?"

Everything inside her ached knowing she'd jeopardized something wonderful. "I see that. And I understand it's hard for you to believe me when I say I won't do it again. Especially when the evidence is so clear that's exactly what I did do, but it was the shame. To be honest, it would have been easier talking about you cheating on me."

She pushed hair off her face. "I'm not new to relationships, Ben. I've lost a child. I've had the hard conversations and dealt with faded love. All I can do is promise you that I won't cut you out again."

Doubt lingered in his eyes—doubt she'd put there. "Georgie ..." He blew out a breath. "I want to believe you."

"I want you to believe me too. I want you to know I've been desperately miserable without you."

All she wanted to do was reach out and touch him, but the fear of rejection kept her fingers tightly laced. "I haven't been able to talk to *anyone* about it. Harry and Xara didn't know about us and the only person who had an inkling we were a couple was Mom. I've been too furious with her for putting us in this situation to talk to her."

With nothing left to lose, she threw all her cards on the table of their tattered relationship. "Please, Ben. Let me show you I'm capable of a mature relationship. I know I have to earn your trust again but surely we can go slowly and ..." Her voice trailed off at the wariness on his face.

Everything inside her sank under the weight of what she'd lost. Time stretched out between them, the silence thick and foreboding, muting the clattering and chattering background noise of the café. What had she expected? For him to just forgive her for all the pain she'd caused him? She was about leave when he finally spoke.

"I guess if I don't let you show me, we're going to be forever faced with the awkwardness of being connected through our parents."

Oh God, how she'd missed his sense of humor. Missed him. She grinned inanely. "There'd be embarrassing Christmas lunches."

"I was thinking more along the lines of excruciating Easters." He grinned at her—the mischievous smile she'd missed so much dancing across his cheeks. "Oh wait, we've already done that."

A laugh bubbled up, but as it broke it became a sob. He stood and pulled her to her feet. Not caring they were in the middle of a busy café, she threw her arms around him and held on tight. She pressed her cheek onto his shoulder and breathed him in, still not able to believe his arms were wrapped tightly around her.

He cradled her against him, his cheek resting on her hair and his hand patting her back. "Hey, you're not making a mess of my meet-the-sisters sweater, are you?"

She raised her tear-stained face and studied the wet spot on his shoulder. "I think I am."

His forefinger traced a line of moisture down her cheek. "Why the hell are we standing here? I know a much better way to make up than having you cry. And it protects my clothes."

Her laugh was half hiccough as he ushered her out of the café and into a nearby delivery alcove. As soon as they were out of sight of passers-by, his warm lips came down onto hers in a kiss that was both gentle and deliciously erotic.

"You'll get us arrested," she said, coming up for air. "Besides, don't you have to meet your sisters?"

He gave a good-natured grimace. "That'd be right. I have a beautiful woman in my arms and yet again my sisters are getting in the way of my love life." He kissed her again. "Come with me."

She blinked in surprise. "To meet your sisters?"

"Yeah. This bloody family mess affects all of us. You might have something to offer them. And vice versa."

She'd been so selfishly preoccupied with her own feelings and those of her sisters, she hadn't really considered the Pedersons' reactions. "How do you feel about Doug, Mom and Michelle?"

His cheeks puffed out and then deflated like a balloon. "It was a hell of a shock. But it's all pretty sad, really. They obviously loved each other."

With a sigh, she dropped her forehead onto his chest. "It answers a *lot* of questions about my mother."

He rubbed her back. "I think Edwina's had it harder than Dad. I can honestly say he loved my mom and I don't feel any anger about him and Edwina. I might have felt differently if Mom was still alive."

"A need to protect her?"

"Yeah." He was quiet for a moment. "I've spent the last month doing a lot of thinking. If Edwina and Dad hadn't been separated back in the day, you and I wouldn't even be here. I think that's part of what's freaking out my sisters. The thing is, it's not like Dad hid Michelle's existence—he didn't even know about her until Easter. I guess I'm interested to meet Michelle if she wants to be met, although according to Dad, that's not looking hopeful."

He pressed a kiss into her hair. "How do you feel about Dad, Edwina and Michelle?"

"That changes on an hourly basis. The first time I met Doug was the day after we'd seduced each other. I was on a lust high and wanted everyone to be just as happy. While Xara and Harry were up in arms over Mom having a lover, I was smugly pleased they'd rediscovered each other."

He winced. "You know I don't think about my father getting any."

She tilted her head back to look at him. "Makes you itchingly uncomfortable?"

"A bit." Comprehension dawned. "Okay, I see your point but—"

"But I should have talked to you. Yes, you're right. You will always be right about that." She pressed a kiss to his chin. "I only found out about Michelle an hour before you did. At the time, I wasn't angry either. I was sorry Mom was forced to go through such a horrible ordeal." She laced her fingers through his. "I keep thinking about Eliza. I lost her to death but Mom lost Michelle to life. To another family. Is that harder?"

It was a rhetorical question but he answered it anyway. "I dunno. It all sounds pretty tough to me."

"True, but death is final. Michelle's alive and Mom's known that —or at least she's suspected—for forty-eight years. I think it means she lurches between hope and despair."

She raised their linked fingers to her mouth and pressed a kiss to his knuckles. "I've been so angry with her for keeping it all a secret. My faulty reasoning was that if I'd known about Doug and Michelle I would have known about you and ... well ... you know. But when I think about Michelle, I don't feel anything really except some curiosity. I guess if we ever meet her it may answer the whole nature versus nurture question. Or not. I was raised in the same house as my eldest sister and we don't have much in common.'

"I'm curious too but my sisters are anxious about their inheritance. Dad's done okay but we're not talking tens of millions."

"Is it really about money? They might be feeling a bit abandoned too."

"Why would they feel abandoned? They're adults."

She laughed at his naiveté. "I'm an adult and I went a bit crazy. Think about it. They lost their mother. Now your dad's met someone else and on top of that he's discovered there's a daughter he didn't know existed. Some of his attention is bound to have shifted away from them. From you."

Ben rubbed the back of his neck. "Dad's still in Mildura a couple of times a month. I suppose in the future that might change." A pleading look entered his eyes. "Please come and help me talk them off the ledge."

Her heart went out to him. "I'd love to come and believe me, I really want to meet your sisters—"

He sighed. "I'm sensing a but."

"I just wonder if we should give them a bit more time to get used to the idea of Michelle before we hit them with us? You know, emotional women and all that."

He brushed her hair behind her ears. "You've probably got a point. But I want a commitment from you that when we tell our siblings we're dating the kid of our parent's lover, we do it together. And I want a date when we're doing it."

"Are you okay if we keep us on the down-low until vacation? That way we can grab some late June winter sunshine in Mildura and tell your sisters before freezing our bums off in Billawarre and telling mine."

He grinned at her. "Too easy. I like the idea of focusing just on us for a bit before we open our relationship up to public scrutiny."

"I can't promise my sisters will be happy about us."

"I can't promise mine will be either but I'll tell you what I've learned so far about family."

"What?"

"Everyone's reaction is unpredictable. Josie's always been the calm one and she's lost the plot about Michelle. Perhaps your sisters will surprise you."

She thought about Harriet. "And pigs might fly."

"We'll take wine."

"Oh yeah," she said, rising on her toes to kiss him again. "Lots and lots of wine."

CHAPTER TWENTY-SIX

Hi Xara,

Sorry I've been mostly off the air and I could only stop for a quick drink when you were in Melbourne. It's been a huge half-semester but vacation in six sleeps. I'm coming down to Billawarre. Any chance of a family lunch at the farm? I've got some news

Georgie xxx

EDWINA SAT at the breakfast table sipping coffee and jotting down a list of things she needed to do for the day. At the same time, she kept an ear out for sounds of movement from Charlotte, who was yet to appear for breakfast. Doug had been in Mildura for a few days but was expected back tonight. It was the winter solstice and the weather in Billawarre was at its bone-chilling best and every time Doug returned from Mildura he waxed lyrical about the warmth of the Sunraysia. To ease his transition back to the cooler climate, she'd planned comfort food for dinner. She had beef cheeks bathing in red wine in the slow cooker and she wrote *Kipfler potatoes* on her shopping list so she could serve fluffy mashed potatoes.

She checked her to-do list and knew she needed to add *call Harriet*. It had been weeks since she'd told Primrose she'd talk to Harriet and despite her numerous attempts to set up a meeting, she was yet to have the tough but necessary conversation. Each time she texted or called, Harriet always had an excuse as to why meeting was impossible.

Edwina recognized the work-related excuses as legitimate. Other reasons were a lot flimsier and far more transparent. It was obvious Harriet didn't want to see her and Edwina was loath to have such a serious conversation over the phone. Not wanting to push Harriet even further away, she'd acquiesced to her excuses, ever hopeful that when she tried again the following week, Harriet would oblige. Harriet had not.

Edwina blew out a breath and wrote, *call Harriet @ 9.00*. The familiar sounds of "Majestic Fanfare" blared from the radio, heralding the morning news, and she realized Charlotte still hadn't made it to breakfast. The night before, Charlotte had told her she was going to school early for a jazz rehearsal. She'd been snapped up by a music group the moment the school discovered she played the saxophone. Had she forgotten to change her alarm?

Edwina made her way down the hall to Charlotte's room and found her dressed in her school uniform but curled up on her bed, sobbing. Edwina's stomach lurched and she closed her eyes for a moment, gathering herself. She knew how easily eviscerating grief and sadness welled up out of the blue. Part of her had been waiting for this to happen to Charlotte and another part had deluded herself that she'd be fine.

Given all the recent changes in her granddaughter's life, she'd been remarkably stoic. She attended school, diligently studied and even took care of her own laundry and ironing, which was more than Harriet had ever done at the same age. She'd asked Edwina to teach her some quick and easy meals and had taken to cooking on

Thursdays when she finished classes by lunchtime. Despite, or perhaps because of, her pregnancy, she carried herself with regal grace—spine straight, shoulders squared and chin slightly tilted upwards—what Edwina recognized as the Mannering shield. Was it learned or in their DNA?

Now that Charlotte was free of her earlier nausea and fatigue she glowed with rude health. Edwina noticed that boys and men turned when she walked past but if Charlotte knew of her impact on them, she didn't mention it. On the odd occasion Charlotte had invited some of her peers to Glenora, they always came and went in a group. Although Charlotte appeared to be part of that group, Edwina recognized in her granddaughter some of her own reticence that pain and stress had instilled in her throughout the years. The carefree, bubbly girl was a fast-maturing woman with far more to worry about than the next test paper or which dress to wear to the prom.

Of course, just as it was with her own daughters, the moment Edwina dared to relax and believe all was calm and Charlotte was coping with the massive changes in her life, her stoicism tumbled.

Edwina sat on the bed. "What's the matter?" Charlotte handed her a crumpled and slightly tear-dampened form. Edwina instantly recognized the hospital's logo. "You have an ultrasound appointment this morning?"

Charlie gave a giant sniff. "At eleven."

Edwina automatically handed her a tissue and bit down on the tempting desire to say, *Don't sniff dear.* "And?"

She blew her nose. "I texted Mom and asked her to come with me. I thought if she saw the baby and heard the heartbeat ..." Fresh tears flowed down her high cheeks and she snorted then hiccuped before wiping her beautiful but troubled eyes.

Oh, Harriet. You foolish girl. Despair mingled with anger, settling as a large and heavy weight in Edwina's chest.

"I'm twenty weeks pregnant, Mardi. Half way. This baby is real now. I feel it kicking. It's her grandchild and—" A strangled sob broke through her fragile control. "I th-th-thought she'd have c-c-come around by now. I've done everything to show her I'm responsible, but she's not even loo-looking. Auntie Xara t-tells her but she ..." She swiped a fresh batch of tears away with the back of her hand. "I just want my mom, Mardi. I miss her so much."

Edwina's heart broke. She gathered her part-child, part-adult granddaughter into her arms, held her tight and wished she could absorb all her anguish and pain. When she'd been the same age, the last person in the world she'd have wanted to be with her was her emotionally moribund and disapproving mother. But for all of Harriet's faults, right up until Charlotte's pregnancy, she'd been a loving and caring mother—albeit slightly controlling—who'd have done just about anything to protect her daughter. Now, she was cutting her nose off to spite her face.

"I know you do, sweetheart." She stroked her hair and made a decision. "I'll talk to her."

Charlotte pulled back, her vivid sky-blue eyes awash with tears but lit with a flash of hope. "Do you think she'll listen?"

Edwina was long past lying about anything. "She's never taken much notice of my advice before." She squared her shoulders. "But that's no reason not to try."

With less than three hours until the appointment, Edwina jettisoned the idea of telephoning Harriet and drove to the clinic, mentally preparing herself to stay strong when she spoke with her. She got a parking spot outside the building and, taking that as a good sign, gripped her handbag and strode to the door. Her hand paused on the chrome handle as she read and absorbed the blue *Sorry, we're closed* sign. Alongside it was another notice announcing the new—reduced—opening hours.

Shock reverberated through her. Harriet was only seeing private patients twice a week now and the rest of the time she was working at the hospital. Edwina had gleaned things were bad, but not this bad, and Harriet hadn't told her otherwise. But then again, Harriet was barely speaking to her.

Faced with the unwanted news, she crossed the road and walked into the hospital. Back in the days when Richard was alive, Karen, the receptionist, had always greeted her as if she was a VIP, making her slightly uncomfortable. Today she faced a stranger and she was grateful for the associated anonymity. It took a moment for the young woman to raise her head.

"Could you please direct me to Ms. Chirnwell?"

The receptionist consulted a list. "She's in general surgery clinic this morning." She wafted a hand in the direction of a long corridor. "Follow the signs."

Before Edwina could thank her, the woman's gaze had returned to her screen. She followed the signs, noting with satisfaction the newly completed renovations. All of the faded 1980's décor, along with the rabbit warren feel, had vanished and a sense of space and light suffused the area. Fortunately, Primrose's middle daughter, Kate, was on duty and Edwina didn't have to say who she was or why she was here without an appointment. On top of everything else, the last thing she needed was an obstreperous staff member.

"Auntie Edwina." Kate greeted her with a welcome hug. "Are you after Harriet? I'll let her know you're here."

Edwina thanked her then took a seat in the only vacant plastic chair. She gave a polite smile and nod to the patients who were waiting.

A tired-looking woman, whose lined face told of a difficult life, glanced at Edwina's tailored woolen coat. "You in the right place, love?"

"If this is the clinic, then yes, I am."

"I hope you brought a book with ya then." She threw down a shabby magazine. "Mind you, if you want to relive the birth of Prince William, you'll be set."

"Gracious." Edwina glanced at a photo of a bonnie blond-haired toddler in a blue romper. "He's a father now himself. Did they find a stash of old magazines during the renovations?"

"Who knows, love." The woman laughed before nodding toward another woman reading a recently released magazine. "All I know is I recognize all of them celebrities in the old mags and none of them ones in the new. You been on the waiting list long?" Fortunately, the woman didn't pause for a reply. "I'm from Camperdown. Two years I've been waitin' and I was stoked when I got the letter but ..." She leaned forward, a conspiratorial look on her face and dropped her voice. "Apparently, this surgeon's husband was the mayor. He stole half the town's money."

"As well as a lot of hers," Edwina said firmly, the lioness of motherhood rising to defend her daughter. She may wish to knock some sense into Harriet over this situation with Charlotte, but she'd defend Harriet every time against scandalmongering.

The woman's eyes lit up at the new tidbit. "Bastard."

"Exactly." Edwina gripped her handbag on her lap. "The important thing is she's a very talented surgeon. You're in good hands."

"Did you hear that?" The woman looked at the patients. "We're in good hands."

"If we ever get to bloody see her," grumbled a man, checking his watch.

Kate reappeared, beckoning to Edwina. She rose and slipped her handbag onto her shoulder.

Surprise and chagrin whipped across the other woman's face. "You're lucky. I've been waiting forty-five minutes."

"I do apologize," Edwina said self-consciously. "I promise I won't keep my daughter long."

"Your daughter?" The woman's face immediately softened. "That's different then. You take all the time you need."

As Edwina walked into the consulting room she heard the woman say, "My Tiffany might not be a lah-de-dah surgeon but I don't have to make no appointment to see her."

Edwina would have laughed if it hadn't been so glaring and achingly true.

"Edwina?" Underneath Harriet's surprise and irritation, she had the grace to look slightly concerned at her mother's unannounced arrival. "Is everything alright?"

Edwina sat in the patient's chair. Harriet avoided the vacant one next to her and took a seat behind the desk. The action placed a wide, wooden barrier between them.

"That depends on your definition of alright. Charlotte is devastated by your refusal to accompany her to her ultrasound appointment."

Every part of Harriet stiffened. "I've made my stance very clear from the start. She knows how I feel about the choice she's making so she can hardly be surprised by my not attending the scan."

"This baby," Edwina started then amended, "your grandchild is going to be a reality in twenty weeks or less. Your daughter wants you involved. Isn't it time for you to rethink your choice?"

Harriet's lips thinned. "I don't think so. Charlotte knew what I expected of her and this is so far removed from that, it doesn't bear thinking about."

"Oh, Harriet. No one's child does what their parents expect."

"I did."

Edwina shook her head and said softly, "You did what your father expected."

Harriet's blue eyes darkened to navy and bored into her. "Of course I did. And why wouldn't I? After all, he was the parent in my life who was there for me. He encouraged me and supported me."

The need to defend herself rose up, breaking over Edwina in a hot sweat. "I wasn't entirely absent, Harriet."

"That's not how I remember it. You were never fully there for any of us and now we know why. To be frank, the reason doesn't help. You gave away one daughter then you failed three more. It's not a good track record, Edwina, so don't come here telling me how to deal with my daughter."

The words slashed, aligning in part with her own beliefs. She dug deep and drew on a kernel of truth she'd spent her life trying to shield from the ravages of doubt. Despite her shortcomings, she knew she hadn't been a total failure as a mother. Granted, she hadn't been a great mother, but she hadn't been a total disaster either. She'd got some things right.

Struggling against the tentacles of self-loathing pulling her hard and fast back toward the black pit of despair she'd been avoiding for weeks, she linked her fingers tightly on her lap. "My track record may be patchy, but I've learned things along the way. Things you need to hear."

Harriet made a derisive sound.

Edwina ignored it. "If you continue shutting out Charlie, she'll stop inviting you in and ..." She thought about her barely-there relationship with Harriet and the silence from Michelle. "Believe me, that's soul destroying. I know Charlie becoming a mother at eighteen is less than ideal but it's not the utter catastrophe you're making it out to be. Today's an opportunity to heal the rift while she wants it healed. Take this chance. Go to the ultrasound."

"There's enough talk about me already without me turning up at the scan."

"Oh, for heaven's sake. You sound just like my mother and that's not a compliment," Edwina said dryly. "The people you love matter far more than the opinions of this town. You're strong enough to withstand gossip, Harriet. What's far more important is that in a few months' time, Charlotte will have a child of her own. When she holds her baby and is consumed by that rush of overwhelming love, she'll get angry with you. She won't understand how you could have ever left her."

Harriet shot to her feet, her palms pressed against the desk. "Isn't that the pot calling the kettle black? Xara tells me that despite getting the letter requesting contact, your missing daughter Michelle hasn't made any."

The attack was swift and it burned with the shocking intensity of acid eating through skin. It didn't help that on one level Edwina knew Harriet was lashing out at her to mask her own pain.

"That's exactly my point," she managed in an almost even voice.

"I've lost a lot and I don't want you to experience the same loss. I'm trying to protect you, Harriet. Mothers do that. Please don't let Mannering pride and Chirnwell arrogance get in the way of ruining what could be a great and unexpected gift."

Harriet strode to the door and opened it with a jerk. "I don't have time for this, Edwina. I have patients stacking up. Goodbye."

Before Edwina could say anything, Harriet was calling out, "Mrs. Rutherford," and Edwina was summarily dismissed, her heartache heavier than when she'd arrived.

THAT NIGHT, hours after Edwina had shared the wondrous moment with Charlotte of seeing the awe-inspiring grainy image of a tiny baby sucking its thumb and hearing her great-grandchild's whooshing and galloping heartbeat, she turned the conversation with Harriet over and over in her mind.

How had it gone pear-shaped so fast? Then again, what had she expected? Ambushing Harriet at work hadn't come close to creating the ideal conditions for a serious conversation nor had it gotten to the nub of the real issue—Charlotte's pregnancy was white noise compared with that. It troubled her that even in death, Richard managed to insert himself so quickly and deftly between her and Harriet in every conversation that mattered. Even in ones that didn't. Alive, he'd been Harriet's hero. Dead, he was her saint and Edwina was her constant disappointment.

"Have you considered telling Harriet the full story?" Doug said, after Charlotte said goodnight.

They were in the library as was their habit now each night around ten. They'd fallen into a routine of sipping a small glass of port before checking their emails. As weeks turned into two months they'd slowly drawn out the drinking of the port, neither of them in a rush to get to the computer and deal with the inevitable disappointment.

"I doubt she'd hear it. If she did she wouldn't believe me." She sighed. "How are your girls doing?"

Sadness seemed to flatten his curls. "Josie's mad as hell with us for upsetting the status quo of her life. Flis was doing okay but now she says she's devastated for Michelle. She wants to meet her so it all feels real. She got pissed off with me when I explained Michelle might decide never to contact us. And Carla's still acting as if nothing's changed and sent me home with cake."

"Sorry."

"Why?" He gave her a wink. "It's great cake."

"Doug, I need you to be serious. I'm sorry I've brought so much dissension into our families."

"Don't say that. Neither of us wanted Michelle to be a secret and our kids are doing what the counselor said would happen. Hell, they're a textbook example. They're mad, they're sad and they're unsettled. Well, all except Ben."

"Thank goodness for Ben. Why do you think he's less affected?"

"No idea." He refilled their glasses. "Perhaps the fact that he's a bloke is the difference. Maybe if Michelle had been a Michael, he'd be the one in a tailspin and the girls would be doing okay."

She grimaced. "I can't help wondering if we've done the right thing. I mean, we've unsettled everyone and for what? I've given up on Michelle ever wanting to meet us and I really don't blame her. I'm the mother who gave her up. Even if I got the chance to tell her why, how do we bridge forty-eight years? We're her parents but we're not. To her we're just two old strangers."

"We wouldn't be strangers if we'd had a choice," he said curtly, sounding unusually angry. "If the chance hadn't been stolen from us and stolen from her, we'd have been her parents. We'd have raised her."

His shoulders suddenly slumped as the fight left him, and he rubbed his face. "I don't have any expectations about any of this, Eddy. I just hope I get the chance to tell her that."

The computer chose that precise moment to ping with incoming mail, reminding them of the reason they were in the library.

"That will just be the nightly digest from our adoption group," Edwina said as Doug rose and fiddled with the mouse. "Let's skip reading it. I'm not up to hearing about anyone else's sad or happy stories tonight."

She stood, setting off an unwelcome ache in her hips, and suddenly felt old. "All I want is to put an end to a tumultuous day. I'm going to bed."

Doug didn't respond—his eyes fixed on the screen.

"Remember to turn out the lights." She leaned in to kiss his cheek.

"It's her," Doug said so softly she barely heard him. "At least I think it is." His hands started patting his pockets. "Jeez, where the hell are my reading glasses? Eddy, can you read it?"

She gripped his hand and leaned in close to the screen, her heart doing somersaults of excited dread. "Oh God. It's really her."

"Don't keep me in suspense. What does it say?"

The email was four short lines but her mouth fumbled the words as her eyes and brain raced ahead. "'Hello. I received a letter from the Tasmanian Department of Health and Human Services telling me you wished to make contact. At this stage, I am only open to email communication from you. Regards, Michelle van Leeuwen.'"

Suddenly light-headed, Edwina sank into the large leather chair. "I can't believe it."

"It's very formal. It's like she's worried if we knew her street address we'd arrive uninvited."

"You can't deny that would be tempting."

"Sure, but we wouldn't do it."

Edwina wasn't convinced she could resist at least scoping out the street and house her daughter lived in on Google Maps. "She doesn't know us. Remember what Tim said? The road is a series of cul de sacs and blind curves. But this email's a start. Oh, Doug." Her throat thickened. "We've found our daughter. *Our daughter.* It's our opportunity to get to know her. For her to know us."

She pressed control + P on the keyboard and the printer hummed into life, spitting out two copies of the brief email. She picked up the pages and handed one to Doug. "Does this make it seem more real?"

He read the words out loud twice and laughed. "I guess it means we have to type out the letter you so carefully wrote."

"Let's do it now." Edwina's weariness vanished under the onslaught of adrenaline. "You read it to me and I'll type."

Laughter and tears flowed and twice she had to stop to blow her nose and wipe her eyes. Twenty minutes later, the letter was finished and she attached a recent photo of the two of them Charlotte had taken on her cell phone.

Edwina squeezed Doug's hand. "Ready?"

A smile of unwavering support lit up his face. "Ready."

Together, they made a heartfelt wish and hit send.

CHAPTER TWENTY-SEVEN

"THANK YOU AND GOODNIGHT," HARRIET SAID TO HER SURGICAL staff as she stripped off her surgical gown and dropped it into the laundry hamper.

Lisa, her instrument nurse, ducked her head and held her arms up in front of her in a cross. "Don't tempt fate."

Harriet was almost too tired to smile. As she'd predicted when she'd gone cap in hand to see Reg Davies three months ago, he'd given her the increased hospital hours she'd requested. The payoff was more than her fair share of graveyard shifts. After a full day of cholecystectomies and laparoscopic gastric bandings, she'd been about to head home when the first emergency of the night arrived. A ruptured appendix had been followed by a bowel obstruction. She'd just finished writing up the notes when a head-on collision had brought in a ruptured spleen. Now it was close to 2:00 a.m. and bed beckoned.

Her cell phone rang and Lisa groaned. "Harriet Chirnwell." She listened to the night unit manager from ICU explaining her concerns about a patient whose condition had been deteriorating all evening. "I'll come straight up."

"What do I set up for this time?" Lisa said in a resigned tone.

"Possible laparotomy. I think Mrs. Nikolovski's got a slow bleed."

"Isn't she Blake's patient?"

"Yes, but he's on days off."

The irony of the situation wasn't lost on Harriet. It was the sauce on top of the humble pie she'd been force-fed since April. She was still Blake's boss but she was also on this bloody schedule and until 7:00 a.m. she had to cover all surgical emergencies, even if they'd been created by her intern.

She ran up the stairs to ICU and after examining the patient, made the decision to return her to theatre for exploratory surgery. While the staff prepped Mrs. Nikolovski, she'd grab a sandwich and a coffee and check her emails in the staff lounge. She was waiting to hear back from her attorney, hopeful she'd have news on the next phase of Project Save Miligili.

Since Charlotte had chosen not to meet with James, he'd refused to be part of the gift deed to make a transfer of love, care and affection and Miligili remained in both their names. Just thinking about the legal name of the transfer made Harriet's blood boil. There was no love, care or affection left between her and James, only angst, hatred and pain.

In a weak moment, she'd lamented to Angela that James had refused to sign over Miligili's title to her and her attorney had been apoplectic.

"You were going to do what?" Angela had screeched down the phone. "Harriet, you're paying me for legal advice so why are you using Google? A transfer of love, care and affection won't protect the house. When James declares bankruptcy, and I'm ninety-nine percent certain he will, then the trustee in bankruptcy will do everything possible to claw back his share."

"Even though I'm the one covering the mortgage?" Harriet had been outraged. *Just covering the mortgage.* She hadn't told anyone that her recent trip to Melbourne had taken her and a large part of her wardrobe to The Collection Boutique in upscale Toorak Road. "Are you saying I'm going to lose the house either way?"

Angela had used legal jargon that always left Harriet feeling that nothing in this mess was clear-cut when she desperately craved simple, clear and concise. "The Family Court will work at finding ways to preserve the property but it doesn't help that your daughter's currently living away from you and your mother is financially supporting her. Reconcile with your daughter and you'll have a stronger chance of keeping the house."

And there lay the problem. Harriet loved her daughter and she loved her home but she couldn't validate Charlotte's choice to have this baby, not even to keep Miligili. Something about doing that tarnished her, the house and its memories. Who was she kidding? James had done a bloody good job smearing those memories and making a mockery of everything they'd shared there as a family. But Miligili was home, history, place—belonging. She was desperate for something solid and unmovable to hold on to in this fluid and eddying chaos.

Stepping into the lounge, she was surprised to find she wasn't alone. An unfamiliar dark-haired man sat reading the paper. He wore scrubs, had a sooty five-o'clock shadow and reading glasses perched halfway down his nose.

He looked up as she walked in, giving her a laconic smile that crinkled the skin around his eyes. "G'day."

"Hello," Harriet said crisply, walking directly to the coffee machine. She had little interest in chit-chat at this ungodly hour, especially with an agency nurse she was unlikely to ever meet again.

"I hear you're having a busy night," he continued conversationally. His drawl was similar to the one the local farmers favored.

She thrust a coffee pod into the machine and pressed the button before tilting her head toward the open newspaper. "Unlike you?" It came out far more tart than she'd intended.

He laughed. "You must be Harriet Chirnwell."

A prickle of offense ran through her. God, she was sick of hospital and town gossip. It was bad enough to be maligned by people who knew her let alone from the ill-informed scrutiny of strangers. "And why must I be she?"

He gave an easy shrug. "Basic deduction. Your name's on the schedule as the on-call general surgeon and your ID clearly states who you are."

She automatically glanced down at her forgotten security lanyard and her umbrage faded. It had been a long time since she'd been known without labels: the estranged wife of the man the press called the Billawarre fraudster; the mother of a pregnant teen; and the daughter of Edwina Mannering; a woman who was turning her back on her heritage. To this unknown man she was just Harriet Chirnwell, general surgeon. As freeing as that was, she didn't like being on the back foot—she knew nothing about him apart from what she saw.

"And you are?"

He stood. "Andrew Willis. I'm the new visiting ortho."

A rush of surprise skittered through her. She'd received the memo from Reg Davies last week and assumed that Andrew Willis would be a newly minted orthopedic surgeon in his early thirties starting his career, not a man in his fifties. She accepted Andrew's proffered hand and returned his firm handshake. Most visiting surgeons were only at the hospital during business hours, working on whittling down the waiting list cases.

"Why are you visiting at 3:00 a.m. and reading the paper?"

"Serendipity."

"Excuse me?"

He resumed his seat. "My operating days are Wednesdays and Thursdays so I stay Wednesday night at that rather over-decorated B & B in Leura Street."

She pictured Andrew amid the all the froufrou and felt herself smile. "Cecily has a certain penchant for ruffles, frills and throw pillows."

"I'd call it an addiction. I always leave craving to do something like chop wood or run ten k. Anything that makes me sweat and feel like a bloke again. Tonight's car accident call saved me from spending another night feeling my masculinity drain away."

"I got the ruptured spleen."

"Nasty. Mine was a fractured femur. Made more sense to operate on him here rather than transporting him to Geelong. Especially as I'm here tomorrow for follow-up."

Enjoying the easy and uncomplicated conversation—something she hadn't experienced with anyone in months—Harriet sat down opposite him with her coffee and offered him a sandwich from the plate. "Common sense doesn't always line up with hospital funding."

"You're not wrong there," he said with feeling. "Fortunately, Reg gave the okay."

"How is he?"

"Reg? Interesting character that one."

"That's one way of describing him." She thought about the way the medical director was using her current situation to his advantage and how he was getting more than his money's worth out of her. She bet Andrew had a much better deal. "And your patient?"

"He's doing okay now. I was just winding down here reading the paper before I head back to the B & B." He smiled again, only this time it held a rueful line. "You know how it is."

Harriet did know. "I find it's pointless trying to sleep when I'm still wired and thinking about the surgery."

"Exactly, and a strange bed with a canopy of ruffles doesn't help things either. Although I guess it won't be strange after a few months."

Even after a few months she hadn't completely come to terms with the bed in the guesthouse. It wasn't that it was uncomfortable—it was, after all, an expensive mattress with a pillow-top cover—but it was more the fact it was empty and devoid of warmth. Hating the direction of her thoughts and not wanting to think about the loneliness that was now a large part of her life, she continued to quiz

Andrew. If she asked him questions, she didn't have to talk about herself.

"Where are you visiting from?"

"I haven't quite decided."

"That's cryptic."

"Not really." Tired gray eyes surveyed her from behind frameless glasses. "I've just sold my Adelaide practice. I grew up in the Wimmera region and I'm not sure if I want a sea change or a tree change. Working here's a good base to explore both."

"Retirement planning?"

"God, no. I've still got kids at uni."

She knew all about the cost of an education. "Seems an odd time to sell your practice."

"Yeah." He rubbed the back of his neck as if he was weighing up his words. "I won't bore you with the details, but in a nutshell, the moment my youngest finished senior year, my wife decided she was finished with our marriage."

"I'm sorry." Harriet heard the automatic response leave her mouth and was surprised by the force of feeling that followed. She was intimate with the shock of discovering one's spouse's feelings and actions were both unfamiliar and utterly unexpected.

He shook his head. "The time for sorry is long past. At the time it caught me by surprise but I've had eighteen months to adjust."

"Does it take that long?"

"This time next year you won't know yourself."

She stared at him, astonished to hear the words and the kind tone in which he'd offered them. For a second they made no sense and then she realized she'd spoken her thoughts out loud. *Stupid, stupid, stupid.*

Quickly scrunching the cling wrap from the sandwiches into a tight ball, she said coolly, "I need to get back to the OR."

He nodded, seemingly unfazed by her abrupt change of tone. "Good to meet you, Harriet."

"Andrew." She was already on her feet and moving fast to the door. Her hand closed around the handle.

"Hey, Harriet."

She reluctantly turned back. "Yes?"

He shot her the same laconic smile he'd greeted her with. "Don't let the bastards get you down."

Her mouth dried and she silently walked away, all her thoughts and words vaporized by the anxiety crawling through her. Andrew Willis knew far more about her than the fact that she was a surgeon. The disappointment that knowledge brought her was disproportionate to the situation, and yet it wasn't. For a few brief minutes, she'd been free of the months of mess that tainted her life and it had been blissfully liberating. How would it feel if it was a permanent state of affairs? Andrew had obviously divested himself of his old life by working here, and he had plans to settle in a new town. She could do the same thing.

The thought galvanized her with more purpose than she'd experienced in a long time. What would it be like to live and work in a new place where she was totally unknown? To walk away from James's perfidy, from Charlotte's disappointing life, from her mother, Doug, and this unknown sister whose mere existence cast a long shadow? The idea of starting over somewhere new without the shackles that currently held her by the throat, took hold. She walked into the OR with her head full of the lingering thoughts that tempted and terrified all at the same time.

"We're ready when you are," Lisa said. "Rod's putting her under now."

"Let's do it." Harriet strode to the sinks and as she scrubbed her skin pink, she lost herself to the familiar needling pain, using it to block her tumultuous thoughts in the same way she'd been doing for months.

"I THINK I'll go and check on the lambs," Steve teased, stealing some cashews from the nibbles platter.

Xara slapped his hand. "Don't you dare leave me here alone."

He rolled his eyes. "What—with your family?"

"I want you here if Harry turns up."

"She's not going to come, Zar." He opened the bottle of champagne Georgie had brought as a gift. "The one thing you can't fault Harriet on is changing her mind on a whim. Once you told her Edwina and Charlie were coming, you lost her."

"I know." Sadness curled through her. "But I couldn't lie to her. Can you imagine the fallout if I'd failed to mention who was coming? Things with Georgie have been rocky enough and just as they've come good I don't want to rock the boat with Harry."

"I don't know why you turn yourself inside out for your family. I let mine sort it out themselves."

"Oh right, and that works so well. Craig hasn't spoken to your father in years." Xara ripped open a packet of camembert cheese. "I'm the voice of reason. I'm trying to support everyone and see both sides. It puts me in the perfect position to try to facilitate understanding and forgiveness."

"You been binging on self-help books again?"

She threw a celery stick at him. "I'm serious. Think about it. Now I know about Michelle, so much of Mom and Dad's relationship makes sense. He wasn't always fair to her and she deserves to be happy with Doug. Georgie and Harry need to stop being selfish and at least consider Mom. It's not all about them, you know. I think today's lunch is a step in the right direction. Now that Georgie's come around to the idea of Michelle, it just leaves Harry."

Steve's grunt was non-committal. "Don't expect too much, okay?"

She knew his comment came from the right place but she bristled nonetheless. "I think you're forgetting I'm a trained mediator."

"Yes, but there's no emotional investment with strangers and talking of strangers, I'm glad Doug brought Ben. It evens up the ratio a bit." He picked up the tray of drinks at the same time Xara lifted the platter. "So, this news of Georgie's. Any ideas?"

"Promotion, maybe? Perhaps she's finally got a job teaching art. Whatever it is, she's excited about it. She's been bouncing since she arrived."

As they walked into the living room, the twins came barreling the other way, dragging Charlotte toward the playroom. "We're showing Charlie our Ninjago dragons."

"Charlie might want to talk to the grown-ups."

The twins looked at her, utterly baffled by the concept.

"It's fine, Auntie Zar, I don't mind. It's not like I can eat soft cheese or drink champagne anyway." She lifted a bowl from Xara's hand and held it aloft. "But I can eat chips."

"Yay!" The twins ran after her.

"Edwina, champagne? Doug, beer or bubbles?" Steve passed around the drinks as Xara followed, offering the nibbles.

"So, Ben." Xara smiled up at him. "Georgie tells me you're teaching at the same school. Talk about a coincidence."

"Mmm hmm." Ben nodded, his mouth full of pâté and cracker.

Steve scanned the room. "I think everyone's got a drink now. Over to you, Georgie."

Georgie's wide smile faltered slightly. "Well, first of all, thanks to Xara and Steve for hosting today."

"Our pleasure." Xara gave her an encouraging smile, wondering why her sister suddenly seemed nervous. "Come on, spit it out. We're all desperate to know what we're celebrating."

Georgie shared a glance with Ben, who'd moved to stand next to her. Now he took a step closer and as he slid his hand into hers, she said, "Ben and I have been dating since the start of March. We've just moved in together."

March? March! A sickening sense of betrayal crawled through Xara and her glass slipped out of her hand, landing on the carpet with a soft thud.

Edwina drained her drink in one gulp.

Doug slapped Ben on the shoulder then he leaned in and kissed Georgie's cheek. "That's great news."

"Thank you," Georgie said gratefully.

Steve laughed and dropped a cloth on the spilled champagne. "Does Harry know?"

Georgie grimaced. "Apparently I've joined Mom, James and Charlie in trashing the family name."

"Oh, I don't know. You might have just done her a favor. This is just the sort of gossip to knock her off the most-talked-about-person-in-town pedestal." He raised his glass to Georgie and Ben. "Ripper news. Congratulations."

"March?" Xara finally found her voice but couldn't prevent her hurt from radiating into it. "That means you were together before Easter. Why didn't you tell me?"

Georgie shrugged apologetically. "It was very new then and—"

"So?" The word shrieked in accusation as Xara thought of all the times in the past two years she'd listened to her sister pour out her heart and soul. Of the support she'd given Georgie after Eliza's death and later when things failed with Jason. Surely it wasn't outrageous to expect Georgie to have told her about this new relationship from the start?

Her breath caught in her throat when her brain caught up with the timeline. "Oh God. You kept dating after you found out that Doug and Mom ..." She couldn't finish as her body involuntarily shuddered. "I don't even want to think about it."

Ben gave her a wry smile and raised his glass to her. "That's how I deal with it, Xara. It works pretty well."

"I know it's a shock," Georgie continued hurriedly, "and if it helps, we had a very rocky month after we discovered Mom and Doug's relationship."

"Helps?"

Georgie sucked in her lips and squared her shoulders. "When we realized their relationship makes us virtually step-siblings but—"

"No." Xara covered her ears.

"Darling, are you absolutely sure about this?" Worry lines deepened on Edwina's face. "You do realize it links the families in a rather complicated way."

"You mean if we broke up it would put a lot of stress on you and Dad," Ben said succinctly.

Edwina sighed, her fingers rolling her pearls. "That makes me sound far more selfish than I am." She glanced at Doug before returning her gaze to Ben. "Believe me, I'm the last person to prevent two people who love each other from being together. I just want you both to be certain you're not rushing things. That you've thought everything through."

"We broke up for a month and it was awful." Georgie's voice pleaded for understanding. "It proved to both of us that we don't want to live our lives apart."

"If it helps," Ben offered, still holding tightly onto Georgie's hand, "we'd already met and fallen in love before we knew anything about Dad and Edwina."

"You fell in love in less than a month?" Xara's voice rose on a wave on incredulity. How could Georgie not tell her something that significant?

Georgie grinned at Ben. "Well, I fell in lust first. He ruined me for anyone else."

"La, la, la," Xara said loudly, refilling her empty glass with a shaking hand.

"Darling, that's probably more information than I needed to know about my stepson and possible son-in-law," Edwina said dryly.

"You've made me proud, son." Doug winked at Ben. "Very proud."

"Righto, Dad," Ben's face pinked under his olive complexion. "That'll do."

"Oh, I don't know..." Steve gave Xara's shoulder a squeeze. "... I'm sure I can mine this situation and get my own back for all those sheep jokes. So, Doug, if your son's now your son-in-law what will that make their kids?"

Georgie blanched and Xara growled, "Shut up, Steve."

"Sorry, Georgie." Steve took a pull on his beer, his face reminiscent of the twins' after they'd been caught out.

"It takes a special woman to get the seal of approval from Ben's sisters, Georgie," Doug said conversationally, filling the uncomfortable silence. "You've scored Olympic gold there."

"Even Ben's sisters knew before me?" Xara shot to her feet, seething at the added injustice. "Well, that's just fabulous. What else haven't you told me?"

"Nothing." Georgie wrung her hands. "This isn't personal, Zar. It just made sense to go to Mildura first and—"

"Not personal?" It felt incredibly personal. "I'm your sister! I was the one there for you after Eliza. After Jason. Not Mom. Not Harry. *Me!* God. And now, after everything, you ..." She struggled for coherency. "You can't even offer me the courtesy of—"

"Ben, Doug, would you like a tour of the farm?" Steve offered loudly while at the same time shooting Xara a take-it-easy look.

It inflamed her outrage. "I've got a better idea. You all stay here and I'll go for a walk."

"I'll come with you," Georgie and Edwina said in unison.

"Please don't." She grabbed her coat and stormed out into the bracing winter air. God, why was she bothering to try to hold things together for her sisters? To keep her family intact and be there for each of them?

Because you're the glue in the middle.

Hah! Right now she was sick of being the glue, sick of trying to see everyone's point of view. Hell, she was sick of the lot of them.

She stomped up the incline, propelled by fury and breathing hard. She stopped at the top of the hill behind the shearing shed. Looking down onto the rocky but fertile volcanic plains she thought about her sisters. She let out a loud and satisfying scream.

CHAPTER TWENTY-EIGHT

"I SHOULD HAVE WORN SOMETHING COLORFUL." EDWINA'S fingers fumbled her pearls as if they were rosary beads. "I look like the wait staff."

"You look beautifully elegant." Doug squeezed her hand. "Most importantly, you look like you."

"You mean slightly aloof, on edge and terrified?"

He smiled at her across the table. "Well, there is that, but I was talking about your grace and style."

"Exactly. It's camouflage."

He shook his head. "Not all of it. Believe me, even when you're stark naked, Eddy, you've got style."

"Shh." Her cheeks burned hot.

"It's alright," Doug soothed, laughter in his voice. "I promise not to talk about sex in front of our daughter."

"How can you be so calm? I'm so jittery my hands shake."

"I'm not calm." His gaze hooked hers and she read apprehension in their chocolate depths. "But teasing you helps."

"What if she's changed her mind?"

"It's too early to worry about that just yet, Ed. Let's look at the facts. Her plane landed on time. According to the traffic app there are no incidents and traffic's flowing well. By my reckoning, Michelle should arrive any minute."

She forced her hand away from her pearls, worried she'd break the string. "What if she didn't get on the plane?"

"That's unlikely. She texted us from the departure lounge."

Edwina lacked Doug's confidence. There were so many steps for Michelle to take between her home in the Perth hills and this Melbourne restaurant. So many opportunities for her to decide not to take the next step, including arriving at the front door of the restaurant and not getting out of the Uber.

Watching the rainbow refractions of the thin winter sunshine bouncing off the silver saltshaker and dancing on the snowy cloth, Edwina tried not to obsess over why Michelle had waited so many weeks to contact them. Or why she'd been reticent with information about herself. Two weeks ago, they'd finally shared a very stilted phone conversation and with much trepidation, Edwina had asked if they could meet in person. Silence greeted the request; a silence that had rolled down the line as loud as thunder and just as frightening. Finally, Michelle broke the silence saying she needed time to think.

Trying not to fall at that first crushing hurdle, they'd waited. Doug had immersed himself in the restoration of a 1960's Ford Mustang and Edwina threw herself into charity work and exhausted herself by minding Tasha and the twins, giving Xara and Steve a much-needed weekend off. She'd welcomed the fatigue; when she was bone tired she couldn't think.

Michelle had telephoned five days later, telling them she didn't want them coming to Perth. Edwina hated the crippling desperation that filled her and had immediately offered to fly Michelle to Victoria. The invitation seemed to take Michelle by surprise and it had taken another two weeks for her to accept, on the proviso they didn't make any plans for the weekend other than meeting for lunch. So here they were on a Friday afternoon in late July, waiting. Edwina felt as if she'd been waiting a lifetime, which of course she had.

Panic skittered in her veins. "Should we have chosen a café?"

Doug ran a finger around the inside of his collar as though it was too tight. "We've been through this a dozen times, Eddy. We needed somewhere quiet. If I can cope with this swanky place, then she can too. For all we know, she might be just as used to swank as you."

"This waiting's as hard as giving her up." A river of heat rolled through her, burning with the intensity of a blowtorch. She lifted her glass of water and pressed it against her cheeks, needing the ice-cold chill to vanquish the hot flush. Her other hand used the menu as a fan.

The maître d' appeared by her side and she tried not to groan. She really wasn't up to coping with solicitousness today.

"Madam."

Doug rose clumsily. "Eddy."

The eagerness and anxiety in his voice made her turn and she too stumbled to her feet. Standing behind the maître d' was a woman of similar height to her. She wore black pants and a long cream top, and she'd wrapped a bright, multi-colored pashmina tightly around her torso like a shield. Or perhaps it was just a Western Australian trying to stay warm in the frigid Melbourne winter air.

Edwina couldn't have cared less about the clothes, her gaze was fixed on the woman's golden skin, dark curly hair and piercing blue eyes. Her hand flew to her mouth, stifling a gasp. *Susan.*

A sepia memory of a tiny baby with dimpled fingers and long cocoa lashes—a baby Edwina had cradled tightly to her chest so long ago—flashed across her mind. Now that baby was a middle-aged woman but there was no mistaking her genetic heritage: she was Doug with hints of Edwina, Harriet and Doug's daughter Josie. Over the years, Edwina had imagined her baby growing but she'd always pictured Susan looking like her, just as her other daughters had grown to look more like her than Richard. This woman who looked familiar yet was a stranger was utterly disconcerting.

Edwina's heart skittered. "You're here," she said softly, her voice quavering.

Michelle gave a faint smile. "I am." Her voice was deep and her accent neither broad nor elocuted.

"Can you give us a few minutes, mate?" Doug dismissed the maître d.

"Certainly, sir." The man melted away as quietly as he'd appeared.

"I thought ... that is ..." Edwina fought for composure. "I'm so glad you're here." Never one for overt displays of affection, she held out both of her hands toward Michelle. "Thank you for coming."

Michelle hesitated, her arms hidden behind the pashmina as if she was hugging herself to keep warm or stay upright. As her hands tangled in the wrap, her handbag slipped, swinging out to hit Edwina on the thigh. "Oh shit." Embarrassment burned in her eyes. "Sorry."

Edwina shook her head. "No need for sorry, Su—Michelle."

Despite practicing for the last three months to call this daughter Michelle, it was excruciatingly difficult when in her heart, she'd always been Susan. It added another layer of separation. "I've had worse things happen.' The quip fell flat.

"Woman hits birthmother at first meeting." A small dimple—Doug's dimple—appeared on her left cheek and her mouth twitched up. "My psych class will read a lot into that."

Edwina laughed, recognizing Doug's humor and she welcomed the brief touch of Michelle's fingers against her own. She wanted more—she wanted to fold this woman into her arms and never let her go, but she couldn't do it. She had no confidence she'd survive a hug if Michelle decided that today's lunch was their only contact and she wasn't certain she'd get through Michelle declining a hug either. Tim had explained that ongoing contact could be sporadic and not to pin everything on the first meeting, but it was so hard not to ride that hope train.

Doug cleared his throat. "Will it overwhelm you if I hug you? You look like you could do with one."

Michelle's smile strengthened. "I think I could cope with that."

Not for the first time, Edwina envied Doug's ease with people.

She watched with a small stab of jealousy as he enveloped their daughter in a bear hug before pulling out a chair for her.

"We can't believe you're here." Doug's voice filled with awe.

Michelle took her seat between them. "I'm not sure I can either."

"You've got my eyes." Edwina couldn't stop gazing at the woman who'd been her baby so very long ago.

"All my life people have commented on my eyes." Michelle fiddled with the edge of the starched serviette. "Does that ... does it happen to you?"

Edwina nodded, ecstatic at the tiny but shared experience. "Yes and it happens to—" Should she say *my other daughters* or *your sisters*? "To your half-sisters."

Michelle visibly startled. "I still can't get my head around the fact I have half-sisters."

"You have a half-brother too. My youngest, Ben." Doug reached for his cell phone. "Is it too early to show you photos?"

"Yes. I think it is," Michelle said firmly, nodding to the waiter pouring her a glass of water. "Could I please have a lemon, lime and bitters?"

"Certainly, ma'am." The waiter checked for other drink orders before retreating.

Edwina glanced at Doug, who gave her a small but resigned smile that said, *Yeah, I know. I rushed her.*

Michelle tugged open her dinner roll with the fervor that comes from needing to do something. "Your letter. This. Everything. It's ... overwhelming."

"Yes." Edwina passed the butter. "If it helps, it's very overwhelming for us too, but in a good way. A wonderful way."

Michelle didn't acknowledge the sentiment but instead slid a pad of butter onto her knife, keeping her eyes fixed firmly on the action. "When I registered two years ago, I wasn't looking for family. I already have a family. A *lovely* one."

The butter knife flashed back and forth against the fluffy white bread as the defensive words landed on Edwina like shot ripping into her skin. The fact this long-lost baby, who she'd thought about every day for almost fifty years, didn't need her juxtaposed with Edwina's enormous relief that loving people had raised her. Joy collided with sadness, leaving her dry mouthed and dizzy.

"Anyway," Michelle continued as if she'd rehearsed a speech and was determined to deliver it without interruption, "I've always known I was adopted. Growing up, Mom and Dad were very open about it. They told me I was the much-loved and longed-for daughter after three boys. I was. I still am." Her mouth moved into a crooked smile—Doug and Ben's smile. "I often felt like I had four fathers."

The smile faded. "None of my brothers are thrilled I've come to meet you. They tried hard to talk me out of it. They're angry and worried about Mom and Dad." She sighed. "I think they feel I've betrayed them in some way. As if they're not enough family for me, which is totally ridiculous. When I married Phil they didn't react like this but ..."

"There's a lot of anger and betrayal going around," Doug said carefully. "We've told my kids and Edwina's about you and they're struggling too. They're not happy with Eddy and me for upending their world. The counselor told us it's pretty normal."

"How did your parents take the news you were meeting us?" Edwina asked, gripping the stem of her wine glass too hard. One child adopted and yet so many people affected.

"I haven't told them yet. I wanted to wait and see how today went."

A wave of shame reinforced with guilt rolled through Edwina, settling heavy in her chest. For years she'd kept Michelle a secret for the sake of others. Now Michelle was keeping her a secret. Although part of her understood, it didn't lessen the hurt.

Michelle stirred her drink, the ice cubes tinkling against the sides of the highball glass. "The thing is, I know that a lot of people who are adopted have this need to find out who their biological parents are. I've never felt like that. I've always felt loved and secure. Smug, even, when I look at some of my friends who grew up with their biological parents and their current fractured relationships."

Doug frowned in bewildered concentration. "I don't understand. If you didn't want to find us, why did you register?"

A flicker of something unreadable crossed her face. "I had a precancerous cyst removed two years ago. It was the first serious medical condition I'd ever had. When my doctor asked me if there was any history of breast cancer in the family, I found myself talking about Mom and Dad and then it hit me. Yes, they're my family. Yes, they love and support me, but they can't help me with this. It rocked me."

Her voice wavered. "It was the first time they couldn't be there for me and I had a pressing need to fill this gap with information. Not just for me but for my daughter."

I have another granddaughter? Edwina pushed away the question for another time and tried to stay focused on the present. "And your health now, Michelle?" she asked anxiously. Was the daughter she'd only just found after all these years in jeopardy?

"I'm fine. I have regular mammograms and nothing else has been detected. The urgent need I had to get the information faded with each good result. That's why it was such a shock to get the letter from Tim saying you were looking for me. I'd never really thought of you beyond the medical history."

Edwina' heart tore—Michelle's desire to meet them was utterly pragmatic. It took her a moment to rally then she grabbed onto the fact that a medical history was something concrete she could do for Michelle. It might be the only mothering thing she ever got to do for this daughter.

"None of the women in my family have had breast cancer," Edwina said. "Doug?"

A pain crossed his face. "Sorry. I don't know much about my family's medical history. All I can tell you is my mother died of a heart attack at fifty."

"I can give you a fairly complete Mannering family medical

history." Edwina gave a tight laugh. "It may be the only advantage of being descended from a dynastic family so proud of their family tree that it rules their lives. It dates back to the 1500's in England."

Michelle's eyes widened. "Wow. That's a long way back. Dad did our family tree, but he became stuck at 1830."

"Your great—"

Tim's voice played in Edwina's head. They'd spoken to him about how best to manage this first meeting. He'd stressed Michelle had her own family and that she and Doug were her biological parents, not her parents. It was a hard pill to swallow when Edwina had never wanted to give away her firstborn child, but the fear of alienating Michelle burned strong.

"Your *biological* great-great-grandfather arrived in Victoria in the 1830's with three brothers and a mob of sheep. I still live in the district where they settled. Your family history's everywhere in Billawarre."

"And your family, Doug?" Michelle turned to him, her guarded demeanor fading slightly. "You said you don't know much of your medical history. Were you adopted too?"

Doug's usually cheerful manner dimmed and Edwina automatically took his hand. Although he spoke often about Sophia and his kids, he never mentioned his mother or extended family.

He cleared his throat. "My maternal great-grandmother was Aboriginal. My mother had Irish blood in her and I believe my father was English, but I never knew the man."

Michelle stared at him, her mouth slackening before her hand rose up to cover it. "Oh. My. God."

Doug flinched. "Does that upset you?"

"No." She shook her head, a baffled look of wonder washing across her face. "In a crazy way, it actually makes sense."

"Growing up people teased you about your curly hair and your tan, right?" Doug gave a sigh.

"No. Never. In fact, my girlfriends have always been envious of my tan." Her eyes sparkled with excitement. "Doug, I work in the

Department of Aboriginal Affairs in Perth. I liaise with community groups helping them write grant submissions and I absolutely love it. I get to travel to communities all over the west and it always invigorates me. Where's our country? Our mob?"

Sadness flickered in Doug's eyes. "I dunno. I was born in outback New South Wales, but I've got no memory of it. I've never been back. It was a different time. My mother moved us around a lot to avoid me being taken."

"Stolen, you mean," Michelle said with chagrin.

"Yeah." Doug downed his beer. "They got me at ten. Put me in a home."

Edwina's mind spun with Doug's revelation and suddenly the reason he never spoke of anything much before coming to Murrumbeet was clear. She stared at the man she loved and the daughter she'd lost, awed by how much they shared.

"You were stolen too, Michelle," she choked out against a tight throat.

The blue of Michelle's eyes darkened to a flinty gray. "Because my father's Aboriginal?"

Edwina shook her head. "No. Because it was 1968 and I was a single mother with no rights." Tears pricked the back of her eyes. "I never wanted to give you up but I was forced to. I got to hold you for an hour and then you were taken from me. I've never forgotten you."

Michelle made a choking sound. "I didn't know ... my parents never said..." She blinked rapidly and reached out to touch Edwina's arm. "I have a son and a daughter. I can't even imagine the pain if they'd been taken from me."

"No," Edwina managed to say softly. "It's every mother's nightmare. It's been my nightmare for a long time." Despite her best efforts, her withheld tears fell silently, tracking down her cheeks. "I can't tell you how relieved I am you've had a happy life."

"Would you like to order now?" the waiter asked cheerfully.

Edwina wanted to both smite him and hug him for the interruption. Although food was the last thing she felt like, she needed a breather from the emotional intensity cloaking them. She chose the salmon simply because it required no other decision-making. Doug ordered more wine and another beer for himself. This time Michelle accepted a glass.

They sat silently with their thoughts until after the waiter had set the fish and steak knives and retreated. Michelle fumbled in her handbag and pulled out a piece of paper covered in large blue handwriting. The loops on the Gs and Ys were identical to Edwina's script.

"I wrote a list of questions I wanted to ask you."

Doug burst into peals of laughter. "Edwina has a list just like it."

Edwina shrugged. "Lists are a way of making sure you don't forget the important things."

Michelle smiled. "I've always made lists. Mom and Dad used to say I was busy organizing them from three."

Edwina thought of Harriet and patted Michelle's hand. "Sorry. It's a Mannering trait."

"I like it. I get a great sense of achievement crossing things off a list." A sheepish look crossed her face. "I've been known to add something I've done that wasn't on the list just so I can get the buzz from crossing it off."

"I know exactly what you mean." Edwina relaxed for the first time. "Do you want to start working through your list?"

THE CONVERSATION over lunch lurched from moments of blissful simpatico to strained and uncomfortable silences and back again. Edwina had loved Susan but Susan had only existed in her mind. Michelle was real and she loved her, but she didn't know her. Edwina wanted to learn everything about her and yet as tidbits about her daughter's childhood were casually revealed it brought back the pain of loss in unending waves. Doug seemed to cope better but he hadn't had years to imagine a baby growing into a woman—no preconceived ideas of their child.

Michelle, too, appeared more relaxed with Doug and far more interested in him.

After viewing Doug's family photos, she said, "You should try to find our mob. You'd still have living cousins and maybe some aunties and uncles who remember your mother and grandmother. I could help you."

Doug murmured something noncommittal while Edwina weathered another knife to her heart. The irony wasn't lost on her. She could give Michelle more Mannering family information than she probably needed but Michelle didn't seem interested in her Anglo-Saxon connections and their pastoral dynasty. Despite that, at the end of lunch, Edwina said, "You're very welcome to spend the weekend with us at Billawarre. You could stay at the motel or with us at Glenora. It's your choice."

"Your daughters all live there?"

"Two of your half-sisters live there." Edwina didn't want to make a distinction between Michelle and her other three daughters. "Georgie lives here in Melbourne." Did she mention Georgie was living with Ben? Probably best to keep that bombshell for another time.

"Today's a lot to process," Michelle said hesitantly. "I'm not ready to meet them."

"No. Of course," Edwina wanted to offer understanding but at the same time dread was building. Would Michelle walk away and she'd lose her all over again?

"Could I ... would you ..." Michelle fiddled with her cell phone. "I don't want to come to Billawarre but can you stay in Melbourne for the weekend? Could I see you both tomorrow?"

Edwina looked at Doug, and together they said, "Yes."

CHAPTER TWENTY-NINE

It was mid-August and lambing season was in full swing. Xara was doing the morning pasture check because Steve had "man flu". To be fair to the poor guy, it had been a rugged virus. He hated being in bed, so the fact that he'd spent two days horizontal was testament to how ill he'd been. He'd now graduated to light duties and was keen to do more, but Xara had insisted he needed another two days before braving the coldest winter they'd had in years.

She'd pointed out that the last thing she needed was him hospitalized with pneumonia while the kids lurched from one winter bug to the next. Last week, all three kids had been home sick and she'd been tempted to paint a black cross on the door. Tasha lacked the robust constitution that blessed the twins so she was still dealing with the sniffles and a wet and hacking cough a smoker would be hard pressed to outdo. She'd left Steve and Tasha home watching kid's TV. Steve quite enjoyed *Bluey*.

The weather was bitter, made more so by the Antarctic southerly blasting across the pasture. The sheep had been busy overnight: two lambs dying from the cold but four were hale and hearty. She'd had to intervene and assist with one delivery when the lamb become stuck.

She'd been able to rescue it and deliver it safely. Unfortunately, due to the large size of the lamb, the ewe had suffered pelvic nerve damage and paralysis. Xara had shot it. She hated that part of farming.

With the dismal job over, she stowed the rifle in the gun locker on the back of the truck then pushed her hands deep into her coat pockets, seeking a tissue to stem her streaming nose. Her fingers collided with a letter that had arrived a few days earlier. She'd read it at the roadside mailbox before shoving it in her pocket. Not that she'd forgotten it—far from it. It wasn't the sort of thing one forgot. She'd left it there because it fell into the too-hard basket and she wasn't certain how best to handle the request contained within.

She should probably discuss it with Georgie. After Xara's "getting real meltdown"—Steve's words, not hers—she and Georgie had sat down with a bottle of wine. They'd talked, listened, cried and laughed.

"I'm sorry I didn't tell you sooner." Georgie's face had filled with regret, "But I couldn't. I freaked out for a bit there. Zar, and I couldn't tell anyone. After, Ben and I needed time to work through stuff."

"I guess I can understand." Xara took a long gulp of wine. "I like Ben, I really do. And I'm thrilled you're happy, but it's going to take time for me to get used to it."

"I'd never do anything intentionally to hurt you. I mean, you've been there for me through all the bad stuff. I get that you probably deserved to be the first person to hear my good news and I'm sorry we went to Mildura first. But I reckon you'd still have freaked out about me loving our mother's lover's son."

"Oh, yeah." She drank more wine. "I'm sorry I made it all about me when it's all about you and Ben. God, I did exactly what I've been accusing you and Harry of doing."

Georgie laughed. "In a weird way, it was kinda reassuring watching you lose it. Sometimes, your logical and rational approach to things makes me feel I'm too emotional."

"I've missed you."

"Me too."

They'd fallen back into their routine of regular texts and occasional phone calls. Xara especially valued them as things between Harriet, Charlotte and Edwina were still at an impasse. She fingered the letter again and made a decision. She'd call Georgie tonight and discuss the contents.

Glancing up at the steel-gray sky, she thought it, the howling wind and the bleating lambs made it all very Gothic. On a playful whim she called out, "Heathcliff!" then laughed.

"Zar-rah!" came back to her on the wind.

She stilled, convinced she was imagining things but then she heard it again. With mud sucking at her rubber boots, she stomped over to the gate and was startled to see Harriet coming toward her, dressed in running gear. Her sister dodged and weaved around the potholes of water on the corrugated surface of Woolscour Lane.

"What on earth are you doing? It's freezing."

Panting, Harriet stopped and bent over, pressing her palms to her thighs as she caught her breath "Exercising. You ... should ... try ... it."

Xara rolled her eyes. "I've just walked the length and breadth of a field and delivered a lamb. If that isn't exercise, I don't know what is."

Harriet laughed. "Fair point. Sorry."

An apology? "Wow, exercise really suits you," Xara teased then remembered the distance to the farm. "Surely you haven't run from Miligili in this weather?"

Harriet dragged her forearm across her forehead. "I needed to run."

Xara took a closer look at her sister. Her face was lined with fatigue and gaunt with misery. She looked older than she had before Easter and despite what was clearly an expensive color treatment in her hair, new silver strands had appeared. Her dominant aura of control didn't have the same sharp and precise cut. For weeks, Xara had been calling and dropping by to check on Harriet, and Harriet had visited the farm more often than she had in the past decade. But whenever Xara asked how she doing, her response was always a clipped and terse, "I'm fine." Today it was clear Harriet was struggling.

Xara had a sudden urge to be the sister to Harriet she'd always wished Harriet could be for her. Slipping off her coat, she threw it over Harriet's shoulders. "Get into the truck before you freeze."

Harriet didn't object and was oddly quiet on the short and bouncy drive back across the fields to the farmhouse. After waving and calling hello to the sick crew on the couch, she turned back to Xara.

"Can I grab a shower?"

"Sure." Xara pulled a towel from the linen closet.

"Thanks. Have you got something I can wear after?"

"I don't have any cool-down clothes. Can you cope with a pair of my baggy sweatpants and an old school hoodie?"

"I think I'll be able to manage without breaking out in a rash." Her mouth tweaked up. "Only just though."

Xara laughed and went off to find the clothes.

She'd just brewed tea when Harriet appeared in the kitchen wearing her comfort clothes with a style Xara could never emulate. A gnarly old resentment surfaced. "Why do you look better in my old clothes than I ever look in my good ones?"

"I don't," Harriet said bluntly, accepting a mug of tea. "You just think I do. For the life of me, I've never understood why."

Because you have a wardrobe full of designer clothes. The thought was petty and she didn't want to dignify it by saying it out loud. But today there was something sad in Harriet's gaze that made her say, "Sorry." For the first time ever, she glimpsed a shift in their relationship and saw a chance for them to move out from under the shadow of their birth order and just be sisters. Friends even, but it could only start with the truth.

"For years, I've been jealous of how much you can afford to spend on clothes. It's ridiculous really, because out here I need a totally different type of wardrobe."

"Well, you don't have to be jealous anymore." Harriet slumped onto a chair in a very uncharacteristic movement. "Two-thirds of my clothes are currently on consignment in Melbourne."

"Oh, Harry." Xara sat next to her, feeling the loss almost as keenly. Sure, she'd had moments of envy but at the same time she gained a lot of pleasure from admiring Harriet's clothes.

Harriet shrugged. "Clothes are the least of my problems. You've seen today's paper?"

"No. It comes with the mail."

"Yesterday my estranged husband appeared in court," she said bitterly. "They've charged him with 1227 counts of theft and fraud and revoked bail. Apparently, there's so much evidence there's no room for all of it at the station. They've had to rent the house next door." She half-laughed, half-snorted and reached for a Tim Tam. "It would be funny if it wasn't so ghastly."

Xara didn't know what was more worrisome—that James had ripped off so many people and was now in custody or that Harriet was eating a Tim Tam. Harriet never succumbed to the irresistible chocolate cookie and usually Xara got a lecture on the calorie load just from offering her one.

Harriet bit down hard but showed no signs she was savoring the milky chocolate coating or the lush, creamy interior. "Zar—" Her voice cracked. "I'm going to lose Miligili."

"No! You can't," Xara heard herself saying, utterly stunned that the situation had devolved to this. "You love that house and all of its Mannering history."

"Loving it isn't enough. Believe me, I've tried everything. Even a marginally dodgy scheme where James transferred the house into my name."

"Not a transfer of love, care and affection? Oh, Harry, why didn't you talk to me?"

"Because, just like Angela, you would have tried to talk me out of it. Anyway it's moot. The bastard's even made that impossible to pull off."

"How? I thought he'd leap at a chance of keeping a stake in the house."

"He had a caveat."

"What did he want?"

Harriet stood and walked to the counter, pouring herself more tea and fingering the fluffy balls of wool on the sheep tea cozy Georgie had knitted. "Do you want a second?"

"No, thanks."

Harriet went to the doorway. "Cup of tea, Steve?"

Tasha squealed. Whether it was in objection to the interruption or something on the screen, it was hard to tell.

"Thanks, but for peace and quiet I'll wait until *Bluey's* finished."

"I can—"

"Harry!" Xara interrupted. Her sister never acted like a hostess when she visited. Usually she sat primly on the edge of a dining chair worried that dust or a rogue squashed pea would stain her clothes. "What did James want in exchange for the transfer?"

Her sister sighed and sat down. "He insisted I convince Charlotte to meet with him."

And you didn't do it. Xara was thrilled and relieved that amid all the crazy and the drama generated by the surprise pregnancy and her refusal to see or talk with Charlotte, in this instance Harriet had put her daughter first. She leaned over and impulsively hugged her big sister. "You did the right thing."

Harriet stiffened. "It's cost me my home."

Xara was struck for the first time how similar Harriet and Edwina were with displays of affection. She drew back from the uncomfortable embrace. "If you'd forced Charlie to meet James, it would have cost you your relationship with her."

"The horse has bolted on that already."

Irritation prickled Xara, making her skin hot and itchy. "No. You're the one who's bolted, but you can turn around and canter back. Charlie's still in the stable."

"Edwina's stable." Air hissed out between Harriet's clenched teeth. "Doesn't it bother you that after years of indifferent mothering, Edwina's suddenly a vessel of maternal feeling? She's clucking around Charlotte like a broody hen. Who knows the display she's putting on for her first-born child?"

The words struck Xara with the dull thud of realization. Harriet was no longer the eldest daughter—Michelle had usurped her. "Are you jealous of your older sister?"

Two pink spots burned on her cheeks. "God, no. What's there to be jealous of? We know only too well what Edwina's like as a mother."

But Harriet had answered too quickly and too savagely to squash Xara's theory. She thought of the letter in her coat pocket and knew no time would be a good time to bring it up so she may as well do it now. "Doug's daughter, Josie, wrote to me. She wants to meet with us and talk about Michelle."

"What's there to talk about? I don't intend to meet my half-sister and from what you've said, she doesn't want to meet us. Problem solved."

"I don't think it's quite as clear cut as all that. Initially, Michelle didn't want to meet us but that was weeks ago. Things are different now."

"So why hasn't she set it up?"

"She's getting a lot of pressure from her brothers not to rock their family boat."

"I like the sound of those brothers. I mean really, what's the point of meeting her? The only common ground we have is a biological connection through our mother. A woman she's known for five weeks."

"How is meeting her any different from going to family reunions and talking to long lost cousins?" Xara used Harriet's zest for the family tree as an argument. "You're the one who's forced us to go to the last three reunions. You lectured us on the importance of knowing where we came from so we can know who we are."

"Yes," Harriet said irritably, "but you grew up knowing you were part Chirnwell and part Mannering. Michelle didn't."

"She hardly had a choice in the matter and neither did Mom. That doesn't stop half of her DNA being Mannering."

"My advice to her is, if she wants to stay in starry-eyed delusional land about her birth mother, perhaps it's best not to meet us. She'd only hear the real stories about Edwina."

Xara ground her teeth. "From what Mom says there's nothing remotely starry-eyed about her. Georgie agrees with me that if Michelle wants to meet us then we should make it happen."

"Of course Georgie agrees. She's got a foot in each camp now she's taken up with Ben."

"It's got nothing to do with Ben," Xara said, thinking about the angry and tormented letter from Josie. "Michelle grew up with three brothers. Perhaps she'd like some sisters."

Harriet snorted. "We fought all the time growing up."

"We bonded over bossing Georgie around."

The quip didn't elicit a smile. "I have no need of another sister, Xara."

"Neither does Doug's daughter Josie." The idea of Josie and Harriet meeting or Skyping, as Josie had suggested, was unsettling. "But I want to meet Michelle."

"Why?" Harriet sounded genuinely mystified.

"Because it will kill the air of mystery surrounding her. And you never know, we might have things in common. We might even like her and her kids."

Harriet's brows rose in an I-don't-think-so arch but before Xara could respond, Tasha squealed loudly. Harriet flinched as always at the high-pitched and penetrating sound.

Xara rose. "That's the I'm-wet-and-uncomfortable squeal. I'll go and change her."

As if reading her mind, Steve called out, "I've got it."

"Thanks," she yelled back then groaned. "I gave the twins a

lecture this morning about yelling from room to room. I've just realized Steve and I are just as bad."

"A house with stone walls puts an end to that," Harriet said, a catch in her voice.

"Are you sure there's nothing else you can try to save Miligili?"

"I've tried everything that's legally, morally and ethically palatable. My estranged husband's a special man," Harriet said acidly. "Despite stealing millions, James has managed to run up a large domestic debt as well, some of which I'm liable for. Angela and I have looked at it all six ways from Sunday. My best option is to sell."

Xara hoped the attorney had covered all the bases. "And the split on the sale price?"

"I'll get a larger percentage. His share will be seized by creditors. Fun times."

The thought of Harriet living in a different house was so foreign to Xara, she could barely wrap her head around it. "I guess you'll move into a smaller place in town?" She suddenly got an idea. "What about the Sandersons' Edwardian? It's beautifully restored with gorgeous pressed-metal ceilings. Oh, and it's close to the lake for running and close to the hospital too."

Harriet sat straighter, her old verve back in the set of her shoulders and the sparkling glint in her eyes. "I quite fancy an Art Deco apartment in Rose Bay. I've applied for a position at Royal Prince Alfred Hospital in Sydney."

Xara's mouth fell open. "Sydney? You hardly know anyone in Sydney."

Harriet gave her a patronizing smile, as if Xara was simple. "I've got school friends there. And I'll get to know people. After all, Sydney's the party town."

An angry wave of indignation oscillated in Xara's chest. "You always said you hated cities and now, just like that—" she snapped her fingers "—you're off to Sydney?"

Harriet's eyes narrowed. "It's hardly 'just like that.' I've been thinking about it for a while. You have no idea how difficult things have been for me these last five months. I deserve a fresh start."

"A fresh start?" Xara lost control. "What planet are you on? You have a pregnant daughter living in Billawarre. How does she fit into your fresh start?"

"I'm hardly abandoning Charlotte to the streets," Harriet said tightly. "She's being well looked after by her grandmother."

"Spare me. You can't honestly sit there and tell me the fact Charlie's got a roof over her head absolves you of all responsibility? I'm not saying the last few months haven't been tough for you. I won't argue that you've worked hard all your life, but you've also had some good luck and good fortune. For years, everything's gone your way. You've had power, prestige and privilege. Life's been pretty cushy for you, Harriet Jane.

"Yes, the town's behaved badly. Yes, what James did to you is unforgivable, but what you're doing to Charlie is pretty bloody unforgivable too. You're running away from the first tough situation you've ever had to face."

Harriet's mouth thinned into a hard and brittle line. "I face tough situations every day at work."

"That's completely different."

"You have no idea what you're talking about."

"Excuse me?" Her hand slammed the table making the Tim Tams rattle on their plate. "Do you really want to go down this path with me?"

Harriet, never one to back down from a fight, held her gaze, her blue eyes deepening to flinty shale gray. Xara imagined that her own looked pretty much the same: silver flashes of angry lightning against a dark blue sky.

"You want to compete with me for life's suckiest moments, Harry? It's not a wise bet. I'll win it hands down. No contest. I have a daughter whose potential was stolen from her before she was born. Her life is so far removed from the dream I held for her it still rips me apart fourteen years later."

"Exactly," Harriet said, nodding in agreement. "You understand then how I feel about Charlotte and this pregnancy."

Xara felt as if her skull was being blasted open by volcanic fury. "No! You don't get to align yourself with me on this one. We don't share the same level of pain about our daughters. My child will never eat, never walk, never talk, never write, never read, never ..." Angry tears built behind her eyes. "You have a healthy, functioning daughter brimming with potential, but you're blind to that because she's not living the life *you* envisaged for her. A life you're trying to impose on her. And because things aren't going your way, you've cut her loose."

"I have not cut her loose." Harriet ground out each word with the precision and sharpness of a diamond cutter. "Charlotte is choosing to live her life without me in it."

Xara threw her hands up as despair fused with utter frustration. "Can you hear yourself? You've put Charlie in an impossible situation. You've asked her to choose you or the baby. I know it's breaking your heart she's pregnant, but life isn't perfect. God, I worked that out years ago. It's messy and complicated and disorganized. People do things that hurt you. People disappoint you and let you down. Family lets you down and that one hurts the most."

"Especially mothers who have a child no one knows about!"

Xara ignored her. This time Harriet didn't get to hide behind her antagonism for Edwina and her idealistic adoration of their father. This time Xara need her sister to face her own behavior. "It's especially devastating when the dream we hold for our child crashes and burns. But sometimes, Harry, in the muck and dross of family life, you stumble over a nugget of gold sparkling brightly amid the imperfections. When that happens, it's magic."

She thought about her daily challenges and a memory from three weeks ago flared into life. The twins had brought home an orphaned lamb. They'd jumped from the truck and rushed straight to their sister, shoving it at her with an enthusiasm borne of love and a desire to include. Tasha's face had lit up in its contorted way, but the constriction hadn't suppressed the pleasure. It was those moments that kept Xara going. Those moments that made all the hardship and pain worthwhile.

"Only you won't ever find those moments of magic if you run away to fucking Sydney!"

"I. Am. Not. Running. Away." The skin on Harriet's face stretched so tightly her cheekbones threatened to break through. Her usually well-modulated voice took on a screech worthy of a parrot. "And you have no idea what I'm going through. You've never lived and worked in a town that hates you."

"Um, Xara." Steve appeared in the doorway. "Everything okay in here?"

"No!" As she yelled at him she heard Harriet's voice echoing her own.

Harriet rose to her feet, her chest heaving. "I came here because I thought you were the one person who'd understand. Obviously, I was erroneous in that assumption."

The pompous surgeon had swooped in, vanquishing all traces of the needy sister. "It's clear I'm no longer welcome. I'll leave."

"Of course you'll leave," Xara said bitterly. "Perish the thought you might actually stay and listen to something I have to say."

"I'll listen, Xara, when it's something worth hearing."

Xara was hurled back in time to the circular arguments they'd shared during their childhood and teenage years. Only this time the argument wasn't about how much shelf space she deserved in the shared wardrobe at Apollo Bay or her right to hang her music posters in the game room. This time it was far more important, but Harriet stood staring at her as she'd always done—aloof, disinterested and slightly disdainful.

Xara crossed her trembling arms. "Off you go then. Run away from your messy, imperfect family who keep letting you down. Go to Sydney. Construct the façade of a perfect life with your friends who are using money to hide their own messy lives. You'll fit right in."

"Now you're just talking nonsense."

Harriet's haughty tone undid her. "Am I? Remember that when

I'm here in Billawarre getting to know your grandchild and you're living 600 miles away."

Harriet's face raged puce and she pushed past Xara, heading toward the back door.

Steve grabbed the truck's keys off the hook. "I'll drive you home."

"I no longer have a home," Harriet said dully before disappearing outside.

Shaking, Xara sank onto a chair, uncertain if she wanted to cry or throw up.

Steve hovered where he stood, clearly undecided if he should stay with his wife or make sure his sister-in-law got home without developing hypothermia.

Alone in the living room, Tasha squealed.

"I'll go," Xara said with a weariness she recognized as being decades old. "You take Harry home, but Steve?"

"Yes."

"I meant every word that I said. Do *not* apologize for me."

"I wouldn't dare."

CHAPTER THIRTY

"An island vacation," Ben had suggested to Georgie late in August when her brain was full of everything she had to do for the school's open house as well as finding time to revamp her resume. "I was thinking the end of September. The first week of school vacation. It will be a getaway from school, our families and the last six crazy months. A complete rest."

The words "complete rest" and "island vacation" had immediately conjured the image of lazing on a golden beach with a good book in one hand and one of those bright colored cocktails with a paper umbrella in the other. More importantly, the beach would be a student-and parent-free zone.

"Sounds like a plan." Since they'd moved in together they'd been making plans. Their dream was to move to the country and buy a house. Currently, they were scouring the internet and the regional newspapers for rural jobs in both public and private schools. Ben was encouraging her to get out of classroom teaching and consider a job where she could explore her art. He'd seen the advertisement for an art therapy job in Bendigo and suggested she apply.

"You're frantic," Ben had said. "Leave the vacation planning to me. I'll organize everything."

"God, I love you." She'd thrown her arms around his neck and kissed him.

Her relationship with Ben was so different from the one with Jason that she often pinched herself. Ben not only filled the obvious hole in her life—he'd filled spaces within her she'd never known existed. Not that they agreed on everything—examples being what constituted a clean sink and a clean bathroom—but instead of becoming stuck in circular arguments, Ben suggested they work to their strengths. He shopped, cooked, ironed and vacuumed. She dusted and cleaned the kitchen and the bathrooms. They daydreamed of paying someone to do all of it for them.

Ben's island vacation idea was now reality and she still loved him, but good God! No part of her definition of a "relaxing island vacation" featured rising at dawn and taking a breath-sucking walk up a precipitous climb. It didn't help that Ben was positively bounding up the track ahead of her looking fit and buff while her hair stuck to her sweaty head, her calves screamed and her heart and lungs threatened to explode. Not caring that the bulk of the hiking group were ahead of her, she took a moment to rest. Her parched throat welcomed the cool water she glugged down fast.

Ben jogged back to her and pressed a protein bar into her hand. "We're almost there. You're doing great."

"This better be worth it. There better not be cloud," Georgie grumbled. "And just so you know, I'm having a spa day tomorrow and being pampered."

He laughed. "I promise you'll remember this walk for longer than you'll remember the spa."

She doubted that. The track was too narrow to walk side by side and as Ben was the faster walker, he went first. She supposed the one benefit of this strenuous hike was that she got to admire his ass as she went. They'd started at sea level, climbing quickly. She'd used the ropes to help haul herself up and soon they'd found themselves in a grove of tall and straight kentia palms.

The next section had freaked her out as she'd gingerly traversed a very narrow track wedged between a mountain on one side and a 300-foot drop to the Tasman Sea on the other. As if nature knew she only had so much stamina, the trail had thankfully flattened out for a mile and they'd strolled over a plateau before climbing again. Now they were above the tree line in a mossy forest.

The summit beckoned and she pushed through her discomfort, keen to get to the top and conquer the walk like the rest of the party. Soon she was gazing out across Lord Howe Island's rainforest toward the rugged volcanic Mt. Lidgbird and down to the spectacular turquoise lagoon. Two providence petrels soared overhead, riding the wind currents, and above them the blue, blue sky went on forever.

"Oh, wow," she managed to splutter despite panting for breath. "It's amazing."

"So are you." Ben grinned at her and whipped off her hat. "Marry me?"

Her oxygen-deprived brain short-circuited as his unexpected question sucked away the little remaining breath. She blinked her sweat-filled eyes, trying to work out if he'd just proposed or if she was having an exercise-induced hallucination.

A knot of worry pulled at his mouth. "Georgie?"

She heaved in air. "Did you ... did you just ask me to marry you?"

He gazed down at her, his eyes filled with love but backlit with a thread of anxiety. "I did. Sorry. I mean, I'm not sorry. Not at all."

He ran a hand through his hair. "Hell, I've stuffed it up. The thing is, I've been planning to ask you for weeks and tonight was the night. I booked us a romantic dinner in the restaurant in the corner window you love so much under the watchful eye of Mt. Gower. But seeing you standing here with wonder and delight on your face, I couldn't wait another minute."

"But I'm bright red, sweaty and I've got hat hair!"

"You're beautiful," he said softly. "Inside and out."

Her heart lurched and she had the craziest sensation she was going to cry. She didn't want to cry—she'd done too much of that in the last two years. "Only a gym teacher would propose on a precipice to a woman who isn't match fit."

"You're fitter and stronger than you ever give yourself credit for." He picked up her hands. "You still haven't answered me. Shall I repeat the question? I can do the official version or the unofficial version. Which do you want?"

"Both." The shock was passing and she wanted to savor every minute of this life-changing moment.

"Okay. Take one. The unofficial version." His eyes twinkled and he cleared his throat. "Hey, babe. You and me. How about it?"

She laughed. "Smooth. Very smooth."

"That's me." His face sobered. "Now the official version. Georgina Elizabeth Chirnwell, will you do me the honor of becoming my wife?"

The old-fashioned words wrapped around her heart with the reassuring warmth of a blanket on a cold night; words she'd waited years to hear and despaired they'd never be spoken. Now she understood why—she'd had to meet Ben first.

"Oh, Ben. I'd love to marry you. The sooner the better." She wrapped her arms around his waist and snuggled in close, tilting her head back to look at him. "But I still get my romantic dinner tonight, right?"

He laughed. "I promise you champagne, the seafood extravaganza, and a ring served with a decadent dessert."

Her heart swelled. "You bought a ring?"

He looked sheepish. "I told you. I'd planned it all perfectly. Then I stuffed it up."

"No, you didn't. You've just doubled the joy. I get to relive it all over again tonight." She gave a shivery squeal. "I can't wait to see the ring. I can't believe you bought me a ring."

"I had help. I got input from Xara and my sisters."

"Clever man."

"I thought it politic on many fronts. Besides, it gave Josie something else to focus on instead of Michelle. Josie loves a wedding."

"A wedding," she said wondrously. "Oh my God, we're really doing this. We're engaged!" She grabbed his hand and tugged him over to the group of hikers who were now sitting in a circle and digging into the gourmet sandwiches packed by the resort kitchen. "Everyone," she said portentously. "You intrepid folk are the first to know. Ben just proposed and I said yes."

To the background of cheers, Georgie kissed her fiancé and thrilled at the sheer joy pulsing through her.

"Welcome to Miligili. And doesn't she look a picture in this glorious spring sunshine?" The realtor's voice boomed over the buzz of the large crowd. "Historically significant, this rare and illustrious home was built by the Mannering pastoral dynasty in 1878. Now nestled on five acres, it boasts beautifully established landscaped gardens, a full-size tennis court, a swimming pool and spa as well as a guesthouse and bluestone stables. Restored and currently owned by a descendent of Thomas Mannering, its superb interiors retain their heritage allure and include soaring ceilings, Baltic pine floors, original leaded glass and decorative designs ..."

Harriet stood at the back of the crowd wearing dark glasses and praying she was inconspicuous. She'd dressed carefully, passing over her usual spring weekend casual wear of knee-high leather boots, caramel twill pants, a long-sleeved striped T-shirt and a jaunty quilted vest. Instead, she'd hauled on Xara's sweatpants and hoodie.

It had physically hurt to put them on, not just because she'd taken a personal vow at seventeen never to be seen out of the house dressed in sweatpants, but because the clothes reminded her of the bitter argument she'd had with her sister. They hadn't spoken since. It wasn't like she and Xara had never argued before—they had and often

—but this time was different. They'd never gone weeks without speaking and Xara's silence had bitten hard. For the first time in her life, Harriet felt completely abandoned.

Despite their differing views, she and Xara had always pulled together on the important things. Every time she thought about Xara's current silence, the root of her anger burned hot. How could Xara believe that she'd never grieved for her over Tasha? Granted, she didn't provide Xara with any hands-on help, but she'd paid for the occasional weekend away for her and Steve, she'd contributed money toward Tasha's new wheelchair and every school vacation she'd lent them Charlotte.

I think that was more Xara helping you out with childcare than the other way around.

She batted away the errant thought with renewed resentment. It was Charlotte's exposure to Tasha and the twins that had made her hell bent on continuing with the pregnancy. Charlotte was thirty-four weeks pregnant now. Not that she'd seen her daughter or her fecund belly, but despite not thinking about the pregnancy, she always seemed to know the gestational week without even trying.

"... Handsome formal sitting and dining rooms, each with marble open fireplaces and bay windows, precede an expansive informal living and dining domain with a tessellated-tiled floor accompanied by a well-appointed kitchen with butler's pantry. The outdoor spaces are accessed through French doors and are ideal for indoor–outdoor entertaining. There are six bedrooms including a luxurious master suite with bedroom, bath and a parents' retreat. The children are looked after too, with a large game room offering fabulous family flexibility."

Harriet peered out from under the knotted cap she'd pulled over her hair—all part of her disguise—and her umbrage grew. The bulk of the crowd weren't here to bid on her beautiful home; they'd come to gawk and pass judgment on her and her taste.

They'd walked over her polished floorboards, slid their fingers across her furniture, probably opened her linen closet and underwear drawers, checked out her bathroom cabinets and commented on the righteousness of the forced sale of her home. With a masochistic bent she hadn't been aware was part of her, she'd lingered in the house during the obligatory open for inspection time before the auction. Apparently, having good taste and money was offensive to many.

"It serves them right. I mean, who needs a house this big?"

"Look at all these bedrooms. Ridiculous. Apparently they only had one kid."

"I heard she's run off the rails just like her father."

"Yeah, well what do you expect? The rich think they're above the law. It's all about power and prestige."

The realtor's voice droned on. "The original attic-style servants' quarters have been converted into two bedrooms. With a total of three bathrooms, a library-cum-study, a cellar, water tanks, automatic gates and a four-car garage, Miligili is a home you want to own. And now I'll introduce you to our auctioneer, Ted Radak."

Harriet had told the realtor she wouldn't be in attendance and would deal with questions by phone. She hadn't wanted the gaze of the town on her, which was why she was incognito. She scanned the throng, which featured almost every demographic in Billawarre from farmers to shopkeepers, hospital cleaners to administrators, with a few teachers thrown in for good measure. James was not among them. He'd written from the detention center when he'd gotten news of the auction: *We can't always get what we want, H. It's just a house.*

Unlike the man she'd married, this new James always found a way to hurt her. Miligili had never been just a house. Now, standing in the crisp morning air watching the bright and cheery daffodils sway in the breeze, she wondered why she was putting herself through the pain of watching what had been her third love—after James and Charlotte—go under the hammer. She'd wondered if Charlotte might have come but she wasn't in the crowd either. None of her family had come. Georgie was out of range on Lord Howe Island but even if she'd been able to call, her youngest sister's long-distance solicitude would have made Harriet miss Xara more.

"Harriet?"

Panic surged through her. How the hell had someone recognized her in this getup and behind large dark sunglasses? *Don't respond and they'll go away.*

"Harriet Chirnwell?" the voice persisted, slightly louder this time.

Shit. She really didn't want him yelling out her name so she turned around slowly. Through her Polaroid glasses she was startled to see Andrew Willis. Acute embarrassment followed; she'd just been outed by a colleague while being dressed like a bag lady. He, on the other hand, had his hands shoved deep inside the pockets of a navy woolen coat. Underneath it he wore jeans and what appeared to be a cream, hand-knitted, cable sweater. He looked like a hatless fisherman.

"Have you lost your boat?"

"It's definitely you." He smiled slowly. "I wasn't certain there for a minute. I'm used to seeing you in scrubs, although it seems you favor the casual look out of hours too."

An unreasonable sense of betrayal gripped her that he, like so many others, had come just to scope out Miligili. She didn't understand why she felt so strongly—it wasn't like they were friends. Apart from some brief conversations with Jenny, he'd been the only other person she'd talked to over the last few weeks. Not that the conversations had been riveting—they'd barely strayed from work-related topics, the weather and the latest knick-knack Cecily had added to his room at the B & B. She'd never mentioned James and the fraud, or Charlotte and the pregnancy, and she definitely hadn't mentioned the auction. Still, this was Billawarre. All it would take was one short conversation with anyone in the hospital and he'd have been told Miligili was hers.

"Come to bid?" she asked tartly.

"Nah," he said easily. "She's a bit big for my needs."

"So, in actual fact, you've joined the rest of the town as a tire kicker."

He didn't even have the grace to look abashed. "I like to think of it as getting a feel for the market."

"This is hardly your market."

"Yeah, okay. You got me." He rolled back and forth on the balls of his feet, his face lined in thought. "Will you accept I have an interest in historic houses?"

"Do you?"

His eyes lit up silver gray, matching Miligili's blue stone, and he pulled out his cell phone. Swiping the screen, he brought up a photo of a glorious Victorian house. "I spent five years restoring her to her former glory."

Harriet studied the picture. The two-story house with long verandas was built out of the distinctive South Australian bluestone. Unlike the blue-gray of the Victorian stone, this was a multi-color mix of browns, blues, grays, sand and ochre. The neat red brickwork surrounding each window punctuated the beautiful mélange of colors and textures. All of it said, "Adelaide."

"She's beautiful."

"Yeah, she is. Part of my heart will forever remain in that house." He closed the screen and slid the cell phone back into his pocket. "I lost her as part of my divorce settlement."

Her heart took a hit on his behalf and she glanced at him over the top of her sunglasses. "Is it supposed to hurt this much?"

He rocked again, his booted feet crunching against the driveway's crushed gravel. "Yep."

She crossed her arms, hating the feel of the bulky hoodie bunching around her middle. "If it was your intention to come today and make me feel better," she said, "it's not working."

He laughed and the sonorous sound rang out with relaxed enjoyment. "I like your frankness, Harriet Chirnwell."

She stared straight ahead, not sure what to make of him. "You'd be in the minority."

"You did a beautiful restoration job on this house. You served her well. You'll always be a part of her history. Hold onto that."

She wanted to say thank you, but her throat was scratchy and her eyes burned. She looked away, blinking rapidly, grateful she was wearing sunglasses.

"Ladies and gentlemen, now we've outlined all the information required by law," the auctioneer said after declaring the obligatory rates and water costs and referring the serious bidders to the contract. "I need to tell you that as well as the people present here today, we have three people bidding by telephone. My assistants—" he indicated three women dressed in almost identical black skirts, white blouses, gray and white patterned scarves and black jackets "—will be relaying their bids to me."

Nausea rolled Harriet's stomach. Miligili was really going on the market. "I don't think I can stay and watch after all."

Andrew gave her shoulder a quick squeeze, the pressure steady and friendly. "You owe it to her. Besides, you'll hate yourself if you don't stay. As much as you don't want to be here, you won't want to miss it either. It's all part of saying goodbye."

She didn't quite know what to make of this man who up until today had only ever talked shop. She went to say a tart, "Nonsense," but instead muttered, "Have you always been insightful?"

"Of course." This time his laugh rang with self-deprecating humor. "Put it this way: getting divorced taught me some things. I thought some of it might be useful to you. Mind you, as difficult as it got for me, I didn't have to face the scrutiny or deal with the vitriol of an entire town."

He gave a small smile. "Sorry. Can't offer you much advice there except keep doing what you're doing."

"Hiding in plain sight in awful clothes?"

"I was thinking more along the lines of turning up to work every day." He winked at her. "Not that you don't rock that particular look, although you haven't got it quite right. You're missing the Ugg boots."

Despite her embarrassment, she felt her lips twitch.

The auctioneer rang his bell. "Let's start the bidding at 1.5 million dollars."

The bids started slowly but quickly sped up. Despite her height, Harriet had trouble working out exactly who was bidding. It soon became apparent the telephone bidders were the serious contenders.

She leaned in close to Andrew so only he could hear her whispered, "It just passed the reserve price."

His very male scent of wool, sweat and mint settled inside her with an ache. He didn't smell anything like James, although memories of that clean, crisp fragrance now made her gag. Andrew's aroma rammed home exactly how long she'd been alone, especially if she counted the months preceding James's arrest. All of it unsettled her and she didn't like feeling unsettled about Andrew. She had enough disconcerting things going on in her life without adding another one. Besides, he wasn't her type.

You've been married to the same man for twenty years. Do you even have a type?

"This property is now on the market," the auctioneer announced, accepting another bid from the assistant Harriet had dubbed Thing One. The bids climbed and then Thing Two shook her head and stepped back, leaving Thing One and Thing Three with bidding clients.

"We have 3.1 million," the auctioneer's voice boomed and Thing Three stepped back, shaking her head. The auctioneer scanned the crowd. "I'll accept thousand-dollar bids."

There was no nodding, no raising of hands nor lifting of fingers. "In that case," the auctioneer continued, "I have 3.1 million dollars going once ... going twice ..." He held a sheaf of rolled papers in his hand and suddenly brought them down on his opposite palm with a slapping sound. "Sold to phone bidder number one."

A polite round of applause broke the crowd's silence and then the twitter of chatter rose, buzzing around Harriet like wasps. The muscles in her thighs quivered, the movement quickly morphing into a fully-fledged shake. "That's that then," she said, trying to sound brisk and in control. The words wobbled.

"Can you take any solace in a decent price?" Andrew asked.

She thought of the stack of creditors' notices locked away from prying eyes in the study's filing cabinet. "It will give me some breathing space."

He nodded thoughtfully. "Good."

She had an odd urge to invite him inside for coffee, but she dismissed the thought as quickly as it landed. "I best go and put on my real clothes and sign the papers." She stuck out her hand as if they were at an official meeting and it was coming to an end. "Thank you for coming."

"No worries." He shook her proffered hand, his expression unreadable. "See you in the trenches, Harriet Chirnwell," then turned and walking back down the drive to Miligili's heritage listed gates. His chirpy whistling floated back to her before the noise of the crowd drowned it out.

Surrounded by people, Harriet felt utterly alone.

CHAPTER THIRTY-ONE

GEORGIE TWEAKED THE BOW ON THE GIFT SHE'D SWATHED IN layers of tissue paper for Charlotte's baby shower. It was the second weekend of October and she still couldn't quite wrap her head around the fact that Charlotte was thirty-five weeks pregnant.

"It looked perfect three tugs ago," Ben said from his prone position on Glenora's guest room's bed.

"Perhaps to your masculine eye." Georgie fingered the turn again, smoothing it as she made three wishes. One for Charlotte. One for her great niece or nephew and one for herself.

She heard a book hit the floor followed by the sound of Ben's feet and then his arms went around her waist. Pulling her against him, he rested his chin on her shoulder. "You're fiddling. What's up? Decided your embroidery is too good for this baby and you're keeping the blanket for ours?"

"We're not even pregnant yet." But she hugged the thought they'd started trying. Prayed she'd be able to conceive quickly given she was about to turn thirty-five and but at the same time trying to keep her fears about pregnancy and babies at a very low ebb.

"I reckon you should buy a body-hugging wedding dress that's so tight it has to be virtually sprayed on. That almost guarantees you'll be a pregnant bride." Ben's arms tightened around her and he kissed her ear, his tongue outlining the shell. "We can start practicing now if you like."

A dart of delicious desire shot through her and she turned in his arms. "I guess as the Chirnwells' spotless reputation is already blotted, being a pregnant bride is just helping along a whole new tradition."

"Georgie?" Xara's voice drifted down the hall. "Where are you? There's work to be done."

Ben gave a good-natured sigh. "I thought you said Harriet was the bossy one."

"She is. At least she was." Georgie thought how flat her eldest sister had sounded on the phone after the auction. "I'm worried about her. I want to check on her and we can do that under the guise of showing her the ring." She gazed yet again at her elegant and sparkling emerald-cut solitaire diamond.

"That's not something I really want to put my hand up for. But I'll do it for you if you think it will help."

She patted his cheek. "Harry's coming around to you. She actually asked me how you were the last time we spoke, and she'll be seriously impressed by this ring."

"A rising approval rating, eh? I should buy a lottery ticket." He sat on the bed and pulled on his socks. "Exactly when are you going to fit in this visit? The baby shower's this afternoon and she's not coming, right?"

Georgie understood his confusion. At the moment it almost took a map and a compass to work out who wasn't talking to whom—and it wasn't just her side of the family. Josie continued being difficult although unlike Harriet, she wavered between cutting herself off from Doug and opening the door to him. It was currently closed to Edwina.

"No. She's not coming." Although Georgie knew Harriet was stubborn, she'd fully expected her to have conceded by now that

Charlotte's baby was real and it wasn't going away. As Harriet and Xara weren't talking, Georgie was the one to urge Harriet to accept this fact. She'd called her the moment they'd gotten back from Lord Howe Island.

"Ben and I are coming to Glenora on the weekend. I'm hoping we can catch up at Charlie's baby shower."

"Did you leave your brain behind on the island?" Harriet asked waspishly.

Georgie, still on an engagement high, refused to let anything dent her joy. "Harry, think of the baby shower as a bridge to heal the rift between you and Charlie. Cross it and bring a gift. She'll be thrilled."

"Next you'll be suggesting I bring gold or frankincense." Harriet had hung up.

Ben tied his shoelaces. "Right, well, we've got dinner with everyone after the shower and it can't be a late night. We need to leave here at seven sharp to make it to Mildura for lunch with the sisters where we continue our ring tour." He looked up and grinned at her. He'd been doing a lot of that since she'd said, "I'd love to marry you."

"I'll visit Harriet between the shower and dinner. You're off the hook. Spend some one-on-one time with your dad and ask him if Michelle's committed to a date to meet us."

"Georgie! There you are." Xara appeared at the door. "I've been looking for you everywhere. There's balloons to be—Oh, hi Ben," she said a little more congenially, "didn't see you there."

"Hey, Xara. Can I help?"

"Can a sheep bleat? I need you up a ladder hanging the baby bunting."

"Daddy's gone a-hunting," Georgie murmured.

Ben kissed her and left the room humming.

"Zar?"

"Yes?"

"You're clutching a list, barking orders and sounding a lot like Harry."

"Oh, God, am I?" A rueful smile crossed Xara's face. "I just want Charlie to have a lovely afternoon but there's so much to do before everyone arrives. Mom and Doug have taken her out for lunch. Steve's keeping the kids occupied but I'm running out of time." She sighed. "We've always given Harry such a hard time but she's the one who knows how to throw a kick-ass party. God, I miss her."

"You could call her."

Xara shook her head. "I'm not being stubborn. You know I'm usually the one to call but this time it's not about some trivial matter. Only Harry can fix this. Only Harry can work out what's more important to her: family or pride. I'll be here if she decides to mend fences, but I can't enable her abandonment of Charlie. Or Mom, for that matter."

"Fair enough. I tried to convince her to come to the shower."

"I can imagine how that conversation went." Xara suddenly jerked off the doorjamb. "Gah! The sausage rolls need to go into the oven. I'm such a novice at this. Why did I send Mom out when she's as good as Harry with parties?"

"Show us your list then." Georgie pushed Xara out the door. "We can do this. And when Harry comes around and we show her the photos, she'll be proud that we color coordinated the decorations. Although she might not forgive us the sausage rolls ..."

"Mardi," Charlotte wailed, her hand gripping the nitrous oxide mouthpiece. "It hurts."

"I know." Edwina stroked Charlotte's sweat-drenched hair.

It was a warm November afternoon and she'd brought Charlotte to the hospital five hours earlier, direct from school. Apparently, she'd been in early labor throughout her chemistry test although she'd thought her intermittent back pain was due to the uncomfortable school chair. It was only when she'd stood up to leave and her waters had broken that she'd made the connection.

"But at least it's pain with a purpose, darling. Deep breaths on the gas."

"I can't do this," Charlotte sobbed.

"Yes, you can." Despite the intervening years, memories of Edwina's first labor rushed back—her alone in a room lying on a narrow bed. Only, it wasn't the tight band of steel contracting around her belly that dominated her recall, it was fear and devastating loss. It was an experience she wouldn't wish on any woman.

At least Charlotte's baby wouldn't be snatched out of her arms and stolen from her. Edwina didn't regret a moment of her support of Charlotte, but she wished she hadn't lost Harriet in the process. Despite having never been close, she felt their estrangement keenly. It seemed her mothering experience was fraught with losing daughters—as babies and as adults—and both ways hurt. She thought about Michelle and although she took solace in her happy childhood and the woman she'd become, it didn't temper the loss of having missed out on so much of her life.

Slowly, very slowly, Michelle was warming to her and Doug. Since their initial meeting in July, they'd Skyped every couple of weeks. She'd mentioned visiting Victoria again, but she still hadn't told her adoptive parents that she'd met her biological parents. Edwina had spent nights lying awake bothered by this and on more than one occasion woken Doug to talk to him about it.

"I feel like Michelle's put us in a secret box and we're only allowed out when she's visiting."

"She's trying to protect her parents," Doug had said sleepily.

"But they know we exist. After all, they raised *our* child."

"And they did a great job."

"I'm not denying that but it's not the point of this discussion. Michelle's not protecting them by keeping us a secret. I've lived with secrets all my life, Doug. I know the damage, hurt and pain they inflict." Her chest was tight and the familiar accompanying burn had taken hold. "Heavens, I'm a perfect example, and my family's the collateral damage."

"Deep breaths, Eddy," he'd said gently as he rolled toward her. "Come here."

She'd sunk into the warmth of his comforting embrace. "I just don't want that sort of pain for Michelle. I don't want her feeling guilty about getting to know us or lying to her parents by omission. I don't want Marieke and Hans discovering she's lied to them. No one should experience that awful gut-wrenching betrayal. And I don't want to feel any shame about wanting a relationship with Michelle. I deserve that."

Doug had been silent for a minute. "It's a sticky situation. You can't rush things."

"But the longer it goes on, the harder it's going to be for all of us. That includes the van Leeuwens. I know I can never be the mother who raised her. I'm not in competition with Marieke but I want to come out of hiding and be known as Michelle's biological mother. I want to find a way to be a part of her life that sits comfortably with all of us."

"Mardi?"

"Yes, darling?" Edwina refocused.

"Has Mom texted?"

It was the same question Charlotte had asked a dozen times since arriving at the hospital. While Carolyn, the midwife, had admitted her granddaughter, the first person Edwina called was Xara. Her middle daughter had arrived at the hospital within the hour and they were taking it in turns to sit with Charlotte. The second call she'd made was to Harriet. It had gone straight to voice mail so she'd left a message and immediately followed up with a text. She'd also rung the hospital's general reception to find out exactly where Harriet was working today. An efficient receptionist told her, "Ms. Chirnwell's in the OR all afternoon. Would you like to leave a message?"

The surgical suite was one floor below them in an adjacent building. Edwina had been tempted to walk there but the memory of the last time she'd approached Harriet at work cautioned her. She'd left a message with the receptionist asking Harriet to call maternity. Hours had passed since that conversation.

"I can go and ask the midwives if she's left a message and check my cell phone. But that means I have to go outside."

"Okay."

"Xara will be back any minute, but I'll ask Carolyn to stay with you." Edwina gave Charlotte's shoulder a squeeze, picked up her handbag, and walked toward the door. She was halfway across the room when Charlotte let out a long, low moan—the visceral sound made by all laboring mammals.

"Mardi. No." She reached out her hand. "I need to use the bathroom. Right now!"

Edwina rang the bell for the midwife. "I think perhaps that's the pressure of the baby's head."

Charlotte's eyes widened into large, blue pools, their depths a mixture of exhaustion, fear and excitement. "I—" But she didn't finish the sentence. Her words got swept away by the all-encompassing guttural moan and heave of her body pushing the baby down the birth canal.

Carolyn pushed open the door and smiled. "That sounds promising, Charlie."

Xara hurried in after her. "Did I miss anything?"

AN HOUR LATER, an exhausted but elated Charlotte sat propped up on a bank of pillows, gazing down at her baby. She'd counted ten toes and ten fingers and now the baby's fingers tightly gripped her own index finger. "He's perfect."

Edwina blinked away tears as she stroked his damp little head. "He is. He's absolutely perfect."

Charlotte gave a small laugh. "I never thought about having a boy. I mean, you had girls and Mom had me ..."

"The twins will be beside themselves having a boy cousin—"

Xara paused in thought. "Or is he a second cousin? Either way, he's going to have big boys to teach him disgusting things like digging for worms and fun things like catching freshwater crayfish."

"Mardi, would you like to hold him?"

"I'd love to." Edwina received the swaddled bundle and was just pressing a kiss to his forehead when Doug stuck his head around the door. "May I come in?"

Charlotte nodded and he walked in holding a huge vase of blue and white hydrangeas and deep blue irises, along with a blue balloon and a teddy bear.

"Congratulations, Charlie-girl. What a champ!" He dropped a kiss on her head.

"Thank you. They're beautiful flowers." Charlotte rested back against the pillows.

"Enjoy all the treats, while you can, Charlie," Xara said pragmatically. "Dirty diapers and baby sick take over soon enough."

"And this is the little fella." Doug pulled up a chair next to Edwina, sliding his hand into hers and squeezing.

Their eyes met and as impossible as it was, she knew they were both trying to share a moment that had been denied them all those years ago. "He's got the Mannering mouth," she said briskly, trying to squash her overwhelming desire to weep.

"Does he have a name yet, Charlie girl?"

Charlotte seemed to sit up higher in the bed. "I know the Mannering tradition is girls are always named after their great-grandmother and boys after their great-grandfather but because you've both been so good to me, I'm tweaking the tradition. His name is Edwin Douglas Richard Chirnwell. Teddy for short."

"Good call, Charlie." Xara hugged her.

"Oh." Edwina's tongue thickened and the backs of her ears burned hot. She blinked and blinked again but it barely stalled the inevitable. She gave up the fight, allowing her hard-fought composure to slip and her tears fall.

"Have I upset you?" Charlotte asked anxiously.

Edwina shook her head, sniffing loudly as Xara bent down and scooped up little Teddy. "No, it's just ..." But emotion tightened her throat and caged her words until she couldn't speak at all.

"Your great-grandma's christening you with her tears," Xara said to the baby.

Edwina tried to draw in a deep breath and stem the flow, but her body had other ideas. Her shoulders shook, her hands trembled, mucous clogged her nose and as she gasped for air, her sobs became a hulking, savage noise.

Doug produced an ironed hankie from his pocket and thrust it into her hands. "You okay?" he asked, his face creased in worry.

"Mom?" Xara's consternation and anxiety radiated off the word. "These are happy tears, right?"

"Mardi, I'm sorry." Charlotte's voice wavered. She sounded close to tears herself.

None of them had seen Edwina cry like this. She'd never allowed herself to cry in front of anyone. Not even Richard—especially not Richard. In the early months after Susan was stolen from her, when tears hovered close to the surface, she'd only allowed them to fall in the privacy of her room. It had been the start of her very controlled public demeanor—the behavior everyone in Billawarre thought was a combination of good breeding, finishing school and innate grace and style. It was the start of her emotional void.

She blew her nose, trying to seize control and reassure Charlotte, Xara and Doug she was alright. But whenever she tried to speak, it sparked another crying jag. She cried for the consolation and comfort that helping Charlotte was giving her and for the joy this wonderful new life—Teddy—brought her. All of it went some way toward tempering the enduring loss of baby Susan.

She mourned for all she, Doug and Michelle had missed out on over the years but at the same time she gave thanks for Harriet, Xara and Georgie. She shed old tears for Tasha and for Eliza. She wept anew for Harriet—for the pain and heartache James had inflicted on her and for the pain and heartache she was inflicting upon herself by cutting Charlotte out of her life. She mourned the now shattered dream that one day she and Harriet would share a closer relationship. It hurt so much to have sacrificed that for Teddy, but like most sacrifices they didn't come with much of a choice. She cried for all her daughters and their families, knowing no one was immune from the legacy of secrets and lies.

"Should we call the nurse?" Charlotte asked, her voice shaking.

"Do we have a paper bag?" Xara glanced around. "She's going to hyperventilate."

Doug's hand gently gripped Edwina's shoulder and his other rested under her chin. "Eddy, look at me."

His face was a blur of creases and lines, salt and pepper stubble and dark, warm eyes. Eyes that understood. A breath shuddered into her lungs and with it came a semblance of calm. She harnessed it and managed to control the next breath. Slowly, her ragged breathing eased and the flow of tears lost their noisy accompaniment. Accepting a damp face cloth from Xara, she pressed her hot face into the cloth, welcoming the cool.

"Better now?" Doug asked quietly.

She nodded. "It seems that becoming a great-grandmother is rather overwhelming," she quipped with a wobbly smile before standing to take Charlotte's hand. Her chest, which often felt like a lead weight was sitting on it, suddenly felt remarkably light. "Darling, I'm honored."

"I'm scared," Charlotte said.

"I'm sorry, I didn't mean to frighten you."

"You didn't. Not really. I mean I'm scared about being a mom." Her large eyes implored. "What if I make a mistake?"

"Darling, motherhood is all about mistakes. It's how we learn."

"But what if I hurt him or—"

"Babies are pretty tough, Charlie." Xara laughed as she passed Teddy back to her. "Once I dropped Hughie and he bounced."

Charlotte looked aghast and Edwina added, "Being a mom is all about love. There will be times when you don't like what Teddy's done and he won't like a decision you've made, but as long as he knows he's loved, it makes up for a lot of blunders."

Does it? Edwina thought about Harriet and the deep and abiding love she felt for her eldest daughter. A love that fear had held back for so long that when it had finally defeated the debilitating barrier, Harriet had found love elsewhere, bonding with her father instead. It was a love inured by the repercussions of secrets and lies and in a misguided attempt to protect her, no one had ever told Harriet the complete truth. She looked down into the large dark eyes of her great-grandson. It was too early to know whose eyes he'd inherited but he was a part of her. She owed him the opportunity to grow up knowing his grandmothers.

Charlotte bit her lip and said softly. "Do you think Mom still loves me?"

"Yes," she said firmly as Xara echoed her. "She loves you very much. She's just struggling to accept you're an adult making your own decisions." She dug her cell phone out of her bag. "I need a photo to show Harriet."

"She probably won't look at it." Charlotte hugged Teddy so tightly he gave a little cry.

"We'll never know if we don't give her the chance," Edwina said with more confidence than she felt. "Smile, Charlie." She snapped the photo.

CHAPTER THIRTY-TWO

Harriet poured herself a glass of wine and took it outside, wanting to be away from the stacks of packing boxes that dominated Miligili's surfaces. With only two weeks until she moved out, she'd intended to spend this evening packing, but she couldn't settle to it. She couldn't settle to anything.

She disliked being distracted and it took a lot to derail her concentration. When she was operating, being preoccupied by anything other than the surgical field in front of her wasn't a good thing and years of training enabled her to tune out distractions. This afternoon had put all her skills to the test. The early evening continued to challenge her.

It had all started when she'd checked her cell phone in between cases at 3:00 p.m. She'd only done it because she was chasing outstanding pathology results for an anxious patient and his family. Instead of hearing the recorded and apologetic voice of the pathologist, she'd heard Edwina's rounded vowels telling her that Charlotte was in labor. Concentrating on anything else since had been an uphill battle.

She'd immediately rung the labor ward to inquire about

Charlotte and been told things were progressing nicely. Harriet had thanked the midwife and rung off without leaving a message. After all, what did one say to a daughter after a seven-month silence?

I hope you finished your exam before the contractions started?

You should be getting ready for summer vacation not motherhood?

Your life's about to change forever?

Despite Harriet's fervent belief eighteen years ago that motherhood wouldn't change her life, Charlotte's arrival had upended it. She'd spent years torn between work and Charlotte's needs, not that she'd ever admitted that to anyone. Female surgeons who wanted to rise through the ranks didn't have that luxury. Men didn't drop everything for a sick child—their wives were at home to deal with the inconvenience.

In London she'd had a nanny and, on the weekends, James. In Billawarre, she'd had Edwina, Xara and James. It hurt to remember the man who'd once been so besotted with his young daughter was the same man who'd wanted to use her to help him repair his shattered reputation.

And now that little girl was having a baby.

The familiar nausea that came whenever she thought about the baby rolled through her. How could Edwina and Xara expect her to embrace it when its existence would make Charlotte's life so hard? She picked up her cell phone for the tenth time in half an hour and checked the time. 19:17. Was Charlotte still in labor? It was very possible. First babies rarely rushed. She'd expected Edwina to have called by now and left an updated message, but her cell remained silent.

It suddenly buzzed in her hand, making her jump.

On-call tonight. Need to avoid froufrou fever. Going to new Lebanese joint with ortho crew. Join us? Andrew.

She stared at the words, surprised and discombobulated. She hadn't received an invitation—social or otherwise—in six months. Before James's actions had knocked her off Billawarre's social pedestal, she'd been someone people sought. She'd had the connections people valued and needed. Invitations had poured in not just from Billawarre and environs but from Geelong and Melbourne too.

She'd been frequently invited as a guest speaker at dinner functions, at opening events, and at fundraisers. Often, she was invited because her name on an attendees' list encouraged others to accept. Part of Nicki's job had been to manage her social calendar so she wasn't double booked. How things had changed. She had few friends in Billawarre now and that was a driving force behind her decision to live in Sydney.

Did you have friends before?

She wanted to say yes, but if this year had taught her anything, it was she'd had acquaintances not friends—people who were either useful to her or vice versa. There was nothing like a scandal to expose expediency over true feeling. Although Jenny had stayed in touch, it had been Xara and Georgie who'd stayed true. Thinking of Xara made her reach for her glass of merlot. Anything to do with her family made her reach for wine. Hoping to divert her thoughts, she re-read Andrew's text.

Apart from the auction, she only saw him at the hospital. And "saw" made it sound like they had a lot more contact than they did. Although he'd increased his hours and was at the hospital more than when he'd started, any time they spent together was minimal. It consisted of brief conversations at the scrub sinks or a quick sandwich and a coffee in the lounge if they happened to be taking a break at the same time.

But when they did chat, his easy company and non-judgmental manner took the edge off her isolation. The other day she'd caught herself glancing at the board to see if he was operating and she'd found herself smiling when she'd overheard his country drawl explaining a procedure to a patient. The sad truth was that the sum total of these brief moments made Andrew the closest thing she had to a friend.

Dear God! She drained her glass and wished she'd brought the bottle outside. Once, if someone had disclosed something like that to her, she'd have considered them to be totally pathetic. She considered the dinner invitation.

It's not a dinner invitation. He's invited you to join a group from the hospital.

Her delight at the surprise text waned as doubt infiltrated. Did she want to spend the evening with a group of orthopedic staff listening to their in-jokes?

She should be so lucky. Based on the headline splashed across the front of yesterday's paper, the likely scenario was a café filled with hostile faces and difficult questions. Every time she thought James's fraud story had faded and she dared to believe she was getting some respite from the ordeal—at least until the court case—the local newspaper found something new to print. It was as if the journalist had a monthly reminder on his cell phone: *Find new dirt on James Minchin.*

Yesterday's headline was Ex-Mayor's Cayman Caper. The article was accompanied by a photo of James and Harriet taken on Seven Mile Beach during their vacation there two years ago. Although she was wearing a hat and dark sunglasses, anyone with a memory that lasted longer than a year would know it was her. The paper had previously used the photo in an advertising feature about travel.

She'd immediately called Angela. "I want that bastard paper sued for defamation."

Her attorney had sighed. "There's no case, Harriet. They haven't defamed you in any way. They haven't even mentioned your name."

But the law didn't live in a small town. The article had brought back the hushed conversations and the pointed stares. Did she really want to go out for dinner tonight and face all that?

I want to know if Charlotte's had the baby.

She didn't want to see the baby, but she needed to know Charlotte was safe and well. She texted an apology to Andrew and was about to call maternity for an update when she heard the distant buzz of the doorbell. It was faster to walk around the veranda than to go through the house.

As she made her way along the beautifully ornate tessellated tiles, she breathed in air redolent with the heady perfume of her Mr. Lincoln roses. It was a familiar late-spring scent and a tug of regret caught her. She'd miss her roses. She'd miss Miligili. She'd miss—

Stop it. There's no family to miss. Dad's dead and everyone else has let you down. Sydney has roses and Rose Bay. It has a harbor to die for and a job that will challenge you. More importantly, there are over four million people living there who don't know you.

"Hello, Harriet."

Her mother's voice cut into her thoughts and she realized with a start it was Edwina standing by the front door. Her usually smooth bob was in disarray, with strands of hair pointing in all directions. Her face was devoid of makeup although there were traces of smudged mascara around her eyes, which were puffy and red. Her linen pants, always pressed with knife pleats, looked like they'd never known the touch of an iron, and her silk blouse had some sort of stain on the shoulder.

A knot of fear clenched her stomach. "Is Charlotte—"

"She's fine," Edwina said quickly. "Very well, in fact."

Harriet's heart slowed to its normal speed and the knotty and prickly distance that was a permanent part of her relationship with her mother re-established itself. "You look like hell."

"I do." Edwina laughed easily. "I could have gone home and freshened up, but I wanted to come straight here to see you. It's been a rather momentous day."

Her wide smile lit up her eyes like sparklers on a birthday cake. It wasn't a smile Harriet associated with her mother. When Edwina smiled it was always done politely and with an air of refined restraint. There was nothing muted about this smile—it was open and full of joy. Harriet's chest cramped as hard as it had the time she'd been winded by a polo mallet. Edwina was happy.

So? It's not like you've never seen her happy before. Except she wasn't certain she'd ever seen her this happy. A slow pain radiated from her gut, although she couldn't tell if it was pain for Edwina or pain for herself. She tried to shrug it away as an irrelevancy.

"So she's had the baby?"

"Yes. The official time was 6:08."

The steel trap around Harriet's heart snapped its jagged teeth shut and she saw spots. She clenched her hands, willing anesthetizing cold to rush in and deaden all her contrary feelings about this baby—a child who'd changed everything for her and for Charlotte. She told herself she didn't need to know any more about the baby other that it was alive and healthy, but she found herself asking, "Boy or girl?"

"A beautiful boy. Edwin. Teddy for short."

She leaned against the veranda post for support. "Named after you and Great-Great-Grandfather?"

"Yes." Edwina hesitated before adding, "And your father's name is in there as well."

Edwin Richard. "So she does have some sense of family tradition after all." She blinked against suddenly itchy eyes.

"It seems so." Edwina reached into her handbag. "Would you like to see a photo?"

Yes. Only a photo would give too much reality to something she only ever wanted to think about in the abstract. "No."

Given the last conversation she'd shared with her mother, she fully expected Edwina to try again and insist she look at the photo of her grand—the baby.

Edwina slipped the cell phone back into her bag and glanced over at the stile. "The wildflowers are beautiful at this time of year."

"The damp spring helped," Harriet said automatically, her mind stuck on Edwina's wordless acquiescence.

"Come for a walk with me on the Stony Rises."

A walk? By default, a walk implied talking and as Edwina had told her the baby was a boy named Edwin, what else was left to say? Not much. Too much had been said at Easter and then at the hospital. Her relationship with Edwina was now so badly fractured that the only course of action was amputation. Going to Sydney would be the final severing.

She'd grown up sharing a private understanding with her father about Edwina. When her mother experienced what he'd always referred to as "an episode" or the "can't copes" he'd give Harriet a conspiratorial smile and say, "We know what your mother's like."

And she'd smile back knowing exactly what he meant and experience that special bond with him. From the age of twelve, she'd felt a mixture of affection and frustration for Edwina's vagueness and melancholy and after her father died, she'd taken over the mantle of responsibility. Everything changed when she'd discovered the reason for her mother's periods of detachment. Michelle.

Now, the mess of feelings for Edwina had coalesced into a seething mass of betrayal—not just for herself but for her sisters and her father. Hadn't any of them been worthy of Edwina's love?

Every time she thought about her mother, Michelle and *that man*, she wanted to punch something and cry. She hated allowing her emotions to rule her so she did what she'd always done—blocked errant thoughts about her mother's other family. She did the same with Charlotte and the pregnancy.

It's Edwin Richard now. A hot and cold chill raced across her skin. She shivered and pulled her light jacket tighter around her.

"Come for a walk," Edwina repeated. "I'd like to say goodbye to Miligili."

"You can do that without me."

"Actually, I can't. Or at least, I don't want to. Xara says you're moving to Sydney and there's some things I want to say before you go."

"I doubt I'll want to hear them."

"It won't be easy for me to say them."

Harriet narrowed her eyes, not prepared to have the same argument she'd already had with Edwina and Xara time and time again. "You can talk until you're blue in the face but I'm not changing my mind about Charlotte and the baby. You wanted her to keep it so they're your responsibility now."

"It's not about Charlie and the baby. It's about me. By default, it's also about you, me and your father."

"I'm not tramping across the Stony Rises with you, Edwina. And I'm not playing games either. Whatever you have to say, you can say it here."

"You're right. I could say it here but I think it's better for both of us if we walk and talk."

"Why?"

"Because ..." She jerked her head toward the Stony Rises. "Both of us are calmer when we're out there."

Her mother's unexpected perspicacity gave her pause. Harriet ran out there to think, to regroup and to try and find a sense of peace that had evaded her for most of the year. Edwina always had her hands in the soil of her garden and she walked in the bush twice a week.

"Mannering love of the land?"

"Precisely." Edwina walked toward the stile. "Coming?"

Harriet watched her climb the three steps, knowing Edwina would take the walk whether she accompanied her or not. In some ways her mother was oddly determined and in other ways totally flaky. But at sixty-five, Edwina had become a force to be reckoned with. Harriet also knew that Edwina had baited her with the mention of her father.

She called out, "Is this going to be some sort of an apology to Dad and me?"

Her mother looked thoughtful. "I suppose it is. In a way."

"In that case ..." As far as she was concerned, Edwina owed her father a long overdue apology. As he wasn't here to accept it, she'd listen on his behalf. Clambering over the stile, she joined her mother on the other side of the barbed wire fence.

Edwina's face changed from anxiety to relief and with a quick nod Harriet accepted as thanks, she struck out sure-footedly across the familiar pasture of her childhood. Harriet kept pace. She'd grown up hearing how when Edwina was a young child her uncle had owned the smaller farm of Miligili. Back then the expansive Murrumbeet property had abutted one of Miligili's boundaries and the cousins had considered the combined lands their private playground. They'd ranged far and wide, camping, picnicking and generally exploring.

"So, Sydney?" Edwina finally broke the silence, her words caught by the breeze.

Harriet tensed. "I didn't come to talk about Sydney."

"No." Edwina skirted a large slab of granite. "I'll just launch into it then, shall I?"

"That's why we're here."

"Right," Edwina said as if she was about to start a Country Women's Association meeting. "I know you feel the loss of your father keenly. And we both know you think I'm a poor second. In some respects, I understand that. I can't offer you the same professional mentoring Richard did, but Harriet, you're my daughter and I love you. I think there've been times in your life when you've doubted that. Especially recently, with everything that's happened. But I've always loved you and I'll continue to love you and your sisters. Nothing changes that. Not even our disapproval of each other's choices."

Edwina paused as if she was giving Harriet space to speak but Harriet wasn't prepared to say anything until she'd worked out where her mother was going with all of this.

"And I did love your father. Granted, at the start I didn't have the same depth of feeling for him that I'd felt for Doug, but when I married him, I committed to doing my best by him."

"You learned to love him? Lucky Dad. God, Edwina, it sounds like you're talking about an arranged marriage."

"That's exactly what it was."

The quietness of her mother's voice chilled her—the words at odds with what Harriet had always believed about her parents' marriage. "Growing up, whenever we asked either you or Dad, we were always told the story of how your eyes met over the champagne fountain at the Young Conservative's ball. How Dad danced with you all night before whisking you off in his yellow Triumph Spitfire." Icy cold anger burned her. "Was it a lie?"

Edwina's gaze met her with sincerity in their depths. "No. All of that's true. It's how we met, but unbeknownst to me, your grandfather had already met Richard and paid for his ticket to the ball specifically to meet me. I quickly became the solution to two problems." The corners of her mouth turned down. "When I returned to Murrumbeet after Michelle, your grandfather wanted to marry me off quick smart before I risked the family name a second time. Richard needed my name and connections to establish his practice. In your father's defense, he didn't pressure me at all. He was actually quite chivalrous and romantic at the start. The pressure to marry came from your grandfather. What Fraser Mannering wanted, he invariably got."

Harriet's disbelieving laugh came back to her on the wind. "For God's sake, Edwina. It was 1969 not 1869. I can't believe you were forced to marry Dad."

"Exactly," her mother said simply, "it was 1969. The social mores in the country hadn't travelled so very far from those of the turn of the century. In the Mannerings' circles, women were still defined by their virginity and their social standing. Although no one knew about the baby, your grandfather considered me tainted goods and a liability. The sooner he could offload me onto a husband and reduce the risk of his political reputation being sullied, the better."

Edwina's voice suddenly took on an acrimonious edge. "The fact he'd had affairs for years and his bullying was likely the reason my mother took refuge in a gin bottle was the double standard he chose to overlook."

Surprise made Harriet blink. "Grandma drank?" Her memories of her grandmother were rather beige in comparison to her larger-than-life grandfather.

"Like a fish," Edwina said pragmatically. "And while we're talking family foibles and secrets, I think it's time you knew that the Mannerings were not the paragons of virtue they've molded history to reflect. Your great uncle gambled far too much on the horses. Your great-great-grandfather had a thing for showgirls, and my great-great-grandmother's sister ran off with an impoverished artist. Of course the family disowned her and she ended up contracting TB and dying destitute. That story was trotted out and told to all Mannering women for generations to keep us in line. Oh, and your great-uncle on my mother's side spent far too much time in the stables with the horses."

"I didn't need to hear that. God, I want to bleach my brain."

"Those stories are the ones I know. I'm sure you'd find a veritable treasure trove of scandal if you went digging."

Harriet didn't want to. She pushed away the hint at bestiality and replaced it with images of the old sepia and black and white photos she'd recently wrapped lovingly in bubble wrap and placed in packing boxes. There were photos of rich men in white tie with their starched shirts and waxed moustaches—serious and stern upstanding members of the community. Pictures of young women in white muslin dresses, older matriarchs dressed in neck-to-toe widow's weeds as well as debutante, ball and wedding photographs. They projected the image of a life of privilege lived with appropriate entitlement.

Her grandfather used to sit her on his knee and tell her stories about the photos. Tell her how special it was to be a Mannering and how the family had played their part in not only shaping the district but in shaping the state of Victoria. She was struggling to align all those generational stories of great things and personal sacrifice with what her mother was telling her.

"How do you know Grandpa had affairs?"

Edwina tucked her hair behind her ears to keep it from blowing into her eyes. "All of us who keep secrets eventually let something slip."

She thought about James. "But the rest of us have to have suspicions to interpret those slips."

"Not always, but in this instance you're right. I was probably on the lookout for something because of the way he treated my mother. Unlike his constituents, I didn't hold your grandfather in quite so high regard."

The words barreled into Harriet. With a jolt, she realized that all her life she'd never heard her mother say "Dad" in reference to her own father. It was always *your grandfather* or *my father*.

Edwina continued, "He was a conniving, scheming bastard who used people. All in all, over the generations, the Mannerings have hidden a great deal of dirty little secrets behind their pillars of respectability and the façade of a spotless life."

"They've done a bloody good job," Harriet said, slightly rattled. "None of those stories have turned up in the official family history."

"No." Edwina bit her lip. "And I was co-opted into the secret keeping. In hindsight, I should have resisted."

"When Dad proposed, he didn't know you'd had a baby, did he?"

"No."

Despite the unsettling information about her ancestors she knew her father and was confident in her assumptions about him. "I thought so. He wouldn't have married you if he'd known."

"Richard would have been torn between the social standing I offered him and the stigma of being with a woman who'd had a child out of wedlock."

The practical words grazed her. "That's unfair."

"Actually, I think it's very fair," Edwina said calmly. "Richard's family didn't have the same level of wealth or respectability as we did and he craved it. He loved the social prestige I gave him and coupled with an esteemed career as a surgeon, he thrived more successfully than he would have without me. Why do you think he threw so many parties?"

"For you," Harriet said hotly, trying to block out Xara's thoughts on their father's parties. "To keep you happy."

Edwina sighed. "The last thing to make or keep me happy is a party. But parties and socializing were exactly what made Richard happy. They make you happy too. Xara and I not so much and Georgie—" She looked thoughtful. "To be honest, I'm not really sure where Georgie sits on the socializing fence. There's a lot I don't know about Georgie. From now on, I intend to do a much better job at finding out."

Harriet wasn't interested in her mother's plans for Georgie. She was here for her father. Her resentment spilled over. "Dad was just trying to find ways to help you out of your blue funks. He might have been able to help you more, even been a little more understanding if he'd known the reason for them."

"He knew."

Harriet's heart lurched at the quiet but penetrating words. "What do you mean he knew? You just told me he didn't know about Michelle."

"He found out when you were six."

The years rolled back. She clearly remembered sharing the private eye rolling and amused despair about Edwina with her father. All of it had said how could Edwina, the wife of a loving man, mother of three girls, living in a beautiful home with plenty of outside help with the house and garden, keep having episodes of the "can't copes"?

Buck up, Edwina. Worse things have happened.

She suddenly felt a bit sick. No! There had to be another reason for his behavior. Her father was a caring man. Only, over the years Harriet had seen and heard many examples of his cavalier approach —accepted it even, because at the time she'd thought there was no good reason for Edwina to be sad. But Edwina was telling her he knew there was a reason. He'd known since she was six.

"You eventually told him?"

Edwina shook her head. "No. I didn't tell him. I've often wondered if things may have been different if I had."

Harriet wasn't interested in musings. She wanted the facts. Needed the facts. "How did he find out?"

"I promise I'll get to that but first I need to tell you about the early years of our marriage. We both worked hard to establish his practice. Obviously, he was talented and good at his job and I introduced him to the—" her fingers formed quotation marks "—"right" people. I kept busy with my volunteering, but I craved a baby and Richard was keen to start a family too.

"For whatever reason, it took me well over a year to fall pregnant with you. I'd almost given up when old Doctor Leonard gave me the good news. I was over the moon and so was your father. The six months before you were born were some of the happiest times we ever shared. We were so excited about starting our family. Neither of us expected me to get severe post-natal depression.

"*Nothing* prepares you for that. All I'd wanted was to be your mother, hold you close and love you. Instead, my body was invaded by a suffocating, choking darkness. I was numb to what was going on around me but at the same time I felt pain and sadness down to my soul." Her voice quavered. "It made me feel worthless. Defective. An utter failure."

Edwina cleared her throat and when she spoke again her voice was firmer. "I spent time in a clinic and when I'd recovered enough and was able to be a mother to you, you were almost one."

Disbelief stopped Harriet's feet and she stared at her mother. "You spent almost a year in a clinic?"

"No. I was there for a few weeks and then your father insisted I come home. He was worried what people would think. He employed a nurse as well as the indomitable Mrs. Abercrombie. She always managed to make me feel even more useless than I already believed I was. But she adored you and your world revolved around her and your father. I was a stranger." Edwina gave a strained laugh. "Of course, like every mother, I blamed myself. I was being punished for giving up Michelle."

"If you'd kept Michelle, then Xara and Georgie and I wouldn't exist," Harriet said tightly, still trying to absorb the news that Edwina had virtually missed her first year.

As a doctor, she knew the theory about bonding and the development of trust that occurred in the first year of life. As a mother, she'd watched it evolve between Charlotte and herself: Charlotte's bright-eyed gaze fixed on her face while she breastfed; the wide smile and gurgly laugh that lit up her baby's face when Harriet walked into the room and Charlotte recognized her. Every time it happened, Harriet had gotten a high from the rush of love that consumed her. Edwina had missed out on all of that.

I missed out too.

A spurt of anger made her stride out. "I clearly remember your postnatal depression after Georgie. Why didn't you ever tell us it had happened before with Xara and me?"

"Shame. Guilt. All the usual suspects." Edwina shoved her hands in the pockets of her jacket as the late spring chill nipped at exposed skin. The sun was now low in the sky, threading its wide fingers of orange and crimson through the clouds in a vivid display of hectic color. "My depression embarrassed your father. He refused to discuss it and he didn't want people talking about it or us." Her mouth tightened. "After all, just like the Mannerings before us, we were an exemplary family with the world at our feet. No chinks in perfection allowed."

The words buffeted Harriet, their bitterness stinging. She wished she could ask her father about all of this. He'd cared for thousands of people as a doctor, and as a father, he'd loved and cared for her. Had he really put public perception ahead of his wife? No. He wouldn't do that.

James's voice, which had thankfully become fainter in recent weeks, suddenly roared back like dragon fire. *With you, everything has to be so fucking perfect.*

She remembered yelling back at him that it wasn't true. And it wasn't; she'd believed it then and she believed it still. Hadn't her father always told her that life was all about hard work? What was it he'd said to her at her graduation? *Remember who you are and where you come from. Keep your guard up and know that success is the result of perfection.*

She felt herself frown. For years she'd remembered that speech quite differently. She'd have staked her life he'd said success was the result of hard work. She pictured him as she always chose to remember him: sitting by the fire in Glenora's library with a book in one hand and a glass of top-shelf whiskey in the other. She always felt close to him in that room with its scent of leather and his favorite paintings. He loved the Arthur Streeton oil of Mt. Elephant that hung behind his desk not only because it was a quintessential piece of Australian art but also because he'd managed to outbid Geoffrey Gunderson, who'd also coveted it.

She saw him raise his glass to her. *Surround yourself with perfection, Harry and everything else follows.*

She choked on a breath.

"Are you alright?"

"Breathed in an insect." She coughed and cleared her throat to add gravitas to the fib.

Edwina passed her water bottle. "The reason there's almost five years between you and Xara is because after postnatal depression with you, I was too scared to have another baby. I was terrified of tumbling into that black morass of despair again.

"Initially, your father felt the same way, but you were such an engaging child that by the time you were three, Richard was keen to try again. I had a lot more confidence in being your mother and I thought I could cope. I saw my doctor and told him my concerns about getting sick again. He brushed them aside, saying the depression was a one-off thing probably caused by fear of the unknown. Now that I knew all about being a mother I'd have to be really unlucky for it to happen twice." Edwina gave another short, sharp laugh. "I proved him wrong."

For the first time in her life, Harriet caught a hint of the anguish Edwina had endured. "I have a vague memory of wearing my red coat and visiting you somewhere after Xara was born."

"You loved that coat. Richard bought it for you in Melbourne from the Georges children's department." Edwina smiled. "Your father always had exceptional taste in clothes."

"He did." She'd loved the way her father had carried himself, the smart way he dressed and the way he and Edwina had always turned heads when they walked into a room. When he'd died, Harriet had asked Edwina for one of his cashmere sweaters. It was one of only a few possessions she was taking to Sydney. Apartments, she was discovering, did not come with a surfeit of storage.

"Unlike the old-school psychiatrist I saw after you were born, the young doctor who treated me with Xara had studied in America. He asked me if I'd ever suffered any trauma in my childhood or my adult life. I almost told him about Susan—I mean Michelle—being stolen from me."

"Why didn't you?"

"It was 1976."

A raft of irritation zipped through Harriet. "So? I need more information than that."

"It means I was a woman with less rights than a man. Added to that, I was married to a doctor. All Richard had to do was ask to read my file and no one would say no to him. He probably didn't even need to ask." She gave herself a shake as if pushing herself back on track. "Anyway, the psychiatrist's question about trauma stayed with me and I promised myself that when I was well, I'd try to get information about my lost daughter. I knew it would be a hard task because back then they changed the birth certificate. But I thought if I could find out if she was alive, healthy and happy, perhaps that would free me of the debilitating depression."

Harriet surprised herself by saying, "That sounds reasonable."

"Thank you. When things were good again, I hired a private investigator. Your father, who in nine years of marriage had never been home before eight on a Thursday night, walked through the door just as the phone rang. He answered the call. Richard could be very persuasive when he wanted to be. To this day I have no idea why the investigator risked his reputation by telling him what I'd hired him to do. Your father was paralytic with rage." She blew out a breath. "I'm surprised you don't remember that fight. All the yelling. It scared me and I was a lot older than six."

Harriet had very little recollection of her parents ever arguing or raising their voices at each other. When Edwina was well, her father would say what he wanted and Edwina would make it happen. When she was sick, he'd just ask Mrs. Abercrombie. As a teen, there'd been a few occasions when she'd been aware of some passive-aggression from Edwina but those episodes hadn't happened often. In fact, she'd always thought quiet harmony was a feature of her parents' marriage. It had certainly contrasted with Auntie Primrose and Uncle David's volcanic one. They didn't care who was in the house when they argued—insults were hurled, doors slammed and feet pounded. Later, there was always the sound of laughter and sex.

Back then, Harriet had assumed that despite Edwina's ups and downs, it was her father's gracious consideration of her mother's illness that made the marriage work. That the reason her parents never argued was because they'd found a way to be happy. Now she was starting to wonder if she had even the remotest understanding of her parents' relationship.

Edwina reached the dry stone wall built on the boundary of Miligili, stopped and gazed out across the Rises. "I told Richard all I needed was information that the child was safe and happy. That if I knew she was safe it might help me with the episodes of depression. Help me cope. Surely that would have been better for us as a family."

"And?" Harriet had a horrible sense she already knew the answer.

"He wouldn't have a bar of it. He was terrified the story would come out and he'd be made to look a fool. Given the investigator told Richard what he was doing instead of protecting my privacy, I had little to combat his argument." She wrapped her arms around her middle as though she was in pain. "Richard told me that if I insisted on continuing the search, he'd have me declared an unfit mother, divorce me and keep you and Xara."

"No," Harriet heard herself say vehemently. "Dad wasn't cruel. He'd only have said it out of shock. And let's face it, finding out that your wife of nine years had a secret love child stashed somewhere would test anyone."

"Harriet," Edwina said wearily, "I'm not placing blame. I'm just telling you what happened." She turned, walking back to the house.

"At least Dad stuck around." Harriet was determined to safeguard her father in his absence. "Another man would have left."

"Am I supposed to be grateful for that?" An unusual flare of anger heated her face. "Michelle was born before I met your father. Did he tell me everything about his life before he met me? Of course he didn't. I accept I'd kept a secret from him but we weren't newlyweds, we'd been married for almost a decade.

"We'd made a life together. I was his wife. I'd loved him, been faithful to him, and I wasn't asking him to accept and raise someone else's child. All I was doing was trying to get well and stay well. I thought as my husband he'd have wished that for me too. For himself. For you and Xara. It was the only thing of great importance to me that I ever asked him and he declined."

Harriet knew what it was like to be betrayed by a spouse and exactly how James's betrayal had affected her. She raged to defend her father but as she tried to rustle up her indignation at Edwina for asking too much of him, she struggled. Everyone had a past and she doubted her father had been a virgin before he'd married. She supposed there was a chance he'd sired a child he'd never known about. Or had known about. She immediately silenced the disturbing thought.

"I'm sorry Dad let you down back then, but he must have made it up to you in other ways over the years. I mean, the two of you were married for forty-three years."

Edwina gave a derisive snort. "Richard didn't leave me, but it wasn't because he forgave me. The man was a conundrum. He mostly stayed for selfish reasons, but I'd be unjust if I didn't mention his love for you and your sisters. Love and duty tangled up with position and power pretty much summed up our marriage.

"By then your father had a thriving practice and a reputation he loved. Despite the recent introduction of no-fault divorce, there was still a stigma attached to it, especially in Billawarre. He'd have lost far too much by divorcing me and he'd worked too hard to get everything he'd wanted. He had social standing, he had money and he had the town's respect. And he loved you and Xara and the idea of family, even if he didn't love me enough. All in all, it was easier for him to stay. And he did, but from that moment, he lived by his own rules."

"What does that mean?" Harriet asked savagely, immediately regretting the question.

She shouldn't be furthering this unwanted destruction of her father—she should be putting a stop to it right now. Miligili homestead was in view. If she started running, she could be inside with the door bolted before Edwina and the words she didn't want to hear reached the veranda. It was a good plan, only her legs refused to pick up speed. It was like being trapped in a careening car with no brakes and no way to escape until it crashed and burned.

"Oh, Harry," Edwina sighed as they clambered over the stile. "I know this is hard. You and Richard had a special bond. It was forged during your first year when I was sick. I experienced a lot of guilt about not being able to mother you during those early months and it built upon itself after each of your sisters was born and I lost more time with you over again.

"I let you see your father through rose-colored glasses. In your eyes he could do no wrong and I never offered you any evidence that contradicted some of your opinions of him or of me." Her mouth wrinkled in a resigned line. "I'm certain Richard offered you plenty of opinions about me and my fragile mental health."

Your mother's a worry. God, I don't know how she'd survive without me.

Your mother's lucky she married me. Another man wouldn't be quite so understanding.

Harriet's hands rose quickly to cover her ears and drown out the words. She wanted to refute that Richard had ever said such things but as she desperately tried to prop up the image of the man she loved so much, she knew she couldn't. Not now. Not since she'd been told her father had known for years about the baby her mother had lost. Not lost. The baby had been stolen from her.

As if sensing Harriet's divided loyalties, Edwina gave her arm a gentle squeeze. "Your father was a talented surgeon, a good doctor, and a loving and doting father. You were lucky to have him."

"I've always known that." But the words rang slightly hollow.

Edwina dropped her hand. "But like the rest of us, he had feet of clay."

"I never saw it." Harriet had the ridiculous sense she'd just lost her father all over again. James had hidden so much from her and now it seemed Richard had too. Did she put the men she loved on pedestals and become blind to their faults?

"Richard and I are both to blame for that," Edwina said sadly. "We kept secrets too. Everything changed the night he found out about Michelle. The perceived partnership I thought we shared became weighted very much in Richard's direction. He held the power. With my history of depression and time in the clinic, I knew if he did file for a divorce, he'd have had no trouble convincing a court I wasn't fit to have custody. While holding that over my head, he punished me for never telling him about Michelle by entering into a series of affairs in Melbourne. He spent the last twenty years with the same woman. An oncologist at the Royal Melbourne Hospital."

Harriet's stomach contents roiled and surged as she suddenly connected this traitorous piece of news with her father's routine. "So his week in Melbourne every month for lecturing and training was a lie?"

"No, of course not. You've got his academic gown. It's just while he was up in Melbourne for that week, he also had a mistress."

Edwina's tone had become practical and matter of fact—conversational even. "Do you remember Patrice Nicols? She came to the funeral and you spent a long time talking with her."

Harriet remembered the conversation because of the strong connection she'd experienced with the woman who'd been open about her admiration for her father. "Oh my God! I thought she was a colleague!" The anguish in her voice carried across the pasture. "She's only five years older than me. She stood with me eating cucumber sandwiches and drinking cups of Darjeeling. She told me how much she respected him. How much he'd be missed."

"You can't fault her for lying. She loved him."

"The accident? Was he with her when—?"

"I'm sorry."

Harriet's legs trembled and her head spun. "I'm going to throw up." She stumbled into the house and into the powder room. Collapsing onto the floor, she hugged the toilet bowl and vomited what was left of her lunch, the wine she'd drunk before Edwina had arrived and the final vestiges of her father—the man she thought she'd known.

CHAPTER THIRTY-THREE

HARRIET WALKED INTO THE KITCHEN TEN MINUTES LATER. She'd washed her face with cold water, gargled with mouthwash and changed into her pajamas. She had an overwhelming need to feel cozy and secure even though she knew it was all just an illusion. "I've got questions."

"Ask while you eat." Edwina was welding a spatula over the sandwich press. She handed Harriet a glass of wine and a plate filled with toasted triangles of Vegemite and cheese. The comfort food of her childhood.

"Did he and Patrice—?" Harriet gulped wine, unable to finish the sentence.

"You have a half-brother. He's in Seventh grade at Scotch College."

"Of course I do." She slapped her forehead with her palm, the news not totally unexpected given her father and Patrice had shared a twenty-year relationship. "But he wasn't at the funeral, was he? I'd have remembered a thirteen-year-old boy."

Edwina served herself a sandwich and switched off the press. "A private viewing was arranged. Patrice preferred it that way."

"She preferred it!" Harriet's shout bounced off the walls. "How could you allow that?"

"Richard was Oscar's father too," Edwina said simply.

The nausea Harriet had experienced when she'd found out about Patrice surged again. She was furious with her father for being in a long-term relationship while still living with her mother, but she was equally aghast that her mother had put up with it for so long.

"How can you be so calm about it? How could you and Dad live your lives together like everything was normal?"

Edwina bit into her own sandwich, her tongue chasing an errant string of cheese. "Normal is a relative term, darling. Richard separated his life into compartments. I belonged to his life in Billawarre with you and your sisters. He had a second life in Melbourne."

Harriet was struggling to keep everything straight. "God, Edwina. Why did you put up with it?"

Edwina flinched at the criticism. "It was a different time, Harry, and as I explained before, I had very little choice. I either accepted life with your father on his terms and found a way to make it work, or I lost everything. I'd already lost one child. I wasn't going to lose you and Xara."

Harriet saw the determined set of her mother's jaw and for the first time glimpsed true strength of character. With aching realization, she saw exactly what Edwina had sacrificed for her and her sisters: an embattled self-esteem and self-respect laid over a lifelong grief for a stolen baby. It would have taken remarkable strength of character to make a disastrous situation like that work. To live in a marriage where your husband lived two lives. Edwina's secret had festered inside the family all of their lives. Only it wasn't just Edwina's secret. Her father had contributed his fair share as well.

"But ..." Harriet faltered, not quite able to ask the question.

Edwina delicately wiped her mouth with a paper serviette and took a sip of wine. "Ask me. I'm an open book. I've lived with the damaging effects of secrets all of my life. I don't want any to exist between you and me or between me and your sisters."

"Georgie?" Harriet said. "How ...? Why?"

Edwina's head tilted slightly and her eyes rolled. In that moment, Harriet recognized herself.

"Yes, of course I know how but ..."

"How could I have sex with Richard?" Edwina said matter-of-factly. "I know it's hard to comprehend but for three weeks out of four, our life was much the same as every other marriage. I refused to spend any time thinking about week four. Besides, I was an expert at not thinking about a lot of things ..." She drank more wine. "Given everything, having another child wasn't something either of us wanted but we're human. Contraception fails. Mistakes happen. Do you remember that vacation we took to Fiji?"

Harriet remembered it well. There'd been snorkeling, swimming and her father's undivided attention—a rare and treasured thing. A framed photo of her parents taken on that trip was still on display at Glenora. Her father looked handsome, tanned and relaxed and her mother looked elegant and genuinely happy.

"We were a long way from Billawarre and our real life," Edwina continued. "Perhaps I imagined that he'd changed or perhaps I was seduced by Fiji." She waved her hand as if both scenarios were preposterous. "The news of the pregnancy two months later brought reality crashing back down onto both of us. Even though we knew what was coming, I never considered a termination and your father never asked me for one. Richard did all the right things and he made sure I had the help I needed. He was there for you and Xara while I battled the demons. He was always there for you."

The complex nature of her parents' relationship baffled Harriet. How could her father be both callous and caring at the same time? How could Edwina have stood it? "What about the other women?"

"To his credit, your father never mentioned them to me and I never asked. In the years before Patrice, I'd occasionally get a phone call from a woman. I always told Richard. They never called again and I imagine he ended things with them quick smart—he didn't want a whiff of scandal making it back here. When he was in Billawarre, his focus was on his family. When he was in Melbourne, his focus was there. On the journeys in between he visited you and your sisters at school. He loved you. None of this changes that."

Harriet had treasured those visits but knowing what she knew now tainted them. "God, Mom! You're defending him?"

"I'm not. He wasn't an ideal husband, but he was a decent and loving father. I don't want you to confuse the two."

Harriet dropped her head into her hands as a throb pounded in her temples. "But what about all the fuss he went to on your birthdays? Those parties were legendary in the district and he always proposed a toast to you. How could you stand the hypocrisy?"

Edwina's chin rose in a classic supercilious Mannering gesture. "I made a choice. You have to remember; I grew up with a philandering father. I knew how the game worked and to be fair, your father was a much nicer person than your grandfather. He was generous with his money and we lived in a beautiful home and I had carte blanche with the garden. I got on with my life and we fell into a pattern. Your father was either a conundrum or a man of his time."

"Are you excusing him?" Harriet asked, horrified.

"No." The emphatic word rang off the walls. "I don't think I ever forgave him for his reaction to my need to find some information about Michelle."

"Then why didn't you leave when Georgie turned eighteen? And why didn't he leave when Patrice had what's his name?"

Edwina smiled gently. "Oscar. Be kind. He's a nice kid. It's not his fault his father kept him a secret from you. When Oscar was born, I fully expected Richard to leave. But I think he feared your reaction and honestly, I don't think he wanted to live with Patrice full time.

"As for me, well, I'd created a good life here. I had friends, the historical society, the Country Women's Association. You'd just moved back from England and Charlie was five. I wanted to be a grandmother." She raised her head and looked her daughter straight in the eye. "Your father was a huge influence in your life and I couldn't fight that. If I'd left, I'd have lost the small part of you that you've allowed me to share. I'd have lost Charlie."

Harriet had no reply. She desperately wanted to talk to Xara. She needed her sister to help her find her way through this. To make sense of it.

"I need fat. Chips, chocolate, ice cream. Anything."

Edwina pulled a family-size block of Cadbury chocolate out of her handbag and passed it to her. "I knew you wouldn't have any in the house."

Harriet's throat tightened as she bit into the milk chocolate and savored the velvety touch and the sweet taste on her tongue. She'd spent a lifetime thinking Edwina had been a relatively ineffectual mother, but she'd gotten it wrong. Despite the periods of time stolen from her by depression, Edwina did know her. She understood her better than she'd ever given her credit for.

Edwina opened more wine and refilled their glasses. "Harry, I grew up in a family whose public face was the polar opposite of what went on in private. I hated the suffocating hypocrisy and boarding school was only a temporary escape. I plotted for a more permanent one where I had control of my life instead of my father controlling it. I wanted out so badly that I thought of little else for my last two years at school. I felt my father owed me something for keeping his family secrets. It took a lot of convincing, but he finally agreed to pay for my university education."

"I had no idea you'd wanted to go to university."

"No, well, you wouldn't. For reasons you now understand, I never talked very much about my life before I met your father. Your grandfather was surprised I wanted to go too. Back then, there'd only been two women in the Mannering extended family to attend university and my father considered both of them to be radical troublemakers. As a politician, he wasn't going to allow any member of the family to rock the foundations of his carefully constructed life. He only agreed to it because he thought there was a good chance I'd meet an eligible husband. After all," she said wryly, "as a Mannering, I couldn't just marry anyone."

Edwina stared down into her wine glass, her brow furrowed in thought. "Not even Rosie knew I'd met Doug, let alone fallen in love with him. We had a plan and it didn't involve getting pregnant until about four or five years later. While he was doing his national service, I'd go to university. When I was twenty-one and no longer needed my parents' permission, we'd marry." She glanced up, sadness clear in her familiar blue eyes. "As you know, it didn't turn out that way."

Wordlessly, Harriet pushed the chocolate back toward her mother. Edwina reached out and covered her hand with her own. "The last thing I ever wanted was a child of mine growing up under the crushing mantle of being a Mannering. Putting family ahead of personal happiness is a huge burden to carry. But I lost control of my life for a long time and when I married Richard, I found myself living a life scarily similar to my mother's. I let Richard wrap us up in the same hypocrisies and take you along in the slipstream.

"I'm sorry your father and I led by false example. I'm sorrier than you can ever know that I allowed you to grow up believing the Mannering rhetoric that privilege, power and perfection brings happiness. That there's no room for mistakes and if you make any they're hidden, ignored or made to go away. I was forced to give up a child for respectability. I paid a high price for secrets and lies and I'm paying it still."

A jet of toxic green jealousy flooded Harriet. "The lost years of Michelle," she muttered, snatching back the chocolate.

"Not only Michelle," Edwina said softly, placing her hand back on Harriet's. "I ache for the lost years with you. Somehow, whether it was experience, medication or a combination of the two, I managed things better with Xara and Georgie. But my depression after your birth created a distance between us that to this day, I've never managed to close."

The heartfelt words hovered over Harriet, making her hot, cold and uncomfortable all at the same time. A kernel of guilt rolled through her at her not infrequent and barely leashed intolerance toward her mother. As much as she didn't want to believe Edwina's story, there was too much truth in it for her to just slough off her father's behavior and bury it under the carpet.

Oh, Dad. She missed him every day. He'd been her mentor and her cheerleader, but he'd also been a man of staunch opinions and a true believer in his own skills. How could he have been so supportive of his daughter and not his wife? More than anything, Harriet wished she could ask him why he'd treated Edwina the way he had. She burned to point out the hypocrisy of his life with Patrice and Oscar when he'd punished Edwina for having a child before she'd even met him. Surely he'd had some regrets about the entire messy situation?

She raised her head and sought her mother's gaze. "I never thought I'd say this, but after what you've told me today, I think I let Dad keep that distance open."

Edwina blinked rapidly and blew her nose before standing up. "Cup of tea?"

"When there's still wine in the bottle and chocolate on the block?" She refilled their glasses. "Edwina, why are you telling me this now? I mean, you could have told us about Patrice and Oscar after Dad's funeral. At that point you scarcely owed him loyalty."

"I was protecting you and your sisters from the pain of a lifetime of lies."

Old anger burned under new pain. "And what? Today you decided you didn't want to protect us anymore?"

"Harriet, I'm your mother. Until my last breath, I'll always do my best to protect you."

A lifetime of regret was evident in the lines around her eyes. "Granted, until now, sometimes my best has been misguided or not up to par. But if I let you go to Sydney laboring under the secrets and lies of your ancestors, I'd be letting you down.

"All your life you've aspired to be as successful and as perfect as the Mannerings who preceded you, only they were riddled with flaws. They valued respectability and feared the judgment of others over individual happiness. They used money and power to force family members to toe their hypocritical line. It's left a path of destruction in its wake and I want it to stop. I want it to stop right now."

The wine was making Harriet woozy. "That sounds very admirable, Edwina, but unless you have a time machine, I don't see how you can stop anything."

"I'm talking about the here and now. I know it's been a tough year for you on so many fronts. I know James stole more than money from you. That the town's judged you far more harshly than you deserve and that Charlie's decision has disappointed you. But you're strong, Harriet. You've survived far more than just malicious gossip."

Harriet ate more chocolate. "I've lost my house and my private practice barely covers the costs of running the rooms. If that's survival, it totally sucks."

"They're possessions, Harry. I'm talking about people. The values of the past forced me to lose a child and that's affected my life and yours. Don't let those values steal Charlie from you. If you do, it's a heartache that will stay with you forever."

Harriet thought about her daughter who right this minute was in hospital with her baby. The usual zip of pain and disappointment caught her under the ribs. "I had such high hopes for Charlotte. She had everything going for her. She's bright, beautiful, smart and when she got pregnant she—" *ruined all my plans for her.*

The wine and chocolate burned in her throat like firewater. For the first time she actually heard herself—heard the words—and they weren't pretty. She'd always justified that pushing Charlotte to win, to achieve high academic grades and insisting she study pre-med was because she wanted the best for her. But now she could see it was all about her need to create a perfect life.

Surround yourself with perfection, Harry and everything else follows.

Oh Dad.

In her own lifelong strive for perfection she'd taken Charlotte along with her. And James? No, she hadn't taken James with her. Despite what he'd said, she knew deep in her heart that he'd been a more than willing partner. He'd joined her on the ride, placing a higher value on power and perfection than on morals.

Xara's voice came back to her. *I know it's breaking your heart that Charlie's pregnant but life isn't perfect.*

She winced, recalling how she'd tried to draw a comparison between Xara's situation with Tasha and her own situation with Charlotte. How could she have done that when her daughter was able bodied, intelligent and determined? Even when Harriet had refused to support Charlotte, she hadn't wavered in her decision to keep the baby. Despite being pregnant, she'd continued her senior year even though it involved changing schools.

Xara had told Harriet that Charlotte had found the change tough. At the time, Harriet had muttered something like, "Nothing like reality to drive home our choices." God help her. She'd been such a selfish cow, punishing Charlotte for choosing her own path. She'd hidden behind her belief she was a loving mother who wanted the best for her child, but her love had come with conditions.

She rubbed her sternum. Her father had imposed conditions on Edwina to get what he wanted. Edwina's father had imposed conditions on her for the same reason and now Harriet was guilty of doing exactly that to Charlotte. She couldn't hide behind her misguided belief that tough love was in Charlotte's best interests. Or that she'd rejected all of Xara's and Edwina's suggestions to heal the rift and that going to Sydney was running away.

She was running from Billawarre. From her messy family. From her daughter's choices that made her ache with worry for her and from the grandchild who scared her more than she wanted to admit.

"Mom?"

"Yes."

"About that photo of Charlotte and her baby. May I see it, please?"

Her mother smiled. "Of course you can. It's exactly why I took it."

CHAPTER THIRTY-FOUR

HARRIET HESITATED IN THE DOORWAY OF CHARLOTTE'S hospital room. She had a screaming hangover from drinking far too much red wine with Edwina and having lain awake most of the night digesting everything she'd learned about her family. The foundations of her life had been violently shaken and after she'd spoken with Charlotte, she and Edwina were going to visit Xara. They'd called Georgie, who was driving to Billawarre tonight. Harriet was dubbing all the visits her "apology tour."

"May I come in?"

Charlotte's head turned sharply and Harriet saw surprise and anxiety cross her daughter's face, stealing the happiness from it. She winced, accepting the blame.

"Have you come to convince me to put Teddy up for adoption?"

As recently as twelve hours ago that would have been exactly her purpose. "No."

"Did you come to see your grandson?"

Harriet tried not to flinch at the word that made her feel unreasonably old. "I came to see you."

"Oh." Charlotte hesitated before indicating the visitor's chair. "Please. Take a seat."

Charlotte sounded exactly like Harriet when she was bringing a patient into the consulting room. She'd used the same tone as Edwina when she greeted a stranger. Harriet didn't know whether to laugh or cry.

"Thank you." Carrying the box she'd brought with her, she crossed the room, set the box down beside the chair and took a seat. "How are you?" Given seven months of estrangement loomed large between them, the question sounded banal.

"Labor hurts like a—It hurts."

"It does."

"But it's so worth it." Charlotte's hand hovered in the crib, caressing her baby's downy head.

Harriet remembered doing exactly the same thing. "It is."

"Do you want to hold him?"

A ripple of anxiety rolled through her. "While he's asleep and quiet, there's something I need to talk to you about."

Charlotte's shoulders immediately tensed. "Xara told me you're going to Sydney."

"That's been the plan, yes."

"When do you leave?"

"Miligili settles in two weeks."

Sadness filled Charlotte's eyes. "It's so weird knowing another family will be living there."

Harriet tapped the lid of the box with her foot. "I know you came and got everything you wanted but when I was packing I found a box of your baby things. A blanket Georgie made you and the bear Xara and Steve gave you. You loved that bear so much ..."

Charlotte indicated a soft toy rabbit with floppy ears and a blue coat. "Xara gave Teddy that. Steve tried to take it back. He said rabbits are vermin and no self-respecting farmer should be giving a baby a rabbit. He and the boys gave Teddy a football."

"Steve's got a point. Although he would have objected just as much to a toy wombat."

"I guess." Charlotte glanced at the box. "Thanks for bringing my baby things."

"You're welcome."

Strained silence filled the room broken only by the snuffling of the sleeping baby. Eventually Charlotte said, "I wasn't sure I'd make it, but I sat all my exams."

"Well done."

Charlotte's eyes narrowed and filled with determination. "I know it's not going to be easy being a single mom but I've spent six months getting as prepared as I possibly can. I've got my driver's license and I did a barista course. I've been working at The Staff of Life café since June and I'm paying Doug back for the secondhand car he bought me. I'm hoping to defer elementary school teaching and start the course part time when Teddy's one."

Her voice developed a steely edge Harriet recognized as her own. "I know I've got Mardi to help me, but most people have some help from their family. I'm not going to be the unskilled disaster or the drain on the public purse you predicted."

Ouch. Harriet accepted the hit. "I know."

Charlotte blinked. "How?"

"Because you come from a long line of strong and determined women." She laced her fingers on her lap. "Charlotte, your pregnancy threw me. No mother puts up their hand and says, 'Pick my daughter to be the teenage mother.'"

"I didn't plan it either, Mom."

"No." She inclined her head toward the crib. "How does he make you feel?"

"Like my heart's going to burst."

Harriet nodded. "That feeling only gets stronger."

"It's hard to imagine."

"I know but that's what happens. You discover you'll scale mountains and fight lions if that's what it takes to protect your child." She leaned forward as if pulled by an invisible string. "All I ever wanted was the best for you. It's what every mother wants for her child. I started out with the best of intentions but somewhere along the way I imposed on you a big dose of Mannering and Chirnwell tradition. The last few years I added in the same hopes and dreams I had for myself when I was your age and ignored what you wanted."

She sighed. "For many years, your father and I were very influential and I've gotten used to having my own way. Your pregnancy wasn't part of my plan for you so I did what I've always done—I tried to change it. I demanded, I cajoled, I pushed and I threatened to get you to comply.

"Your aunts and your grandmother told me what I was doing was wrong, but I refused point blank to acknowledge it. I completely disagreed with them when they said I was putting unreasonable demands on you. I reasoned that as I was your mother, I knew best. I thought I was saving you from yourself."

She looked straight into her daughter's beautiful face. "I've only recently realized how ugly and obnoxious I've been. I was wrong. I'm sorry."

Charlotte's mouth fell open. "You're apologizing?"

Harriet tried to laugh at Charlotte's disbelieving voice but the sound came out as a strangled moan. "I know it's hard to believe, but yes. I'm very sorry for putting you in an impossible position."

"Th-thank you." Charlotte's gaze moved to her sleeping son. "What made you change your mind? Is it because Teddy's here? Now you want to be a grandmother?"

"God, no." The words rushed out before she could stop them. Charlotte's face fell and she hastily tried to explain. "If I'm honest, the idea of being a grandmother scares me to death. I'm not a natural with children, you know that. Generally I prefer them once they can walk and talk."

"He'll do that eventually. If you like, I can let you know when it happens. Maybe you can fly down from Sydney."

"That would be great but I won't have to travel quite that far. I don't have a new address yet but when I do, it will be in Billawarre."

"You're staying? Wow, you are full of surprises today, Mom." A smile warmed her words.

"And your grandmother was full of surprises yesterday. It's a long story, and I'll tell you all about it another day, but she finally got through to me that if I go to Sydney, I'll lose any chance of being part of your life. I'll lose you." Her voice broke. 'I couldn't bear that. If I'm here, at least I can share the parts of your life you're prepared to share with me. I realize it's going to take time for you to forgive me but—"

"Oh, Mom." Charlotte closed the gap between them, throwing her arms around her neck as tears streamed down her face. "I've missed you so much."

Harriet hugged her back just as hard, letting her own tears fall. "I've missed you more," she choked out, realizing she'd just quoted one of Charlotte's favorite childhood stories.

Charlotte made an inarticulate sound then sniffed violently. "Mom, it's been so hard without you. Everything changed. Suddenly, Dad screwed over the town and you refused to talk to me. At first I couldn't believe you'd cut me out of your life. I mean, you've always made me feel special and loved and I kept expecting you to change your mind. I felt so bad at disappointing you, but at the same time, I felt as if I didn't matter to you anymore."

Harriet's heart quivered as if a blunt knife had just stabbed it multiple times. She'd inflicted so much pain on the person she loved most in the world and for what? Pride? Conceit? For the false reputation of a family imbued with devastating secrets? "I'm sorry. So very, very, sorry."

Charlotte reached for a tissue and blew her nose. "I really wanted to hate you, Mom and I tried. My part-time job, getting my license, going to school ... I did all of it to prove you wrong. Prove to myself that you were wrong about me. It was Mardi who kept saying, 'Give her time. She loves you.' I found it hard to believe."

Harriet knew she'd caused her daughter untold grief but a balm of relief was finally beginning to assuage the agony. Charlotte was open to forgiving her and she wanted nothing more than to build a bridge and cross to meet her on the other side. "I didn't make it easy for you."

Her thoughts strayed to Edwina and her sisters. "I don't think I've made it particularly easy for anyone to love me this year."

"It's been a pretty hard year for all of us. Dad too."

Harriet's forgiveness only went so far. "Your father's in jail because he chose to steal money."

"I know." Charlotte's fingers plucked at the cotton bedspread. "In January, I thought I was pretty mature but I had no clue. It's everything that's happened since then that's made me grow up fast. You were partly right when you called me a princess. I was scared to tell you I was pregnant but I honestly thought you'd yell for a bit then calm down and things would go back to normal. Well, as normal as they could be without Dad at Miligili. I assumed you'd pay for everything like you've always done and look after me and the baby."

She raised her head, her tear-stained cheeks full of apology. "I was wrong to expect all of that."

Harriet's heart filled with gratitude. "Thank you."

"When I moved in with Mardi she gave me an allowance and immediately asked me to pay some of it back for board and expenses. I was pretty shocked. The allowance you and Dad gave me was always just for me. Mardi made me pay for my toiletries too. Mom, do you know how much you pay for your shampoo?" Her critical tone was that of a recent budgeting convert.

Harriet had no clue. Her hairdresser just lumped the cost of her hair care products in with the price of her haircut, color and waxing. She justified the exorbitant total as another business expense because she needed to look well presented for work. "I'm not sure."

"Well, it's heaps. I changed brands and saved seventeen dollars a bottle," Charlotte said triumphantly. "And Doug's been helping me budget. He set up a program and I type in every cent I spend so I can see where the money's going." A rueful smile crossed her face. "It's very unforgiving. I couldn't hide from the amount I was spending on makeup."

Despite her delight that Charlotte had a newfound appreciation for the value of a dollar, a familiar antipathy coiled inside her like a snake ready to strike. It happened whenever Doug was mentioned. It had never bothered her before—truth be told, she'd embraced it—but today it arrived uninvited.

She tried hard to fight it. "It sounds like he's been very helpful."

Charlotte rolled her eyes. "You sound just like Mardi when she's frustrated with the horticultural society. Mom, you have to get to know Doug. He's a really good guy and he makes Mardi happy. Gramps would want her to be happy."

Harriet made an involuntarily and incomprehensible noise, then took a quick breath and recovered. Everything she'd learned yesterday was so fresh in her mind that the blood of it was still running. Now wasn't the time to tell Charlotte about her grandfather and his other life, but she'd tell her sometime this week. After all, didn't everyone deserve to know they had a half-uncle younger than themselves?

Harriet shrugged off the need to be sarcastic. "You're right. Your grandmother deserves to be happy."

"I know Doug's nothing like Gramps," Charlotte said earnestly, "but you need to stop comparing them. Give Doug a chance. You might just discover you like him."

The idea was foreign to her. Then again, so much of what she'd believed to be true about her family—past and present—was equally unfamiliar. The gap between what she'd believed about her father and the reality wounded her the most. "I promise I'll stop comparing Doug with your grandfather."

The heated determination in her startled Charlotte and she laughed. "It's okay, Mom. I believe you. And I'll hold you to it when you lapse and give Doug a hard time."

"Along with Mardi and my sisters." Harriet smoothed her skirt over her thighs, taking a moment to assemble her thoughts. "Darling, I can't promise that I'll ever be an easy person. I can't promise that I won't have strong opinions about your plans or that I'll even approve of them, but I can promise you this. I won't ever make you choose between your life plans and me again. I want to support you to achieve your goals.

"It's not going to be easy for me to change and it won't happen overnight. After all, I've spent eighteen years telling you what to do. But I'm going to work hard at trying to listen and hear you. And even harder than that, I'm working on hearing Mardi's, Xara's and Georgie's opinions too. Please be patient with me while I learn how to be the mother of an adult daughter. I'm going to need your help."

Charlotte reached for her hand. "I'm going to need your help too."

Fear churned, but she had to say this now before Charlotte got any unrealistic expectations. "I'm sorry, Charlotte, but I can't be the sort of grandmother who's a full-time carer."

"Mom, I know that. You've got a full-on career. You didn't stay home full time with me, and I don't expect you to do that for Teddy either. Help comes in lots of different ways." She kissed the top of her son's head. "I want to be the best mother to Teddy."

Harriet thought about Edwina's best and how up until yesterday she'd always thought it fell well short of the mark. She reflected on her own mothering failures—especially over the last few months. Illness was the reason her mother's best had wavered and Harriet had no such excuse. She'd placed all the wrong values ahead of Charlotte.

"Every mother wants to be the best they can be, but sometimes that best is hampered by the circumstances they find themselves in."

Charlotte frowned. "Are you saying I can't be the best because I'm a single mother?"

"No." She gripped Charlotte's hand tightly, scared their fragile reconciliation might shatter before it had started. "Not at all. What I'm trying to say is that I let my dreams for you get in the way of me doing my best for you. If it wasn't for Mardi, I would have gone to

Sydney and let those ridiculous dreams of mine destroy our relationship."

"Mardi's seriously wise," Charlotte said sincerely. "I mean, can you imagine how hard it must have been for her when they took Michelle away?"

In the wee hours of the morning, all Harriet had thought about was her mother. "I don't think we can ever truly understand what it's been like for her to live with that level of pain."

The baby whimpered and Charlotte immediately picked up the swaddled bundle. "I know you're allergic to babies, Mom, but do you want to hold him for a minute. Just to say hello?"

A squad of butterflies fluttered in her stomach. It was ridiculous to be scared of a baby. "He hasn't got any teeth so I guess he can't bite," she joked, sounding far more certain than she felt.

As she accepted the baby, she surprised herself by automatically crooking her left arm, supporting his head. Apparently, she hadn't forgotten how to hold a newborn after all. He was tiny; the weight and length of the large salmon she'd bought last Christmas. A smattering of fine blond hair covered his head and one of his tiny, dimpled hands had escaped from the blanket and was pressed up against his cheek. He was innocent, new and unsullied by life. Lucky kid.

"Harriet Jane Mannering Chirnwell meet your grandson, Edwin Douglas Richard," Charlotte said proudly.

"Edwin Douglas Richard?" Harriet repeated slowly.

"I thought about James but ... I'm still really confused about how I feel about Dad. And we all miss Gramps, especially you, so I thought it was a nice way to remember him."

Yesterday, Harriet would have been foaming at the mouth that Doug's name was part of Teddy's let alone that it preceded her father's. Today, it seemed improbably appropriate. She wondered if Charlotte would change her mind about including Richard when she learned the truth about her grandfather.

"There's no rush to decide. You've got sixty days before you have to register the birth."

Teddy chose that moment to open his eyes. Like all newborn's, his were a very dark blue. He gazed up at her, his little pixie face creased in a concentrated stare as if he was trying to remember where he'd seen her before.

"He's got your forehead and I'm assuming that's his biological father's nose?"

Charlotte laughed. "Don't worry. He'll grow into it. Hamish is very good looking."

"Have you told him about his son?"

"Of course. I called him last night. He's flying out to Bali in the morning for summer vacation but he's visiting as soon as he gets back."

"And his parents?"

Charlotte shrugged. "They're still living in Qatar, but they'll be in Melbourne for Christmas and in Lorne during January. They've invited me to their beach house and they're following my Instagram account for photos."

"Should I meet them?"

"Maybe. I'd like you to meet Hamish."

Harriet slid her finger across Teddy's palm and it closed tightly around her finger. She knew it was purely a reflex action and that every baby did it, but it didn't stop the rush of love and joy pouring through her. "Hello, little one," she said softly. "I'm Harriet."

He stared at her for a little bit longer, as if absorbing a fascinating piece of news, and then he suddenly screwed up his face and spit up colostrum. She laughed and wiped away the mess. "You're a cheeky one. You're testing my patience already."

He opened his mouth wide, his little pink tongue vibrating. A loud and ear-piercing cry filled the room. "And on that note ..." She quickly handed Teddy back to his mother but she knew he'd already taken a piece of her heart.

While the midwife helped Charlotte attach Teddy to her breast,

Harriet decided she needed to find a name he could call her. She shuddered at the thought of Nana, Gran and Grandma. Mardi was taken and Harriet was too much of a mouthful. Oma? Naini? MorMor? Bubbe? She fished out her cell phone, opened a browser and googled, "trendy names for grandmothers." She clicked on a link, scanned it and laughed.

Charlotte glanced up from her hungry son who was busy slurping his way to fulfillment. "What's so funny?"

"I think I've found the perfect name for Teddy to call me."

"What's that?"

"Glamma."

IT WAS THE EYES.

Edwina swallowed hard, emotion rushing her with the power of swirling floodwaters, threatening to knock her off her feet. As she glanced at her daughters, who all had very different personalities, she saw the obvious DNA they shared and the one thing they all had in common: blue eyes. Not baby blue or the intensive blue of the vast and endless country sky they'd been conceived under. No, it was an electric blue tempered with a distinctive violet ring around the iris.

Her eyes.

Eyes that could sparkle so brightly that heads turned in their direction as if drawn by an invisible force. Eyes that captured snapshots of places and people with the click and clarity of a camera shutter and then stored them as carefully as a museum curator. Eyes that shed tears of sorrow and despair when those images bleached to an indistinct reddish-brown, turning the features of much-loved faces into blurred memories.

Edwina welcomed the intensity of her daughters' gaze on her now. A new sibling always brought a combination of joy and anxiety into a family and her daughters' eyes conveyed all of that and more. Excitement thrummed through her and she automatically tightened her arm around the daughter who was gazing silently at her with bright and inquisitive eyes.

She cleared her throat, raised her head and said quietly, "Girls, I'd like you to meet your sister, Michelle. Michelle, I'd like you to meet Harriet, Xara and Georgie. Your sisters."

"Hello." Harriet stepped forward, offering Michelle a glass of champagne. "You have no idea what a relief it is to know I'm no longer the oldest."

"I'm not here to steal your role," Michelle said hurriedly. "In fact I—"

"Oh, no." Harriet gave a dismissive wave. "You're not stealing it. I'm giving it to you. I tumbled off my sanctimonious-big-sister perch recently and I really don't want to climb back on. It turns out it's a lot more fun being one of the middle daughters."

Georgie laughed and tapped her glass against Michelle's. "I agree. I was the youngest for years and even though I don't get to boss our recently discovered little half-brother about very often, he officially bumped me out of holding the youngest position. I'm forever grateful to him. Now I get to remind these two that I'm a grown up with opinions they need to listen to."

"I've always been the middle child," Xara said equably. "I played up and had a lot more fun growing up than Harry. Thankfully, she's making up for lost time. But it doesn't seem fair to foist the responsibilities of the first born onto you unless you want a crack at it?"

Michelle glanced at them, her face part bewilderment, part anxiety and part delight. "I don't have any experience with sisters. I'm only used to having brothers and I think they're a lot less complicated. I used to bribe them with food."

"Oh, that works with sisters too." Harriet laughed. "Georgie has a penchant for Swiss chocolate and Xara will agree to almost anything for French champagne. It's her kryptonite but sadly, I can no longer afford the real stuff so I've lost my power over her."

Michelle laughed. "And what about you, Harriet?"

"Harry has far too much self-discipline to be bribed with food or drink," Xara said. "But she can be tempted by a particular shade of lipstick and designer shoes.

"That sounds a bit out of my league," Michelle said.

"Sadly, it's out of mine too, at the moment," Harriet said. "I'm surprised at how little I miss the shoes. I got a bigger kick out of buying Teddy a pair of crocheted booties from the good ladies at the hospital's auxiliary than I did for my last pair of Christian Louboutins."

A wistful look entered Michelle's eyes. "Growing up, did you share your clothes and shoes?"

Xara snorted. "Harry was a closet hog. Her clothes barely left any room for mine but I wasn't allowed to wear anything of hers."

"It didn't stop you," Harriet said without rancor before turning to Michelle. "And I bet your brothers didn't nick your lipstick, unless of course your adopted family has as many secrets as ours."

"I'm not aware of any cross dressers," Edwina said thoughtfully, "although who really knows? Their valets probably knew and either loyalty or money kept them quiet. There are a few women in the family who never married. Some because of a lack of men after the wars but I've always wondered if the maiden aunts who lived for years with a close female friend were lesbians."

Michelle sat down next to her. "I've been browsing that Mannering family history book you gave me and nothing like that's mentioned. To be honest, it's a bit dry."

Harriet cut some brie and placed it on a cracker with some pear spread. "Grandpa had a very selective memory when he wrote that book. Edwina and I are currently writing an up-to-date version that tells it like it was and how it is. We're not hiding secrets anymore."

"I'm adding to the mayhem by marrying your half-brother and my de facto stepbrother. If Edwina ever makes an honest man of Doug, we can drop the de facto," Georgie teased.

"After years of living a life that was expected of me, I'm living the life I want." Edwina raised her glass to Georgie.

"Michelle, we're adding you to the family tree along with my father's son Oscar and my grandson, Teddy," Harriet said. "And we're searching the ranches' records to see if we can pinpoint other Mannering love children."

"That's a much nicer term than illegitimate," Michelle said with feeling. "But how can you tell if a child was a love child?"

"If they're children of female employees and their education was paid for by the ranch that's a fair indication," Xara said. "So are small bequeaths in wills. Before the First World War, ranch life was pretty isolated. The Mannerings tended to look after their staff especially if they gotten knocked up by one of their own. We could have unacknowledged cousins all over the place."

"Put it this way, I'm expecting a lot of new faces at the next Mannering extended family reunion," Harriet said with a laugh.

Doug came up behind Edwina and whispered, "How's it going?"

Edwina stood and they withdrew from the room giving the sisters a chance to talk alone. "So much better than if it had happened a few months ago. But it's early days. As far as I'm concerned, it's enough that Michelle wants to spend some time with you and me. She doesn't have to throw herself into this huge extended family if she doesn't want to. It's a lot to ask."

"Part of me understands, but, Eddy, just once, wouldn't it be great to have all our kids and their families together in the same space?" Doug's eyes twinkled. "Ben and Georgie's wedding is the perfect event."

"Everyone includes Oscar," she reminded him. "Patrice is surprisingly keen for him to get to know his nieces and nephews."

"And great-nephew. As far as I'm concerned, the more the merrier."

"Doug Pederson, you're such a romantic. It could be a total disaster."

"I've seen weddings melt down over lesser things than a few illegitimate kids."

"We can only hope there are no more surprises."

"At least with our mob, everything's out in the open."

Our mob. "I've been thinking—"

"Should I be worried?"

"Always," she teased. "But on a serious note, I've been thinking about Michelle. She's discovered an entire set of relatives and ancestors she never knew she had. I've been able to give her a very detailed family history and she's been polite about it, but she's not really interested. It doesn't bother me. Heaven knows, I struggle with some of the things that have happened in the family. But I've noticed she's really interested in knowing more about your family."

He frowned, confusion moving along the creases of his forehead. "She's met the kids."

"I'm not talking about your family with Sophia. I'm talking about your mother's family. Are you interested in trying to find out if any of your aunties or uncles or cousins are still alive?"

He rubbed the back of his neck. "I dunno, Eddy. It's been a lifetime since then."

"Have Michelle's questions made you think about it just a little?"

"A bit. But ..." This time he dragged his hand through his hair.

"If you want to start searching, I'd love to help. That is, I'll help if you want my help." She gave him what she hoped was an encouraging smile. "I've never been to the back of Bourke."

"I was born in Wilcannia. It's southwest of Bourke."

"I haven't been southwest of Bourke either. We could visit all the places you remember your mother and grandmother said they'd lived or had family living."

"It wouldn't be fair to leave Charlie and Teddy on their own just yet and we did offer to help. Harriet's getting better with Teddy, but her job makes her unreliable."

"I didn't mean that we take off tomorrow," she said gently, recognizing his apprehension. "And I'm not talking about being away for months at a time. I'm thinking a series of short trips with time in Mildura and Billawarre in between. Besides, we can't leave until after Georgie and Ben's wedding. I've made some inquiries—"

"Inquiries? Jeez, Eddy."

She heard frustration or was it fear? On the one hand she understood but on the other she thought it was important he start looking for his mother's family while there was the possibility of people still being alive who remembered his mother. "Have I done the wrong thing?"

"I dunno. It's all a bit of a surprise." Consternation crossed his face. "You haven't mentioned this to Georgie or Michelle have you?"

She shook her head. "It's your decision, Doug. I only mentioned it because I get the impression finding Michelle has brought back memories for you and sparked a lot of unanswered questions."

He sighed heavily. "I see my mother in her. The way she walks. Her smile. The frown line between her eyes. She's much the same age as Mom was when she died."

"I think she'd be keen to help you."

Apprehension flickered. "Before I do anything, I'd need to talk to the other kids. See how they feel about it."

"They might want to help too. They've got a gap in their story as well."

"I always thought it was easier to forget," he said sadly. "Thought it would make life easier. When I married Sophia, people just assumed I was Italian. I got some grief for that but it was nothing compared to what I'd have got for being Aboriginal. Mildura in the seventies was pretty unforgiving and I had a family to support. The business would have suffered."

"You won't get any judgment from me, Doug. We do what we have to do at the time, but times change." She slipped her hands into his. "Our families are like a jigsaw puzzle with missing pieces. You helped me fill my missing piece by finding Michelle. I can never thank you enough for standing with me while we did that. Now I want to help you fill in some of the missing pieces in your family puzzle."

"You want me to do this?"

"Only if you want to. But that said, Michelle's got a bee in her bonnet about country. I have a feeling she might try doing it on her own and that worries me only because it might upset your girls and Ben. If you make the decision to explore this, it makes you the linchpin for the family, which is as it should be. It's your story."

"My story." He puffed out a long breath. "Crikey. There's stuff I haven't thought about in years. All the moving. The orphanage ..."

"There are people you can talk to if you need to."

His brown eyes sought hers, filled with love. "You're a special woman, Eddy."

"I'm not special. But I'm lucky."

"How do you figure that?"

"I've been blessed with second chances. I've been blessed with you."

He grinned. "Well, when you put it like that." He kissed her. "I feel exactly the same way."

She cupped his cheek. "Even if you're surrounded by women?"

"Your daughters, my daughters and our daughter are going to keep life interesting. There's nothing wrong with that."

She laughed. "Nothing indeed."

EPILOGUE

Harriet walked through Glenora's French doors and dropped her keys in the dish on the dresser before placing the small pile of mail next to it. It was early afternoon and Teddy was sitting on a mat sucking the ear of the toy rabbit Steve had dubbed Mixie. When he saw her, he squealed, dropped the toy and put out his arms to be picked up.

"Hello, darling boy. You really are the best thing for my ego. Not everyone's quite so excited to see me." She scooped him up, hugging him close before feeling a distinctive dampness seeping through his baby jeans. "Saved that big wee for me, did you?" She held him away from her silk blouse and walked over to the change table while he kicked his plump legs in delight.

"Oh, great, you're home." Charlotte stood in the doorway holding a laundry basket filled with Teddy's clothes. "I was hoping you wouldn't have any emergencies."

Harriet had been trialing having Wednesday afternoons off and sometimes it worked and sometimes it didn't. "Today was blessedly straightforward. I picked up the mail. Mardi has to be the only person who still writes postcards. This one's a picture of the Wilcannia post office."

Charlotte set down the basket and picked up the postcard. "She says Wilcannia's Barkindji country—" she sounded out the unfamiliar word "—and that goes all the way to Wentworth. Isn't that near Mildura?"

Harriet slid a plastic apron over her head before undoing Teddy's diaper. She'd learned the hard way that when given the chance, little boys could spray far and wide. "Your geography's better than mine."

"What?" Charlotte pressed her hand to her chest in faux shock. "You don't look at the map Doug left us every time you open the refrigerator?" She peered at the names. "It's only twenty miles from Mildura. Wow, he was living close to his country all this time."

"Only if his mother originally came from there. From what I understand, a lot of Aboriginal people were removed from their land and taken to Wilcannia in the early twentieth century. She could have come from anywhere."

Charlotte continued reading. "They've found someone who thinks they remember Doug's mother. There might be family in Cobar, Tilpa or Bourke." Her cell phone beeped. "Michelle's posted a selfie taken in the back of the car and titled it, 'Are we there yet?' Her daughter's left a comment saying, 'Now you know how I feel.'" She slipped her cellphone back into her pocket. "We didn't do family road trips, did we?"

"God, no." Harriet picked up Teddy. "Driving to Melbourne airport to start the vacation takes long enough."

"I got a letter from Dad today."

"Oh?" Harriet had reached a place where she no longer flinched when she thought about her ex-husband. James was ten months into his five-year sentence. Once the court case had finished in March, the town's reaction to her had thawed considerably. She was slowly rebuilding her practice, but she'd been surprised to discover she had no desire to return to the frenetic pace of the past. Equally surprising was how much she enjoyed some spare time in her week to read, exercise and to spend with Teddy.

Charlotte had visited James in prison once, taking Teddy to meet him. It had almost killed Harriet to think of an innocent little baby inside a jail, but she'd only vented to Xara. They'd walked—she'd stomped—around the pasture while she'd ranted and raved until she ran out of breath and rancor. All Xara had said was, "You know what you need to do."

She'd driven home to Glenora. "Charlotte, Beechworth's a five-hour drive with a baby. I'm not setting a foot inside that prison but if you want me to come and share the driving with you then I will."

Charlotte had accepted. By overlooking the reason for the trip, Harriet had enjoyed the time in the car, along with the glorious autumnal colors of the Ovens Valley.

"Dad doesn't have much news."

"That's hardly surprising."

"He's been working with Landcare."

Harriet nodded and resettled Teddy on the blanket, circling him with toys. She didn't need to know any more. "What are your plans for this afternoon while I play with this gorgeous boy? Reading? Taking a walk on your own?"

"Actually..." Charlotte reached for a blue folder labeled *Teddy's Name Day*. "Can you help me with this?"

"Planning a party?" She grinned. "Now, that sounds right up my alley." Edwina had been right—she loved throwing parties and socializing. She missed it. "Have you finalized the guest list?"

"Almost. I've invited the great aunties."

Harriet couldn't hide her surprise. "All six of them?"

"They probably won't come but I wanted them to know they're welcome. I love how Doug's daughters have that great Italian enthusiasm for children. You have to admit, it makes us look a bit restrained and emotionally stunted."

"Blame your dour Scottish Presbyterian ancestors."

Charlotte tapped her pen against the list as if she was considering a dilemma. "And I've invited Andrew."

"Excuse me?"

"You heard. I've invited Andrew. He's here heaps so it makes sense."

"He's here because Doug's a classic car broker and he's selling his MG," Harriet said, irritation rising.

"Yeah, but he likes you, Mom. Can't you see that?"

Harriet did see that, but his manner with her had never progressed beyond easy camaraderie—something she appreciated. "Just because you're reading Jane Austen at the moment doesn't mean you have to read more into our friendship than exists."

Charlotte rolled her eyes. "Georgie, Xara and I had a conference call the other night all about it and they agree with me. He watches you just like Steve watches Xara, and Ben watches Georgie, and Doug—"

"Stop." She held up her hand. "I will not have my daughter matchmaking for me."

"Why not? I'm an adult daughter, remember?"

Harriet ground her teeth. "Not when it comes to my love life."

"You don't have a love life, Mom." Charlotte sounded exasperated. "And isn't it time you did? I mean, you and Dad are over and although I'm sad about it, I get it. It's too hard to fix. And you're officially divorced. To be honest, I thought you and Andrew would have hooked up two months ago."

"Hooked up?" She broke out in a cold sweat at the thought. "Dear God, Charlotte, I'm not nineteen. And I haven't been on a date since 1992. The whole idea terrifies me."

"Nothing scares you, Mom."

"Oh, Charlotte." How she missed the optimism and naiveté of youth. "Plenty of things scare me. This conversation for one."

Charlotte laughed. "Do you remember when Teddy was teething and I was exhausted? You and Andrew took him for a long walk until he fell asleep?"

She remembered. It had been one of many walks—not all of them known to Charlotte. "Hmm," she murmured noncommittally.

"You were gone for ninety minutes. You had coffee. That's a date."

"No, that's two friends spending time together."

"Oh, please." Charlotte jumped up. "He's single. You're single. You're both doctors. You have heaps in common. He's asking your advice about houses and he's taken you to six house inspections in the last three months."

"That would be because he's buying a house." Harriet stood too and searched the fridge as much to move as to look for something for lunch.

"But is he? Don't you think it's odd he's never actually bid on any of the houses or made an offer?"

"No. Houses are very personal. They have to speak to you."

"Exactly, and none of them have spoken to you."

"I'm not the one buying." She slapped slices of cold roast beef onto whole wheat bread. She'd delayed buying a house in Billawarre. With Charlotte starting university next year, she'd need a place to live and Harriet was considering buying an investment property in Melbourne. Right now, living at Glenora was working well. She had two rooms: her bedroom and a room she'd decorated as a quiet space.

Edwina had offered her the exclusive use of the library but as it was filled with strong memories of her father, it no longer offered the same sense of peace it once had. Her conflicted feelings for Richard still warred inside her and she'd decided the best way to deal with them was to acknowledge her disappointment with him in regard to Edwina, but to hold on to the love, support and advice he'd always shown her. With that in mind, she'd moved some of his books into her sitting room along with photos of him and the framed MBBS and Fellow of The Royal College of Surgeons certificates.

Living in her childhood home was giving her the opportunity to get to know her mother through a new set of eyes. Harriet had always thought of herself as being more like her father, but she now recognized she and Edwina shared many traits. It was probably why they clashed. There were still times when they differed but once when she'd have rolled her eyes and dismissed Edwina's point of view out of hand, she now had a clearer idea of the source of her mother's opinion. It lent itself to negotiation and conciliation.

And then there was Doug. It turned out he loved a good debate. Without too much skin in the game, the two of them sparred, often taking an opposing view from their own beliefs just to see how far they could run with it. Harriet enjoyed the intellectual stimulation. Doug had been remarkably generous to Charlotte with his time and sage advice. He still divided his time between Billawarre and his family and business in Mildura. Now Teddy was six months old, Edwina joined him there. Family, Harriet had learned, was a continuous balancing act to keep everyone happy.

The sound of footsteps on the gravel path made her glance up from the sandwich and she caught sight of black and silver hair and rimless glasses. Surprise fizzed. "Did you invite Andrew over?" she hissed at Charlotte.

Her daughter, who was picking up Teddy, ignored her and greeted the doctor with a smile. "Hi, Andrew."

He clucked a dribbling Teddy under the chin. "G'day, mate."

Teddy shrieked in delight and reached for his glasses. Andrew ducked and turned.

"G'day, Harriet. You ready to go?"

Increasingly suspicious, Harriet glared at Charlotte. "Go where?"

"I'll see you two later." Charlotte hastily buckled Teddy into the stroller. "Have fun. Bye."

"Charlotte!" But her daughter had crossed the threshold and was marching down the long gravel drive.

Andrew looked between the retreating Charlotte and Harriet, his expression confused. "Have I missed something?"

"I think we both have," she muttered as she sliced the sandwich in half with a satisfying cut. As she offered him half, she realized how often they shared sandwiches. "Where are we going?"

"Golf."

"Golf? Why?"

"Because you invited me."

"Remind me to kill my daughter when she gets home."

He grinned. "Not sure what that's got to do with golf, but okay."

For months, she'd felt at ease in Andrew's company but now her skin burned hot with embarrassment. She pressed a glass against the fridge's chilled water dispenser and downed the contents quickly.

"Want to fill me in?"

Not really. "God, I hate games."

"Then why did you suggest golf? I have to say I thought it was a bit odd. In the year I've known you, I've never heard you mention golf before."

"I used to play but I haven't since James ... Well, you know. I stopped doing a lot of things fifteen months ago."

"So you do like golf?"

"I prefer tennis."

He rubbed his chin. "I have no idea what the hell is going on."

She pressed her fingertips to her forehead, took a deep breath then raised her head to look into his kind and rugged face. He wasn't GQ-model handsome but there was a sincerity about him she found very attractive. "I didn't invite you to play golf."

"But I got a text from you." He pulled out his cell phone.

"I'm sorry. I'm ninety-nine percent certain Charlotte sent that text."

"She wants you to play golf?"

"She ..." Her cheeks burned so hot they'd light dry pasture. "I'm sorry. She's got it into her head that I should spend more time with you."

His wide mouth lifted into a broad smile. "Does she? You've got a remarkable daughter."

"I've got an interfering daughter." Irony struck her. Charlotte had just turned the tables by making decisions for her without consultation. "I'm sorry if she's made you feel awkward. That's the very last thing I'd ever want. Your friendship this last year has meant a lot to me and Charlotte's clearly overstepped the mark."

"Oh, I don't know." He rubbed his jaw. "I think spending more time together is something worth considering."

Surprise and delight zipped through her along with a soupçon of anxiety. "You do?"

"I do. What are your thoughts?"

Harriet was struggling to string a single thought together. The unforeseen breakdown of her marriage had shocked and traumatized her, and for a long time the idea of being involved in another relationship was too hard to imagine. And scary. She wasn't easy to live with.

"You aren't put off by my perfectionist tendencies?"

He laughed and walked around the kitchen counter until he was standing very close to her and gazing down at her with shining gray eyes. He smelt of shoe polish, a dash of antiseptic and the freshness of salt. A tingle whooshed along her skin, waking up her mothballed libido.

"You're a lot more relaxed than when I first met you."

"Am I?"

"Hell, yes. The first time we met, you had me for breakfast and your staff were petrified of you. Last week I heard you crack a joke with them. And you smile more now. You laugh more. And for all the hot air you spout about being allergic to children, Teddy's wrapped you around his chubby fist and you love it."

He slid his hand along her cheek. "All in all, Harriet Chirnwell, you're very pleasant company."

Something inside her let go and a few of her anxieties went with it. Andrew knew her foibles and yet he still wanted to be with her. "You're very pleasant company too." She kissed his smiling mouth.

His arms wrapped around her, pulling her in against him and he returned the kiss with a depth and intensity that made her knees sag and her body sing. When he released her mouth, she said, "So this spending more time together, does it have to be golf?"

His eyes were smoky gray. "Do you have a better suggestion?"

"I think I do." She took his hand and started walking toward her bedroom.

"Harriet?"

"Yes."

"I'm not going to remind you to kill Charlotte."

She laughed and delight rolled through her. Fifteen months ago she'd never have imagined her life as it was now. Nor that it could be good in ways she'd never considered positive. But she'd finally found those nuggets of gold sparkling brightly amid the imperfections. She'd found moments of magic.

It was enough.

ALSO BY FIONA LOWE

Daughter of Mine

Birthright

Home Fires

Just An Ordinary Family

A Home Like Ours

Coming in 2022

A Family of Strangers

Join My Newsletter

For a free novella, *Summer of Mine;* Doug and Edwina's summer of 1967, please join my VIP Readers newsletter. You'll also be the first to hear about new releases, book sales, competitions and giveaways. Register at

fionalowe.com

Did you know **BookBub** has a new release alert? You can check out the latest deals and get an email when I release my next book by following me at

bookbub.com/authors/fiona-lowe

ABOUT THE AUTHOR

FIONA LOWE has been a midwife, a sexual health counselor and a family support worker; an ideal career for an author who writes novels about family and relationships. She spent her early years in Papua New Guinea where, without television, reading was the entertainment and it set up a lifelong love of books. Although she often re-wrote the endings of books in her head, it was the birth of her first child that prompted her to write her first novel. A recipient of the prestigious USA RITA® award and the Australian RuBY award, Fiona writes books that are set in small country towns. They feature real people facing difficult choices and explore how family ties and relationships impact on their decisions.

When she's not writing stories, she's a distracted wife, mother of two "ginger" sons, a volunteer in her community, guardian of eighty rose bushes, slave to a cat, and is often found collapsed on the couch with wine. You can find her at her website, fionalowe.com, and on Facebook, Twitter, Instagram and Goodreads.

ACKNOWLEDGMENTS

All books rest on the goodwill of many and *Daughter of Mine* is no different. Many thanks to Clare Webb for her honesty and openness, and sharing with me the daily routine, the joys and the heartache of mothering a disabled child. Thanks to David Webb Ware for letting me tramp over his farm and pepper him with questions about sheep and life on the land and a big thank you to Sarah for feeding me. Richard Anderson put me in contact with Linton Drever who, cheerfully lent me his family law expertise and helped me make a plot point work. Michael Coghlan advised me on criminal law, gently pointing out what I wanted to do wouldn't happen in the real world and helped me come up with a more realistic solution. I appreciate all the assistance and advice. Any mistakes are mine.

Noel Russell kindly took the time to explain hospital funding to me after his wife shoved her cell phone unexpectedly into his hand and said, "Talk to Fiona." My beautiful sister, Sue Peterken, a passionate educator, shared with me stories of the day-to-day life of an elementary school teacher. In this 2020 edition, Norma Blake and Norm Lowe helped me convert some of the more confusing Australian expressions into more accessible US-speak for American readers and Debbie Haines did a final read through. Thank you all so much!

The Lowe men, Norm, Sandon and Barton, put up with me lurching from excitement to despair and back again as I tried to pull the longest book I've ever written into a coherent story. Thanks for the fun road trips around the Stony Rises and the western district of Victoria. For happily coming to open garden days, visiting historic homes and taking all the great photos that helped keep me in the district long after we got home.

Thanks go Annabel Blay and Kylie Mason who took a raw manuscript, smoothed it out and made it into the book you're holding today. Editing is never easy or fun and I appreciated the encouraging words during those times when I thought I'd never dig myself out of what seemed to me to be a big fat mess.

Last, but by no means least, a huge thank you to all my readers. I know the choice of books is large and your book buying budget not quite as big. I much appreciate your choice in purchasing this book with your hard-earned money. I hope you enjoy *Daughter Of Mine*. If you do, please subscribe to my newsletter at fionalowe.com. You can also find me on Facebook, Twitter, Instagram, Pinterest or email me at fiona@fionalowe.com.

BOOK CLUB QUESTIONS

BOOK CLUB DISCUSSION QUESTIONS FOR DAUGHTER OF MINE

What you hold onto, holds onto you.

—John Maclean

- Why is perfection so important to Harriet?
- "You lectured us on the importance of knowing where we come from, so we know who we are," Xara says to Harriet. Do our ancestors have anything to do with who we are?
- Do you think that the birth order of the sisters plays any role in their personalities?
- Adult children are often challenged when their parents recouple. What issues confront them?
- Edwina gave up a child in 1968 for respectability and paid a high price for keeping secrets and lies. In today's

society what are the social taboos that force families to keep secrets?

- Michelle is hesitant about getting to know her biological parents. What are some of the dilemmas faced by children who experienced closed adoption?
- Does society today judge single women who choose to be parents? Does age, socio-economic and educative status of the woman play a role?
- Xara and Harriet have very different mothering experiences. Do they have any understanding of the other's challenges?

Printed in Great Britain
by Amazon

82141956R00263